PRAISE FOR "LIGHTS & SHADOWS"

This is the book I've been looking for! Doria writes deep characters that face down an evil bigger than this world. A real page-turner. I loved every moment of reading it and related to the characters. Doria hits all the genre high notes while exploring a side of detective fiction that breathes humanity and reality into its supernatural roots. Don't miss this one!

— RICHARD C. FRANKLIN, AUTHOR OF
DEFECTOR

I don't often read mystery thrillers but I'm glad I made an exception for Lights and Shadows. An absolutely smashing read! Kept me turning pages as fast as I could! I guarantee no one will see the ending coming before it does. And when it does--it's a doozy!

— RICK SHERMAN, AUTHOR OF *NIGHT BUS*
AND *MAKE OVER*

A great read! I literally could not put the book down! The author kept me wanting to read more at the end of each chapter. Story flows effortlessly and the characters are interesting and multi-faceted. Mr. Doria has a bright future ahead of him. I am looking forward to reading the sequel.

— M. GOLDFARB, FRANKLIN LAKES, NEW
JERSEY

Joe Doria just made my list of favorite new authors! I was emotionally involved in the characters and loved the twists and turns of the plot. This book is hard to put down!

— DANNY BROCK, HONOLULU, HAWAII

I literally read this book from start to finish without stopping! Joe Doria is a master storyteller. As a retired law enforcement officer, I enjoyed the realistic writing, the vivid sights, sounds, and heart stopping details! I can't wait to read more Aaron Wyler books!

— MICHAEL BAKER, FARMINGTON, UTAH

I could not turn the pages fast enough I was so eager to discover where it led me. I love getting lost in a good book. I hope there's a sequel!

— DON MARKHAM, SARATOGA SPRINGS, UTAH

Author Joe Doria weaves a tail of suspense and mystery a thousand years in the making. You'll not go wrong following ex-New York City cop Aaron Wyler as he sorts through theft, power, suicide, and greed to solve not only the unsolvable crime at hand but also the challenges of raising a son on his own and healing his own heart.

— D.B. HOGAN, BOUNTIFUL, UTAH

Educates and entertains and weaves many different story threads together to an unexpected conclusion. It will linger in your thoughts until you race to the end! Great for audiences looking for something good, clean, and entertaining. A great read!

— L. WHIPPLE, SIMPSONVILLE, SOUTH CAROLINA

LIGHTS & SHADOWS

LIGHTS & SHADOWS

AARON WYLER, BOOK 1

JOE DORIA

Copyright © 2023 by Joe Doria

All rights reserved.

No part of this book may be reproduced in any form or by any electronic or mechanical means, including information storage and retrieval systems, without written permission from the author, except for the use of brief quotations in a book review.

The characters and events in this book are fictitious. Any similarity to real persons, living or dead, is coincidental and not intended by the author.

Published by Knox Court Press, Inc.

Cover Design by Jerry Todd

Interior Design by Dave Pasquantonio

Edited by Kevin Breen

ISBN (print): 979-8-9873758-0-8

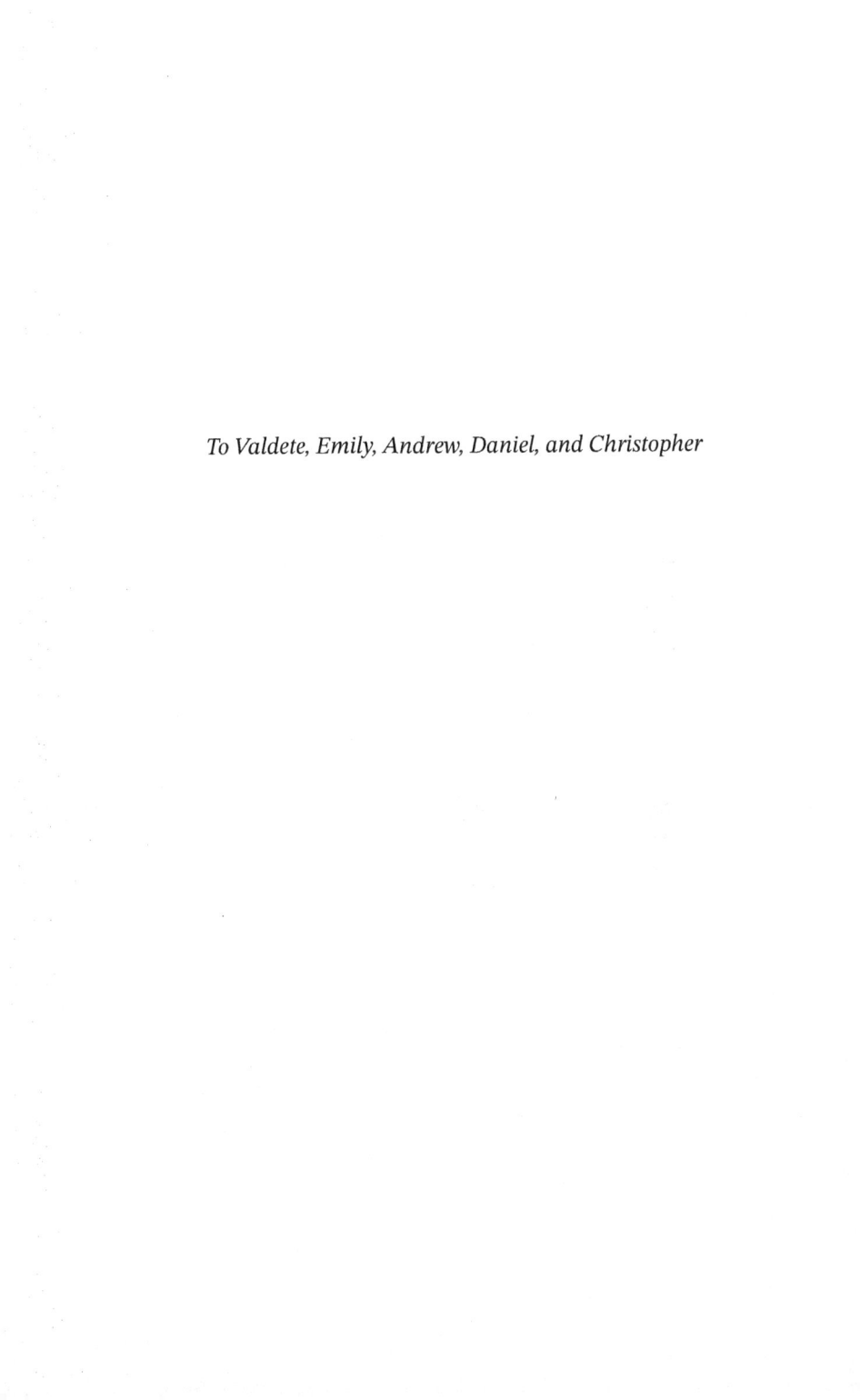

To Valdete, Emily, Andrew, Daniel, and Christopher

PROLOGUE

Michelle Wooten lay alone in her hammock, staring into the pitch blackness, listening to the shrieks and screams that filled the darkness all around her. She had learned that the jungle is much louder at night than during the day. Two weeks ago, her first night in the rainforest, she had been so exhausted that she fell asleep right away in spite of the discomfort of the hammock that swayed in response to her slightest move. But as soon as night fell, the jungle came alive, and she was jarred awake by the sounds of howler monkeys, macaws, frogs, birds, and other unknown animals that haunted her imagination. She and some of the other kids on the expedition had begun using earplugs at night in order to sleep. But tonight, Michelle wasn't using the earplugs because she wasn't trying to sleep. She was waiting.

Three weeks ago, she had been in her dorm lounge at the University of Utah, eating pizza and watching *The Bachelorette* with friends. Now, she was stretched between two trees in a remote, unexplored forest, deep in the jungles of Honduras, swallowed up by the complete and total darkness of the jungle night, with no internet, no phone signal, and no connection to the life she had known for nineteen years. Although the individual hammocks were spaced only about twenty yards apart, the dense foliage created a sense of total isolation. Michelle had never felt so alone, or so afraid.

Her parents had warned her—pleaded with her—not to go. But their protests had only fueled her determination and strengthened her resolve, like gasoline on a fire. If only she had listened to them, she wouldn't be here now, wondering if she would ever see them, or anyone else, again.

When she first heard about the expedition several months ago, it had sounded like an amazing opportunity, something to eventually put on her resume and talk about one day at dinner parties. She had always lived, she thought, a sheltered life, protected and shielded from the kinds of real-life experiences that seemed to make other people interesting and well-rounded. She was sick and tired of the bland, Utah way of things, where everyone thought and acted the same. She wanted to taste life, to gain experience, to be a part of the real world for once instead of the artificial one created for her by her parents and the Church.

Her decision to come on this archeological expedition was the first time in her life that she had openly defied her parents. There had been yelling, and tears, and things were said that shouldn't have been said. In the end, she had surprised her parents, and herself, by holding her ground and asserting her independence.

But what had started out as an exciting adventure had turned into a nightmare. She would give anything now to be back in her parents' house, lying on the couch watching TV, or sitting at the kitchen table playing a dumb board game with her family.

She turned on her flashlight and checked her watch. It was time. She and a few of the others had decided to meet at the center of camp for a private conference. The secret meeting would take place in the middle of the night, in hopes that both Lorenzo and Diego would be asleep.

Michelle gripped the small handle of the zipper and got ready.

Then, in a burst of practiced motion, she unzipped the mosquito netting, climbed out, and quickly zipped the net back up again. She had become an expert at getting in and out of her hammock quickly ever since the night when she made the mistake of leaving the seam in the netting unzipped while she went to the bathroom. She was gone for only a few minutes, but in that short time, sand flies had swarmed into the opening and tormented her the rest of the night. They had been told that some sand flies carried a form of leprosy.

Her long, snake gaiter boots were next to the hammock, placed upside down on stakes driven into the ground to keep spiders and scorpions from crawling inside. She shook the boots out to make sure they were empty before putting them on, then began her journey.

As she walked, her flashlight illuminated the moving floor of the rainforest, alive with cockroaches and green spider eyes. Years ago, while staying in a rented cabin by a lake during a family vacation, she and her sister Tammy had encountered a single, small cockroach in one of the closets, They had both run away screaming. Now, there were hundreds, maybe thousands, crawling all around her, crunching under her boots as she walked.

She proceeded slowly and carefully, knowing that she was risking her life with each step forward. Brushing up against the wrong tree could cause a shower of poisonous red ants to rain down on her hair and neck. Some members of the group had heard jaguars growling at night, and there was talk of something called quickmud, which could swallow a person alive. And of course, there were the snakes. Back at the hotel in Catacamas, before they entered the jungle, they had been shown horrible pictures of legs and feet eaten down to the bone by the venom of the fer-de-lance, the deadliest snake in Central and South America.

It took her about ten minutes to reach the center of camp, a small gathering place that had been cleared out with machetes where a few plastic folding tables had been set up under tarps. There was a camp stove there where they boiled water to mix with the bland, disgusting freeze-dried meal packets that were their only food.

About a half-dozen people were already there, huddled together in the light of a lantern, speaking in low voices. The meeting had begun, and Michelle stepped up wordlessly to join the small circle.

"Things have been wrong here from the start," Steven was whispering, just loud enough for the others to hear. Steven was the most experienced of the dozen or so college kids who had been recruited for the expedition. Michelle really liked and respected Steven. He was tall and kind and spoke fluent Spanish, having served his mission here in Honduras. He was also a graduate student in archeology who had been on other digs, including one in Mexico.

"What do you mean wrong?" asked Scott in a challenging voice.

"From the beginning these guys haven't been following basic practices and procedures for doing real archeological research. I don't think either of them have ever been on a real dig before. I've tried to talk to them, and believe me, they don't know what they're doing."

Michelle knew that Steven was talking about Lorenzo and Diego, the two professional guides who were in charge of the group. Back at the hotel in Catacamas, Mr. Dordevic, the Project Director, had been so nice to all of them. He had made what they were doing sound so exciting, a thrilling adventure of archeological discovery that would also strengthen their faith and testimonies. But as soon as they entered the jungles of Mosquitia with Lorenzo and Diego, everything had changed. During the day, they treated all the student volunteers like slave laborers, yelling and swearing at them. At night they got drunk and either ignored them completely or made creepy passes at the girls.

"And they won't let any of us look at the map they're using," said Doug.

"That's right. I've asked to look at the map several times," added Steven.

"Maybe they don't want you to see the map for some reason," said Scott. "That doesn't mean anything. You're not in charge, Steven. They are."

Michelle hated Scott. He seemed threatened by Steven, who was a natural leader, and always had to disagree with everything Steven said if only to make some stupid point about not taking orders from him.

"Can't we just get out of here and go home?" one of the other girls asked, on the verge of tears.

"There's no way in or out of here except by helicopter, and only Diego and Lorenzo have the SAT phones to call for a pickup," said Scott, shutting her down.

"I think we'll be okay as long as we stick together," Steven added, reassuringly.

"What if things get worse?" asked Doug.

"If things get worse, we might have to get our hands on one of those SAT phones."

"What are you talking about? Staging some sort of mutiny in the jungle?" Scott sneered. "You'll get us all killed!"

"Keep your voice down, Scott!" whispered Doug.

"Look, the thing I'm worried most about right now is what happened yesterday," said Steven. They all knew what he was talking about.

"Steven's right," Michelle said. "There's something wrong with that thing they found. I felt something strange as soon as they found it. I think…it's evil."

Scotty laughed and said, "Give me a break!"

"I felt it, too," another boy agreed.

"So did I," added another.

"What was it, did anyone see it?"

"I was in the group that found it," said Doug. Suddenly, everyone grew silent and turned their attention to Doug, like Boy Scouts listening to a ghost story around a campfire. "A few of us were digging, on the other side of that big rock, and we hit something about four feet down. We kept digging around it, then we used a couple of hand brushes to clear away the dirt."

"What was it?" asked Michelle.

"It was a stone box," Doug said ominously, as looks were exchanged in the circle.

"How big was it?" Steven asked.

"I don't know. About the size of a mini fridge."

"Did you open it?" Michelle asked.

"As soon as we uncovered it, Diego came over and ordered all of us to back off. He and Lorenzo did the rest of the digging. They wouldn't let anyone else near it."

"What do you think is inside it?" asked another one of the girls, sounding terrified.

"I don't know," said Doug. "But I felt something too, as soon as we uncovered it. Something ... not right. Like, it wasn't just a stone box. It was as if it had a ... presence or something. It's hard to describe. It's like it had some dark force or power or something."

Scott forced a derisive chuckle, but everyone else was deadly silent.

"Whatever it is, I think it's the thing they've been looking for," said Steven.

"What do you mean?" asked Doug.

"I think we've all been lied to," explained Steven. "I think, from the start, they've been looking for that box. That's what this whole expedition has been about. That's why they ignored that city three days ago."

"That was not a city!" said Scott. "It was a grass field."

"It was roughly a hundred square meters of unnaturally flat terrain, bordered on all sides by large stones," continued Steven, ignoring Scott and speaking to the group. "And there were dirt mounds all around it that looked manmade to me. It could have been a public square, maybe even an ancient plaza or a small city like Copan or Xunantunich. It was potentially a major find. No serious dig would have passed that by."

"So, what are you saying?" asked Doug.

"What I'm saying is this," Steven continued, glancing around the circle and into the eyes of each person there. "I don't know why we are here, but I do know this: We are not on an archeological expedition."

There was silence for several moments as the implications of Steven's words sunk in.

"So, what are we doing here?" Michelle asked, her voice trembling with fear.

For a long time the question hung in the air, unanswered.

And then finally, Doug spoke.

"I know what I'm going to do," he said. "I'm going to find out what is in that box."

CHAPTER 1

Aaron Wyler was picking up the pieces. He bent over carefully and retrieved a jagged piece of the plane's fuselage, adding it to the pile of fragments he was already cradling in his arms like firewood. Parts and pieces had been flung surprisingly far in all directions, a wing here, a wheel strut there. As he walked along the grassy slope in Roosevelt Park, scanning the ground for the scattered debris from his son's remote-control airplane, Wyler mused that the scene looked very much like a real aviation disaster in miniature, minus fire and smoke and the horror of human carnage.

His thin, wiry frame was just under six feet, and his high forehead was topped by curly black hair that, although usually cut short, had begun to sprout disorderly curls and corkscrews. That, along with the dark shade of stubble accenting his narrow, olive-skinned face, paid homage to the fact that he had recently taken a step back from normalcy and routine.

Aaron spotted a piece of the cockpit and headed toward it, taking long, sluggish strides that mirrored his mood. For the first time in months, his son Gabe had been excited about something, and Wyler had hoped this might be a turning point, that he might start to move past what had happened and begin to reconnect with the real world, and with him. Now, after this mishap, Wyler worried they were back to square one.

The idea of learning to fly model airplanes had come two months ago, after Dr. Schoenwald suggested that a hobby for Gabe might help with his therapy. When the suggestion was first made, however, Wyler had gotten defensive.

"Doctor, I quit my job. We left the city and bought a house up here. I spend every day with him. We go to movies, ballgames, the zoo. His day is full of activities. I don't see what more I can do, and frankly I don't see how coming here every week is really helping him. He's just not doing any better."

Schoenwald had ignored his outburst and patiently explained that all those activities were *passive*. What Gabe needed was a hobby that would occupy and focus his mind; something enjoyable, but something new that would require effort and concentration; something that would stimulate his mind and help his brain to naturally let go of the traumatic memory that haunted him. Schoenwald had suggested learning to play a musical instrument, a small construction project, or painting.

But later that night, as Wyler was alone in the living room watching a movie, he had another idea. He had seen *The Final Countdown* many times before. It was far from a great movie, but it had a unique plot and it was one of Wyler's guilty favorites. In the movie, Kirk Douglas plays the captain of a modern-day aircraft carrier that goes through a strange storm at sea and is thrown back in time to December 6th, 1941. The captain and crew are faced with an interesting moral and ethical dilemma: Do they use their modern weaponry and firepower to defend Pearl Harbor from the attack only they know is coming, or do they let history take its course? Of course, they choose to fight, and it was during a scene when two F-14 Tomcats dogfight a pair of World War II era Zeros that Wyler got the idea.

The next day he and Gabe made their first trip to Vortex Hobbies in downtown Poughkeepsie. Since then, he and Gabe had spent a part of almost every day at Roosevelt Park learning together to fly remote-controlled planes. Controlling the aircraft through take-off, flight, and landing proved much harder and more complicated than Wyler would have imagined, but they stuck with it together, and in the process, he could see his son slowly coming back to life.

They had started with simple models with rear propellers and Styrofoam wings that were forgiving if crashed, then had moved on to more advanced designs. Today, they had tried to take things up a notch with the P-38 Lightning. It was larger and heavier than anything they had flown before, and it had taken them days working together in the garage to assemble it. Wyler was a World War II buff and he had always loved this particular plane. It's unusual design—a cockpit nacelle flanked by two large twin booms on either side and the tails connected behind—made it look like three planes merged into one.

When the silver-colored plane had first begun to rumble down the narrow concrete path that they used as a runway, Wyler had held his breath. The plane started off slowly, shaking and jittering on the bumpy pavement like a bundle of nerves. But then, as it picked up speed, it smoothed out and seemed to gain confidence. Gabe stood beside him in a bubble of intense concentration, his hands firmly gripping the control box. Both their bodies rotated in unison as the plane sped noisily past them, the loud roar of the battery-powered engine totally out of proportion to the plane's size. As the four-foot wingspan approached the sea of grass at the end of the concrete, the plane's unique double tail, which had led the Germans to nickname it "the fork-tailed devil," suddenly left the ground. A moment later, the plane lifted unsteadily off the path and soared into the air.

Wyler relaxed a little as he watched the replica climb higher and then bank slightly to the left, porpoising up and down on the wind. He glanced down at Gabe's face, and although he wasn't smiling—that would have been too much to hope for—his son's eyes were wide with excitement. After taking the plane through several complicated maneuvers, Gabe slowly turned it back in their direction. "Dad, watch," Gabe said as he guided the plane in for a landing. To Wyler, those two words represented a breakthrough. Gabe was excited, and proud of what he was doing. He was making a connection—finally reaching out through the dense fog that had blanketed them both for almost a year.

"Bring it down easy, son," said Wyler, as the large plane descended toward the path, rocking unsteadily from side to side.

And then, suddenly, just a few feet from the ground, the nose of the plane dipped unexpectedly, the wing waddled, and the plane touched down at an awkward angle. A moment later it was cartwheeling violently along the pavement, spitting pieces in different directions as it broke apart.

Having collected all the fragments he could find, Wyler approached the car and popped the trunk. Gabe was sitting by himself in the front passenger seat, playing a handheld video game. He didn't even look up as Wyler passed. Gabe's dark hair was long and stringy and, when his head was down, hung like closed curtains over his face, hiding him from the world.

"Maybe Eugene can fix it," Wyler offered as they drove away from the park. He didn't really think Eugene or anyone else could fix it, but he felt he needed to say something positive. Gabe's only response was a silent, uninterested nod with no eye contact.

About fifteen minutes later, they entered Vortex Hobbies. The store was a gathering place for model enthusiasts of all kinds, and the shelves were filled with airplanes, boats, drones, rockets, and cars. Wyler and Gabe walked past the long sales counter on the right and continued beyond the showroom toward the back of the store. Eugene, a white-haired man wearing faded jeans and a khaki field jacket was, as always, perched on his stool, his worktable strewn with parts and tools and wrinkled tubes of glue. As they approached, Eugene glanced up from the boat he was tinkering with and saw the shattered bundle in Wyler's arms.

"Looks like the P-38 had a bit of a bumpy landing," he said as his eyes returned to his work. They had met Eugene on their first visit to the store two months ago, and he had taken them under his wing. He had suggested starter kits, taught them basic assembly, advised them on control boxes, helped with repairs when needed, and had even come to their home a few times to give them flying lessons.

Wyler tried to gingerly deposit the scraps on Eugene's worktable, but they ended up falling out of his arms in a heap.

"I crashed it," Gabe said in a voice of defeat. Wyler noted, without surprise, that Gabe's first words since the crash were spoken to Eugene, and not to his dad.

Eugene picked up a piece of the wing and stared at it. "This doesn't seem too bad." He examined a few larger fragments while mumbling technobabble to himself as Wyler nodded along, pretending to follow.

"Do you think there's any hope?" Wyler asked.

"There's always hope," Eugene answered brightly. And then, leaning down and across the table to Gabe, he said with a grin, "But before we talk about that, tell me what it was like—before the crash!"

Gabe's eyes instantly brightened as he excitedly recounted the story of the plane's brief but glorious flight, seeming to forget entirely about how it ended. Eugene had a special bond with Gabe, a natural chemistry which Wyler both appreciated and secretly envied.

When Gabe was done, Eugene said, "Gabe, why don't you go practice your landings while I chat with your dad a bit?"

Gabe complied, leaving Wyler and Eugene alone at the workbench.

"You don't really think you can fix it, do you?"

"I can try," Eugene said, surveying the debris on the table with wide eyes that reflected the challenge.

"Thanks, Eugene. You really do have a way with him," Wyler said, turning to look at Gabe. His son was already practicing on the flight simulator that was set up like an arcade game at the front of the store.

"Actually, I was hoping you would come in today. There's something I wanted to talk to you about."

"Sure. What's up?" asked Wyler, turning back to face Eugene.

"Didn't you say you were a detective of some kind?" Eugene asked.

Wyler was caught off-guard by the question, and he didn't answer right away. His mind quickly scanned through all their past conversations, searching for the details of what he had told Eugene about himself.

"No, not really. I mean, I used to be with the NYPD. But not anymore."

"Oh." Eugene nodded, as if considering the new information. "The reason I mention it is I have a friend that I was hoping you could talk to. She's a neighbor of mine. Lives in my building."

"What's the problem?" Wyler asked, more out of politeness than curiosity.

"Well, she has a brother in Manhattan. Or had a brother, I should say. He died a few days ago. Committed suicide."

"I'm sorry to hear that," said Wyler, guardedly.

"The thing is, she doesn't think it was suicide. She thinks he was murdered."

CHAPTER 2

After quietly peeking into Gabe's bedroom to make sure he was asleep, Wyler descended the staircase, passing the framed picture of himself and Jessica and Gabe that hung on the wall. He didn't look at the picture, but he felt its presence tugging at him as he went by.

When he and Gabe had moved into the house last year, he wasn't sure how to handle the pictures issue. Of course he didn't want to erase the memory of Jessica from Gabe's life, but on the other hand, the walls and shelves of their Manhattan apartment had been filled with framed photos of the three of them. He wasn't sure if rehanging all those pictures in their new home was the right thing to do, especially since they had moved here in large part to forget. There was no handbook for these kinds of decisions, and he ended up simply hanging some pictures and boxing others. As with most decisions he'd made regarding Gabe since Jessica's death, he had wrestled over it endlessly, reluctantly decided, then immediately started second guessing himself.

On his way to the living room, Wyler stowed Gabe's shoes in the hall closet and reset a fallen couch pillow. Reaching behind a row of books in the bookcase, he fished out a lighter, ashtray, and pack of cigarettes, then settled into a large leather chair by the window and picked up the TV remote. He lit the daily cigarette he allowed himself and began watching *The Seven Samurai* where he had left off the night before. He had been picking at the movie for several days. It was the scene where the samurai first arrive in the village they've been hired to protect, and the villagers are all cowering in their homes, afraid to come out to greet them. Offended by their behavior, the young hot-headed samurai played by Toshiro Mifune begins wildly ringing the village alarm, forcing the villagers to scramble out of their homes and beg for protection.

Wyler's father had worked as a film projectionist in Manhattan for thirty years at famous cinemas like St. Mark's Theatre and Film Forum before he and one of Wyler's uncles opened a revival theater of their own in the Park Slope neighborhood of Brooklyn , specializing in art films and foreign and American classics. Growing up, both Wyler and his older brother Marty worked weekends and summers at the theater. They passed the time together making fun of corny old Hollywood classics and pretentious foreign films. One time, Marty's whispered running commentary on *The Seventh Seal* made Wyler laugh so hard he wet his pants in the projection booth. But after Marty left for college Wyler stopped laughing and started watching, and before long his father's love for all kinds of movies began to rub off. When Gabe was younger, Wyler had tried to share his passion for classic and foreign films with his son, but he had long since given up. These days, it was hard enough to get Gabe to tear himself away from video games and YouTube to watch a new movie with him, let alone a subtitled black-and-white movie in Japanese.

Their house was in Rhinebeck, New York, about a hundred miles north of New York City. It was a large house with a history. According to local lore, it had served as a post office and an inn at different times. It was much more space than a forty-two-year-old man and an eleven-year-old boy required, but Wyler chose it because he felt he and Gabe needed a place where they could be separate, protected from the outside world, a kind of cocoon they could both hide in until they were ready to emerge.

A shaft of orange lamp light illuminated his exhaled smoke, and as Wyler studied the changing cloud patterns that hung lazily in the air, his attention drifted from the movie to the conversation he had earlier with Eugene in the hobby shop.

"She thinks he was murdered," Eugene had said, speaking of his neighbor's conviction that her brother had not committed suicide. Wyler had seen this many times before. After a suicide, family members and friends often went looking for another answer, something to ease their personal guilt or pain.

"Eugene, I'm sorry about what happened with your neighbor, but believe me, if the cops say suicide, it was suicide."

"That's exactly what I've been telling her," Eugene said. "I just think, if she heard it from someone like you, it would mean more. She's really upset. Would you be willing to just talk to her?"

"I'm not in law enforcement anymore. There's really nothing I can do." At that point he had walked away, collected Gabe, and left the shop abruptly.

Wyler drank in another drag and let it out slowly, creating a new swirling smoke cloud that merged and danced with the one already hanging in the air. How had Eugene known about his law enforcement background? He didn't remember discussing it with him, but he could be wrong. There had been so many meandering conversations over the past months that it was possible he could have mentioned it. Still, the fact that he couldn't remember doing so bothered him. It was the kind of annoying loose end he would have obsessed about in his previous career.

Aaron Wyler had joined the New York City Police Department eighteen years ago, back in 2001. In September. It was a decision that couldn't have been anticipated even a month earlier.

He had earned a bachelor's degree from Brooklyn College and had just graduated from law school at St. John's University in Queens when 9/11 happened. That morning, he was at his father's movie theater in Brooklyn where he had been working part-time while preparing to take the bar exam. He was cleaning the bathrooms when he heard a loud scream coming from the front of the house. At first, he thought his father might be testing a print of one of the old Universal horror films they kept in stock for Halloween, but then he heard his father's anguished voice moaning "Oh God!" over and over. Wyler rushed to the lobby and found his father standing in the private office behind the concession stand, staring at the small TV on his desk. Wyler didn't understand what was happening. It was a live news feed, but no one was speaking, and the screen was filled with smoke, dust, and debris. His father was staring transfixed at the images, sobbing. And then, a few moments later, the footage was replayed, and the horrible realization of what he was seeing filled Wyler's heart with shock and disbelief. As he watched the footage of the North Tower of the World Trade Center collapsing onto itself, he felt his father's unsteady hand on his arm, as if grasping for a lifeline.

The previous year, after graduating from SUNY Binghamton, Marty had moved back to the city to take a job as a junior bond broker at one of the most prestigious financial services companies in New York, Cantor Fitzgerald. His office was on the 103rd floor of the North Tower.

To this day Wyler doesn't remember consciously making the decision to go, but within seconds he found himself on the street outside the theater hurrying to the subway platform. He learned later that all the trains in New York stopped running at about 10:20 a.m., but by that time he had already made it to what would become known to the world as Ground Zero. He spent the next several days, alongside hundreds of others, fighting his way through the chaos and debris and his own tears as part of the makeshift rescue effort.

As time passed, the desperate hope that Marty would be one of the miraculous survivors slowly drained out of him. Only later would they learn the tragic news that every one of the 658 Cantor Fitzgerald employees that showed up for work that day had died in the attack.

In addition to the emotional impact of losing the person closest to him, Wyler also experienced the collective trauma shared by all New Yorkers in the aftermath of those events. The iconic Manhattan skyline, which provided a sense of identity and purpose to all those who lived there, like some kind of vast, architectural talisman, had been violently assaulted, maimed and scarred. Every New Yorker felt the wound deeply and personally.

Wyler remembered very little about the week that followed, except the eerie silence. The city's usual soundtrack of car horns, boom boxes, sirens, and street chatter was gone. People went about their business in a solemn, quiet state of shock, overshadowed by the mushroom cloud of dust particles that darkened the sky over Manhattan for days following the attack.

But that same mushroom cloud had the opposite effect on Wyler. The combination of his brother's death, the time he spent at Ground Zero, and the overall psychic shock of the 9/11 experience, had somehow brought clarity to his own life. By the end of the month he had abandoned his plan to become a lawyer and joined the New York City Police Department. It was a decision that he knew disappointed his grieving mother profoundly. Helen Wyler had worked as a paralegal in a big New York law firm, and Wyler knew his mother dreamed that he would someday become like the high-powered attorneys she had worked with. Still, he had never been more sure of a decision in his life.

Wyler rose quickly in the NYPD. After spending time on the street and then in narcotics, he made detective and was assigned to the squad located in Manhattan's Midtown South Precinct. He spent three years at Midtown South, investigating murders, rapes, robberies, burglaries, and other crimes that took place within the precinct's boundaries, which included Times Square.

Even though Wyler's rapid ascent to gold shield had raised some eyebrows, Wyler himself wasn't satisfied. From the beginning, he knew what he wanted to do in the department. He had joined the NYPD in direct response to 9/11, and he wanted to avenge those events by keeping New York City safe and secure in the future. By the end of the decade, he had gotten what he had been working toward from the start. He was a detective in the Counterterrorism Bureau.

Following 9/11, the New York City Police Department had taken the unusual step of organizing its own in-house counterterrorism task force. The move was strongly resented by the FBI, the CIA, and the Pentagon, the organizations traditionally responsible for combating terrorism. But in a short time the NYPD Counterterrorism Bureau became one of the most powerful and technologically advanced counterterrorism operations in the world, larger even than the FBI in terms of sheer manpower. The federal agencies that had initially scoffed at the concept began cooperating and collaborating with the NYPD, actively sharing resources and intelligence.

As a detective in Midtown South, Wyler had been focused on solving crimes that had already taken place. His work in counterterrorism required a completely different set of skills. The focus was on prevention, and success meant stopping things before they happened, not solving crimes after the fact. Every unchecked plot was a potential catastrophe. Although the cell responsible for 9/11 had long been rolled up by the time Wyler joined the bureau, there were plenty of new and active threats. New York was both the communications and financial capital of the world, and buildings like the United Nations, the New York Stock Exchange, and the new Freedom Tower—not to mention the city's hundreds of bridges and tunnels—made it the most target-rich environment on the planet.

Wyler had spent the past few years of his career with the NYPD thwarting car bombs, cyberattacks, active shooter plots, and attacks involving chemical, biological, and radiological weapons. He served on the Joint Terrorism Task Force which included members of the NYPD as well as agents from the FBI and the CIA. Since many terrorist plots originated overseas, the NYPD Counterterrorism Bureau sent officers to foreign countries, and Wyler had spent time in Madrid, Tel Aviv, Mumbai, and other places, partnering with local police and sharing training and intelligence.

But his career in law enforcement ended abruptly just over a year ago, when he resigned from the department shortly after the death of his wife, Jessica.

The doorbell rang, interrupting Wyler's train of thought. He paused the movie and mashed his cigarette into the ashtray, then glanced at the clock on the wall. It was almost 11:00 p.m. Before getting out of the chair, Wyler drew back the window curtain slightly and saw Eugene from Vortex Hobbies standing just outside his front door. In his arms, he held the P-38 Lightning airplane that Gabe had crashed. It had been miraculously reassembled to mint condition. Wyler was stunned by the plane's resurrection.

Eugene caught Wyler peeking through the window and waved to him, grinning. He held the fixed airplane up like a trophy. Wyler smiled and waved back, then went down to open the door.

CHAPTER 3

Three nights later, Wyler sat at a table toward the back of the cafeteria on the ground floor of Westchester Medical Center, nursing a cup of coffee and waiting. He checked his phone and saw that it was almost 9:00 p.m. The summer day was over, but the late-setting sun still threw low shafts of muted light through the hospital windows, cloaking the room in a depressing, dull haze. Wyler noticed that only two other tables were occupied: one by some patient's grim-faced loved ones, and one by a few hospital staffers in scrubs on break.

A few minutes past nine, a woman wearing blue pull-tie nurse pants and a polka-dotted top walked purposefully into the seating area, bypassing the food and the cash register. Her eyes scanned the room and picked up Wyler, who gave a tentative wave.

"Sarah Miller?" Wyler asked as she approached the table. Wyler estimated her age to be mid-thirties. Her hair was long, but done-up, and she wore no makeup.

"Yes. Mr. Wyler?"

They shook hands, and although she forced a polite half smile, Wyler immediately picked up a tough, world-weary vibe.

"I appreciate you being willing to talk to me, and for meeting me here," she began politely. "My hours are so crazy, it's hard to get away."

"It's not a problem. As it happens, I'm pretty flexible these days."

There was a pause, as if neither of them knew quite how to get started.

"Can I get you a cup of coffee or something?" asked Wyler.

"I'm fine, thanks. I don't have too much time."

She looked at Wyler as if sizing him up.

"Eugene said you might be able to help." She said it as though she didn't believe it and was challenging Wyler to prove her wrong. "I've tried to deal with the police, but they won't listen to me. The detectives assigned have been completely useless." She waved her hand in a dismissive gesture.

Wyler took a sip of his coffee, sensing that his name would probably soon be added to her list of useless people. He had agreed to meet with Sarah Miller as a favor to Eugene, but he had no intention of doing anything other than politely hearing her out.

"I don't see how they can call themselves detectives. They've already closed the case."

She grimaced, as if the chip on her shoulder was causing her physical pain.

"I was sorry to hear about your brother," Wyler offered, hoping to move things forward. At the mention of her brother, Sarah Miller's body changed immediately. Her shoulders slumped, and she stared down at the empty table.

"He was my only sibling. I'm—I was—three years older. There was just the two of us growing up together."

Her eyes reddened as her cheeks flushed with sadness.

"Did you grow up around here?"

"West Point," she said, regaining her composure and looking

up at Wyler. "My father taught at the military academy. He was the deputy head of math and sciences there."

"So, he was in the army?"

"Oh yes," she said, with an emphasis that Wyler couldn't quite read. "He was a lieutenant colonel. My mother was also a schoolteacher, but not at the academy. She taught English at Poughkeepsie Day. My father died a few years ago. Lung cancer. My mom sold the house and moved to a condo in Arizona to get away from the snow."

Wyler waited, giving her time to get there. Years of experience had taught him the power of uncomfortable silence when questioning witnesses and suspects. Let them talk, even ramble, and eventually the truth comes out.

"Peter was a wonderful brother. He was very kind and loving and sensitive."

Wyler gave her a moment, then asked, "Why don't you tell me about him?"

"Well, Peter was kind of a lost soul for many years. After high school, he went to a few colleges, but it never worked out. He tried a lot of different things. For a while, he wanted to be an actor, then a professional dancer. He moved to the city to try to break in. But, like a lot of people, he found the reality of it was just too hard. He was always dreaming big."

"What did your parents think of his big dreams?"

"I think my mom was secretly supportive, but my dad, that was another story. He and Peter fought all the time. I don't want you to get the wrong impression of my father. He was a good man, very loving in his own way. But Peter was his only son, and he always expected him to follow in his footsteps. There was a lot of tension there, and not just from my dad. Peter played his part, too, believe me. I think he went out of his way to push my father's buttons."

She seemed to get lost in the memory for a moment, so Wyler brought her back.

"You said Peter *had* been a lost soul. Does that mean he eventually found himself?"

"Oh, definitely. He decided to become a chef. He was always an excellent cook. A few years ago, he moved back up here, and got into the CIA."

Wyler was momentarily taken aback, but then recovered. "The Culinary Institute of America, in Hyde Park?" he asked.

She nodded. "He did really well there, and after he graduated, he moved back to Manhattan and worked at a bunch of different restaurants. You know, trying to break in."

"When was this?" asked Wyler.

"That was about three years ago."

"How did he do?"

"It was hard. Harder than he thought it would be. He hated having to pay his dues and wait his turn. I thought he was too impatient. He was doing really well. For a while, he was one of the sous chefs at The Empire Grille."

Wyler nodded, impressed. The Empire Grille was a top rated, upscale restaurant near Lincoln Center. "Sounds like he was doing very well for an up-and-coming chef."

"He was, but he hated it there. The executive chef was a real Gordon Ramsey type who bullied Peter and everyone else, so he left The Empire Grille last year and took a job as the head chef at Nine."

"Nine?"

"It's a small bistro on 2nd Avenue in the East Village. A big step down from The Empire Grille, but at least he was in charge."

"So, was he happier there?"

"No, it was actually worse. He thought he would be running the kitchen, but the place had two owners that were very hands-on about the menu. They were totally inflexible. They refused to let Peter try anything new or take any chances. Peter was the head chef, but he wasn't able to do what he wanted, to really show his stuff. He was miserable there. He got really depressed."

Sarah suddenly looked at Wyler defiantly. "I know what you're thinking, but he wasn't depressed when he died."

"Why do you say that?" Wyler asked.

"Because his whole life changed completely last month, after he met Scottie Hibble."

"Scottie Hibble?" Wyler asked.

"You've never heard of Scottie Hibble? Maybe there is some hope for humanity," she said with a mocking sneer.

"Who is he?"

"He's actually pretty famous. He's this young, hotshot entrepreneur. He's the founder of RopeLine."

Another blank stare from Wyler.

"It's one of the hottest things right now. It's this invitation-only app that gives you access to exclusive clubs and events. You party with celebrities—supermodels, rappers, that kind of thing. It's huge, if that's what you're into." Sarah Miller obviously wasn't.

"So, how did Peter meet him?"

"I actually don't know, but somehow they met, and he and Scottie Hibble became friends."

"You said meeting this guy changed Peter's life completely. How?"

"Well, Scottie totally believed in Peter. He thought he was going to be the next big thing. He was going to help make him a famous chef. Scottie was going to set Peter up in his own restaurant."

"And all of this happened right before Peter died?"

"Yes. That's how I know Peter didn't jump off that balcony. All his dreams were suddenly coming true. He was going to open his own restaurant and finally get to do things his way. He was never happier."

Wyler listened sympathetically, but he had enough experience with suicides to know that an outward façade of happiness often masked pain and torment buried deep inside.

"How close were you to your brother?"

"We were close," Sarah answered, a bit too quickly. Wyler wondered how close they could have been, with Peter in Manhattan and Sarah up in Dutchess County, an hour and a half by train or car. "Well, we didn't get to see each other as often as I would have liked," she added, as if reading Wyler's thoughts. "Both my husband and I work crazy hours. He's a realtor. We have three kids. We don't get into the city much. But Peter and I talked on the phone a lot. We talked the night of the ... the night he died. He and Scottie Hibble had spent the day scouting properties for the restaurant. Peter was convinced they had found the perfect place. I've never heard him so excited, so happy. And then," she paused, taking a paper napkin from the box on the table and preemptively dabbing her red eyes, "I got a call at around midnight from the police, telling me he had jumped from the balcony of his apartment."

Wyler took another sip of his coffee, giving her time to compose herself.

"Was Peter seeing someone at the time of his death, maybe a girlfriend?"

She shook her head. "He was always too focused on his work, on achieving his dreams."

"What about ... a boyfriend?" he asked carefully.

"Of course not," she answered quickly, with a defensive edge to her voice that communicated more than she probably intended.

Wyler let a little more time pass, then decided it was time to lower the boom.

"Look, Sarah. I know this is really difficult to accept, but sometimes people who seem perfectly fine on the outside may be going through something on the inside, something that they don't share, even with the people closest to them. It might surprise you to learn this, but most of the time, close friends and family of people who commit suicide are totally shocked by it. They didn't see it coming. They're left with unanswered questions and feelings of guilt, that they should have known, that they should have been able to do something about it."

"You sound just like those detectives who were assigned to the case," she said bitterly. "Look, I can pay you," she continued. "I'm not asking you to do this for free."

"Do what?" Wyler asked.

"I want to hire you. You're a private detective, aren't you?"

A laugh almost escaped him, but luckily he caught it in time.

"I'm a retired police officer, and yes, I was a detective. But I don't really think that's what you need. If the detectives assigned to the case are convinced it was a suicide, then I'm sure that's what it was. As painful and difficult as that may be to accept."

Sarah lowered her head. Wyler couldn't tell if it was a gesture of defeat or if she was steeling herself for round two, so he turned to look out the window to give her some privacy. Out of respect, he resisted the urge to check the time on his cellphone while he waited.

"I know that Peter was murdered," Sarah said slowly, still fixing her stare at the tabletop. "And," she continued, "I know who killed him."

"Who do you think killed him?" asked Wyler.

She raised her head and looked at Wyler with pleading eyes. For a long moment, neither of them said anything. When she finally spoke, it was in a fierce, quiet whisper.

"God," she said.

CHAPTER 4

Wyler studied the face of Sarah Miller. He had years of experience dealing with religious fanatics, and although he knew the nurse sitting across from him wasn't a terrorist, her bizarre statement set off an internal alarm.

"I know how crazy that sounds," she offered, almost as an apology. "But please, hear me out."

Wyler nodded, signaling her to continue.

"There's a whole part of the story I haven't told you," she began, lowering her voice to a conspiratorial whisper, even though all the tables near them were deserted. "I haven't told it to anyone, actually. But I want you to hear it before you decide to help me or not."

"I'm listening," said Wyler.

Sarah Miller didn't speak right away. She stared at Wyler, as if looking for some assurance in his face, some clue that would help her resolve her inner conflict. But after a few moments of wrestling with her decision, she made her choice and began speaking.

"My family has a secret. Actually, it goes back over a thousand years."

She paused, as if expecting a reaction from Wyler, but there was none.

"Are you a religious person, Mr. Wyler?"

Wyler took a moment before answering.

"I'm Jewish," he replied truthfully, but in a clipped tone that suggested no more details were coming. The answer seemed to satisfy her, and she continued.

"We're Catholic," she said.

"What does this have to do with –"

"Peter had something with him when he died."

"What did he have?"

"An ancient, religious artifact."

Wyler gave her a questioning look, which she answered.

"Miller is my married name. My maiden name is Lisonbee. My family has an English ancestor named John Lisonbee who went on one of the crusades to the Holy Land with Richard the Lionheart. At that time, Richard was given a sacred gemstone by a Jewish priest in gratitude for fighting to free Jerusalem from Saladin and the Muslim invaders. According to family legend, King Richard, in turn, gave the gemstone to our ancestor, John Lisonbee. That was in 1191. This gemstone has been a part of my family ever since. I know it's hard to believe, but this stone has been passed down in my family from father to son for almost a thousand years."

She paused and took out her cellphone. After a few moments of tapping and scrolling, she handed the phone to Wyler. On the screen was a picture of a shiny, oval-shaped black gemstone, cradled in what looked like a miniature treasure box.

"It's an onyx stone," she said.

"What does this have to do with your brother's death?" Wyler asked, handing the phone back.

"Before he died, my father gave the stone to Peter. It was the first time either of us heard the story. He told us that our family had been chosen by God to be caretakers of the stone."

"Caretakers? I don't understand."

"Well, according to the story, the stone is very special. It's been passed down by biblical prophets from the time of Moses. Our father shared all this with us just before he died. It surprised us. Even though we went to Mass regularly, I never really considered my father to be a spiritual man. My dad was a scientist, so to hear him talk this way ... It just wasn't like him. But you could tell that he took the covenant of the stone very seriously."

"The covenant of the stone?"

"That's what he called it. Our family was supposed to protect the stone. I don't really know from what. I don't think he knew either. But he made it clear that possession of the stone should never leave our family, and it could never be used for ... personal gain."

"What do you mean?"

"Well, if the story is true, that stone would be worth a lot of money. My father was very proud of the fact that during all the years our ancestors guarded it, no one had ever tried to sell the stone or use it to get rich. We were not a wealthy family, but my father kept the covenant of the stone, and he expected Peter to do the same."

"And did he?"

She paused and grimaced, as if in pain.

"Yes, until last month," she said. "I told you how miserable and depressed my brother was. He was desperate. He was convinced the only way out was to start his own restaurant, but he didn't have the money to do that. In New York City, are you kidding? There was no way. So, he decided he was going to sell the stone."

She said the last part with a mix of anger and disappointment. For a moment, she seemed to physically buckle under the strain of juggling all the conflicting emotions about her brother, but then she recovered and continued.

"Last month, he had another fight with the owners of Nine, the restaurant where he worked. A big blow-up over something he wanted to add to the menu. Peter called me after and told me he was done. His birthday was the next day—he was turning thirty—and he said he was going to give himself a present. He told me he was going to sell the stone and get the money to open his own restaurant."

"What did you say to him?"

"I was very angry. I didn't think it was right. I mean, I'm not sure what I believed about the stone, but our family had protected it for almost a thousand years. You don't take something like that lightly. Our father believed there was something special about the stone, that it was very sacred and holy, and he was not a superstitious man, Mr. Wyler. But Peter," she sighed heavily. "He was so impulsive. He saw the stone as his only hope of getting what he wanted, and he didn't care about anything else. I think, in a perverse way, the fact that it was in direct defiance of our father's dying wishes actually made it more appealing to him. We fought about it."

"You said he had it when he died. Did you convince him not to sell it?"

"No, he wouldn't listen to me. The day after he called me, he took the stone to get it appraised. He had every intention of selling it and getting the money."

"So, what happened?"

"He met Scottie Hibble. After that, he didn't need to sell the stone anymore. He was going to get what he wanted without it."

Sarah paused while Wyler considered what she had said.

"Do you really think God killed your brother?" Wyler asked.

"I don't mean that literally, Mr. Wyler. But I know this. A short time after deciding to sell the stone, Peter was dead. You may think I'm silly or crazy or deluded, but I think he was punished. Punished by God. He broke the covenant that our family had kept for almost a thousand years, and now, he's dead."

Tears threatened the corners of her eyes again, and she pulled a few more paper napkins from the box on the table.

"And there's one more thing," she said. "Peter kept the stone in his apartment, in a box my father had given him. The night he died, after the police called and told me what had happened, I went to his apartment that same night, and the stone was gone."

There was a pause as Wyler considered the implications of this.

"I know this is hard to consider," he began, softly, "but isn't it possible that Peter actually did go ahead and sell the stone, like you said, to get the money for his restaurant? He could have made the whole thing up about meeting Scottie Hibble because he knew how you felt about it."

She took a moment , as if trying to assemble images in her mind to match this alternate theory, but then she shook her head quickly like a teacher erasing a wrong answer on a chalkboard.

"No, that's not what happened. I know that. When we spoke that night, he swore to me that he didn't sell it. He knew how upset I was about it, and I know he wouldn't have lied to me."

"How do you know?"

"He *swore* to me, Mr. Wyler, on The Bible. My brother wasn't religious, but I know his heart. He would never have done that if it weren't true. Besides, he texted me a picture of the stone the night he died. That was the picture I showed you."

"Why would he do that?" Wyler asked.

"He knew how upset I was about his plan to sell it. He wanted to assure me that he still had it."

"He could have taken that picture anytime and just sent it to you that night."

"But if that's true, and he did sell the stone, then where's the money? He had no cash in his apartment, and only a few hundred dollars in the bank when he died."

Wyler paused to take all this in. There certainly were some unanswered questions, but he wasn't sure what she expected of him.

"Did Peter leave a note?"

"You mean, like a suicide note? No. There was no note. Because it wasn't a suicide."

"So, what exactly do you think happened, to Peter, and to this stone?"

"That's what I want you to find out."

CHAPTER 5

Wyler sat in his car with the engine running, scribbling notes as fast as he could. The car was parked outside a CVS pharmacy a few blocks from the hospital. Wyler had stopped there and rushed in to buy a notebook and pen. Now, he was busy trying to record all the details of his conversation with Sarah Miller while they were still fresh in his mind. Back in the day, he never would have conducted an interview without taking meticulous notes, or better yet, recording the entire conversation. But his meeting with Sarah Miller was not supposed to be part of an investigation. It was a favor to a friend, a courtesy to ease someone's pain. And so, he had come unprepared. Now he was scrambling to make up for his mistake.

The sky was dark and there was a low rumble off in the distance. When Wyler finished writing, he flicked off the car's overhead light and sat for a moment, thinking things over. He had agreed to look into Peter Lisonbee's death. That's exactly how he put it. "Let me look into it," he had said. He made it sound casual and low-key. He would make a few calls. Talk to some people he knew. Make a few discreet inquiries. He avoided using the word *investigation*. He didn't want to get her hopes up. He wanted to manage her expectations, because he still believed, at the end of the day, they were looking at a suicide.

Even so, there were some elements of her story that interested him. And not just the ancient religious stone, as fascinating as that was. No, there were some loose ends that bothered him. For starters, there was no suicide note. Of course not everyone leaves a note, but the fact is most do. Then there was the strange timing of his meeting with Scottie Hibble. Peter Lisonbee had gone out, trying to sell this strange family heirloom, and then he happened to meet a millionaire who promised to make his dreams come true, thereby removing the need for him to sell the stone. Could be a coincidence, but Wyler didn't trust coincidence. And then there was the texted picture of the stone, sent just a few hours before his death. That's a strange thing to do, right before taking your own life. Was there some hidden meaning to the picture? Was he trying to send his sister a message? If so, what? Had he actually taken the picture that night? And where was the stone now? Had someone stolen it? Had he given it to someone? In spite of Sarah Lisonbee's assurances about her brother, he had to consider the possibility that the entire Scottie Hibble part of the story had been invented by Peter to avoid admitting to his sister that he had sold the stone. But if that were true, and he had sold it, then where was the money?

In the end, there were enough unresolved questions surrounding the circumstances of Peter Lisonbee's death that Wyler had offered to help.

Raindrops began to tap on the car. Since Wyler wasn't driving, he left the wipers off and watched the drops collect on the windshield. There was another reason he had agreed to help Sarah Miller that was harder to admit to himself. The truth was, Wyler's life had been pretty empty and unfulfilling lately. When he had retired from the force following Jessica's death, he had done so to spend more time with Gabe. The circumstances of Jessica's death had traumatized Gabe, and Wyler knew his son needed his undivided attention and support. But even though he loved being with Gabe, he was also frustrated. For all the time and attention he lavished on Gabe, his son didn't seem to be making much progress. Sometimes, it felt like they were both just stuck.

On the other hand, Wyler wasn't sure he would be able to recognize progress in Gabe even if he saw it. Maybe Gabe wasn't even the problem in the equation. As usual, whenever he took time to think about Gabe and his situation, there was another truth lurking beneath the surface, waiting to be confronted: His own feelings about his wife's death.

About her suicide.

When it had first happened, Wyler had tabled his own feelings. Gabe needed a full-time father, and he couldn't afford the luxury of rummaging through whatever unresolved emotions he might be harboring. They could wait. *He* could wait. Gabe and his well-being were all that mattered.

But, just as Dr. Schoenwald had suggested that Gabe find an activity to occupy his mind, Wyler realized that he, too, needed something to focus on. He wasn't turning away from his son, but he needed a distraction. As he had sat in that hospital cafeteria, listening to Sarah Miller, something had happened. Parts of his brain that had lain dormant were cranking to life again, and he had to admit that it felt good.

That's why, at the end of their meeting, Wyler had agreed to help. She had tried to offer him money again, but he had refused. For one thing, he didn't want Sarah Miller as his "client." He didn't want her thinking she had hired him, and that he was therefore beholden to her in any way. There was also the issue of legality. He was not a licensed private investigator in the state of New York, and things could get very messy if he took money and things went south. Of course, if he wanted to hang out a shingle he could. Lots of private detectives were ex-cops. He had plenty of

NYPD colleagues that had gone that route. But Wyler had no real interest in doing that. And the truth was, he didn't need the money.

Wyler's wife Jessica had been a very wealthy woman. Her father, Charles Maitland, had made a fortune manufacturing industrial drill bits used in oil and gas exploration. Jessica had a sizable trust fund, and she had left everything to Wyler. Although it had never been part of his life's plan to accumulate a lot of money, Wyler unexpectedly found himself, for all intents and purposes, well-off. More than well-off. Rich, actually. The truth was, unless he acted very foolishly, he would never have to work again. Not that he planned to remain idle for the rest of his life. He just hadn't thought it through. He had no long-term plans at this point. For now, his only focus was Gabe.

As the rain started to pick up, Wyler closed the notebook. He thought he had captured all the relevant details of his meeting with Sarah Miller, and the outline of a plan for investigating the death of Peter Lisonbee was beginning to form in his mind.

He turned on the headlights and windshield wipers, pulled out of the parking lot, and headed for home.

CHAPTER 6

Peter Lisonbee's apartment was in the West Village, a small neighborhood in lower Manhattan on the western slope of New York's Greenwich Village. The area was famous for its bohemian culture and was home to several small theaters, off-beat art galleries, and trendy, hole-in-the-wall restaurants. The neighborhood was a magnet for the young, hip, and strange. The colorful residents of the West Village tended to live in low-rise brownstones sandwiched together and divided into apartments or artist lofts. Peter Lisonbee lived in one of the few high-rise buildings in the neighborhood—an old residential apartment complex on Perry Street called The Gateway. It was from his apartment's balcony on the fourteenth floor that Peter had jumped to his death ten days earlier.

Wyler stood in front of the building, craning his neck to gaze at the long tapering column of balconies that rose into the sky. It was almost noon, and he had to shield his eyes. He had gotten an early start, but between the train ride from Poughkeepsie to Grand Central and then another subway ride to the Village, it had taken him over two hours to get here. He could have taken a cab, but Wyler hated riding in cabs in Manhattan. He couldn't stand being stuck in traffic knowing that beneath him subways were shooting through their tunnels unimpeded. Of course, subway cars often sat stuck in the tunnels for several minutes at a time or even longer, but you pick your poison.

Wyler counted out thirteen floors to find the fourteenth floor, where Peter Lisonbee lived. He assumed that, like most New York City buildings, the numbering of floors skipped from twelve to fourteen, omitting the unlucky number thirteen altogether. He fixed his eyes momentarily on the fourteenth floor, then let them drop slowly to the pavement in front of him. There was still some discoloration where the FDNY had obviously power blasted the blood from the sidewalk over a week ago. Wyler repeated the gesture, looking up again to the balconies on fourteen, then slowly down to the ground. He tried to imagine the fall. He had been to dozens of similar locations all around the city where jumpers had met their end. Although guns and ropes were far more popular in the heartland, the number of tall buildings in Manhattan made jumping the easiest and by far the most popular method of taking one's life in the big city, and Wyler had witnessed the grisly results many times.

By the time he had reached the site of the collapse of the Twin Towers on September 11th, both buildings had already fallen. Wyler had been part of the makeshift team of professional first responders and volunteers that spent the next two weeks picking through the rubble and debris, searching desperately for survivors, but mostly just finding and removing the remains of the dead. It was an awful process. Hours of backbreaking, bone-aching physical labor punctuated by shocking moments of gruesome discovery. But of all the horrors that Wyler witnessed that week, nothing compared to the bodies of those who had jumped to their deaths that day. Terrible as it was to uncover the broken, twisted bodies of those who had been burned alive and buried beneath the rubble and ash, the bodies of the jumpers were even more disturbing. Wyler had tried many times to imagine the awful scenes that must have played out inside those two buildings. People seeing their friends and coworkers consumed in flames before their eyes, listening to their chilling death screams as the wall of smoke inched closer and closer. About two hundred people that day had chosen to escape the burning heat and suffocating smoke by jumping to a certain death. Some had held hands and jumped together. These bodies were more than just maimed and broken. They were completely pulverized. Smashed to oblivion. In some cases, no longer even recognizable as human beings. For years he was haunted by the thought that his brother may have ended his life as one of those misshapen abominations.

But there had been no flames in Peter Lisonbee's apartment ten nights ago. Wyler knew of no imminent danger that had forced this young man with a promising future to climb over that balcony and jump. If, in fact, he did jump.

Wyler walked toward the building's double glass door entrance and went in. The spacious lobby was unfurnished except for a small security desk manned by an overweight doorman flipping the pages of a tabloid newspaper. A large sculpture hung from the lobby ceiling, one of those modern art mobiles made up of hundreds of tinted, translucent shapes dangling from wires. Wyler passed under it and headed toward the elevator, noting that the guy at the security desk didn't even raise his head. His job was obviously more about signing for packages and letting in various tradesmen than it was about building security.

The elevator doors opened, and two women got out at different speeds. One was dressed for a yoga class and the other, older woman was carrying a big pot with a tall tree-like plant of some kind. Wyler stepped into the empty elevator and pushed the number fourteen. Before the doors closed, he saw the top of the older woman's plant brush the bottom of the hanging lobby sculpture, causing a cluster of shapes to sway and clink together.

As he rode up to the fourteenth floor, he thought of what he might find. It had been almost two weeks since Peter's death, and he knew the crime scene would be far from clean. It had no doubt been trampled through by the officers and detectives who initially responded to the call. Still, it was possible the initial investigators had missed something, and Wyler was anxious to see things with his own eyes.

Wyler stepped out on fourteen and headed toward a door midway down the corridor crisscrossed with yellow police tape. The apartment with the tape was 14-L, Peter Lisonbee's. Wyler took out a pair of blue latex gloves and put them on. The scene was already contaminated, but he wouldn't add to it. He carefully unhooked both strips of police tape on one side and let the ends drop out of the way. Before proceeding, he paused for a moment to consider what he had just done. Removing police tape was something he had done hundreds of times before as a cop. But he was no longer a cop, he was a civilian, and by removing the tape, he had committed a crime.

Next, he took out the key that Sarah Miller had given him, opened the door, and stepped, unauthorized, into an official crime scene. Crime number two. Oh, well. In for a penny.

It was a medium-sized loft, with a small entranceway leading into a large open space that served as both living room and bedroom. A modest kitchen was off to one side, and next to that was a door that Wyler assumed led to a bathroom. No lights were on, but the room had plenty of sunlight coming in from the far wall where a sliding glass door led onto a small terrace.

As he closed the door, he noticed that it had an old-fashioned chain lock which had been broken. He examined it. The small round head of the rusted chain was still hanging in the sliding slot on the door, and there was a jagged strip of painted wood dangling from the other end. A divot in the doorframe matched the wood hanging from the chain. Someone had broken through the door, smashing through the chain lock to get into the apartment. Probably the police officers who had responded to the call. If the door had been locked and the chain fastened when Peter jumped, that meant he was alone in the apartment. A point for suicide.

Wyler paused in the entranceway by the kitchen and scanned the room. At first blush, it was a typical New York starter apartment, similar to thousands scattered all over the five boroughs that housed ambitious dreamers like Peter with a willingness to start at the bottom. It was neater than he had expected from a bachelor living alone. The bed was made, and there were no clothes hanging over chairs or socks on the floor. In fact, there was nothing out of the ordinary. No sign of a struggle or frenzied search for money, drugs, or other valuables. There was, in fact, nothing about the physical surroundings that seemed to justify the sense of foreboding that Wyler was suddenly experiencing.

He knew it wasn't the fact that a death had recently occurred here. Wyler had visited the scenes of hundreds of crimes, including several brutal murders.. He was well acquainted with the aftermath of death, and he had personally felt the trace elements of shock and terror that sometimes hung in the air in such places. But what he was feeling now was an entirely different sensation. As he simultaneously scanned his surroundings and also his own psyche for the source of the unusual feeling, it suddenly occurred to him that the last crime scene he had visited had been inside of his own apartment, over a year ago

This flash of memory and what it represented forced him to immediately regain focus and begin working the scene.

A framed photograph on the wall next to the bed suddenly became a needed lifeline, and he walked over to get a closer look. Wyler stood in front of the picture and studied it. It showed a large group of people dressed in white excitedly tossing chef hats into the air. Some were college age, but many were older. Peter's graduation from the Culinary Institute of America.

There was another, smaller photograph in a frame on the nightstand next to the bed, and Wyler picked it up. In this picture, three friends in chef hats hung off each other, clutching their diplomas and smiling goofily. There was a woman with brown skin and black hair who looked possibly Middle Eastern, a young African American man, and another young man in the middle. It had probably been taken on the same day as the picture on the wall. Wyler stared at the young man in the photograph. Peter Lisonbee, in better times. He was smaller and slighter than the two friends who towered over him on either side. Wyler removed the picture from the frame.

Setting down the empty frame, he noticed a smartphone was also on the nightstand. This was another clear sign that the investigators who responded to this scene did not seriously consider any cause of death other than suicide. In a murder investigation, the victim's phone would have been taken into evidence and all recent contacts thoroughly scrutinized. Wyler picked up the phone to examine it. He was surprised to find that the phone was plugged in and charging. He disconnected the charger and slipped both the phone and the picture into his pocket. Crime number three. He was on a spree.

Wyler's eyes next went to Peter's bed. The two bed pillows had been propped up portrait-style against the headboard, and several stacks of papers were assembled in a half-moon pattern on the bed. Wyler imagined Peter sitting cross-legged on the bed, working on some project. He picked up one of the thin stacks of papers on the bed and shuffled through it. The papers in the first stack contained typed lists of food items. Although some of the words were unfamiliar to him, he guessed he was looking at a list of salads. There were lots of handwritten notes scribbled in the margins, with various things circled and others crossed out. A few items were both circled *and* crossed out. He picked up the next stack and found a similar list, this time with seafood items like sea urchin, striped bass, and Dover sole. It looked like, on the night he died, Peter had been planning the menu for the new restaurant he was going to open.

A plate of Chinese food sat on the nightstand on the other side of the bed. Wyler crossed to the far side of the room to examine the plate more closely. The plate was perched halfway over the edge of the nightstand, like it had been put aside hurriedly and then forgotten about. Although he couldn't be sure, it seemed to Wyler that the food had barely been touched. A blue ballpoint pen was sitting next to the plate. Wyler picked up the pen by bracing it between his two gloved index fingers. The head of the pen had not been retracted by the clicker on the back. He placed the pen back down on the nightstand.

He went to the kitchen next. It was not a separate room but consisted of cabinetry and counters built into a corner of the open space. There was also a small rectangular island with two stools. Three open Chinese food take-out boxes were on the island counter, as well as a plastic bag with a menu and a few fortune cookies stuffed inside. There was a receipt stapled to the side of the bag, but no date stamp on the receipt.

Wyler saw another bag on the counter next to the sink and went to have a closer look. It was a tote bag with two long strap handles. The bag was green and had the words Verdure Grocery stitched on the side in ornate lettering that morphed into vegetation. Wyler examined the contents of the bag without removing them. There was a bottle of olive oil, a brand of fancy bottled pasta sauce he had never heard of, a tin of coffee, a small bag of red potatoes, and a container of liquid laundry detergent. Near the bottom of the bag, he found another receipt. This one showed both the date and time of the purchase. According to the receipt, Peter Lisonbee had gone shopping just a few hours before killing himself.

Wyler left the kitchen and walked over to a computer desk that sat directly across from the bed. The desk had a glass top that sat on a wooden frame. There was a large computer monitor, a printer, and two speakers on the desk. Several disconnected cords all pointed to an empty space in the middle of the desk that Wyler assumed represented a missing laptop.

A single row of wooden drawers hung under the desk—a long middle drawer flanked by two larger side drawers. Wyler opened the middle drawer and found a messy assortment of utility bills, take-out menus, ad flyers, and other loose papers. There were also two maroon-colored booklets that Wyler immediately recognized as Zagat restaurant guides. He quickly flipped through them to see if anything was hidden in the pages, but there was nothing.

He closed the middle drawer and pulled open the first side drawer. There were more menus in this drawer, but these were not disposable take-out menus. They were large, hard-backed restaurant menus from some of the top restaurants in the city: Le Bernardin, Gramercy Tavern, Union Square Café, and a place Wyler had never heard of called Covington Bistro. Wyler wondered how Peter had gotten a hold of these. Did he steal them? Buy them online? Or was there an underground network of up-and-coming chefs who traded such things?

Inside the final desk drawer, Wyler found a ream of white computer paper, an opened box of envelopes, a roll of stamps, and a few boxes of printer ink cartridges. Deeper in the drawer, sitting behind the ream of paper, was a small jewelry box. It was exactly where Sarah Miller had told him it would be.

Wyler picked up the box. It was heavier than he thought it

would be. It appeared to be made of bronze and was decorated with ornate flourishes on the lid and side. The box had four carved feet that looked like small animal claws, maybe a bear's or a lion's. Wyler opened the lid and, as expected, found it empty.

After finding nothing of interest in the bathroom, Wyler opened the sliding glass door and stepped out onto the apartment's terrace. It was narrow, with room for a few plants and maybe a couple of small deck chairs. But Peter had none of these on his terrace. The railing was made up of black metal bars and thick wire mesh. Wyler stood at the railing and looked down. On the sidewalk directly below, New Yorkers of different varieties were going about their day, crisscrossing obliviously over the very spot where Peter Lisonbee's falling body had hit the ground.

As he stared down at the spot, Wyler remembered a man in San Francisco who, years ago, had jumped off the Golden Gate Bridge, intending to commit suicide. After plunging over two hundred feet to the water, he had somehow survived. The man became a minor celebrity for a while and told his story to TV stations and newspapers. He claimed that immediately after he jumped, he had regretted his decision. The moment he went over the railing, the hopelessness and despair that had prompted his suicide attempt just vanished. During the few seconds of his fall, he somehow was able to see his life clearly for the first time. He suddenly wanted to live and, miraculously, was given that second chance. Wyler wondered how many others who committed suicide had similarly longed, at the last minute, for a second chance that never came.

As he stepped off the terrace and back into Peter's apartment, the strange sensation of foreboding returned to him, only it felt stronger this time. It was a sensation he had felt only a few times before. He imagined that a similar feeling must possess soldiers in wartime who suddenly find themselves behind enemy lines. It was a deep, sixth sense, like an inner animal instinct, warning of danger.

Wyler had felt something very similar a few years ago as he entered an abandoned basement apartment in Camden, New Jersey. The three Pakistani men who shared the apartment were part of a small terrorist cell. Wyler and his partner had arrested all three of them hours earlier at a chemical manufacturer in Delaware. For over a year, Wyler had been part of an effort to identify and monitor various businesses in and around New York whose products or services might potentially be exploited by terrorist groups. Companies selling chemicals and acids that could be used to make bombs were of obvious interest, but the net Wyler and his team cast was much wider. It included self-storage facilities, propane gas vendors, exterminators, hardware stores, cell phone vendors, truck rental companies, and even plastic surgeons. Wyler and others on the task force had spent several months working with the owners of these businesses, helping to educate their employees on how to spot suspicious behavior and buying patterns. Their efforts had paid off when they were contacted by an employee of a chemical company in Delaware. The employee reported that three men had initiated a purchase of several thousand dollars' worth of hydrogen peroxide, nitrate fertilizer, and sodium carbonate—three telltale components of a homemade bomb. When the three men had returned to the company two days later to pick up their purchase, Wyler and his team were waiting.

Several hours after the arrest, Wyler had been the first to enter the apartment the three men shared. It was a basement apartment connected to a dilapidated three-story house in a distressed part of town. Inside the squalid apartment, they had found several bombs in various stages of completion as well as bomb-making manuals and several notebooks in Urdu. A computer that was confiscated later revealed details of a plot for the synchronized bombing of several high-profile New York City hotels.

Wyler had never forgotten the feeling that had come over him when he first stepped into that apartment. The place was dark and dingy, with all the windows blacked out by towels and sheets that had been taped up or nailed to the walls. But aside from the physical darkness, there was another darkness present. Palpable traces of evil could be felt like an actual presence. It was not the kind of thing you put in an official report, but it was also not the kind of thing you ever forgot. Wyler had spoken later to his partner, Ray Shimura, who was with him at the time, and he had felt it as well.

Now, standing alone in the middle of Peter Lisonbee's studio apartment in the West Village, Wyler experienced a similar sense of malevolence. He decided he had seen everything he needed to see in Peter Lisonbee's apartment.

A few minutes later, Wyler was back in the lobby standing in front of the security desk where the chubby doorman was still absorbed in his newspaper. After waiting awkwardly for the guy to look up, Wyler spoke.

"Could I talk to you a minute?"

"What's up?" the guy responded, his eyes still glued to his paper.

"Do you mind if I ask you a few questions?"

He kept his head down but raised his eyes to look at Wyler. He was Hispanic, with a round face covered in stubble and a bushy black mustache turned down at the edges.

"Are you a cop?"

"I'm a friend—I *was* a friend—of Peter Lisonbee, in 14-L."

There was a delayed three-part reaction as the guy processed the name, made the connection to recent events, and then studied Wyler's face.

"I've never seen you around here before."

"I've never been here before. I'm a friend of the family. Can I ask you a few questions?"

"I don't know, man. I don't think I'm supposed to be talking about what happened."

Wyler got the message. He took out his wallet.

"I would really appreciate it." Wyler said, laying down two twenties on the open newspaper. "Were you working the night Peter jumped?"

He closed the paper over the bills and leaned forward, suddenly eager to talk. "Yeah, I was. The whole thing was unreal. I was sittin' right here. I heard someone screaming out in the street, and then a second later there was this *sound*. It was loud. Like an explosion or something. I thought it was a car crash. I went out there and he was..." He shook his head slowly and sadly. "It was pretty bad." He shook it again, this time quickly, like he was trying to get the memory out of his head.

"You said you heard someone screaming before you heard the sound of—before the body hit the pavement?"

"That's right."

"So, someone saw him jump?"

"I guess. I don't know."

"Did you see anyone outside the building, someone who could have seen it happen?"

"I don't think so. When I saw what happened, I just turned and ran back inside to get the cops."

The statement caught Wyler off guard.

"What do you mean? There were cops already in the building?"

"Yeah. Dr. Labelle, in 14-E, stabbed his wife the same night."

"Are you telling me someone was murdered in this building the same night, on the same floor, that Peter Lisonbee committed suicide?"

"Nah, she didn't die. She's okay. I guess they were having a fight, and he stuck her with a kitchen knife. Really surprised me. They've lived here for years. He's a nice guy. So is she, but I guess he snapped or something. That's why I won't get married."

"When did this happen?"

"Right at the same time. The cops had just gone up the elevator when the guy jumped, so I ran up to get them. It was a messed-up scene. Mrs. Labelle was standing there bleeding, Dr. Labelle was crying like a baby. He's the one who called the cops. I ran in and told them—the cops—what happened. One of them went with me to 14-L. The door was locked so the cop kicked the door in, like in the movies."

"Don't you have a pass key?"

"There's one in the office, but I didn't have it on me."

"Was anyone in the apartment when you broke in?"

"14-L? No, it was empty, far as I could see."

"Had anyone come to see him that night?"

"Not that I know of, but there's a lot of in and out on Saturday nights. People can pretty much come and go. This isn't Trump Tower."

A middle-aged bald man in a jogging suit entered the building and crossed to the elevator, and the doorman suddenly went back to reading his paper. Wyler took a step back from the desk and studied the lobby, trying to recreate in his mind the chaos of the scene that night. The elevator opened and the jogger got in. As soon as the door closed, the doorman stood up and came around the desk to Wyler.

"You want to hear something else that's crazy? The next day, on Sunday, they found Mrs. Fogelman dead in her apartment, 13-A."

"Mrs. Fogelman?"

"She's an old woman. Lives alone. She's been in the building for over thirty years. They say she had a heart attack the night before, around the same time all this other stuff happened. Crazy, right?"

Wyler was stunned by what he had just heard. According to the doorman, three incidents—a suicide, an attempted murder, and a natural death—had all occurred in the same building, on the same day, at approximately the same time.

CHAPTER 7

A few minutes later, Wyler was walking east through Washington Square Park, heading toward the other side of Greenwich Village and the restaurant Nine, where Peter Lisonbee had worked. It was a summer afternoon, and the park was crowded with students, tourists, dog walkers, skateboarders, chess players, street performers, food vendors, and drug dealers. The typical Village soup. He hadn't been in the city for months, and he found the sights, sounds, and smells somehow reassuring. New York hadn't changed in his absence.

He turned left on Broadway, heading north, then turned right and continued east on 8th Street, crossing into the East Village. Unlike the West Village's confusing maze of crooked, intersecting streets, the East Village looked more like the rest of Manhattan, with taller buildings and wider streets laid out in a simple grid that was easy to navigate. Nine was right on the corner of 9th Street and 2nd Avenue, and Wyler had no trouble finding the restaurant.

The place was filled with a noisy lunch crowd, and Wyler immediately regretted not timing his visit better. The staff wouldn't be able to talk to him during a busy shift. He was considering coming back later when a waitress approached him.

"One?" she asked.

Wyler was led to a narrow two-person table by a window and left alone with a menu. The place was a cozy rectangular box, lit brightly by sunlight streaming in through several floor-to-ceiling windows intersecting a red brick wall. A long booth ran the length of the opposite wall, with tables spaced every few feet and chairs set up across from the booth seats.

He decided he might as well eat. There was a burger on the menu advertised as a "100% Grass-fed Variety Burger" with an asterisk next to the word "variety." Small print beneath read "brisket, chuck, heart, liver, and bone marrow," and he wondered how different those ingredients were from the burgers he usually ate. When the waitress came back, he ordered the Variety Burger with cheese and onions. She took the order and sped off quickly before he had time to close his mouth. He would definitely have to wait for the lunch crowd to thin out before asking any questions.

While he sat and waited, he made a mental inventory of the information he had gathered from Peter Lisonbee's apartment. Unfortunately, his visit there had generated more questions than answers. . Why would someone planning to commit suicide go shopping a few hours before, and buy laundry detergent? Why would he charge his phone? Of course, it was possible that he wasn't planning to commit suicide and something had happened to change things, but what? From what he had seen, Peter had spent the evening at home alone, planning the menu for his future restaurant. Not exactly the behavior of someone hopeless and suicidal. But if it wasn't suicide, what was it? Murder? Did someone visit Peter that night and throw him off the balcony to his death? If so, who? And why? And how did they manage to slip out through a chain-locked door? And what was he to make of the strange fact that two other incidents – a death and an attempted murder—had occurred at roughly the same time? The "only in New York" cliché only stretched so far.

It was obvious from the moment Wyler had walked into the apartment that the responding officers had totally mishandled the crime scene. There were no signs of forensics, no dusting for fingerprints. In fact, there was no evidence whatsoever that the apartment had been processed as a crime scene at all. Wyler knew from his own experience that police officers responding to a death often relaxed immediately when they heard the word "suicide." This was, unfortunately, especially true with the NYPD. It was a harsh but unavoidable reality that cops in cities with high murder rates like New York welcomed any death that could be classified as natural causes or suicide. As a result, when things looked like a suicide, the investigators were not highly motivated to prove otherwise. Sometimes, conclusions were jumped to. Procedures were often sloppy or overlooked entirely. Certain tests were not conducted. Few photographs were taken. Wyler was convinced this had happened the night of Peter Lisonbee's death, and it infuriated him. Wyler's approach as a detective was completely different. He made no assumptions and took no shortcuts. This wasn't high-minded ethics; it was practical, seasoned experience. Wyler had seen many lazy cops forced to explain why basic procedures weren't followed and critical evidence overlooked when their initial assumptions were contradicted by more astute medical examiners.

Wyler waited almost twenty-five minutes for his order, and when it finally arrived he was starving. He ate quickly, finding that a Grass-fed Variety Burger tasted exactly like a normal burger. When the waitress came back with his check and to ask him if there was anything else, he decided to stall a bit longer by ordering dessert. By the time she came back with his sour cream walnut cake with raspberries, Wyler noticed there were some empty tables.

As she placed the dessert plate in front of him, he said, "Would you mind if I asked you a question?"

She paused and looked at him with raised eyebrows that said, "your move." She was African American and looked about thirty. Her name badge said "Destiny."

"I was wondering if you knew Peter Lisonbee."

"Yes, I knew Peter." The way she said it made it sound like a question back to him.

"I'm a friend of Peter's family. Could I talk to you for a minute?"

"About what?"

"I'm just trying to find out what happened to him."

She paused, then nodded again, more sympathetically this time.

"How well did you know him, Destiny?"

"Are you a cop or something?"

"Something like that."

She seemed to accept this, and said, "He worked here for almost a year. I've been here for five years, so I knew him all that time."

"Were you friends?"

"We got along. He got along with everyone mostly, but I'm not sure he had any friends."

"You say mostly everyone. Was there anyone he didn't get along with?"

"Well," she began, lowering her voice to a stage whisper, "there was always a lot of tension between him and Layne and Jerry. They're the owners."

She glanced to the front of the restaurant, and Wyler followed her eyes to a short, balding middle-aged man standing by the front entrance. The guy looked fidgety and nervous. Wyler assumed this was either Layne or Jerry.

"How bad did it get?"

"Peter was very intense, and he had a vision of how he wanted to do things, and so he clashed a lot with Layne and Jerry. I don't think it was personal or anything. Peter was kind of arrogant. He thought he should be in charge of everything." She stopped and seemed to feel guilty for having spoken ill of the dead. "The truth was, he really wasn't happy here."

"Were you surprised when you found out what happened?"

"We were all shocked by it. No one expected that. Especially with the whole Scottie Hibble thing and him opening his own restaurant."

"So you heard about that?"

"Of course. I was here the night that Scottie came in."

"They met here, at the restaurant?" Wyler asked, surprised.

"Yes. Scottie Hibble and a bunch of his friends came in late one night. Peter cooked for them. He made stuff that wasn't on the menu, special for them. I think he wanted to impress them—to impress Hibble. And it worked. Scottie Hibble kept saying how he had discovered the next great New York chef, and he was going to make Peter rich and famous. It was pretty amazing."

As Wyler thought about this, he glanced around the restaurant, picturing the scene in his mind.

"Do you remember what time they came in?" Wyler asked.

"It was late. Just before one, I think. They had been out partying."

"How do you know that?"

She pulled a face and gave Wyler a look.

"Were they drunk, or on drugs?" Wyler persisted.

"No comment," she said with a half-laugh.

"It's important, Destiny."

"They were on something, but I don't know what it was. What does that matter anyway?"

"By any chance do you remember the date that Scottie Hibble came in?"

She looked off briefly, searching her mental databank.

"I don't know the exact date, but I know it was the same day as Peter's birthday. We had a cake and sang happy birthday to him earlier in the night. I remember because I went and got the cake from Veniero's. Then, when the whole Scottie Hibble thing happened, everyone was saying how cool it was that he had gotten his big break on his birthday."

Wyler carefully considered this new information.

"Look, I really need to get back to work," she said. "To be honest, I didn't really know Peter that well. I don't think anyone here did. But that doesn't mean I wasn't sorry about what happened." She shook her head slowly, with genuine pity and sadness.

"If I wait, could I ask you a few more questions?"

"I don't know how long it will be."

"I don't mind."

Destiny left and tended to other tables while Wyler sat and considered what she had told him. According to Sarah Miller, Peter had gone to get the gemstone appraised on his birthday, as a present to himself. Now, Wyler was learning, the life-changing meeting with Scottie Hibble had taken place later the very same day. Was there some connection?

When Destiny came back about ten minutes later, they talked more about Peter. Wyler tried to press for more information about him—his habits, friends, and personal life –but it was clear that Destiny was a work acquaintance with no real insight into Peter Lisonbee's life outside the restaurant.

After paying his bill and leaving a generous tip, Wyler introduced himself to the nervous balding man in front who turned out to be Layne, one of the owners. He had a receding fringe of short gray hair and a flat, pushed-in face like a bulldog. Wyler explained who he was and what he was doing, then asked about Peter.

"Peter was a great chef. Really, really great," Layne said, shaking his head sadly and waving a big hairy hand back and forth to emphasize the point. He spoke in a thick accent that Wyler thought might be Polish or Hungarian. "But he was very hard-headed. He was young! He wanted everything now, now, now! He didn't want to listen to anyone. It got difficult, to be honest. He had a temper! But, you ask me could he cook? He could cook! That's why we hired him. So young. Very sad! He was a good boy! He had a good future. I kept telling him, stay here and learn. You don't have to be here forever! You've got plenty of time to make your big mark on the world! We had a tough time with him, but I told Jerry, this kid is worth the trouble. He's good. Business picked up because of him. Why shouldn't I say it? But then, he did what he did. Why? What do these kids have to be so sad and depressed about? Everyone's depressed! Why? It doesn't make sense. Life has troubles. We all have troubles. But there's good, too. When we heard, we were all very, very sad." He went on like that for bit, and Wyler sensed the man wasn't hiding anything. Layne was one of those people who had no natural facility for lying.

He asked Layne's permission to speak to the other employees, and after a quick glance around the restaurant at all the empty tables, he agreed. Wyler ended up spending another hour at Nine, talking to the other members of the wait staff and to the cooks and dishwashers in back. Nothing he heard added any detail to what he had learned from Destiny. They all painted a similar picture of a talented but somewhat difficult young man, a private person who didn't socialize much, a person very intense and driven to achieve his ambitions.

It was almost 2:00 p.m. when Wyler left the restaurant, convinced that Peter Lisonbee hadn't taken the time to get close to anyone, at least not to any of his coworkers at Nine. He walked out and was turning down the sidewalk when a voice stopped him.

"You're asking about Peter?"

Wyler turned and saw a young man dressed in black pants and a dirty white smock. He was sitting by himself in the restaurant's outdoor patio area, slouched over a chair. Wyler had seen him washing dishes in the back, but he had disappeared before Wyler could question him.

"Did you know him?" Wyler asked, stepping up to the waist-high lattice fence. He looked to be in his twenties, with black, slicked-back hair, a long droopy face, and big sad eyes that made him look like an Italian James Dean.

"We used to be friends," the young man said, taking a puff of a cigarette.

"Close friends?"

The kid shrugged.

"You said you *used* to be friends? Did something happen to change that?"

"Scottie Hibble." He took another long puff. Wyler waited for more, but this kid needed prompting.

"What's your name?"

"Paul."

"Paul, how did Scottie Hibble change your friendship with Peter?"

"*He* changed, you know, after he met Scottie."

"You mean Peter? How did he change?"

"We used to hang out. Peter knew I wanted to be a chef someday, and he really encouraged me. He used to teach me things, after hours. Spend time with me. He thought I had a lot of potential. And then, as soon as he met Hibble, he totally changed. He was obsessed with that guy. All he talked about when he came to work was Scottie Hibble, about how he was getting his own restaurant, and how Scottie Hibble was this incredible guy who was going to make him this famous chef. He didn't have time for me anymore. He turned into a jerk."

Wyler was suddenly very interested in this young man. He was the only person at Nine who seemed to have forged any kind of bond with Peter. Wyler's mind spun off in different directions, exploring various scenarios and possibilities. Suddenly, Paul stood up.

"Break's over," he said, flicking the cigarette away with a practiced flair.

Before he reached the door, Wyler called to him.

"Paul, would you mind answering one more question?"

The boy turned back.

"Just so you know, I've asked this same question to everyone else here," Wyler lied. "Would you mind telling me where you were on the Saturday night that Peter died, August 17th?"

"That's easy," he said. "I was up in Niagara Falls, on my honeymoon. My girlfriend and I got married that day."

The kid reached under his smock and pulled out his wallet, then removed a picture and handed it to Wyler. It was Paul in a tacky blue prom-like tuxedo. He stood next to a plump young redhead in a white wedding dress.

"Congratulations," Wyler said. The kid pocketed the picture, turned, and went back into the restaurant.

CHAPTER 8

The headquarters of RopeLine were located downtown on the seventh floor of the old Western Union Building in Tribeca. The twenty-four-story Art Deco building was a city landmark that Wyler knew well, as it had briefly housed the offices of the Department of Corrections in the early 2000s. After the DOC moved out, it was taken over by internet providers and telecommunication companies. Over the past decade, the building had become one of the most important internet hubs on earth, housing endless miles of fiber optic cable and tons of electrical equipment that connected internet and communication networks from all over the world. Wyler thought the unusual architectural design, with different rectangular levels rising toward a center peak, made the building look like something a kid had made out of Legos.

Wyler entered the cavernous brick-and-bronze lobby that ran the entire block between Hudson and West Broadway and approached the security desk. After signing in and showing his ID, he was waved through to the elevator, which he took to the seventh floor. Wyler had called the offices of RopeLine from the train during the ninety-minute ride down from Poughkeepsie that morning, and after explaining who he was to five different people, he managed to make an appointment to see Scottie Hibble at 2:40 p.m.

The offices of RopeLine had the kind of trendy, cubicle-free layout that was popular with start-ups and tech companies looking to attract millennials. Instead of desks and traditional workstations, colorful sofas and ergonomic chairs were grouped together in various lounge areas in the center of the room, surrounded by drafting tables, standing desks, and benches. There was an open kitchen and a bar off to one side, and a cushioned window seat with scattered throw pillows that ran corner to corner. One wall was a giant chalkboard filled with a mix of writing and elaborate doodles. Wyler didn't see anyone over thirty, and no one was dressed in business attire. The décor, the people, and the overall vibe felt to Wyler more like a college student union than a place of business.

There was no reception area, so for a while Wyler just stood near the front, awkwardly hoping to be noticed. He had never felt so old. Two people were at the chalkboard wall, working on something. Eventually, one of them—a tall, curly-haired kid wearing a t-shirt and, for some reason, a scarf—noticed Wyler and called out, "Ashley!"

A moment later, a young woman appeared from the back and approached Wyler.

"Are you Mr. Wyler? I'm Ashley Lang. I work with Scottie."

She was dressed more professionally than the others, in a white shirt and dark business suit, and she seemed genuinely excited to see him. She had a bright, innocent smile without a trace of PR phoniness. She was also very attractive, with long brown hair and a curvy, petite figure. Wyler guessed she couldn't have been much older than twenty.

"I have an appointment with Mr. Hibble."

"Yes, we spoke on the phone this morning. Unfortunately,

Scottie is at a photo shoot and he's running a bit behind." As she said it, she glanced down at an iPad like it knew Hibble's exact whereabouts. Maybe it did. "He should be just a few more minutes. I'm so sorry about that. If you'll follow me, we have a conference room where you can wait."

She led Wyler to a rectangular glass room, and Wyler took a seat at a long conference table. Ashley Lang lingered with him in the room, hugging the iPad to her chest like a clipboard.

"You said on the phone that you were a detective of some kind?"

"Until very recently I was a detective with the NYPD."

"And can you tell me a little bit more about why you need to speak with Scottie?" She said it with an awkward smile that both established and apologized for her gatekeeper role.

"I'd like to talk to him about Peter Lisonbee."

She nodded ambiguously, giving no indication that the name was familiar to her.

"Mr. Hibble and Mr. Lisonbee were involved in a business deal," Wyler explained. "They were planning to open a restaurant together, until Peter committed suicide ten days ago."

"Oh, I didn't know. I'm so sorry to hear that." She reflexively reached out a hand to him, as if Wyler had suffered a personal loss.

"I'd like to ask him a few questions about Peter."

After a short pause, she said, "But you're no longer a police officer?"

"That's correct. I'm acting on behalf of the Lisonbee family."

Ashley Lang continued to smile, but the room seemed to cool slightly. For the first time, Wyler felt the awkwardness of his position. For years, as an officer of the NYPD, he had wielded official authority. His police badge was more than just identification. It connected him to the institutions of power in a way that all people, regardless of wealth or status, had to respect and respond to. Now, he suddenly felt naked and exposed—out on his own. It was not a comfortable feeling.

"Can I get you something? We have mineral water, fresh juices, coffee, tea, espresso."

"I'm fine. Thank you, though."

Wyler turned away from Ashley Lang and looked out through the glass walls of the conference room, observing the activity going on in the rest of the office.

"This is a very busy time," she said, stepping up to the window. "We are only a few weeks away from Bonfire, and Scottie is out on a promotional shoot right now, down at the South Street Seaport."

"Bonfire?"

"You haven't heard?" she asked with big eyes, excited to share the important news. "Bonfire is an event that we're sponsoring this weekend. We've all been working on it for months. Celebrities and other influencers from all over the world will be coming together for a four-day festival of music, ideas, and dialogue about some of the biggest problems facing us right now."

"Such as?"

"Well," she pulled out a chair and sat down at the table, "We are going to be talking about climate change, poverty, racism, gender equality. Lots of other topics as well. The whole thing is Scottie's vision. You see, he started RopeLine with the idea of giving regular people access to celebrities. Now, he wants to bring together the world's powerful and important people in order to harness their creativity and intellect, to put it all in the service of some of the world's biggest problems. It's really an amazing idea. Scottie is a unique individual. He's really a genius, but he's more than that. He really cares about the issues confronting people."

She said all this with passion and excitement in her voice. Normally, Wyler would have found her naïve idealism and hero worship annoying and off-putting, but there was something about this girl that was so sincere that Wyler couldn't help but feel affection toward her. Here was a young woman who was working at a job that gave her a sense of mission and purpose. More power to her, Wyler thought. There was plenty of time for cynicism later. .

"Sounds exciting," Wyler said.

"The purpose of Bonfire is to bring together the most powerful and influential people on our planet in order to foster a unified and sustainable commitment to human growth and change. It's all Scottie's vision. It started with RopeLine, and now Bonfire is the next step."

Wyler remembered Sarah Miller talking about the RopeLine app when they first met. To him, it sounded like an elite club for the in crowd, the kind of thing he detested. He had grown up in a working-class family in Brooklyn, but even after he married into wealth, he never felt comfortable in certain circles. This Bonfire event sounded like a lavish weekend getaway for rich people masquerading as lofty altruism.

"So, where is this festival taking place?"

"On a private island in the Bahamas. It's very exciting. We are all working twenty-four seven to prepare for the event."

Some more time passed, and Wyler checked his phone and saw that it was almost 3:00 p.m. She saw him do it, and said, "We were expecting them to be back an hour ago."

"I understand. It's not a problem."

"If you want, we could reschedule for next week, after Bonfire. It might be easier then."

"I really don't mind waiting. It's important that I speak to him."

Suddenly they were interrupted by a flurry of noise and movement out on the floor. Wyler turned and saw that a small group of people had just walked into the office, creating a buzz of excitement and activity.

"Looks like they're back. Excuse me." Ashley Lang stood and

left the conference room, leaving Wyler to watch through the glass. To his great surprise, Wyler saw Wally Burgess standing with the group that had just come in. Burgess played for the Brooklyn Nets and was easily one of the top five forwards in the NBA right now. He was wearing a black suit and sunglasses and at six feet ten inches, towered over the throng. Jack Wade, the A-list actor who was famous for drug busts and beating up reporters, was standing next to Burgess. Wade had starred in a string of summer blockbusters about a radioactive asteroid that smashes into earth and shrinks the whole human race down to the size of action figures. Wyler had taken Gabe to the first one years ago but had skipped all the sequels. There was also a couple of super-models that Wyler knew by sight but not name, and a small camera crew trying to record everything.

All the company's employees had gathered near the entrance to gawk and soak up the celebrity vibe. As the group moved from the entrance to the main office space, Wyler was surprised to notice that the center of gravity was not Wally Burgess, Jack Wade, or the supermodels, but a short young man in his early twenties wearing a white dress shirt, a blue blazer, jeans, and tennis shoes. The man was slightly overweight and had a boyish face which he tried to compensate for with some stalled beard growth. Still, he carried himself with more movie-star swagger than any of the celebrities who were with him, including Jack Wade. Wyler guessed this must be Scottie Hibble.

As the group of VIPs moved to the large window that over-looked Tribeca, the crowd closed ranks around them, forming an impromptu horseshoe with Scottie Hibble at the center. Things suddenly quieted down, and Wyler could see Hibble addressing the troops. The crowd listened with rapt attention, then erupted in cheers and applause. Curious, Wyler opened the door of the conference room just enough to eavesdrop.

"And that's not all!" Hibble was saying. "We heard from

several more people last night and this morning. Ashley! Ashley! Where's Ashley!" Hibble's high-pitched voice sounded almost pre-pubescent, but he spoke with authority and his charisma seemed to captivate everyone around him. Ashley Lang fought her way to the front and stood by Hibble. "Where's the list?" he asked melodramatically.

"It's right here," Ashley began tapping and swiping on her iPad, while Hibble continued shouting for "the list" like a king at a banquet demanding more wine. Wyler wondered if he might actually be drunk or high on something, but he had no frame of reference to judge. This could be how Hibble always acted.

Ashley Lang suddenly became the center of attention as the crowd began chanting along with Hibble: "The List! The List!" As Wyler watched her frantically search for the right file on her tablet, he felt sorry for her. She was obviously uncomfortable being the center of attention.

Finally, she handed the iPad to Hibble, and he began reading a list of names. After each name was announced, the crowd cheered and applauded wildly. Wyler knew about half of the names on the list, which included well-known actors, musicians, authors, TV personalities, athletes, politicians, and business leaders, mixed with lots of other names Wyler didn't recognize.

"This is going to be the biggest and most important gathering of influencers that has ever taken place on this planet!" Hibble yelled out after reading the names. "Nothing like this has ever happened before! By the sheer force of our will, we are going to change the world!"

As excited whoops and hollers filled the room, Hibble's gaze drifted to Wyler, who stood stoically watching him from the conference room. Wyler's unfamiliar presence seemed to bother Hibble, as if a non-believer had snuck into a sacred ceremony. Hibble's mood seemed to change instantly, and when he half-jokingly commanded everyone to get back to work, the crowd dispersed in a cloud of nervous giggles.

Wyler kept watching as Hibble motioned Ashley Lang over to him. They huddled and had a hushed exchange which prompted a glance from Hibble in Wyler's direction. Hibble's face was reddening in anger as he listened to the girl's explanation, but then he cut her off and began to berate her. Wyler couldn't hear the words, but he didn't have to. He could tell from Ashley Lang's pained expression that she was absorbing an onslaught of verbal abuse, and his gut told him this was probably a common occurrence. At one point, Hibble put his hand on her arm and squeezed, and Wyler was tempted to rush forward and body slam the little punk against the wall.

A few moments later, Scottie Hibble walked toward the conference room where Wyler was waiting, followed by Ashley Lang. She was smiling gamely, but her face was flushed with embarrassment.

"How can I help you?" The words sounded more like an attack than a greeting.

"Mr. Hibble, I'm Aaron Wyler. I wonder if I could ask you a few questions about Peter Lisonbee."

"I'm really busy today. A staff member made the appointment with you without informing me, but today is actually not a good day."

"This won't take long," Wyler responded.

Hibble stared at Wyler for a moment, squinting and studying him like he was a problem that needed to be solved, then he turned to Lang.

"Give Wally and Jack and the others a tour of the space and then take them to the large conference room and show them the footage we shot last week on the island. I'll be there in a few minutes."

Before walking off, Lang flashed Wyler an annoyed look

which he guessed was more for Hibble's benefit, an attempt to show her boss that she was back with the program. As Hibble watched her go, he shook his head and sighed audibly as if to convey how patiently he was bearing the heavy burdens so unfairly placed upon him.

"I appreciate you taking the time to talk with me," Wyler offered flatly.

Hibble looked to Wyler, pretended to smile, then extended his arm toward the conference room in an exaggerated gesture of hospitality. Everyone seemed to be acting out parts.

Wyler sat down at the conference table while Hibble retrieved a beer from a refrigerated cabinet in the corner of the room.

"So, what's this about? Ashley said you used to be cop or something?"

"That's right. I'm retired NYPD."

Hibble plopped down in a chair across from Wyler and put his feet up on the table as if trying to show how unimpressed he was with Wyler's credentials. Close up, Scottie Hibble looked even younger. He had matted bed hair and acne blemishes under his beard fuzz.

"What's your interest in Peter?" Hibble asked as he casually took a swig of beer.

"I'm a friend of the family," Wyler said.

"You knew Peter?" He seemed surprised, possibly even concerned, about the possibility.

"No. I know his sister, Sarah. She asked me to look into what happened to Peter."

"What's there to look into? He killed himself." It was said without any emotion, as if he were reporting that Peter Lisonbee had simply gone on vacation.

"How did you meet Peter?"

Hibble didn't respond at first. But then, after a few moments, he shrugged his shoulders and spoke. "It was a Friday night, and a few of us were out partying late. We were hungry and on a whim, we happened to stop for a bite at this crummy little restaurant in the Village. Peter was the chef there and he made us this amazing meal—none of it on the menu. I mean, it was like the best thing I had ever tasted."

"What did he make you?"

"I'm not a foodie," Hibble punctuated the statement with a self-satisfied grin for some reason. When Wyler didn't react, he concentrated and continued. "There was a paella with different kinds of fish—shrimp and other stuff. There was a steak sandwich with caramelized onions and veggies and this dipping sauce that was out of this world. A salad with some sort of honey, I don't remember what else was in it. Oh, and pineapple fried rice. And for dessert he made this lemon meringue pie with all these different layers."

"Sounds delicious," offered Wyler.

"Yeah, it was." He took a pull on his beer, as if washing down the remembered dinner.

"So, based on this meal, you decided to go into business with Peter?"

"Why not? The guy was a star, anyone with brains could see that." Hibble must have read some skepticism in Wyler's face. "Is something wrong?"

"No, not at all. It's just that Peter must have made quite an impression. You said yourself, you're not a foodie. But based on this one meal you suddenly decided to go into the restaurant business with a person you just met. Even with all the other things you have going on, like RopeLine and Brushfire."

"Bonfire," Hibble corrected him. "You know, this is starting to feel like an interrogation or something. Do I need to call one of my lawyers?" He chuckled as if he had made a joke.

"I apologize if that's how it's coming across. Old habits. I'm just trying to put together a picture of what was going on in

Peter's life at the time he died. You have to admit that meeting you turned out to be a life-changing event for him."

"When I see an opportunity, I take it. I don't wait for someone else, I don't hesitate. I act. It might seem sudden or spontaneous, but believe me, that's what successful people do." He opened his arms, like he was teaching Wyler a valuable life lesson.

"So, during the month or so between the time you met Peter and his death, how many times did you see him?"

"You're making it sound like you think Peter's death was more than what the police have said." *What the police have said.* Wyler found Hibble's choice of words interesting. "Is there something you know that I don't?" Hibble added.

Wyler decided to change tactics.

"Not at all. To be honest, I'm just doing a favor for his sister. Peter was her only sibling, and she's trying to figure out what might have led to...what happened."

"I saw Peter a few times," Hibble said, relaxing. "We looked at a couple of potential spaces for the restaurant, but they didn't feel right so we kept looking."

"Really? I was under the impression that you had already found a place."

"Who gave you that impression?"

Instead of answering Hibble, he let his own question hang out there, forcing Hibble to wonder how much Wyler already knew.

"Well, it's true we were getting pretty close to a place. Actually, on the day he killed himself, we went to see a place in Chelsea that we were both kind of excited about. It's too bad what happened. It could have been amazing."

"Did you spend time with him socially, or was it just business?"

"Business, pleasure, for me everything sort of mixes together."

"How much time did you spend together?"

"Not much. I have a lot going on right now, as you can see."

Suddenly seeming restless, Hibble dropped his feet from the table to the floor. "Actually, I've got some important people waiting for me."

Wyler ignored him and continued. "You said you were with Peter on the day he died."

"So?"

"I was just wondering, how did Peter seem to you that day?"

"What do you mean?"

"Well, was he acting strangely? Did he seem upset about something, or depressed?"

"Look, you want to know what killed Peter? I'll tell you." Hibble leaned toward Wyler across the table. "Fear of success."

"Fear of success?" asked Wyler.

"That's right. I've seen it all my life in people. You see, everyone thinks they want to succeed. But the truth is, deep down, most people don't. People tell themselves that they have the talent and brains to be on top, if only they could catch one lucky break. Life is unfair, blah blah blah. It's a convenient attitude, because it helps them deal with all their unfulfilled dreams and ambitions. But the truth is, most people, deep down, know they're not good enough, and if they ever got near real success, it would terrify them."

"And you think that's what happened to Peter?"

"I know it. Peter had talent. He had skill. But when I suddenly offered him an opportunity to prove it by having his own restaurant, he choked. He panicked. Deep down, he was terrified that he wasn't good enough. Peter was afraid to face the fact that he might not be the secret, undiscovered genius he always told himself he was. The truth is, the whole notion of hidden, undiscovered talent is a myth. People in this world rise just as far and as high as they can and should. Everyone is exactly as successful as they deserve to be. Period."

"I see," said Wyler.

"It's true in any profession. Look at you. You worked for the NYPD, right? I'll bet you daydreamed about running the whole show—chief of police, or maybe even mayor or something, right? Of course you did. You probably looked at your superiors and thought of everything they did wrong and what you would do differently, am I right? But if the opportunity ever fell in your lap to step up, you'd probably panic. Fear and insecurity would kick in, and you'd realize you weren't up to it. I'm not trying to be insulting or anything. I'm just saying that there is a reason why some people are exceptional and others aren't. I'm sure you were a very competent detective."

Wyler nodded politely, but in truth he felt sorry for Hibble. Here was a young man who had achieved tremendous success at an early age, and unfortunately, his success had frozen his emotional development, removing from his life the kinds of challenges, disappointments, and setbacks that lead normal people to examine themselves, to learn, and to grow.

"So, you think Peter committed suicide out of fear and insecurity?"

"What else?" Hibble said flippantly as he got to his feet. "Look, I've got to go. Hopefully this helped with whatever you are trying to figure out."

And with that, Scottie Hibble walked out of the room, leaving Wyler alone.

CHAPTER 9

Wyler stepped into the viewing room and immediately regretted it. He was taking a shortcut he had used before and didn't realize a family would be there. There were three of them, a man and two women, all roughly the same age, huddled together. The trio looked through the large glass window that separated the viewing room from the room on the other side, nicknamed the "showroom" by the mortuary technicians. All three of them jerked their heads toward Wyler when he entered. They were anxious and stressed, and the cheeks of both women were wet from tears. Wyler felt ashamed for intruding on such a private moment, and he was about to leave when the double doors in the showroom swung open and a gurney was wheeled in. Wyler was trapped now. He didn't dare leave and risk distracting from what was happening, so he simply shrunk into the back corner and tried to seem invisible.

On the other side of the glass, the gurney was wheeled up to the viewing window by a technician accompanied by Gail Toussaint, the woman Wyler had come here to see. Toussaint was one of about thirty medical examiners that served New York County, otherwise known as Manhattan. She was a tall, muscular woman in her mid-fifties, with dark brown skin and short, curly black hair. She wore a white lab coat down to her knees and thick, blue-rimmed glasses that made her eyes appear to bulge out like a frog's.

Gail nodded to the mortuary tech, and the man carefully lifted a white sheet just enough to reveal the lifeless head and shoulders of an elderly African American woman. One of the women in the viewing room burst into tears and buried her face in the man's shoulder, while the other woman began to moan sickly. Wyler wasn't sure of the relationships. They could all be siblings, children of the old woman, or maybe the man was married to one of the women. In any case, their worst fears had just been confirmed.

Wyler caught Gail's eye through the glass and she gave him a discreet nod. As the tech wheeled the gurney away from the window, Gail passed through a connecting door and approached the grieving family. She was a large woman, and she spread her long arms like wings, wide enough to embrace all three of them. They accepted the gesture as if Gail were one of the family. Wyler greatly admired Gail for this special quality. Although she dealt with death day in and day out, she had avoided the occupational hazard of developing a cavalier attitude toward it. As the tears began to subside, Gail tenderly shepherded the family out of the viewing room.

Less than a minute later, Gail was back, this time with a big smile on her face.

"Aaron!"

"How are you, Gail?"

She swallowed him up in one her famous hugs. They had not seen each other since Jessica's funeral.

"Same as ever. How are you? How's Poughkeepsie?" Gail's accent was the French Caribbean blend from her native country, Haiti.

"Rhinebeck, actually, just north of Poughkeepsie. What was that?" he asked, pointing with his chin toward the viewing window.

"Heat stroke. Died alone in her apartment. No AC. We're averaging about three a day like that. It's been a long, hot summer."

Wyler nodded, acknowledging the sadness of it. They stared at each other for a few silent moments as thoughts and feelings passed between them that didn't require words. Gail Toussaint was more than just a colleague. She was a close friend—a friend who had been responsible, indirectly, for his marriage to Jessica Maitland.

Wyler had gotten to know Gail during his time as a detective at the Midtown South precinct. About 70,000 people die every year in New York City, which comes to about 200 people a day. Most of those bodies go unexamined by the Medical Examiner's office, but any deaths that are deemed suspicious in some way are taken to the ME. This includes murders, suicides, people in good health who die suddenly, or any other death that seems unusual. Wyler had worked on many cases with Gail, and they had formed a strong friendship.

After Wyler was transferred to the Counterterrorism Bureau, one of his first assignments had to do with the detection of radiological weapons. A radioactive device isn't necessarily more dangerous or lethal than a conventional bomb, but the presence of radioactivity can leave a long-term impact. If such a device were detonated at JFK, or the New York Stock Exchange, or in Times Square, it could potentially render the location uninhabitable for months, even years.

For this reason, even before 9/11, cops in New York City carried radiation detection devices clipped to their belts like pagers. These small devices picked up traces of radioactivity that could indicate the presence of a bomb. At least in theory. Unfortunately, almost all the positive signals picked up by these devices had been caused by cancer patients who had undergone radiation therapy. One woman from India who had traveled to New York for treatment was stopped in Times Square seven times by different police officers. Wyler, assigned to find a way to improve the system and eliminate false positives, decided to consult with a cancer physician about the problem. Gail Toussaint had referred him to a close friend of hers, a pediatric oncologist at Sloan Kettering named Jessica Maitland. They got together several times over the course of a few months, and although they didn't make much headway with the radiation pagers, they developed an unlikely friendship. Wyler felt an easy chemistry with this renowned cancer doctor that he had never experienced with any other woman. . Eventually, he worked up the courage to ask her out.

"How's Gabe?" Gail asked with tenderness.

"He's fine. The change of scenery has been good for him. You'll have to come up sometime."

She stared at Wyler, and the large eyes behind her glasses seemed to penetrate his soul.

"What?" he asked, suddenly uncomfortable.

"How are you, really?"

"I'm fine."

"No, you're not. I can tell."

"Gail."

Neither spoke for a bit, and Gail seemed to study him, like he was a cadaver whose secrets she was trying to unlock.

"You're broken on the inside. You know that?"

Wyler didn't respond.

"You've got to let go of your anger, honey."

"I'm not angry, Gail." But there was anger in his voice as he said it.

Gail chuckled ruefully, then shook her head sadly.

"As long as you ignore it and pretend it's not there, it's going to eat away at you like a parasite."

Wyler searched desperately for something to say, some glib comment that would deflect her words, but nothing came.

"You've got to forgive her, Aaron," Gail whispered. "That's the only way you'll ever find peace."

Wyler felt his heart racing. It was suddenly uncomfortably hot, and he realized he was breathing rapidly. "I can't do this, Gail," Wyler finally managed to say in a flat, stony voice.

Gail looked lovingly at Wyler and said, "Okay. Just remember you're not alone. You've got plenty of people who love you and who are here for you, when you're ready."

After a pause, Wyler acknowledged the offer with a nod, and by silent, mutual agreement, the subject was dropped.

"I pulled the autopsy report on that suicide in the Village you asked me about. Let's talk back in the office." Gail turned and scanned her ID card, which clicked open a door to a corridor.

"Who did the cut?" asked Wyler as they walked down the hall, relieved to be talking about something else.

"Fernando."

Wyler didn't have much direct experience with Fernando Serrano, one of the other medical examiners, but he had a good reputation. They came to another door, and Gail swiped her ID badge again. Wyler followed Gail into a refrigerated room with high walls divided into stainless steel drawers that looked like large filing cabinets.

"He's not still here, is he?"

"Oh no, he was released for burial right after the autopsy."

They passed through a set of swinging double doors and entered the pathology lab. The smell of the room immediately hit Wyler, though he tried to hide his reaction. He had been in this and other autopsy rooms dozens—perhaps hundreds—of times before, but he had never gotten used to the smell. It was a unique odor, combining the stale, acrid scent of death with the sharp aroma of powerful disinfectants.

Wyler followed Toussaint to a small office at the far end of the pathology lab, where she sat down behind a chipped wooden desk. There were no windows, and the office was poorly lit, gloomy, and cramped.

"Here it is," said Gail, picking up an open file on the desk.

He waited while Gail examined the contents of the folder. She read quickly, mumbling to herself, and laid several photographs from the file on the desk. Wyler leaned forward and picked up the pictures. The first shot was of Peter Lisonbee's lifeless, discolored body on the examination table in the lab, followed by several close-up pictures of his injuries. There were various bruises and scrapes all over the body, and the left side of the face was partially collapsed, obviously crushed by the fall.

"COD?" asked Wyler.

Gail flipped a page in the file and read from it. "Fracture of the thoracolumbar spine, severe head trauma, crushed thorax." She looked up at Wyler. "Take your pick. Hard to pinpoint and isolate one injury as the cause of death when so many parts of the body are affected simultaneously."

"I assume the MOD was listed as suicide?" Unlike the cause of death, which referred specifically to the physical injuries or disease that led to a person's death, the manner of death was a determination of how those injuries came about—homicide, suicide, accident, natural causes, or undetermined.

"That's right," replied Gail.

"Histamine levels?" Wyler asked, and Gail looked up at him, surprised.

"You think someone killed him and threw him over the balcony?" she asked. Histamine levels in a wound could indicate that the injury took place postmortem—after someone was already dead.

"I don't think anything. I'm just asking questions."

Gail again scanned the report.

"The levels are all normal."

Wyler examined four pictures showing the backs and palms of Peter Lisonbee's hands.

"Any skin or blood under the fingernails?" he asked.

"Defensive wounds? None are listed here."

"Was there anything in the tox report?"

Gail turned to the last page in the file.

"Nothing really. No drugs. Blood alcohol was under .02."

Wyler came to the end of the photos, then straightened them like a deck of cards and put them back on the desk. He would have liked to compare these shots with photos taken at the crime scene, but those pictures would be in the police file, not the autopsy report.

"Huh," murmured Gail, still reading the paperwork.

"What is it?" asked Wyler.

"There's something interesting here."

Wyler waited as Gail flipped one page and continued reading.

"Well?" asked Wyler.

"It's probably nothing, but I'm just looking at this blood report."

"You said it was clean."

"It was, for alcohol and drugs. But according to this, he had high levels of troponin in his blood."

"Troponin? What's that?" asked Wyler.

"It's an enzyme that's released in the blood, usually during a heart attack."

"You're saying he had a heart attack?"

She shook her head slowly, still reading the file.

"No, I'm not. Heart attacks are caused by arterial blockage. There's none of that here. He was a healthy, drug-free thirty-year-old kid."

"So, how do you explain the enzyme, the trop –"

"Troponin."

She sat quietly for a while, staring at some fixed point in space, lost in her own thoughts.

"Hold on," she said, finally coming out of the trance.

She began flipping through all the papers in the file, then began shuffling through the stack of photos on the desk.

"Shoot, it's not here."

"What's not there?"

She ignored Wyler and logged in to her computer. She leaned over and checked the number written on the file, then began typing on her keyboard.

"Only some of the pictures are printed for the paper file, but all of them will be in here."

"What pictures? What are you looking for?"

She tuned Wyler out and continued typing and clicking.

"Here it is," she said finally, staring at the screen and nodding her head with a satisfied grin. "That's what I thought."

"What is it, Gail?"

"See for yourself."

She swung her monitor around so Wyler could see it. On the screen was a photograph of a human heart in a chrome laboratory dish. Wyler knew that during every autopsy, all the vital organs were removed, weighed, and photographed, but he didn't get the significance.

"So, that's Peter Lisonbee's heart?" Wyler asked.

"That's right."

"I'm not following you, Gail. To me, it looks normal, like a heart."

"Look here," she said, grabbing a pencil from an empty coffee mug and pointing to the screen with the eraser. "You see how there's a slight swelling near the left ventricle?"

Wyler leaned in close.

"It looks like this kid experienced Takotsubo cardiomyopathy right before his death."

"I didn't go to medical school, Gail," Wyler said, frustrated.

"Takotsubo cardiomyopathy is a cardiac event that causes the left ventricle to change shape, to swell abnormally. It makes the ventricle look like a Japanese fishing pot used to catch octopus, called a Takotsubo. Symptomatically, it's a lot like a heart attack—chest pains, shortness of breath. That would explain the troponin."

"Why wasn't this in the autopsy report?"

"It wasn't directly related to the cause of death."

Wyler glanced back to the picture of Peter Lisonbee's heart on the screen. "What caused it?" he asked.

"It's almost always caused by the same thing: an extreme emotional stress event."

Wyler considered this carefully. "Could it have happened during the fall itself?" he asked. "You know, he jumps off the balcony, then he's suddenly hit by the shock of realizing he's about to die. That sounds like a stress event to me."

But Gail was shaking her head before he could finish. "Not a chance," she said. "Cardiomyopathy can come on fast, but not that fast. Even if he had jumped off the top of the Empire State Building, there wouldn't have been time for this swelling to occur. This definitely happened before his death."

"How long before?"

Gail shrugged. "Impossible to say, but based on the enzyme levels..." she moved her head side to side like a metronome, "I would say it was pretty recent. A few days before, maybe even hours."

"What about minutes? Could it have happened right before he jumped?"

She nodded. "Theoretically, yes. It could have been just a few minutes."

Wyler was mulling over the implications of this when Gail stood up.

"I've enjoyed this Aaron, but we are jammed up today and I need to be getting back."

"Thanks Gail," Wyler said, standing. "Just one more thing—it'll only take a second. There was another death in that building on the same night. An older woman."

"Last name?"

"Fogelman."

"Doesn't ring a bell." She leaned down and typed the name into her computer. "Nothing under that name has come through here in the last month. How old was she?"

Wyler shook his head. "I don't know."

"Well, if there was anything suspicious about it, she would have come to us. Probably just natural causes. Heart attack, or maybe heat stroke. Like I said, it's been a long, hot summer."

CHAPTER 10

The detectives who had caught the Peter Lisonbee suicide were Rob Moretti and Mark Bonavitch of the 6th Precinct. Wyler didn't know either man, which wasn't surprising. The NYPD was the largest police force in the world with over thirty thousand cops. But Wyler had reached Detective Moretti by phone from the train that morning and, in a conversation that lasted less than a minute, he explained who he was and made an appointment to stop by the precinct. He was careful on the phone with Moretti, positioning his involvement as a reluctant favor to a friend, which, at the time, had the virtue of being true.

But after just one day, Wyler's attitude toward the case had evolved. There were facts that he didn't think fit into the theory of a simple suicide, and he was coming to believe that there might be more to Peter Lisonbee's death than met the eye.

Wyler walked into the precinct on 10th Street and, after checking in with the desk sergeant in the lobby, took a side stairwell up to the second floor. About halfway down a corridor, he found a door labeled Detective Squad. There were six desks in the room configured into three groups, with each desk pushed up against and facing another. It was almost 6:00 p.m. and the place was deserted, except for two detectives sitting across from each other at the desks farthest from the door. One of them noticed Wyler and waved him over. As Wyler approached, the same detective stood up from his desk.

"Rob Moretti," he said, shaking Wyler's hand. Moretti was on the small side, with black hair, big ears, and a large nose.

"Thanks for giving me a few minutes, detective."

"My partner, Mark Bonavitch." Moretti pointed with his head toward the other man.

"Detective," nodded Wyler.

Bonavitch was bald and fat and about 20 years older than Moretti. He didn't return or acknowledge Wyler's greeting. Instead, he simply leaned back in his chair and folded his hands across his ample belly.

"Grab a seat," said Moretti, and Wyler rolled a chair over from one of the other desks.

"So, you said on the phone you wanted to talk about the Lisonbee suicide?" began Moretti.

"That's right."

"There's not a lot to talk about. It's pretty straightforward."

Wyler knew he had to tread lightly.

"Yes, that's how it looks to me, too. I just had a couple of questions about it."

"And what's your interest in it?" asked Moretti.

"Well, as I mentioned, his sister, Sarah Miller—"

"That broad!" Bonavitch scoffed. "You're mixed up with her? She's nuts."

"I'm not 'mixed up' with her," Wyler explained. "She's a friend of a friend and she asked me to look into it."

"We've spoken to her many times," offered Moretti. "She's having a hard time accepting that her brother would take his own life."

"I agree, but I also think it's more than that."

"What do you mean?"

"Well, for one thing, there's a family heirloom, a valuable gemstone, that's missing from the apartment."

"The door was locked and bolted from the inside. A uniform on the scene had to bust it down," said Moretti. "No other valuables were missing from the place. And the sister herself said he was looking to sell the stone to raise some fast cash. It all adds up."

"Two and two," Bonavitch added.

"Well, he told his sister that he had decided not to sell it." Wyler realized as he said it that it was a weak point. Moretti was right. The absence of the jewel could easily be explained by Peter Lisonbee having sold the stone and lying to his sister about it.

"Anything else?" asked Moretti.

"Well, I went over to the apartment this morning."

"You accessed the crime scene? How'd you get in?" snapped Bonavitch.

"With a key from the next of kin. There wasn't any tape on the door," Wyler lied.

"You're not on the job anymore!" Bonavitch said, sitting up and leaning toward Wyler. "We could bag you and tag you right now."

"We were gonna lift the seal anyway," Moretti said, playing peacemaker. "So, what about the scene didn't you like?"

"Well, a bunch of little things. The guy had just gone shopping a few hours before. He bought laundry detergent. That struck me as pretty unusual for someone about to kill himself."

"That's your beef? Laundry detergent?" sneered Bonavitch. Wyler ignored the remark. Unfortunately, he knew lots of cops like Bonavitch. Paranoid and emotionally immature. Any questions about their work were viewed as personal attacks.

"And then there was his cellphone," Wyler continued, to Moretti.

"What about it?" asked Moretti.

"Well, he was charging it. Strange thing to do if he knew he wasn't going to be around to use it."

Neither Moretti nor Bonavitch responded, so Wyler pressed forward.

"And there was no note," Wyler added.

"C'mon, detective," Moretti said, addressing him as a colleague. "You know they don't always leave a note."

"Of course I do, but I spoke to some of the people who worked with him. This guy was not depressed. He wasn't on drugs. In fact, he had just caught his big break. He was about to open his own restaurant. I don't think this kid was looking for an exit ramp. He was planning his future—literally, right there on his bed, that night. And then, to just commit suicide, for no reason, like on a whim? It just doesn't make sense."

"Sometimes it doesn't make sense," Moretti said calmly. "Things happen all the time that can't be explained. You've spent, what, a day or two looking into this guy? You don't really know him. And guess what? Neither do I. And neither do his friends or his sister or anyone else. If this job's taught me anything, it's that no one knows anybody. I mean, who knows what was going on inside this kid, what private demons he might have had?"

Wyler nodded along. He had to. He had given his own version of the same speech to Sarah Miller the night before.

"I know what you're thinking but trust me, we didn't jump the gun on this," continued Moretti. "We talked to the sister. We talked to his friends at the restaurant. Just like you did."

"Did you talk to Scottie Hibble?"

"Who?" snarled Bonavitch, twisting his face in derision. That question alone told Wyler there had been no serious investigation. They had taken everything at face value.

"His business partner," Wyler said, facing down Bonavitch.

"Hibble was the one investing in Lisonbee's restaurant. I met with him today."

"And?" asked Moretti.

"And, I'm not sure his story adds up."

"What story?" said Bonavitch. "The kid was home alone. Locked in tight. And he jumped. That's it. That's the only story here."

"Did you know he had an extreme stress event that led to cardiomyopathy right before he jumped?" Wyler was stretching the point on the timing, but he felt cornered and desperate.

"Who told you that?" asked Bonavitch, lowering his voice to a threatening tone. Wyler immediately realized his mistake. He hadn't intended to mention Gail's cooperation with him, but Bonavitch's insults and barbs had pushed him to blurt out more than he wanted.

"Gail Toussaint," Wyler said casually.

"That was Serrano's cut!" Bonavitch suddenly erupted. "What's she doing with her hands in it?" He began to curse Gail Toussaint with a stream of misogynistic expletives.

Wyler looked at Moretti, hoping for some support, but his stupidity had cost him the benefit of the doubt Moretti had been giving him.

"Anything else?" asked Moretti, but Wyler saw no point in going on. The meeting had gone completely sideways.

"Pathetic," Bonavitch shook his head in disgust at Wyler.

"Mark," Moretti said in a warning voice to his partner.

"No, man. This is too much!"

"Calm down."

"No, I've had it with this guy!"

"What's your problem?" asked Wyler, turning on Bonavitch. "I'm not second-guessing you guys. I'm just asking some questions."

"Look man, I'm sorry for what happened to your old lady, but that doesn't give you—"

"What did you just say?" Wyler cut in, but Bonavitch kept going.

"—the right to come in here and stick your nose in this case. You got issues to resolve with your wife's suicide? Go find a shrink!"

"That's enough!" Moretti said.

Wyler was speechless, the wind suddenly knocked out of him.

"After we spoke this morning, I made a few calls," Moretti explained. "Spoke to a friend of mine at Midtown South. He told me what happened with your wife, about why you pulled the pin a year ago."

"My wife's death has nothing to do with this," said Wyler, but it was more to himself than to them. He was in a daze, shocked by Bonavitch's words.

"Okay, whatever you say," said Moretti, showing his palms in surrender. "It just seemed a little odd that you would be so interested in a suicide case so soon after...well, we were just trying to figure out what was going on."

"I told you what was going on. I'm doing a favor for a friend. That's it."

"Okay, okay. I got it," said Moretti, but Bonavitch wasn't ready to let it go. He let loose a mocking snort, and suddenly Wyler was on his feet. Bonavitch jumped up quickly to counter the move, knocking his chair over in the process.

"You want to do something, Wyler?" demanded Bonavitch.

"Knock it off, both of you!" yelled Moretti, trying to restore order as the two men glared at each other. Bonavitch was tall and wide, but Wyler wasn't backing down. "Mark, head over to the Blind Tiger. I'll meet you there in fifteen. Wyler, please sit down." But both men seemed unwilling to unfreeze the stand-off. "Detective, please!" said Moretti. "There's something you need to see."

Wyler, breathing heavily from the adrenaline, turned to

Moretti.

"What? What is it?" he asked.

Moretti waited as Bonavitch picked his chair off the ground, grabbed his suit coat, then headed for the door. Once Bonavitch was gone, Wyler and Moretti sat down again.

"There's a video."

"Of what?" asked Wyler.

"Of Peter Lisonbee's suicide."

"*It's on video?*" Wyler was incredulous.

"We didn't have it at first." Moretti turned to his computer and began clicking and typing. "Came in a few days later. Group of kids out that night, bar hopping in the Village."

Wyler rolled his chair closer to Moretti. On his screen, a small window was open and frozen on the blurry first frame of a video. Moretti clicked his mouse, and the image unfroze.

At first the video was hard to follow. It was a jerky cellphone recording of a group of kids in their early twenties walking down a New York City street at night. As the friends shambled down the sidewalk, the girl holding the phone interviewed the other kids about how drunk they were and where they should go next. At one point, they stopped at an intersection, and the camera zoomed in on one member of the gang, a skinny kid with shaggy hair and a goatee. Then, one of the girls in the group said, "Hey, what is that?" and another one said, "Look up there!" Next the phone jerked upward and zoomed in on the building across the street. The camera watched as a lone man on a balcony climbed carefully over the balcony railing. The girl making the recording said, "What is that guy doing?" The camera zoomed in further, causing the image to slip in and out of focus several times, but the picture was clear long enough for Wyler to identify the young man on the balcony. It was Peter Lisonbee. A moment later, the man let go of the railing. Screams distorted the audio as the man fell fourteen stories to the pavement.

CHAPTER 11

Wyler had planned to stop at Zabar's deli on the Upper West Side to pick up some chocolate cheese strudel as a surprise for Gabe before heading home, but after his disastrous meeting with Moretti and Bonavitch, he went straight to Grand Central. Now, he sat brooding in his seat, staring blankly out the window at the east shore of the Hudson River as the Metro-North train rolled toward Poughkeepsie. The sun was just beginning to set behind the low green hills on the far side of the river, but the picturesque scenery was wasted on Wyler. He was in a foul mood.

The NYPD was a huge, complex organization, hampered by outdated procedures, reams of paperwork, competing silos of influence, and a bloated bureaucracy. But when it came to gossip, it was a streamlined model of efficiency. Wyler had no doubt that word of his meltdown would quickly spread, embellished for negative effect by Bonavitch and Moretti. He imagined the reactions of various colleagues. There would be laughter and derision from some, and pity from others. Wyler didn't know which bothered him more, but he felt that both reactions were richly deserved.

As soon as Moretti had shown him the cellphone video, Wyler

realized that he had been wasting his time. He had spent an entire day investigating a non-mystery. And more than that, he had made a fool of himself in the process. How could his judgment have been so off? And then, for a grand finale, he had humiliated himself by letting Bonavitch goad him into a childish schoolyard standoff.

He kept thinking about what Bonavitch had said. He hated the dumb oaf, but he hated even more the painful suspicion growing inside him that the guy was right. Was he really trying to "work out his issues" through the Peter Lisonbee case? Was it a coincidence that he had volunteered to investigate an unexplained suicide? Was there something in Sarah Miller's grief and confusion over her brother's death that had triggered him on a hidden, unconscious level?

He thought of Sarah Miller. He would have to meet with her again, for no other reason than to bring whatever it was he was doing for her to a formal end. When they had first met, he had been sensitive and patient, willing to entertain her suspicions. This time, he intended to confront her directly with the hard truth about her brother's death. Before leaving the 6th Precinct, Wyler had convinced Rob Moretti to email him the video of Peter Lisonbee's suicide. If necessary, Wyler would show it to her. He hoped he wouldn't have to.

The train began to lose momentum, and the conductor announced the stop at Beacon over the PA system. Wyler was just a few stops from home. As the train pulled into the station, the doors opened with a hydraulic hiss, and the car he was in shed another small batch of people. When the train had left Grand Central at 7:45 p.m., it had been packed with commuters crammed into every seat and aisle, but over the past hour the crowd had steadily thinned out, stop by stop.

As the train lurched forward, Wyler noticed someone at the opposite end of the car waving to him. It was Eugene, from the hobby shop. He had probably been on the train since Grand Central, masked by the forest of people. Wyler waved back, and soon Eugene was gathering his things and heading over to him. Wyler was in no mood for company, but there was nothing he could do. He was a sitting duck.

"Hey stranger!" Eugene said as he approached.

"How are you?" answered Wyler as Eugene plopped down in the empty seat across from his. Eugene had a large plastic shopping bag filled with a couple of bulky packages.

"Doing some shopping in Manhattan?"

"Queens, actually," replied Eugene. "There's a hobby shop there I go to from time to time. Much bigger than anything up our way. Actually, I have something here for Gabe."

"Eugene, you don't have to do that."

"I know. I wasn't planning on it. I went there mostly for parts and supplies. But I saw this in the shop, and something told me you and Gabe would appreciate it."

As he spoke, Eugene clumsily withdrew a large box from his bag. Wyler was gearing up to repeat his protest, but then he saw the picture on the box.

"Is that a Fisher XP-75 Eagle?" Wyler asked in astonishment.

Eugene grinned and handed it to Wyler. Wyler accepted it carefully, examining the box like it was a fragile artifact, his eyes glistening with wonder. "I can't believe it. I had no idea anyone had made this."

"It's a rare find."

"These were experimental. They never actually flew in combat. It was always one of my favorite designs." Wyler spoke with the giddy excitement of all buffs and hobbyists given an opportunity to share their passion. "They started working on this early in the war because they needed a plane that could gain altitude very quickly. It used two propellers rotating in opposite directions. But just as it was coming out of prototype, they canceled it and replaced it with the P-51 Mustang. I can't believe you found this!"

Wyler awoke from his reverie and moved to hand the box back to Eugene.

"We really can't accept this."

But Eugene pushed the package back to him.

"It's yours. And Gabe's."

"Eugene!"

"Sorry. Nothing I can do about it!" Eugene was giggling, savoring Wyler's discomfort.

"I don't know what to say." Wyler looked at the box, shaking his head in awe.

"So, how did things go with Sarah?"

For a moment, Wyler was caught off guard by the question. The airplane had transported him to a different mental place entirely.

"I'm afraid there's really not much to it beyond what the police have already told her," he said. "That's where I'm coming from now, actually. I spent the day in the city looking into it."

"Really? That sounds interesting."

"Yes, but like I said, it's pretty straightforward."

"Well, it was kind of you to look into it. I'm sure she'll appreciate that."

"I actually need to call her. I'm not looking forward to the conversation."

"Well, hopefully what you did will at least help her to move on and accept things," said Eugene. There was silence for a few moments filled only by the intermittent sound of the train wheels clicking rhythmically on the tracks.

"Do you mind if I ask you a question?" said Eugene.

"Of course. I mean, go ahead."

"Well, I'm just curious. You know, I'm fascinated by, well,

what I mean is, how do you go about looking into something like this? Is it okay to ask that?"

"Sure. I started out this morning by going to the apartment, you know, her brother's apartment, where it happened."

Eugene whistled softly. "And did you find anything interesting? Any clues or evidence?"

"Well, no. Not really." Wyler remembered the many inconsistencies he had discovered in the apartment, but he didn't feel like rehashing them with Eugene, especially after what happened with Moretti and Bonavitch.

"So, what did you do after the apartment?" asked Eugene.

"I went to the restaurant where Peter worked and spoke to some of his coworkers."

"What did they say?"

"They were all pretty surprised by Peter's suicide. According to them, he wasn't outwardly depressed or suicidal in any way. The exact opposite in fact. None of them saw this coming. It was a complete shock."

"Is that usual, for a suicide?"

"Well, no, actually. It's not usual. What I mean is, when someone commits suicide, people close to the person, loved ones, are almost always initially in a state of shock and disbelief. But then, in retrospect, they look back and see the warning signs, warning signs that they minimized or ignored. That often leads to intense feelings of guilt that just add to the grief of the loss." Wyler said all this with a clinical detachment, but deep down he was aware of the painful, personal irony of his words.

"But that wasn't the case here?" asked Eugene.

"No, it wasn't," Wyler said, suddenly grateful for Eugene's company and questions. "None of the people who knew Peter seemed to have any sense that he was hurting or close to taking his own life." As he made the statement out loud to Eugene, the truth of this fact seemed to crystallize in Wyler's mind. It was something that simply didn't fit. It was an anomaly, hanging out there, unresolved. Why did Peter Lisonbee commit suicide? It suddenly bothered him that he had no plausible explanation to offer Sarah Miller.

"So, what did you do after that? Sorry for all the questions, but this is fascinating."

"I spoke to a man named Scottie Hibble who had planned to go into business with Peter."

"And what did he have to say about it?"

"Well, his opinion was that Peter was riddled with insecurities and fear of success and that's why he killed himself."

"Huh," said Eugene. "So he didn't agree with the others you spoke to at the restaurant?"

"No, he didn't," said Wyler. "In fact, his whole view of Peter was dramatically different from the picture painted by everyone else who knew him."

"Well, maybe he was more sensitive or intuitive than the others," offered Eugene.

"Not this guy," said Wyler with a derisive chuckle. Scottie Hibble was as callous and shallow an individual as Wyler had ever encountered. Now that he thought about it, it seemed like Hibble had tried very hard to push his own theory of the case on Wyler. Now, Wyler wondered why.

The train pulled into the New Hamburg station and a few more people got off. For some reason their conversation paused along with the train and didn't resume until after they were underway again. The conductor announced that Poughkeepsie would be the next and final stop.

"So, what did you do next?" asked Eugene.

"I went to the medical examiner's office to discuss the autopsy."

"You actually saw the body?" Eugene whispered with both shock and excitement.

"No, I just reviewed the autopsy report with one of the medical examiners."

"Anything interesting?"

"There were no drugs in his system, and no signs of violence or foul play of any kind on the body, other than the injuries sustained in the fall."

Wyler left out the information about the unusual cardiac event Peter Lisonbee experienced before his death. He was too tired to explain it and wasn't sure himself what it meant.

"After that, I went to the 6th Precinct and spoke to the detectives assigned to the case."

"What did they say?"

"They showed me a video of Peter Lisonbee's suicide."

"There's a video?"

"It's a cellphone video taken by some people on the street that night. It captured the whole thing."

After a moment, Eugene spoke in a quiet voice. "Wow. So, I guess that's it."

There was silence between them for a while. Wyler looked out the window. It was dark now. He checked the time on his phone and saw that it was almost 9:30 p.m. He realized he hadn't eaten since his burger at Nine several hours ago, and he was hungry.

"But, what about the missing gemstone?" Eugene asked, breaking the silence.

"I'm not sure it is missing," answered Wyler.

"What do you mean?"

"Well, Peter admitted he was thinking of selling it, and the police are convinced that's what he did."

"Is that what *you* think?"

Wyler thought about Eugene's question but was interrupted by the PA system announcing their arrival in Poughkeepsie.

"Do you need a lift?" Wyler asked, as the train pulled into the station. "I've got my car."

"No, I'm just a few blocks from here."

"You're going to walk?"

"After a day in the city, I need the fresh air."

They both stood up and prepared to exit.

"Well thank you again for this," said Wyler, holding up the box. "Gabe is going to be so excited."

"Thank you for being so patient and answering so many questions. Your work is fascinating to someone like me."

They got off the train and continued walking together along the platform.

"Could you stand one more question?" Eugene asked.

"Of course."

"Here's my probably very silly question: What is it that makes a good detective, in real life?"

"What do you mean?"

"Well, on TV, the detectives are all so clever. They outsmart the bad guys by noticing things everyone else overlooks. Each mystery is like a riddle that only the detective is smart enough to figure out. That's fun to watch on TV, but is that really how it is?"

"Not at all," Wyler said with a laugh as they walked down the platform steps into the outdoor parking lot.

"So, what does it take, in real life? I'm just curious. What's the difference between a normal police officer and someone like you?"

"That's not a silly question at all. It's actually an excellent question."

"So, what's the answer?" pressed Eugene.

They reached Wyler's car and stood beside it while Wyler considered Eugene's question.

"Well, I've worked with lots of detectives over the years, and the good ones, regardless of their backgrounds or personalities, all share some of the same basic qualities. You have to be tireless, for one. It's a hard job that usually just boils down to legwork and luck. You talk to lots of people, you make the calls, you follow the leads, you keep asking questions and digging. And you have to be curious. What I mean is, you can't always take things at face value. You need to be willing to question everything and keep an open mind."

"So, is that it?"

Wyler thought some more.

"No. The truth is, if I had to sum up in one word what makes a good detective, what really sets a detective apart from other cops, the word would be instinct. A detective has to have good natural instincts. Come to think of it, that's probably why really great detectives are so rare. The vital quality is one you can't teach. Sometimes all you have is your own gut feelings telling you which path to take, what direction to follow, even when all the evidence is pointing somewhere else."

"I see. Well, that is fascinating. Thank you for indulging my curiosity. I'll let you get back to Gabe. Goodnight, Aaron."

As Wyler watched Eugene stroll leisurely in the direction of Main Street, he reflected upon what he had just said about a detective's instinct, and how it applied to the Peter Lisonbee case. The cellphone video seemed to close the case. Peter Lisonbee had committed suicide. It was right there, recorded for anyone to see. And yet, all his professional instincts, developed and honed through years of experience, told him that there was more to it.

He thought back to his first conversation with Sarah Miller, about the gemstone her family had handed down and protected for so many years. She was not a religious fanatic as far as he could tell, but the stone obviously meant a great deal to her, and to her family.

He stood for a while by his car, feeling the crisp night air blowing in from the Hudson, and came to a decision. Something about his conversation with Eugene had clarified things in his mind. He may never come to understand why Peter Lisonbee leapt off that balcony, but he decided he would keep working on the case and try to find the missing gemstone. If Peter Lisonbee had sold it, he would find out to whom. If someone had stolen it, he would track them down. He could do that much for Sarah Miller, and for the whole Lisonbee family who had kept their own strange faith with the gemstone all those years. What did Sarah call it, the covenant of the stone? Getting the gemstone back, or at least finding out where it was, might give her some comfort and allow her to move on.

As he got in his car and drove home, he felt suddenly invigorated, and a new plan for the investigation began to form in his mind.

CHAPTER 12

When Wyler got home, he found Amy, the Vassar student who babysat Gabe regularly, on the couch watching TV. As Wyler tapped through the Venmo app to pay her, she volunteered a summary of her day with Gabe, which included a trip to the mall and the latest Spider-Man movie, which Gabe had already seen twice. Dinner had been a DoorDash delivery from Tamarind, the best Indian place in town, and Wyler was glad to hear there were leftovers.

After she left, Wyler went upstairs and found Gabe in his room, sitting at his computer with headphones on, playing Rocket League, a video game where soccer is played by cars instead of people. It was one of the few games Wyler himself had tried to play with his son, but he could never get the hang of it. Wyler stood by the door, unnoticed, watching him for a bit.

"Hey," Wyler said when there was a break in the game.

Gabe slid the headphones down to his neck and half turned in his chair.

"What's that?" asked Gabe, noticing the box in Wyler's hand.

"It's a gift from Eugene. I saw him on the train coming home."

Wyler handed the box to Gabe. "It's an RC plane based on one of my favorite World War II planes. The XP-75 Eagle."

"Cool," said Gabe. "Do you want to start on it tomorrow?"

"Actually, I wanted to talk to you about tomorrow. How would you feel about staying with Mimi for a few days? I called her on my way home, and she would love to see you."

"Sure. Why?"

"Well, this thing I'm doing, it may take a bit longer than I thought."

"So, are you working again?"

"No, not really. Like I said. I'm just helping someone out." Wyler hadn't told Gabe any details about what he was doing. This wasn't new. As a detective working in counterterrorism, a boundary had to separate his work from his family life. The problem was, since his job consumed his thoughts even when he wasn't at work, this boundary ended up putting stress on his marriage. At first, Jessica had understood and accepted his need for discretion, but over time, the constant need for secrecy had contributed to the gulf that eventually grew between them. He sometimes wondered, in retrospect, if he had overdone it, if the wall he built around his professional life had hidden other parts of himself, parts that he should have shared willingly.

"So, we'll take the train in together in the morning, and I'll drop you off at Mimi's place."

"Okay." Gabe swiveled back to face his monitor. As usual, Wyler couldn't read his son's reaction. He had no idea if Gabe was pleased, excited, disappointed, resentful, or indifferent to the plan he had proposed. On the outside, his son seemed to take everything in stride, but Wyler had no idea if this was how he really felt, or if it was a façade hiding other feelings. Life father, like son.

"You should pack for a few days."

Wyler went to the kitchen to rummage through the leftover Indian food. He made himself a plate and stuck it in the microwave, then went back upstairs to get his laptop. He passed his son's bedroom on the way and was glad to see Gabe stuffing clothes into a duffel bag. He grabbed his laptop off the desk in his room and went back downstairs. He got his food from the microwave and a beer from the fridge, then sat down at the dining room table to get to work.

Mentally, he had to change gears, as the focus of the investigation was no longer Peter Lisonbee's suicide, but the location of the missing gemstone. He took a bite of food, then picked up his phone and opened the picture of the gemstone that Sarah Miller had texted to him after their meeting. He hadn't looked carefully at it before, but now he used his fingers to zoom in slightly.

The stone was black and slightly elongated, like a robin's egg. It sat on a bed of white cloth inside the small jewelry box he had found empty in Peter's apartment that morning. He zoomed in further. The stone seemed to have an inner oval, raised in low relief above the surface of the stone, creating an outer rim like the brim of a hat. He tried to zoom in a little further, but the picture blurred when he did.

Wyler's working assumption was that Peter Lisonbee had indeed sold the gemstone to raise money, which is why the stone was not in his apartment at the time of his death. Wyler had to admit that Moretti and Bonavitch were correct about this being the most likely explanation. Before he could explore other possibilities, he needed to prove, or disprove, this theory. That meant tracking down where he had sold it, and to whom. During their meeting in the hospital cafeteria, Wyler had asked Sarah Miller if she had any idea where her brother might have taken the gemstone, but she didn't. That left the possibilities wide open, in a city with thousands of jewelry retailers.

Wyler had a decent working knowledge of the gem and jewelry business from his work in counterterrorism. New York was the nerve center of the U.S. jewelry industry, with over 80% of all diamonds bought and sold in the country filtering through Manhattan's diamond district, which was actually just one block on 47th Street between 5th and 6th Avenues. The street was home to hundreds of businesses, large and small, where dealers, designers, and middlemen bought and sold not only diamonds, but other precious metals and gems. Although the district was dominated by Jewish merchants, in recent years other ethnicities had made inroads.

Since most of the high-volume transactions were cash based and conducted in upstairs offices away from the public showrooms, the potential for money laundering was an obvious concern of law enforcement. Drug cartels had a long history of using diamonds to wash dirty money, but after it was discovered that Al Qaeda had converted millions of dollars into diamonds right before 9/11, the FBI and other agencies began to worry that money could be funneled to and from terrorist groups via jewelry retailers in the U.S. Years earlier, Wyler himself had been a member of a joint task force with the FBI that uncovered a plot to smuggle portable Russian-made surface-to-air missiles into the country using a diamond district retailer as a front. The bust had made national news.

Wyler considered contacting Frank Slemmer, the executive director of the American Gem Trade Association, to discuss the Peter Lisonbee gemstone. Slemmer had worked with law enforcement to develop policies and practices to combat money laundering in the industry, and Wyler had gotten to know him. Slemmer would certainly know where to have an antique gemstone appraised in New York.

But then Wyler thought better of it. Peter Lisonbee didn't have any high-level contacts in the jewel industry. He needed to put himself in Peter's place and try to work the problem as he would have.

He did a Google search using the words "gemstone" and

"appraisal" and "New York," thinking this might be how Peter Lisonbee had started. The search generated a list of companies, followed by another list of websites and online articles. Wyler clicked the "view all" button to expand the list of companies. This action generated a map feature on the right that showed the locations of the businesses.

It seemed to be mix of jewelry retailers and companies that specialized only in appraisals. Once again, he tried to think like Peter Lisonbee. Would he go to an appraisal company first or a retailer? An appraisal company would no doubt provide a more accurate estimate, but would probably take longer, whereas a retailer might be willing to make a quick cash offer.

He decided to simply organize the search geographically. He redid the Google search, this time using the address of Peter Lisonbee's apartment building as ground zero. A newly constituted list appeared. He clicked print and, after a moment, heard the printer in his upstairs bedroom whirring to life. Tomorrow, he would go store to store, trying to track Peter's movements. He knew the chances of success were slim, but that didn't discourage him. That was the job. You made assumptions, worked a theory, and if that didn't work out, you regrouped and tried a new angle. In reality, detective work was rarely exciting or glamorous. It was a never-ending numbers game that more often than not didn't pay off.

With his plan for tomorrow worked out, Wyler decided to check his email. Waiting in his inbox was the message from Rob Moretti. The message itself was blank, containing only the official signature line identifying Rob Moretti as a detective with the NYPD's 6th Precinct. But attached to the email was a video file.

At that point, Gabe walked into the kitchen. Wyler waited while his son made himself a bowl of cereal, then went back upstairs to his room. Once he heard the door to Gabe's room close, Wyler clicked on the email attachment, which opened the video file on his screen. He maximized the window, then clicked the play button.

Once again, Wyler watched the group of friends stumble drunkenly down the street, enjoying their night out in the Village, oblivious to what was about to happen. Once again, he saw the group stop at the corner, debating where to go next, then get distracted by something. As the jittery handheld footage swiveled to the building across the street and zoomed in, Wyler again saw the dark figure on the balcony, slipping in and out of focus but clearly visible as Peter Lisonbee. Then he watched the figure let go of the railing and plunge downward to the street below.

When he viewed the clip with Moretti earlier, they had stopped there, right after Peter's jump. But now, the video continued, and Wyler kept watching. For several seconds after the fall, the images on the screen were chaotic and impossible to decipher, as the person holding the phone seemed to be running. Shocked cries and screams could be heard all around.

Eventually, the image came into focus again. The camera was on the other side of the street now, just outside Peter's building, overlooking the crowd of people that had gathered. The phone was panning frantically from left to right. Some Good Samaritans were trying to keep everyone back. At one point, the entrance to the apartment building was visible, and Wyler saw the doorman he had spoken to that morning running back into the building, just as he said he did. Another man, probably a tenant from the building, walked out onto the street and headed off in the opposite direction.

And then, the camera panned back to the crowd.. Once again, the image became blurry and unintelligible as the person holding the phone tried to move closer to the grisly center of attraction. There was pushing and yelling and then the clip abruptly ended.

Wyler sat and stared at the frozen image on the screen for several seconds. There was something in the footage he had just viewed that bothered him, but he didn't know what it was. This had happened to him a few times before in his career. Some incongruous detail at a crime scene, or in a witness statement, or in an autopsy report, had lodged in his subconscious mind, nagging at him without revealing itself. He mentally played the footage back in his mind, slowly, frame by frame, searching for the piece of information that stuck out, that didn't fit.

But he couldn't find it.

CHAPTER 13

The building where Gabe's grandmother lived was on West 57th Street, just south of Central Park and adjacent to Carnegie Hall. The next morning, as Wyler and Gabe stepped out of the cab in front of the luxury high-rise, Wyler felt his usual apprehension about seeing Jessica's mother.

Nora Maitland was a somewhat eccentric character with a larger-than-life personality. Before her marriage to Jessica's father, she had been an actress, singer, and dancer, with small parts in several Broadway musicals in the 1970s. Wyler knew one of them was about P.T. Barnum because when the movie *The Greatest Showman* came out, Nora had gone on and on about what a travesty it was in comparison to the Broadway show she had been in years before.

During his marriage, Wyler had gotten along well with his mother-in-law. In fact, they had grown close. But since Jessica's death, Wyler hadn't known quite how to face Nora. Although he regularly dropped Gabe off for weekends and overnights, Wyler had stayed at arm's length and kept their interactions to a minimum. He wasn't sure if it was guilt, or worry that Nora might, deep down, blame him for her daughter's decision to take her own life.

They entered the building through glass double doors held open by two uniformed doormen. A third doorman behind a reception desk in the palatial lobby flashed a smile of recognition. "Go right on up. She's expecting you." Wyler had grown up in a middle-class Brooklyn neighborhood and never felt truly comfortable in the opulent, upscale building where Jessica was raised. Jessica enjoyed teasing him about his awkwardness. To her, it was simply her childhood home like anyone else's.

They rode the elevator up to the fifteenth floor, then walked down the wide corridor to the end of the hall. As usual, Nora had left the door open for them.

"Hello?" announced Wyler as they stepped into the marble foyer then continued past a bubbling water feature and down two stone steps into the living room. The cavernous two-story apartment was decorated in an eclectic clash of styles that reflected Nora Maitland's offbeat personality. Some furniture was stately and elegant, other pieces were comfortable and homey. Paintings and sculptures by famous artists fought for attention beside some of Nora's own handiwork. There were Persian rugs on the floor, Japanese tapestries on the walls, and shelves crammed with assorted trinkets and knickknacks. Overall, the effect was a cross between a posh salon and cluttered antique store.

"I'm in here!" Nora called from a large sunroom just off the living room.

Nora had lived in the apartment alone ever since Jessica moved out years ago. Charles Maitland, Nora's husband and Jessica's father, had died of pancreatic cancer when Jessica was thirteen. The drill-bit millionaire had been a financial backer of a Broadway show that Nora was in. They met, fell in love, and got married despite the age difference (he was at least twenty years older). A year later, Jessica was born. When Jessica arrived, Nora quit show business for good to devote herself entirely to her daughter. In spite of being a minor Broadway star with a promising career, Wyler had never heard an ounce of regret from Nora about her choices.

"Gabie Babie!" Nora called out as they stepped into the amateur art studio. The glass encased room was flooded with sunlight and crowded with easels, brushes, jars, containers, and other creative debris.

"Hi Mimi!" said Gabe. Nora was standing at a craft table kneading a giant wad of modeling clay. She was approaching seventy but looked younger, with short, curly brown hair that had streaks of gray running through it. "What are you working on?"

"I don't know yet," replied Nora. "An artist, during the creative act, should always be asking himself, 'what is this?' and then let the work itself give the answer." She paused and scrutinized the lump in front of her. "So far, this guy isn't talking."

When Jessica had introduced Wyler to her mother, he was surprised at how different they were. Jessica was the smartest person Wyler had ever met, a brilliant physician and intellectual with a sly, deadpan wit. Her mother's kooky, theatrical personality was a shock at first, but he soon came to admire and appreciate her. He never saw Jessica as happy as when she was with her mom, and they were never together very long before some private joke would send them both into a hysterical laughing jag that often ended in tears.

"How was your ride in?" Nora asked as she rinsed her hands in a chrome sink.

"It was fine," replied Wyler. "Cabbie from Grand Central was a madman."

"Well, that's half the fun, isn't it?" Nora dried her hands on a paint-stained smock and came over to inspect and greet them properly. She wrapped her arms around her grandson and gave him a giant hug. It started off bouncy and fun but then settled into something more tender. Wyler gave them space by looking out the window at the apartment's amazing view of Central Park. When, after a few moments, Gabe didn't squirm or break away, Wyler realized that his son must be starved for this kind of physical affection. As he stared at the rectangular expanse of lush greenery stretching out below him, a sharp pang of shame shot through him. One more log on the fire of his guilt.

"We are going to have a blast!" Nora finally declared as she released Gabe. Next, she embraced Wyler. "How are you, Aaron?"

"Thank you for doing this on such short notice," said Wyler, gently evading.

Nora scoffed audibly. "Are you kidding? What else do I have to do?"

Nora hooked her arms through theirs and led them back into the living room like Dorothy with the Scarecrow and Tin Man. "Now, I know you have work to do Aaron, but I'm hoping you'll at least stay for lunch. I've made reservations at this new Korean place everyone's talking about."

"Unfortunately, I've got to run," he said. "I've got a whole day ahead of me and I need to get started."

Nora made an exaggerated frowny face, but then quickly switched gears.

"Oh, well. What time should we expect you tonight?"

"Actually, I booked a room at a hotel in Times Square."

"What?" Nora stopped in her tracks.

"I'm probably going to go late. I didn't want to bother you."

Nora looked at Wyler suspiciously, then turned to Gabe.

"Gabe, if you head upstairs, you'll find a new piece of furniture in your room. I think it's called the Emperor Workstation 200 or something like that," she said playfully.

"No way!" Gabe dropped his bag and ran up the spiral staircase, taking two at a time.

"The Emperor what?" asked Wyler.

"It's nothing. It's a new gaming chair. Now listen, Aaron," she said, turning to face him.

"How much?"

"Never mind that. I want to talk to you."

"How much, Nora?"

"A few thousand," she shrugged.

"Nora!" Wyler said, lodging his usual protest even though he knew it was impossible to stop her from spoiling her only grandson.

"I want you to stay here with us tonight."

"Nora, I appreciate the invitation, but I can't."

"What is this thing you're doing? You sounded so cryptic over the phone."

"I can't really talk about it."

"You're not getting involved with terrorists again, are you?" Nora asked with unfeigned dread, and when Wyler didn't answer right away, she moved closer and gripped his arm tenderly. "Aaron, you have to be careful. You're the only thing he has left in this world. He needs you." She released his arm and began fussing with his collar and tie. "And news flash, kiddo. I need you too." Suddenly, there were tears in Nora's eyes. "You are always welcome here, Aaron. This is your home, as much as it was hers. Do you understand that?" Aaron nodded but said nothing. "I want to spend time with you. I want to talk to you. And I want *you* to talk to *me*. About *her*."

Wyler fought back a surge of emotion. "We need to share the love that we both had for her, with each other. No one loved her like you and I did."

She forced a smile as a single tear slid down her cheek. Wyler realized at that moment that he had wasted months secretly misjudging Nora and harboring fears about resentment that wasn't there. But he could find no words to match the storm of feelings suddenly welling up inside him.

"I'm not doing anything with terrorists," he said softly, after a moment. "I'm just helping out a friend."

Nora smiled and nodded, accepting his answer as he had intended. It was a partial concession and, for the moment, the best he could do.

CHAPTER 14

"Where to next, boss?" asked the cabbie from the front seat.

So far, the search for the stone had hit a series of dead ends. Wyler had already visited fourteen jewelers on his list, but no one had recognized the photo of Peter Lisonbee or the jewel displayed on Wyler's cellphone.

"Gimme a minute."

"You're the boss," came the cheerful response from the front seat.

After leaving Nora's apartment, Wyler had walked over to Seventh Avenue and hailed a cab. As they drove downtown towards the West Village, Wyler explained to the cabbie, a young man with light brown skin and a thin mustache who wore a Sikh's turban, that he had several stops to make. Wyler offered a generous tip if he would wait for him at each stop, keeping the meter running, of course. So far, Wyler's bad luck had turned into a financial windfall for the cabbie.

He thought he had mapped his game plan logically, plotting a circular search pattern that fanned out from Peter Lisonbee's apartment in the West Village. But as the circle grew wider, it was becoming clear that he was on the wrong track. He realized now that his approach had probably been flawed from the start. Manhattan did not lend itself to circular search patterns. The city was laid out as a rectangular grid, with streets and avenues that crisscrossed at right angles. And most people didn't ride around in cabs with running meters; they walked or rode the subway. Although there were some cross-town subway lines, most city trains ran north and south along the Avenues. That meant Peter Lisonbee probably would have hunted for jewelry stores on the west side of Manhattan using the subway lines closest to him. And yet Wyler's ill-conceived strategy had landed him on 2nd Avenue, all the way on the East Side.

"Let's head back over to 8th Avenue," said Wyler, refolding the map.

After about forty minutes of stop-and-crawl congestion along narrow cross-town streets made narrower by several unloading delivery trucks, they finally approached 8th Avenue. "Just turn north and head uptown," instructed Wyler, as the cabbie made a right turn off 14th and accelerated into the wide, flowing artery of 8th Avenue traffic. Peter Lisonbee had lived in the West Village, near the A, C, and E trains that ran along 8th Avenue, and Wyler had decided to focus his search here. As they headed uptown, they passed two jewelry stores Wyler had already visited earlier that morning. But when they crossed 34th Street, Wyler told the cabbie to slow down. He scooted over to the uncomfortable middle hump of the back seat bench and began scanning both sides of the street, looking left and right, searching the small businesses and buildings for any places Peter Lisonbee might have taken the stone.

New York City is famous for being a diverse patchwork of separate communities and ethnic enclaves. Neighborhoods like Little Italy and Chinatown are well known, but there's also a Little Dominican Republic, a Little Poland, a Little India, and a Little Pakistan. There's the Ukrainians of Brighton Beach, the

Italians of Bensonhurst, the Hassidic Jews of Borough Park, Williamsburg, and Crown Heights. Not to mention Greenwich Village, Harlem, Hell's Kitchen, the Upper East Side, the Upper West Side—all micro-societies with their own identity and subculture. But as Wyler studied the storefronts passing outside his cab window, it occurred to him that each square block of Manhattan was like a neighborhood unto itself, with the same basic assortment of shops and services showing up over and over in a repeating pattern.

They continued cruising uptown for several blocks, until Wyler saw something that caught his attention. He made a quick decision. "Pull over here," he said suddenly.

Wyler got out of the cab and leaned in through the front passenger window.

"I'm going to head down this block on foot. I may grab lunch. Could you be back here in about thirty minutes?"

He saw the young man hesitate. This was New York, and everybody's scam radar was flipped on. Wyler pulled out his wallet.

"This is everything I owe you up to now, plus the tip we talked about. If you want, you can keep it running, go grab lunch yourself, and meet me back here in thirty. If not, that's okay too. Up to you."

The young man leaned over and took the bills from Wyler's hand.

"See you in thirty," he said with a smile.

A few minutes later, Wyler walked into Covington Bistro. It was a small, upscale restaurant with oil paintings, wood-paneled walls, chandeliers, and white tablecloths. Wyler approached an attractive young hostess standing behind a podium.

"One for lunch," said Wyler. Only a few scattered tables were occupied, and he had no problem getting seated. As he slid into a booth, the hostess handed him a menu. It was the same menu that Wyler had seen in Peter Lisonbee's apartment, with *Covington Bistro* in raised gold cursive lettering on the cover. He had spotted the restaurant from the cab and remembered that one of the hardback menus in Peter Lisonbee's collection had come from here. He had wondered then how a young, up-and-coming chef would get a hold of real menus from exclusive restaurants.

Although he was here playing an investigative hunch, he was hungry and still had to eat, so when the waiter came, he ordered a bone-in ribeye. While he waited, he took out his phone and sent a text to Gabe.

> How are you? Having fun with Mimi? Did you guys go to that Korean place for lunch?

He soon saw the three blinking dots under his message that he assumed meant the other person was reading it. But then, a moment later, the blinking dots disappeared, and no response came. Wyler wondered what that meant. Was Gabe in the middle of something, like a video game or a movie? Or did he just not feel like talking with his dad? His mind flashed back to the morning, to the tender hug Gabe had shared with his grandmother. Why was there a wall between him and his son? Did Gabe blame him for what happened? He resolved that when he got back to Rhinebeck he was going to confront Dr. Schoenwald about the situation.

It only took Wyler about ten minutes to eat his steak. Like all restaurant steaks, it was good but not great. Wyler had eaten at some of the best steak places in New York—Peter Lugar, Smith and Wollensky—but he still thought that the steaks he grilled himself at home topped them all. The waiter had dropped off the check as Wyler was finishing, and now Wyler slipped his credit card into the folder's little plastic slot. A moment later, the waiter came by to collect it. While he was gone from the table, Wyler thought through his next move.

"Is there anything else I can do for you?" asked the young man when he returned with the check.

"Yes, there is actually," said Wyler. He opened the check folder and picked up the pen. "I'm wondering if I could speak to the sous chef?"

The waiter, a thin young man with shaggy blond hair wearing a white shirt and black bowtie, looked puzzled.

"You want to talk to the chef?"

"Not the chef, the sous chef."

For a moment, the young man froze. This was obviously something he had never heard before, and he didn't know how to respond. But Wyler was prepared for this reaction, and to help things along, he held the little folder with the check open for the young man to see. The boy looked down at what was written in the tip line, and his mouth dropped open.

"I would really appreciate it," said Wyler.

"Just a moment," the waiter said, and he disappeared into the bowels of the restaurant. Wyler had mixed feelings about "bribing" the young man for his help, but on the other hand, what choice did he have? He no longer had a badge he could flash to get people to cooperate, so he had to improvise. Thank heaven for drill bits.

As he waited, Wyler tried to imagine how the boy was handling his request. Would he try to speak privately to the sous chef without the chef knowing? A request to speak with, and compliment, a chef was common enough. But a request from a customer to speak to an underling might be taken as an insult by a prima donna chef.

Several minutes passed, and no one emerged from the back. Maybe no one would. It was a long shot and a potential dead end, but Wyler's working theory was that Peter Lisonbee, who had been a sous chef at The Empire Grille, might know sous chefs at other upscale restaurants in the city. Maybe the one who worked here had given him the menu he kept in his apartment. Maybe they were friends. Maybe he would know more about Peter than those who worked with him at Nine. Lots of maybe's, but if the theory didn't pan out, at least he had gotten lunch out of it.

The young waiter finally emerged from the back of the house, balancing a tray of food on his shoulder. He passed Wyler without so much as a side glance and headed for a table in the far corner. As the young man laid plates down before an elderly couple, Wyler kept watching him, hoping for eye contact or some other signal. He was about to cut his losses and leave when a young woman in a white apron and chef's cap suddenly stood in front of him.

"You wanted to see me?" she asked. She was young, probably in her twenties, with brown skin, large brown eyes, and black hair. She looked Middle Eastern, possibly Indian. Wyler recognized her immediately as the girl from the framed picture that was on Peter Lisonbee's nightstand, the same picture he had in his pocket now.

"Yes, I did," said Wyler.

"What is this about?" She was small in stature, bordering on petite, and there was a clipped edge to her tone. This was not the excited young graduate aping for the camera with her friends. Wyler wondered if the tough veneer had always been there, or if the pressure of a busy New York kitchen had hardened her.

"It's about Peter Lisonbee."

Wyler read a strong reaction to the name, even though she clearly tried to suppress it.

"Who are you?"

"Can you sit down?" Wyler gestured to the other side of the booth. When she stood her ground, Wyler continued. "My name is Aaron Wyler. I'm an ex-cop. A detective. NYPD. Peter Lisonbee's sister asked me to look into his death."

She glanced back to the kitchen, then slid into the booth across from Wyler.

"What took you so long?"

"What do you mean?"

"Peter didn't commit *suicide*." She spat the last word out like it tasted bad. Wyler was surprised by the conviction in her voice. She was the first person he had spoken to, other than Sarah Miller, to suggest that the police had gotten it wrong.

"What is your name?"

She took a moment, as if assessing the risk of giving her name, then said, "Subi."

"Subi, why do you say that Peter didn't commit suicide?"

Instead of answering right away, she began fidgeting with the origami-folded cloth napkin on the table.

"Did you know Peter?" she finally asked.

"No, I didn't."

"Very few people did."

"Were you one of them?"

"I thought I was, until this happened…"

"What do you mean?"

"The Peter I knew never would have jumped off that balcony."

Wyler waited, but instead of continuing, she seemed to retreat into a private world.

"How did you meet Peter?" Wyler asked, trying to lure her back in.

"We met at the Culinary Institute, up in Hyde Park."

"What was he like?"

She shook her head, and a hint of a smile formed. "He was the best chef in our class. And the most driven."

"How did you become friends?"

"He saved me," she said, raising her head to look Wyler in the eye.

"What do you mean?"

"The CIA is one of the hardest culinary schools in the country—in the world—to get into. It's like, the Harvard Law of cooking schools. And after you get in—*if* you get in—the pressure is intense. It's super competitive. A lot of people end up dropping out. They just can't take the stress."

"How did Peter handle it?"

"Handle it? He thrived on it. He was like on a different plane than the rest of us. He was special. He never had any doubts about himself. Don't get me wrong, we all started out that way. The place only takes the best of the best, so everyone shows up super cocky, thinking they're going to be the next Alain Ducasse. But once you get there, all that changes pretty fast. You've been told all your life you're the best at something, and after a week at CIA you realize how stiff the competition really is. Some people can't make the adjustment. They crumble."

"Is that what happened to you?"

"It would have happened to me if it hadn't been for Peter. My first year there totally kicked my butt. I was a mess. I was ready to give up and go home, but Peter wouldn't let me. He saw that I was struggling, and he made it his business to make sure I kept going. He spent hours with me during his spare time, cooking with me and reteaching me everything we had already learned in classes and labs. He would say, 'You are not going back to Sri Lanka without a chef's hat on your head!'"

"Sri Lanka?"

"That's where I'm from. My family sacrificed a lot so I could go to CIA. I mean, we weren't poor, but it was a big sacrifice, for sure. Peter knew that. He knew how much it meant—not just to me, but to my family—that I succeed, and he just would not let me fail."

Wyler wondered just how close the two of them had gotten.

"We were just friends," she said, guessing his thoughts. "I don't think he dated anyone while we were there. He was just totally focused on his goal."

"And what was that?"

"To own his own restaurant in New York. I mean, that's everyone's dream at the beginning, but then most people scale their ambitions back down to reality."

"But not Peter."

"Peter didn't have to scale anything back. He was the best. He knew it. The teachers knew it. The other students knew it. He was definitely headed for big things."

"So, what happened?"

She slowly shook her head and went back to playing with the napkin.

"It doesn't make any sense. Peter was on track. I mean, less than a year out of school and he was a sous chef at Empire Grille! That's phenomenal. But even there he hated to be in anyone's shadow, so he went to this smaller place downtown where he could be head chef. And then he meets Scottie Hibble, and suddenly they're scouting locations for Peter's own restaurant. It's unreal! Everything was falling into place for him. And he deserved it too. A lot of us have ambition, but Peter had the talent to back it up."

"I met with Scottie Hibble. I spoke to him about Peter. He thinks, deep down, Peter was insecure and afraid of success. He says that's why Peter took his own life."

"No way, no way," she said, shaking her head emphatically. "That was not Peter. He was finally about to achieve the goal he had been working so hard for. There's no way he would throw it away like that."

"I understand what you're saying, but I also know that sometimes the image people project of themselves does not reflect everything that's going on inside of them. There are inner demons that haunt people that others, even people close to them, never see."

"I know Peter. I mean, I knew Peter. He wasn't like that. When his dad died, he was really torn up inside. He and his dad did not have a great relationship. He spent that whole weekend in my dorm room, crying, talking, really opening up to me about what he was feeling. We were very close , and he was hurting, bad. My point is, he didn't keep it inside. Now compare that to this."

She took out her cellphone and tapped and scrolled until she found what she was looking for, then showed it to Wyler. It was a text message.

> Been out all day with SH looking at places. There's a warehouse in Chelsea that he made an offer on! I want you to see! It's on 15th between 7th and 8th. Are you free tomorrow? Not too early because I'm going to be up all night working on the menu. I'm totally rethinking having same appetizer menu for lunch and dinner. Keep going back and forth. Your thoughts please??

Wyler stared at the message. The time stamp right above the block of text said Saturday, August 17th, 7:04 p.m. The name above the text said Peter.

"He sent that the same night, just a couple of hours before..." Her voice trailed off. "There's no way he committed suicide. I just know it. If there was something going on, something bothering him, he would have told me."

Wyler thought of the video depicting Peter Lisonbee's suicide jump. Wyler knew the video was cold hard fact, objective and irrefutable. And yet, try as he might, he could not build a bridge of logic from the Peter Lisonbee who sent this text message to the Peter Lisonbee who leapt from his balcony a few hours later.

"Did you show this to the police?"

She scoffed. "They never even contacted me."

She started to get up from the table.

"Look, I've got to get back and start prepping for dinner."

"Could I ask you one more thing? Did Peter ever talk to you about a gemstone?"

"Oh, yeah, the one that his family passed down?"

"Yes, that's the one. This might seem like a strange question, and please don't take this the wrong way, but do you know where it is?"

"Me? No. Why, is it missing?"

"It wasn't in Peter's apartment. I'm trying to locate it. It means a lot to the family."

"I don't know anything about that. I mean, I knew that he was looking to sell it before he hooked up with Scottie Hibble. He thought it was worth a lot and he was hoping to use the money to start his own place."

"Do you have any idea where he might have taken it to get appraised?"

"Yes, I do actually. We took it to this place in Brooklyn."

"You went with him?"

"Yeah, I was with him when he dropped it off."

"You mean, he left it there?"

"They were going to run some tests on it or something."

"When was this exactly?"

"It was July 12th. The only reason I remember the date is because it was Peter's birthday. He just turned thirty, and he decided that selling the gemstone and jumpstarting his career was going to be his present to himself."

Her statement confirmed what Wyler was told by Sarah Miller.

"Do you know if he ever got the results or picked up the stone?"

"I honestly don't know. I assumed he did, but after he met Scottie Hibble, his whole plan changed. We never talked about it again."

"This is very important. Do you remember the name of the place you went?"

Wyler waited while she searched her memory. "It had a really long name, very official sounding. Something like Jewelry Society or Laboratory—that wasn't it, but it was something like that."

Wyler took the folded-up internet pages from his pocket and began rifling through them.

"You said it was in Brooklyn?"

"Yes. Look, I've really got to get back."

He frantically scanned each page, and then found something.

"Was it the New York Gemological Appraisal Institute?"

"That's it! That's the one where we went. Look, I'm sorry. I've got to go. I hope you find out what really happened to Peter. He doesn't deserve to be remembered like this."

And with that, she disappeared back into the kitchen.

CHAPTER 15

It was almost 4:30 p.m. when Wyler finally bid farewell to the Sikh cabbie who had been his chauffeur for the day. They parted company on the northwest corner of Grand Army Plaza, just across from the huge granite arch that serves as the main entrance to Prospect Park in Brooklyn. Wyler paid him and this time told him not to wait, sending him off a much wealthier man than he had been when Wyler had flagged him down that morning.

Grand Army Plaza, though located in the heart of Brooklyn, had a European feel, with its towering arch, classical statues, sculptured fountains, and circular thoroughfare. As Wyler approached the New York Gemological Institute, a four-story, glass-and-stone structure just off the plaza, he saw a thin Asian man in a crisp suit checking his watch impatiently outside the institute's entrance.

"I know you people have been waiting thousands of years, but the rest of us like to keep a schedule," the man said.

"Hey, I'm a civilian now. I don't have the Blues and Twos to get me through traffic," replied Wyler, using cop jargon for the blue lights and two-tone horn of a police siren.

The two men hugged and slapped each other's backs in the

requisite display of macho affection. Ray Shimura had been Wyler's last, and best, partner in the NYPD. They had worked together in the Counterterrorism Bureau for almost four years before Wyler left the force. Ray was ten years younger than Wyler and, Wyler thought, about ten times smarter. A graduate of Yale who spoke seven languages fluently, Shimura was considered an oddball by many other cops, partly due to his background, and partly due to his own mercurial personality. A third-generation immigrant, Ray had a patriotic streak made all the more impressive considering his paternal grandparents had met at a Japanese internment camp in Arizona during World War II. As they broke from the embrace, Ray looked solemnly into his old partner's eyes.

"How are you, brother?"

Wyler deflected the genuine concern in the question with a stock reply. "I'm doing good. Look, it's almost 4:30 and I don't know what time this place closes, so let me give you the quick rundown of why we're here."

When Wyler had called Ray from the cab asking for his assistance, he had painted in broad strokes. Now, he took a few minutes to fill in the details.

"So, you think this gemstone you're looking for is still in there?" asked Ray, after listening to the whole story.

"I think it's a possibility."

"And what if it is? There's no way we're walking out of there with the thing."

"Of course not, but at least the sister would know it hadn't been stolen, and she could then take appropriate steps to get it back. We should get in there."

Wyler turned and started for the entrance, but Ray didn't follow him.

"What's wrong?"

"Why don't you just call up the sister and tell her the stone is probably in there? She can come down with legal authority and pick it up. No muss, no fuss."

When Wyler didn't answer right away, Ray gave him a look.

"What's really going on here, partner?"

"Nothing. At least, nothing I can go into right now." Shimura continued to stare at him, until he added, pleadingly, "Just trust me on this." To that, Shimura nodded and followed him in.

The lobby of the New York Gemological Appraisal Institute was empty when Wyler and Shimura entered. The place had the sterile décor of a doctor's waiting room: white walls, florescent lights, and blue upholstered chairs with chrome armrests. A receptionist area, partitioned from the lobby by two thick glass windows, was also empty, but there was a phone on a shelf beneath the glass and a small sign that read "Pick Up Phone for Service." As soon as Wyler picked up the receiver, a phone began to ring on the other end. Shimura took the receiver from Wyler and held it to his own ear with a wink.

Wyler heard the faint female voice answer on the other end.

"Yes, this is Detective Ray Shimura with the New York City Police Department. I would like to speak with the person in charge if that is possible."

A few minutes later, Wyler and Ray were being escorted down a long corridor by a woman in a white lab coat. The corridor looked out onto a large open workspace that resembled a laboratory. A dozen or so people in lab coats sat examining gems and jewels. Wyler had seen many jewelers examine precious gems through a single-piece eye loupe, but the people here were using large microscopes, futuristic goggles, magnifying scopes attached to flexible metal arms, and a variety of other equipment and instruments Wyler had never seen before.

At the end of the corridor, they were escorted into an office where a pudgy man in a tan suit and red bowtie was standing behind a desk waiting for them. He was alert and slightly nervous in the normal way most people react when the police show up unexpectedly.

"How may I help you gentleman?"

Wyler let Ray take the lead.

"I'm Detective Shimura and this is my partner, Detective Wyler." Ray opened his badge holder and handed it to the man with a slight bow. "And, may we ask your name?"

"Arthur Robeson. I'm the director here." Robeson removed dark-rimmed glasses from his inside pocket and made a show of carefully examining the ID. Wyler noticed Robeson had a fastidious manner that didn't match his flabby body. "Thank you, Alice," he said, still studying Shimura's badge like it was a precious gem. The woman left and closed the door.

"What is this about?" Robeson said, finally handing the badge back to Ray and gesturing for them to sit down.

"If you don't mind, we'd like to ask a few questions about a certain gemstone that was brought here for appraisal last month." When interviewing suspects or speaking to others in authority, Ray Shimura often employed the cliched courtesy and halting phrases that many Americans expected from Asians. This tickled Wyler, who enjoyed watching people being manipulated without knowing it. Of course, when speaking with Wyler, Shimura dropped the accent and sounded like a vintage New York cop from a Sydney Lumet movie.

Shimura's soft tone seemed to relax Robeson. He leaned back in his chair and spoke more casually, like he was back in control.

"I'm not sure I can provide any information to you about our clients."

A slight pause from Ray indicated he was passing the ball to Wyler. They were picking up their old rhythms of working together.

"Well, this client is dead, and the jewel is now missing. We'd really appreciate any cooperation you could give us."

Wyler waited while the man's discretion battled his curiosity. Curiosity won.

"What was the name?" Robeson said, turning to his computer and typing.

"Peter Lisonbee," said Wyler.

Robeson immediately stopped typing and turned back to the detectives.

"Did you say Peter Lisonbee?"

"That's right."

Robeson paused, then picked up the phone receiver on his desk and pushed a button as Wyler and Shimura exchanged a look.

"Howard, will you come into my office please?"

The phone was connected to an internal PA system and Wyler could hear the announcement echo behind him in the work room they had passed on their way in. The three of them waited in silence until, a few moments later, an older man wearing a white shirt and black vest entered the office. The man had a curly gray beard and long, graying side curls that hung down each side of his face. Wyler recognized him as a Haredi, or ultra-Orthodox, Jew.

"This is Howard Gelb, one of our most experienced gemologists. Howard, these men are from the police. They are here about the Lisonbee stone." He said the last two words as if they held special significance.

Both Wyler and Ray turned in their chairs to face the man, who was lingering by the door.

"What can you tell us about it?" asked Wyler.

The man looked to Robeson, as if asking permission.

"Go ahead, Howard."

The man shuffled over to a credenza against the wall and perched on it. "The Lisonbee stone," he said quietly, as if the words were charged with meaning. "The Lisonbee stone is the most remarkable stone I've ever encountered."

"Why is that?" asked Wyler.

"Many reasons. Many, many reasons," the man said softly, with a faraway look in his eyes. "To be honest, the stone itself is nothing very special. A semi-precious sardonyx. Not much intrinsic value." He shrugged with his arms, to emphasize the point.

"So, what makes it so remarkable?" asked Ray.

"Well, let's start with the inscription."

"There's an inscription?" asked Wyler, surprised. There was no inscription on the stone in the picture he had, though it may not have been visible from that angle.

"Yes, there is. Just two letters, in ancient Hebrew."

"That's interesting, but why is it so remarkable?" asked Ray.

"It is remarkable, gentlemen, because there is no known technology—ancient or modern—that could have made the inscription."

There was silence for a moment as this statement sunk in.

"What do you mean?" asked Wyler. "Gemstones and jewels get engraved with inscriptions all the time."

"True, true," the old man said, nodding in agreement. "Of course, to engrave an inscription on any precious stone, you must cut into the surface of the stone. In the case of the Lisonbee stone, there is no cut. To my knowledge, there is no artisan or machine on earth that could have produced that inscription without cutting into the surface of the stone."

Both Wyler and Ray looked puzzled.

"You see," the old man continued, "the inscription in the Lisonbee stone was somehow engraved into the center, or heart, of the stone. The lack of any apparent sign of interference with the surface makes the existence of the writing an inexplicable phenomenon."

"Well, no offense," said Ray, "but just because you're not

aware of how it was done, doesn't mean it couldn't have been done."

"We didn't just rely on Howard," Robeson interjected. "We contacted Richard Merkle at the Gemstones Laboratory of Johannesburg. He's the leading expert in the world on onyx stones. He flew in at our expense just to examine the Lisonbee stone. He spent two days here, studying it. He was able to date the production of the stone to about the 5th century BC."

"But," added the old man, gesturing excitedly. "He was unable to explain the mystery of the engraving!"

"How sure are you that it *is* an engraving?" asked Wyler. "Is it possible the markings formed naturally and only resemble letters by coincidence?"

In response to Wyler, Robeson began typing on his computer and clicking his mouse. He then swiveled his monitor around so that the two detectives could see the screen.

"This a picture of the stone taken by photomicrography."

"Yes, see there," the old man stood and approached the monitor. "The markings would not be visible to the naked eye, but with the right light source, the surface becomes translucent, and the interior markings become visible. As you can see, the definition and clarity of the markings make it virtually impossible that they formed naturally."

Wyler stared at the screen but couldn't make much of it. He thought it might be the same stone in his cellphone picture, but the extreme close-up view made it hard to be sure. In the picture on the computer screen, intense light was being directed at the stone which made it look almost like an X-ray. Distinct markings were clearly visible, but they weren't recognizable as Hebrew characters to Wyler, at least not the Hebrew he was familiar with.

"We consulted a professor of ancient languages at Columbia," Robeson interjected. "He identified it as a paleo Hebraic script dating back over two thousand years."

"You said it was two letters. What letters are they?" asked Wyler.

Robeson glanced up to Howard Gelb, and the old man said, "These two characters from the ancient Hebrew alphabet do not have a direct corollary in English, but they do signify something very specific."

"What do they say?" asked Wyler.

"*Ha-Urim veha-Tummin.*"

The words had a vaguely familiar ring to Wyler, but he couldn't place them. "My Hebrew is rusty," he admitted.

"Traditionally, the phrase is translated into English as *Lights and Perfections*."

"Traditionally? You mean you've encountered the words before?" asked Wyler.

"Of course."

"Where?"

"References to the Urim and Thummim can be found throughout the Torah and the Talmud. Also the Hebrew Bible," the old man said with a smile.

Wyler quickly scanned his memory of childhood religious instruction but came up empty.

"The Urim and Thummim were part of the *choshen mishpat*," the old man explained. "The breastplate worn by the Temple High Priest."

Wyler thought back to the story he had been told by Sarah Miller, of the Jewish High Priest giving a sacred gemstone to Richard the Lionheart as a gift. He hadn't considered that the story might actually be true.

"You see," the old man said, walking to the center of the room and occupying it like a stage, "in ancient Israel, the High Priest wore a rectangular breastplate made of gold over his heart, and within this breastplate were twelve different jewels, embedded in four rows along three columns." The old man crisscrossed his chest with his hand to demonstrate. "Each of these jewels was forged from a different precious stone—Carnelian, Chrysolite, Beryl, Turquoise, Topaz, Jasper, Emerald, and so on. Each jewel represented one of the twelve tribes of Israel."

Although the specifics weren't familiar to him, Wyler had seen pictures of ancient Jewish priests wearing elaborate robes and garments. He also knew that many articles of Jewish clothing held special meaning and significance.

"Now, according to scripture," the man continued, "two *additional* stones were placed somewhere within the breastplate, hidden from view. These stones!" he announced, with a flourish, "were called the Urim and Thummim."

"You said the twelve jewels on the front represented the twelve tribes of Israel," Shimura interrupted. "What did these two other stones represent?"

"These stones were special. The High Priest, dating back to the time of Moses, used these stones to communicate directly with God! The priest could ask questions and receive answers from the stones. You see, these gemstones contained the power of prophecy."

The room was silent for several moments, and then Wyler spoke.

"Are you saying that the gemstone brought to you by Peter Lisonbee was one of these Urim and Thummim stones?"

The old man grinned and shrugged, as if putting the question back to Wyler.

"Is the stone still here?" asked Ray.

Robeson seemed surprised by the question.

"The Lisonbee stone? Of course not."

"So, Peter Lisonbee did come back to pick it up?" asked Wyler.

"No, it wasn't him."

"You mean, someone other than Peter Lisonbee picked up the stone?"

"That's right," said Robeson.

"Who?" asked Wyler.

"His sister."

About ten minutes later, Wyler, Shimura, and Howard Gelb stood crowded around a small monitor in a room the size of a walk-in closet while Robeson cued up the security camera footage.

"Okay, this is Wednesday, August 21st," he said. Wyler silently noted the significance of the date. It was four days after Peter Lisonbee's death.

The image on the screen showed the lobby area where Wyler and Ray had come in. As the image fast forwarded, various figures entered the office, raced to and from the reception window, sat down and jumped up, all in a madcap frenzy of sped-up motion.

"There, right there!" exclaimed Robeson, using a round knob to take the footage back a little, then resuming the playback at normal speed. On the screen, a slender, petite woman in a dark pantsuit entered the lobby. She had blond hair tied behind her head in a bun and wore oversized sunglasses that obscured the upper half of her face, making it difficult to tell her age.

"That woman is not Peter Lisonbee's sister," Wyler observed.

The woman approached the reception window and began speaking to a girl in a white lab coat on the other side of the glass. In the silent pantomime on the screen, it seemed the woman was telling the girl an elaborate, sad story, which she punctuated with tears and a handkerchief. Wyler leaned in closer to study the image on the screen.

"You recognize her?" asked Ray.

"No," he answered, shaking his head.

"She told us her brother had committed suicide. She was very upset, but she had all the proper identification and paperwork, including power of attorney and the five-digit pin number we give to all our clients."

"This doesn't make sense," said Ray. "Why would someone go through an elaborate scheme like this to steal a piece of jewelry that you guys said was basically worthless?"

"I said that the stone itself had very little *intrinsic* value," said the old man. "But that's very different from saying the stone is worthless. If this is a Urim and Thummim stone, then it's value cannot be estimated. It's priceless!"

Here, Robeson cut in.

"We did of course prepare an appraisal and certification of the stone, which was what we were hired to do. You see, many companies offer an appraisal without certification, but we provide both. A certification by a registered gemological technician verifies a gemstone's characteristics and quality, so an appraisal without certification is really just a subjective –"

"What was the appraised value?" Wyler interrupted impatiently.

"Based on the age of the stone and it's unique properties, we appraised it's value at between eleven point five and twelve million dollars."

CHAPTER 16

A police detective could get away with having a cluttered, disorganized desk (most did), and even a messy apartment (Wyler had seen many). They could be sloppy in dress and grooming (though few actually were—in Wyler's experience there were no Columbo's). But the mind was different. Regardless of outward appearance, a detective had to have a highly organized mind. When working a case, a detective's mind functioned like a warehouse, gathering and storing knowledge that needed to be constantly maintained and inventoried. There were established facts, unproven facts, and placeholders where facts were needed. There was physical evidence, forensic evidence, and circumstantial evidence. There was eyewitness testimony, hearsay, opinion, and speculation. Numbers, data, and statistics had to be collected and collated without knowing what might prove important. This included dates, times, ages, and addresses. Even the temperature of a room or speed of a car could prove important. (The key piece of evidence in one of Wyler's early cases had been the price of a bottle of wine.) Information had to be grouped by various categories and levels of relevance that were constantly shifting and changing as more information came in. Even false statements and deliberate misinformation couldn't be discarded as it might hold a vital insight. On top of all that, the character, personality, and motives of every person involved had to be continually analyzed, evaluated, and reevaluated. And all this had to be done while leaving mental space for the detective's own evolving theories of the case.

But as Wyler sat inside the number 3 subway train rumbling toward Manhattan, he found himself totally unable to organize the facts he had into any workable theory of the case. As much as he tried to mentally sort and index the information, his thoughts remained unfocused and erratic. Either there were still too many missing pieces to make any sense of it, or he had lost the ability to think like a detective. This idea sent a silent shockwave of panic through his system.

When he first met with Sarah Miller and heard the story of the religious gemstone, he had immediately dismissed it as family folklore, interesting only for what it said about the motivations and actions of the people who believed it. But now, he was faced with scientific evidence that seemed to corroborate large parts of the story. Could it actually be the truth? And if it was true, what were the broader implications? Was the theft of the gemstone, coming just days after Peter Lisonbee's death, somehow linked to the stone's religious significance, or was it simply motivated by profit? The key to finding that out was uncovering the identity of the mystery woman who had posed as Peter Lisonbee's sister.

When they had walked out of the New York Gemological Appraisal Institute, Ray had wanted to immediately contact the Major Case Squad of the NYPD. The MCS was set up to handle crimes that were considered beyond the scope of normal squads, including thefts of $100,000 or more. Ray felt an obligation to report what they had uncovered, but Wyler had convinced him to hold off for now, since no crime had actually been reported. In the meantime, Ray had a copy of the security footage and would run it through facial recognition software and search for a match. As a member of the Counterterrorism Bureau, Ray had access to a database linked to law enforcement agencies all over the world.

The brakes of the subway car produced the familiar, ear-splitting screech as the train wound its way around a sharp curve in the tunnel, causing all the passengers to sway in unison.

A few moments later, the train pulled into the Borough Hall station, and the doors slid open with the usual two-note chime. No one in the car got off the train, but a few people got on, including a young man wearing a long black cassock and priest's collar. Wyler assumed he was a Catholic priest based on the law of averages, even though he knew other sects used similar clerical clothing. The young priest carried a backpack slung over one shoulder like a student and sat down on the other side of the car, kitty-corner to Wyler.

As the train lurched forward, the priest unzipped his backpack, removed a worn paperback book, and began to read. For some reason, Wyler couldn't take his eyes off the young man. He had boyish facial stubble and couldn't have been much older than twenty. Wyler noted with interest he was reading *The Sirens of Titan* by Kurt Vonnegut. Vonnegut was one of Wyler's favorite authors, and he knew the book well. It was a science fiction novel that he had read for the first time as an undergraduate, when he was close to the same age as the young priest sitting across from him. In the book, it turns out that all of human history and civilization has been manipulated by an alien species for the sole purpose of sending a one-word message to a robot from their planet who has been stranded for centuries on one of Jupiter's moons. It was a comically nihilistic view of human existence, totally incompatible with Catholicism or any other religion, and yet the boy priest seemed oblivious to the incongruity as he sat, engrossed in the story. Wyler wondered what had led the man to choose this path at such a young age. Did he have a strong religious upbringing, or had he experienced some kind of personal conversion? Was it genuine faith, or was he choosing to escape from the real world for some reason? Maybe the true motive was buried deep in his subconscious, unknown even to himself. Or maybe he was just trying to do some good in this world. Who was Wyler to judge?

All this led Wyler to reflect on his own religious upbringing. As Reform Jews, his parents had emphasized intellect and reason and the Torah's ethical teachings more than faith in God. They observed the ritual and ceremony of Judaism, going to Temple on the High Holy Days, Rosh Hashanah and Yom Kippur, and his father conducted a Passover seder at their home every year. On that day, Wyler's aunts, uncles, and cousins would gather for the ceremonial feast and retelling of the ancient story of the liberation of the Israelites from slavery in Egypt. When he was twelve, Wyler began attending Hebrew school in a small classroom on the second floor of their synagogue to prepare for his bar mitzvah, the coming-of-age ritual marking a boy's passage to manhood and accountability under Jewish law. His teacher, Dr. Katz, was a volunteer from the congregation—a kind and soft-spoken dentist with thick glasses who always passed out hard candy. The lessons did not have much impact on Wyler. He was supposed to recite an entire portion, or *parashah*, of the Torah at his bar mitzvah ceremony, but he struggled so much with the Hebrew that when the day finally came, all he could manage was a few brief lines. Even then, he needed whispered promptings from the Rabbi. Sitting shiva with his parents after his brother Marty died was the last religious experience he could remember that held any meaning for him.

But although these experiences evoked fond and poignant memories centered on family and tradition, they hadn't served to forge an inner belief system that was now a central part of Wyler's life. Jessica had been raised a Presbyterian, but it wasn't really a conflict since neither of them felt strongly about their inherited beliefs. Gabe got to celebrate both Hanukkah and Christmas growing up, but other than that, his life had been mostly free of religious guidance or instruction. Wyler wondered now if that had been a mistake. Perhaps if he and Jessica had sought to instill in their son a belief in something greater, he might have been better prepared to deal with what had happened.

As the train emerged from the dark tunnel and began pulling into the Clark Street station, the last stop in Brooklyn, an unexpected feeling came over Wyler. It was an urge that struck him suddenly, without any warning or buildup. It was probably brought on by the melancholy of his thoughts and reflections, but he didn't take time to analyze it. Instead, he acted.

As the train slowed to a stop, Wyler stood up from his seat. Instead of continuing to Manhattan, he would get off the train here at Clark Street. He would go back one stop to Borough Hall and there, transfer to the R train. The R train could then take him to Greenwood Cemetery, where his wife was buried.

As the doors to the car slid open, Wyler stepped out, turned left, and headed to the staircase at the far side of the underground platform. The stairs led to a tunneled walkway that served as a bridge to the other side of the station where he could catch a train going in the opposite direction, back to Borough Hall and the R train. The walkway was deserted, and his footsteps echoed off the tunnel's concrete walls as he walked.

When he came down the stairs, he found the platform deserted except for a Hispanic woman who looked nine months pregnant. Wyler walked to the middle of the platform and peered down the dark tunnel, hoping to see or hear a sign the train was near. Glancing at his phone, he saw that it was just before 7:00 p.m. Not that it mattered. New York subway trains didn't abide by any published schedule. They just came when they came, every few minutes during peak hours, less frequently on nights and weekends.

The waiting forced Wyler to analyze what he was doing. He had only visited Jessica's grave a few times since her burial. Why the sudden urge to do so now?

This morning, as they were preparing to leave to come into the city, Gabe had asked him if they would visit the cemetery. "Are we going to see Mom?" he had said, as if Jessica were still alive and just living apart from them.

"I'm not sure if I'll be able to. Maybe Mimi can take you," he had answered.

Since they had moved to Rhinebeck, Wyler had a solid excuse for not visiting Jessica's grave. They lived almost two hours away, and besides, his focus for the moment was on Gabe and helping him pick up the pieces. That had to be the priority. But that didn't explain why he had deflected Gabe's question so quickly. They were going to be in the city for a few days, and of course Gabe would want to visit his mother's grave. Why didn't he just say yes? More to the point, why didn't he think of it himself?

His thoughts were interrupted by the sounds of footsteps echoing through the same tunnel walkway that he had passed through a minute ago. A man appeared at the top of the stairs and descended the concrete steps to the platform. A moment later, he was followed by a second man. They did not seem to be together, as the first man walked slowly passed Wyler and took up a position on his right, while the other man stopped at the bottom of the stairs, positioning himself on Wyler's left flank.

Wyler recognized both men as having been passengers on the Manhattan-bound train he had just been on. This immediately struck Wyler as highly unusual. Wyler's sudden decision—to exit that train, cross over the platform, and take a train in the opposite direction—was akin to making a U-turn in a car. The move itself wasn't that unusual, but if two other cars suddenly mimicked your maneuver, you would wonder about it.

The first man was a bald, overweight man in sweatpants. His hands were stuffed into the pockets of a cheap windbreaker. He had wire-rimmed glasses, a mustache, and a thin strip of a beard that bordered one of his two chins like a hairy belt.

The second man, on Wyler's left, was much younger. He was thin and gangly, with a weasel-like face pockmarked with acne and stringy hair that looked dirty and greasy.

From deep inside the train tunnel, the grinding and rattling sounds of an approaching train grew in volume.

The men on either side of Wyler seemed to be from two different worlds. One was fat and middle-aged, the other looked like a scrawny hillbilly. Was it possible they were working together, following him, or was he being paranoid?

There was one way to find out.

Wyler walked to the edge of the platform, preparing himself to board the train when it stopped. Both men on either side of him did the same thing, as did the pregnant woman who was also on the platform.

A few moments later, the southbound number 3 train entered the station. As soon as it stopped, the doors slid open with a chime. Several tired New Yorkers coming home from work filed off and headed for the stairs that led up to the street.

When the doors were clear, the pregnant woman stepped onto the train.

Wyler didn't move.

He glanced quickly to his left and right and saw that both men had moved to board the train, but they both stopped and stepped back when they noticed that Wyler wasn't getting on.

Confirmation.

Wyler let the doors close, and soon the train began to pull

away, disappearing headfirst into the tunnel and leaving Wyler alone on the platform with his two new friends.

"Okay boys, how do you want to do this?" Wyler said with practiced weariness. The truth was he was exposed and vulnerable and he knew it. He felt the absence of his Glock 22 like a missing limb.

The fat man to Wyler's right froze, and Wyler saw fear and panic in his eyes. The hillbilly turned to face Wyler, one side of his mouth curled into a deranged, crooked smile, like he was looking forward to what came next. Although Wyler's remark was meant to throw them off-balance, inside he was on high alert. Neither of these guys seemed to fit the profile of a professional tough guy, but they were unknowns and therefore potentially dangerous. Wyler wasn't about to take any chances.

Both men took steps toward Wyler, carefully closing in like hunters with dangerous prey. Wyler moved slowly away from the edge of the platform, creating a triangle.

"Aaron Eli Wyler," said the hillbilly, moving forward menacingly and flashing an uneven set of tobacco-stained teeth. Wyler was taken aback by the use of his full name, but quickly set that aside as the hillbilly reached behind his back and withdrew a six-inch hunting knife with a serrated edge. Wyler immediately tensed up and crouched into a defensive stance facing the hillbilly, but in doing so he took his eyes off the fat one, a mistake he paid for the next moment when a cord from behind suddenly gripped his neck. Wyler just managed to slip two fingers under the cord before it tightened to choke him.

"Hey!" someone shouted, and Wyler saw two men in their twenties stopped halfway down the concrete stairs. They were dressed to go clubbing and they stood frozen, watching the melee in horror. The hillbilly saw them too and decided to speed things up. He rushed toward Wyler with the knife. Out of options, Wyler violently jerked his head backward and head-butted the fat man.

This caused the cord around his neck to slacken just in time for Wyler to slip his fingers out of the noose and grab the hillbilly's wrist with both hands as it jabbed wildly for his gut.

Wyler heard more yelling from the stairs as he and the hillbilly wrestled for the control of the knife. The hillbilly broke free of Wyler's grip, and Wyler moved backward in quick awkward steps, desperately trying to avoid the thrusting knife edge like the head of a striking cobra. Out of the corner of Wyler's eye, he saw the fat man doubled over with blood pouring out of his nose.

Just then the hillbilly changed tactics and brought the knife up in preparation for a downward kill stroke like the mother in *Psycho*. This was a mistake, as it gave Wyler an opening to reach up with both hands and grab his wrist, blocking the move. With all four of their arms braced upward like tent poles, Wyler was able to bring his knee forward and smash it into the hillbilly's ribcage. He instantly doubled over and as he did, Wyler violently yanked the man's arm forward and twisted his wrist. Wyler felt the bone snap, and the hillbilly dropped the knife and began howling in pain.

Just then, something with the blunt force of a crosstown bus plowed into Wyler and sent him flying. He fell to the ground in a contorted lump, the wind knocked out of him. A moment later, he looked up and saw the fat man pick up the hillbilly's hunting knife. Wyler frantically backed up on his hands and feet like a crab as the man stomped quickly forward with crazed determination, his oversized belly quivering and his doughy face drenched with sweat and blood.

As he reached Wyler, he fell on him in a full body slam like a professional wrestler. Wyler was able to grab his arm and pivot out of the way at the last second. For what seemed like an hour but what was probably just a few seconds, they struggled and fought and rolled on the ground, locked together in a violent tug of war for the knife. The fat man's face, flushed and straining, was inches from Wyler's. In a confused, dreamlike rush, Wyler saw flashes of bystanders and heard people shouting as the edge of the knife inched closer to his cheek. The man grunted and snarled viciously as he fought to bring the knife down into Wyler's face.

And then, Wyler turned the man's size against him by accelerating past one of their rolls and using the extra momentum to toss him to the side. The man rolled free of Wyler and then Wyler saw his huge frame disappear over the edge of the platform.

Several people screamed. As Wyler struggled to stand, a bystander offered a hand up. Wyler looked over and saw that a group of three other bystanders had the hillbilly in custody. Wyler stumbled over to the edge of the platform and looked down onto the tracks. The huge body of his attacker was sprawled out awkwardly on the train tracks. Wyler noticed the knife had been thrown out of reach.

"Come on, get up!" said Wyler, struggling for breath.

The man lay there, staring up at Wyler, huffing and puffing, and Wyler saw that the expression on his face had changed completely. All the murderous rage had drained out of him, almost as if he had woken from a trance.

"Get out of there!" cried Wyler, but the man just shook his head, sadly, and didn't move.

And then, once again, from deep within the tunnel, the metal clanking sounds of an approaching train were heard.

Soon, bystanders were lined up along the edge of the platform, screaming for the man to get up and climb out of the pit, as the sounds of the approaching train grew louder and louder. For several seconds, the man lay there, unmoving, as if resigned to the horrible justice of his fate. But then, as the train noise began to shake the station and light appeared in the tunnel, the man had a sudden change of heart and quickly scrambled to his feet. With the train bearing down, he tried desperately to claw his way up and onto the platform. Many hands reached down to help him, some grabbing on, but he was too big and unwieldy, and kept falling back. And then the train suddenly burst through the tunnel and entered the station. The man abandoned the wall and began running awkwardly down the tracks, pathetically trying to outrun the train as the shouting and screaming from the crowd of onlookers intensified. But it was no use. Even as the steel brakes screeched and the emergency whistle let out a deafening wail, the deadly momentum of the train overtook the man and devoured him.

CHAPTER 17

It was almost 11:00 p.m. Wyler sat alone in a small witness interrogation room inside Brooklyn's 88th precinct, waiting. He tried flexing the fingers of his right hand, but they were stiff and painful. He hoped there wasn't any permanent damage. An EMT at the scene had wrapped his hand in a bandage to stop the bleeding. Wyler didn't remember the knife cutting his hand several times. He hadn't even known he was wounded until one of the uniformed police officers who questioned him suggested he get his hand looked at. Wyler had looked down and was confused to see his right hand dripping with blood. At first he thought it must be the blood of one of his attackers. He hadn't felt anything at the time but now, several hours later, the pain was starting to kick in.

The whole thing had happened so fast that his memory of it was a frenzied blur. Wyler thought back to one of his self-defense instructors at the police academy, a short, bald, muscular Frenchman who had worked with the French secret service. Wyler remembered the sobering speech he gave on the first day of class. He told the group of shocked cadets, in a thick French accent, that almost all martial arts training was useless in real-life situations. He said that in the sudden and unexpected stress of a real-world attack, when your life is in actual danger, most people instantly forget everything they've learned and just fight on pure instinct. People with years of martial arts training in the gym and in the ring will start wildly throwing punches like kids in a schoolyard. He told them that it takes about twenty years of training for martial arts to become instinctual enough to be of use in a real life-and-death encounter.

Now, Wyler had learned the hard way that this was true. Although martial arts and self-defense were never a passion of his like they were for some officers, he had attended many training courses over the years. He had practiced with partners and instructors, demonstrated proficiency, and passed every class. And yet, a few hours ago, he had nearly lost his life in a wild, uncontrolled brawl with two determined amateurs, one middle aged and overweight and the other muscle-weak and scrawny. Luckily for him, whoever sent them didn't splurge on someone with actual fighting skills. But would his luck hold out?

The door to the interrogation room popped open and a tall woman with long brown hair entered the room. She wore a pantsuit with a gold badge clipped to her waist and carried a manila folder and a cup of coffee.

"You find out anything?" asked Wyler.

"Oh yeah," she said, sitting across from Wyler and placing the coffee cup in front of him on the table. Wyler had known Cheryl Branford since the academy, but they had lost touch in recent years. He didn't know she was posted to the 88th until she showed up on the subway platform.

"So, what've you got?" asked Wyler, taking a sip of the coffee. Instead of answering, Cheryl just smiled at Wyler and shook her head. "What?" he asked.

"What are you into, Aaron?"

"What do you mean?"

"Well, you've got some very interesting friends," she said, opening the file.

Wyler had been officially released earlier in the evening after several witnesses had corroborated his version of events, but he had asked Cheryl if he could hang out and wait. He wanted to learn more about the identity of his attackers.

"Do you know who the little one is?" she asked.

"No, I told you, I've never seen him before."

"Do the names Shane and Bobby Willis ring a bell?"

"No."

"The Pine Mountain Murders?"

Wyler slowly set down the coffee and searched his memory. The words definitely struck a chord somewhere in his mind, but he couldn't place it.

"Oklahoma, eight years ago," Cheryl continued, glancing down at one of the pages in the folder. "Two brothers killed their entire family. Mom, dad, two little brothers aged five and twelve, and two sisters, eleven and nine. They butchered everyone. Cut their throats. Only survivor was the youngest sister, two years old. She slept through the whole thing."

As Wyler listened silently, he felt his entire body tense up.

"The older brother, Shane, was seventeen. Charged as an adult. He's still serving life without the possibility at a state max in Oklahoma. The younger one, Bobby, was only fifteen at the time. They let him plead to assault with intent."

"Don't tell me," said Wyler.

Cheryl nodded. "Little Bobby was released last week from Joseph Harp Correctional Center in Lexington, Oklahoma. What does this guy want with you, Aaron?"

"I have no idea. It doesn't make any sense."

"This kid spends the last eight years in prison. He gets out last week, hops a bus to the Big Apple, then randomly shows up on subway platform and goes after an ex-NYPD detective with a hunting knife. You can't think of any connection, any reason for this?"

Wyler considered the question carefully before answering. "None," he finally said.

"Well, you were with CTB. Maybe he was radicalized on the inside."

"At Joseph Harp Correctional Center in Oklahoma?"

"It's one theory. We're going to check who he did time with. See if you have any old friends there. It's a long shot, but we don't have much else."

"Is he talking?" Wyler asked.

"Oh, he's talking. We can't shut him up. The problem is none of it makes sense."

"What's he saying?"

"Bunch of insane gibberish."

"What kind of gibberish?"

"Boilerplate. You know, good and evil, Bible verses. Apocalyptic warnings. Your basic the-devil-made-me-do-it crap. This is one messed up kid. He's kind of scary, actually."

Wyler thought about this. "What about the other one? Did you find out who he was?"

"Wasn't hard. He had ID on him. We just had to peel it off his body."

Wyler's mind flashed back to the gruesome moment the train ran over the man.

"Who is he?"

"He *was* Warren Payson," she said, turning to another page in the folder. "Age forty-eight, of Morristown, New Jersey. Lived alone. Worked as a supervisor at the local recycling center."

"Does he have a sheet?"

"No criminal record. Model citizen. Pillar of the community—until the New Jersey State Police tossed his apartment an hour ago and found some very interesting pictures. Of children. Boxes and boxes. It was like a warehouse in there."

Wyler was silent for several moments while he took this in. He had hoped that learning about his attackers would shed some light on things. Instead, it was having the opposite effect.

"Right now, there's no connection between these two. No overlaps in their backgrounds. No touch points of any kind. It doesn't make any kind of sense."

Cheryl closed the file and leaned back in the chair. She stared at Wyler in silence for a bit, and when she spoke again, her tone had changed from cop to friend. "I was really sorry to hear about your wife, Aaron."

Wyler nodded. "Thanks, Cheryl."

"Her name was Jessica, right?"

"Yeah. Jessica."

"Look, I'm going to be wrapping things up here in a few minutes. You wanna go grab a drink? Catch up?"

"I'd love to. Just not tonight."

"I get it."

"Another time though, okay?"

Cheryl nodded, then stood up to go. "We'll keep trying, Aaron, but for now it just looks like you were in the wrong place at the wrong time. Unless, of course, there's something you're not telling me."

Wyler was silent. Up until now, he had withheld information but had avoided outright lying. He had said that he was in town so his son could visit his mother-in-law and had come out to Brooklyn to see his old partner, Ray Shimura. He justified his truth-but-not-the-whole-truth strategy by telling himself there was no correlation between the Lisonbee case and the seemingly random, inexplicable attack. He had only chosen to withhold one key piece of information. He hadn't disclosed to Cheryl the fact that Bobby Willis, the kid with the hunting knife, had called him by his full name, including his middle name, which was known to only a handful of people.

"Nothing I can think of," said Wyler, shaking his head slowly.

CHAPTER 18

About an hour later, an NYPD squad car dropped Wyler off at his hotel. He had paid for an extra day and checked in that morning before dropping Gabe off, so his overnight bag was waiting for him in his room. He had dozed off a few times in the backseat during the ride from Brooklyn and had planned to go right to bed, but now that he was in his room, he couldn't resist taking out his laptop.

Sitting at the small desk in the room, he typed the biblical name of the gemstone used by Howard Gelb, the old jeweler, into his search engine. The first thing Google did was correct his spelling, changing it to *Urim and Thummim*.

The top result was, unsurprisingly, from Wikipedia. He clicked on it and read the first paragraph of the entry. What he read seemed to confirm the old man's story. According to Wikipedia, Urim and Thummim were ancient biblical stones or objects that were part of a hoshem, or breastplate. The objects were somehow used by the Jewish High Priest to receive revelations from God and answer spiritual questions. Wyler tried unsuccessfully to imagine how two gemstones fastened to a breastplate could do this.

After scanning the rest of the Wikipedia entry, Wyler clicked back to the Google results page to see what else was listed. There were links to the Jewish Encyclopedia, the Jewish Virtual Library, and other Jewish websites. But to his surprise, many of the Google results mentioned "Latter-day Saints" and "Mormonism." He was pretty sure they were the same thing, but he wasn't positive. He knew almost nothing about Mormonism, other than what he had read in the news when Mitt Romney had run for president. He wondered what the connection was. Why would a Google search for an ancient gemstone mentioned in the Torah and the Hebrew Bible generate so many results having to do with the Mormon Church?

Instead of trying to answer this question, he went back to the search bar and typed in the words Pine Mountain Murders.

What he read was horrible and disturbing. The Willis family, consisting of the two parents and seven children, had lived in the small rural town of Pine Mountain, Oklahoma. According to neighbors, the family had kept mostly to themselves. The parents didn't allow the children to play with other kids in the neighborhood, and all the children were home-schooled. On the evening of October 9th, 2013, the two oldest children, Shane and Bobby, lured their eleven-year-old sister into their bedroom, where they cut her throat. The two then went on a rampage through the house, murdering their parents and four of their siblings with various knives and one small hatchet. The mother, who tried to fight back, was found lying by the downstairs sofa with over fifty stab wounds to her body. The youngest child, a two-year-old sister, was later found by police sleeping in her bed, unharmed. In court, the boys admitted that they had been talking about and planning the crime for years.

A series of unpleasant questions swirled in Wyler's mind. Why had Bobby Willis tried to kill him? Wyler knew that it was not, as Cheryl Branford said, a matter of being in the wrong place at the wrong time. Bobby Willis knew him and called him by name. His full name. Where could he have gotten that information? Had someone sent him to kill Wyler? Did it have to do with the Lisonbee case, or was it related to something else entirely, some dark ghost from a past case coming back to haunt him now?

And what of the second assailant, the creepy New Jersey recycling center supervisor leading a perverse double life who seemed to have no connection to Willis, or to Wyler? Where did he fit in? Like a river cruise through an unchartered jungle, every turn he took just seemed to open up new unexplored tributaries of confusion.

Agitated by what he had read and unable to sleep, Wyler got up and decided to get some fresh air. He left the hotel and headed toward Times Square, hoping the short walk might clear his head and help him relax. It was almost 1:00 am, but there was still plenty of foot traffic on the street.

He found an open pizza place on the corner of Broadway and 47th Street and went in. He ordered a slice and a Coke, then sat down at a table tucked in the back corner to eat. He sat with his back to the wall, which gave him a view of the entire restaurant, as well as an unobstructed view of the entrance onto Broadway. He wondered if that was why he had chosen this particular table. Every table in the place was empty, but he had chosen the one with a strategic vantage point. Was he getting paranoid?

The truth was, he had been feeling deeply unsettled even before the attack on the subway platform earlier that night. When had it started? He mentally retraced his steps and found himself back in Peter Lisonbee's apartment. He had felt something there. Or, more accurately, he had sensed something. It had nothing to do with the apartment itself or anything in it, but there were invisible trace elements of something present that had reminded him of that grungy hole in Camden, New Jersey where terrorists had plotted. He had dismissed the comparison at the time, but he now realized the feeling had lingered inside him, leaving him subconsciously disconcerted and agitated ever since.

His work in counterterrorism had required him to develop a sixth sense, an internal radar that picked up a certain kind of organized malevolence, hiding in the shadows of everyday life. Why would that internal radar, honed through years of experience, be activating now?

He thought back to his two subway attackers. There was something so...businesslike about their attack. Even though the Willis kid had mentioned his name, it didn't seem personal. The kid had crazy in his eyes, that was unmistakable. But it was a special kind of crazy that had nothing to do with Wyler. It was a kind of crazy Wyler had seen before only in the eyes of Middle Eastern terrorists. It was crazy with a larger sense of mission, of purpose. There was something similar with the fat one. He didn't have the same look in his eyes, but there was something about his clumsy demeanor during the attack that made it seem like he had come by his motivation secondhand, like he was just following orders. But whose orders? Were both of these men somehow connected to something much bigger and more complex? Some invisible, unseen web of...of what?

Wyler left his slice half-eaten and walked out of the pizza place.

It was almost 2:00 am by the time Wyler reached the lobby of Nora Maitland's apartment building on West 57th Street. Since the graveyard shift doorman didn't know him, Wyler had to wait while the guy called upstairs to announce him.

"Name?" the doorman asked him.

"Aaron Wyler," he replied grumpily, over-pronouncing the name. He was embarrassed at having to wake up his mother-in-law, and considered just telling the guy to forget it.

"An Aaron Wyler is here," the doorman said into the phone

and then, after a short pause, he put the receiver down. "Go right on up."

As Wyler rode up in the elevator, he began to mentally prepare for the conversation that was coming. His mother-in-law would be understandably curious about his unexpected, middle-of-the-night arrival, especially after he had made such a point this morning of staying in a hotel. What would he tell her about why he was here? Did he even know himself?

The elevator door opened, and Wyler immediately saw that Nora was waiting for him by the door to her apartment at the end of the hall. He started walking toward her. She was wearing a long silk robe and at first seemed pleased to see him, but her happy expression melted into fear as he got closer.

"What happened?" she asked as he approached, staring at the bandage on his hand. He had forgotten about the bandage.

"Everything's fine," he said, accepting a welcome hug. But as they broke their embrace, she took his bandaged hand in hers and examined it tenderly. Her eyes were full of worry and concern, but she waited until they were inside the apartment, sitting together in the living room, before pressing further.

"What happened? Are you okay?"

"Just an accident," he lied. "Where's Gabe?"

"He fell asleep in the screening room about an hour ago."

Nora had a screening room with huge comfy recliners, and Gabe would probably sleep through the night in there.

"I'm sorry for getting you up," he said.

She scoffed and dismissed that with a wave of the hand.

"I was up, actually. Finishing the movie."

"What were you guys watching?"

"*Vertigo*."

"You got Gabe to watch an old movie?"

"I make him watch one every time he comes," she mock whispered. "He's seen Sunset Boulevard, Casablanca, Singing in the Rain."

"I'm impressed."

"I think he likes them. Does that surprise you so much? He's his father's son, after all."

Wyler secretly wished this were true but knew that it wasn't.

"How is Gabe, Aaron?" she asked, with quiet, heartfelt concern in her voice.

"I don't know him, Nora. I have no idea what he's thinking or feeling."

"Said the parents of every teenager ever."

"First of all, he's not a teenager, yet. Second of all, it's more than that. I thought quitting my job would bring us closer together, but all it's done is make the problem between us more obvious."

Nora let a few moments pass, then said, "Aaron, I don't know what you're expecting, but believe me, the fact that you quit your job to be with him, that matters to him. Deep down, he knows what that means, and he'll always remember it."

Wyler nodded, then let some time pass by turning to admire the stunning view of city lights from the window. Eventually, he turned back to Nora and found her watching him, patient and attentive. She knew he had something to say, but she wasn't going to force anything.

"I was attacked earlier tonight. Two men tried to kill me," he finally said, surprised by his own bluntness. Wyler expected shock and hysterics, but instead, she just nodded solemnly.

"Tell me about it," Nora said, her voice still and calm.

Wyler told the story of the attack, starting with the subway ride back to Manhattan and his sudden decision to visit Greenwood Cemetery. When he got to the description of the attack itself, her whole face seemed to contract with alarm, but she didn't interrupt, which impressed Wyler. He continued, and she listened, horrified, hanging on every word, as he described the grisly death under the wheels of the subway train, and when he revealed the identities of the two men, she shook her head in awed disbelief.

"If I hadn't suddenly gotten off that train, I probably never would have spotted them. They could have followed me and taken me completely by surprise."

"Why would these men want to kill you?"

"Right now, I have no idea. There's no connection between them, and no known connection between either of them and me. It doesn't make any sense."

"Do you think it has something to do with this thing you're working on?"

"I've been asking myself that all night. I honestly don't know, but if it doesn't, it's quite a coincidence. And good detectives don't believe in coincidences."

"Can you tell me anything about the case?"

Wyler carefully considered the question. He realized that the rules he had followed throughout his career didn't apply anymore. He wasn't working in any official capacity. He also wasn't a private detective with a paying client whose privacy he was obliged to protect. Essentially, he was private citizen helping out a friend.

"Yes, actually, I can."

And he did. He began by recounting his initial conversation with Sarah Miller. This time, Nora interrupted with several questions.

"So, their family kept this stone and protected it for almost a thousand years?"

"If you believe her story, yes."

"And she thinks her brother's death was somehow connected to the fact that he decided to sell the stone?"

He nodded, then continued, describing his visit to Peter Lisonbee's apartment, his conversations at Nine, and his meeting with Scottie Hibble.

"That little creep," sneered Nora, when Hibble's name was mentioned.

"You know him?"

"I've met him a couple of times. He's a worm who tries to suck up to rich people and celebrities. I keep getting invited to this thing he's doing next week on that island. I don't know how I got on his list."

"That's just proof you're an influencer," Wyler said.

"A what?"

"Never mind."

He continued sharing in detail all the events of the past few days, covering the coroner, the suicide video, and the visit to the Brooklyn jewelry lab. He shared with her the things that Howard Gelb, the old gemologist, had said about the Lisonbee stone.

"So, this old jeweler said the stone is supposed to have power from God?"

"That's what he said. These stones are mentioned in The Bible, and they're supposed to have special powers or something."

"What kind of powers?"

"I don't really know. Power to receive messages from God, or something like that."

Nora looked off somewhere, as if trying to imagine how this might work, and Wyler continued the story, finishing where he had begun, with the attack in the subway. He found it was very helpful, even therapeutic, to talk to someone, and he was pleased to discover that Nora was a good listener, thoughtful and attentive.

When he finished talking, silence settled over them, punctuated only by the eerie ticking of an unseen grandfather clock.

"Who do you think this woman is, the one who stole the gemstone?" she asked.

"I have no idea. Ray is going to do a facial recognition search, but the thing I can't figure out is how she knew about the stone in the first place. According to Sarah Miller, no one outside the family knew anything about it."

"Well, I don't think that part is a mystery," Nora said. Wyler looked questioningly at her, and she continued. "You said that this gemstone had been kept secret, handed down through generations of one family for almost a thousand years. This family had been entrusted to protect the stone, almost like sacred guardians. The sister called it a covenant, right?"

"That's right."

"So, every member of the family who was given possession of this stone kept that covenant, up until Peter Lisonbee."

"Yes, so?"

"So, Peter Lisonbee violated that covenant, and in doing so, I think he somehow forfeited the veil of secrecy that had protected the stone all these years."

"What are you saying?"

"What I'm saying is, as soon as Peter Lisonbee went public, all bets were off. The stone, hidden for so many years by God's power or whatever you want to call it, was suddenly in play and up for grabs for...darker forces to step in."

"So, you're saying that some kind of alarm bell sounded in Hell as soon as he went to get the jewel appraised?"

"Why not?"

"I deal in facts, Nora, not superstition. Facts have to connect to one another to form a chain of logic that can be proven."

"There are more things in Heaven and Earth, Horatio, than are dreamt of in your philosophy."

Wyler recognized the quote from *Hamlet*, but he wasn't buying it.

"If you ask me, Horatio was right to be skeptical of Hamlet."

"Maybe, but I think you've stumbled into a case unlike any

you have ever been involved with. You're a detective, trained to think in a logical, linear way, like you said. Well, those very instincts may be tripping you up here, preventing you from seeing the bigger picture."

"Which is?"

"Which is something you may not be able to understand or explain using logic alone. You're dealing with something that may not be of this world. You said yourself that the experts at the jewelry place couldn't explain the stone or its markings. What if you took it as a working assumption that everything the sister and the old jeweler said about the stone was actually true? Wouldn't that explain a lot of things?"

Wyler considered this.

"I know it's a cliché, but unless you're able to take a leap of faith and allow for the possibility that there are forces at work here beyond your normal understanding, you might be left with random bits and pieces that never fit together."

"I didn't know you were such a spiritual person, Nora," he said, teasingly.

"Actually, I've always been deeply religious." She said this with a conviction that surprised Wyler.

"Really?"

"Oh, yes. My parents were very devout. We went to Church every week, and Sunday school, and my mother used to read Bible stories to me at night when I was a girl."

"I never knew that," Wyler said quietly. His thoughts turned to Jessica, and he wondered why she seemed not to share any of her mother's faith and convictions.

"I tried to share my faith with Jessica," she continued, wistfully, as if in response to his thoughts. "I used to read Bible stories to her at night, like my mother did for me. But then, when Charles got sick, it was such a traumatic time, so painful, for both of us." Nora's eyes began to redden as she struggled to contain the sudden onslaught of emotion. "When he died, I just wanted to distract her. We went to Europe, on a cruise. I tried to fill the void in her life with other things, hoping to make up for what she had lost. Nothing I tried worked, until she discovered science, and decided she was going to be a doctor. She was only fifteen, but once she settled on that path, there was no stopping her."

They smiled together at the shared memory of Jessica, and Wyler imagined the determined fifteen-year-old girl, mapping out the rest of her life with perfect clarity and conviction.

"She was a remarkable person," he said.

"She was so close to her father. Charles was a wonderful man, Aaron. You would have loved him. And he would have adored you."

She wiped her eyes, and after some time passed, Wyler moved to stand up.

"Can I take you up on your invitation to stay here? The exhaustion is starting to kick in."

Nora stood and went to him. She put her hands on his shoulders, and looked into his eyes.

"Aaron, she loved you and Gabe."

Wyler nodded, but said nothing.

"Listen to me," she said, in a tender, quiet whisper. "What happened, what she did, had nothing to do with you."

Wyler averted his eyes and started to squirm. He suddenly felt like a trapped animal, and his fight-or-flight instinct was driving him to break free and run away.

"You're not to blame in any way. You know that, don't you?"

"No, actually, I don't know that," Wyler said, his voice cracking with emotion. "But it doesn't matter now."

"Of course it matters. She was ill, Aaron, in her mind, and that illness warped her view of things. It distorted everything, until she wasn't herself anymore."

"I don't want to talk about this right now, Nora. I'm exhausted, and I need sleep."

He began to pull away, but she physically held on and restrained him.

"Aaron, I think she saved your life tonight."

"What are you talking about?" Wyler asked, a tinge of anger rising in his voice.

"You said that if you hadn't gotten off that train, you wouldn't have spotted those two men. They could have surprised you, attacked you, without any warning, and killed you."

"So?"

"Why did you get off that train, Aaron? You said you had a sudden urge, out of nowhere, to visit Jessica's grave. You haven't done that in a year. But right at that very moment, you felt prompted by a desire to see Jessica, to be with her, and it was that feeling, that instinct that came upon you out of the blue, that ended up saving your life. You said detectives aren't supposed to believe in coincidences. I don't think this was one."

A few minutes later, Wyler found Gabe asleep in the screening room, stretched out on one of the room's luxury reclining movie chairs as the Alfred Hitchcock movie *Vertigo* played up on the large screen. The movie was more than halfway through, and Jimmy Stewart's character was in a dress salon, obsessively trying to buy his new girlfriend the exact same dress worn by his dead girlfriend, not knowing yet that they were actually the same woman.

He went over to his son and watched him as he slept, the flickering lights from the movie screen reflecting off his still, pale face. His heart ached for his son and all he had passed through. Wyler wished there were some way he could take away the pain and spare his son the trauma of having to go through the rest of his life remembering...that day. Finding his mother like that was a memory no child should ever have to carry. It was cruel and unfair.

As he stared at Gabe's chest rising and falling in the slow, easy rhythms of sleep, he longed to reach out and hold him. He wanted to embrace his son, to tell him how much he loved him, but part of him simply didn't know how. He was not raised in a household that expressed love and affection often or easily. He did not doubt his parents loved him and his brother, but they didn't say "I love you" the way parents did now, several times a day. Not that he was neglected. He just felt his parents' love in other ways, through the time they spent with him and his brother, and through the conversations they had, and through the care they took to provide for and protect them. There was discipline when needed, but there was also kindness, laughter, and genuine affection, even if the love part was not verbalized. Looking back now, with the hindsight of years of experience, he was able to appreciate his parents more than he ever did growing up. A police officer in New York City serves as a daily eyewitness to human misery and heartbreak, to families ripped apart forever by brief flashes of violence and anger, to children whose lives become permanently scarred by the actions of those charged with safeguarding them. Wyler's parents had provided for and protected him and his brother. He instinctually knew his parents loved him without daily hugs and I love you's. That had been enough for Wyler. Could it be enough for Gabe?

Wyler sat on the arm of the chair where Gabe was sleeping. He was drowsy and desperately needed sleep, but he wanted a few more minutes with his son. Somehow, it helped just to be near him, and he soon felt the anxiety and stress of the day's events drain from his body. Sitting next to his son, his mind began to relax, to rest. He wondered if, somehow, his subconscious had known that this was what he needed, and that it had driven him here for this reason.

Up on the screen, the Jimmy Stewart character was now in a hotel room with his girlfriend, played by Kim Novak. They were arguing over his insistence that she redo her hair to match the exact style of the woman he thinks he killed. He had already forced her to change her appearance in every way, by coloring her hair and buying a new wardrobe. Wyler had always admired Stewart's performance in this film. He was a movie star best known for playing wholesome, good guy roles, but his portrayal in *Vertigo* of a man driven mad by a psychotic obsession was, in Wyler's opinion, his best performance.

Wyler stared, mesmerized, at the screen as the Kim Novak character emerged from the bathroom, as if from a mist of memory, having finally perfected the physical transformation forced on her by Stewart in order to satisfy his maniacal obsession. Stewart and Novak then embraced, bathed in a weird, hallucinogenic light show as the camera spun around them and the music swelled to a heart-wrenching crescendo.

And then, suddenly, Wyler stood up. He stared into the darkness, trying to process what had just clicked in his mind. He took out his phone and dialed. After several rings, the line finally connected.

"What time is it?" Ray Shimura's voice was groggy from sleep.

"You can forget about the facial recognition search."

"What? Why? What's going on?"

"I know who the mystery woman is, the one who picked up the gemstone."

CHAPTER 19

Two days later, Wyler and Ray Shimura were standing by the back wall of a large studio in Midtown Manhattan, observing a live television broadcast. Four giant studio cameras manned by operators with bulging headphones were pointed like a firing squad toward a raised platform with four chairs. Scottie Hibble was seated on the platform next to three very famous people: Maggie Wells-Walling, an actress who had several hit TV sitcoms, Paulo Almeida, the Brazilian tennis champion who had recently won both the U.S. Open and Wimbledon, and Layton Howe, the young tech billionaire who was constantly in the tabloids for dating supermodels and movie stars. Behind them, an enormous jumbotron made up of several smaller screens flashed pictures and video clips, while the static center screen showed only the Bonfire logo.

"Thanks for having us, Julie," Hibble said excitedly to no one visible. There was a pause of several seconds, and then Hibble continued speaking. "Well, the idea for Bonfire came about organically, really. I've spent time with a lot of famous and powerful people, like the ones sitting next to me, and one thing I've noticed is they all share a sense of personal responsibility, a strong desire to help create a better future, not just for themselves but for the entire planet. So, over the years, the idea began to grow in my mind that if somehow we could bring these people together and focus their energy and influence for good, it could have an impact unlike anything we've ever seen before. That's what Bonfire is all about."

After another pause of several seconds, Maggie Wells-Walling began to speak.

"That's absolutely right, Julie, this is about bringing people together at a time when people are being torn apart in so many ways."

It was only 9:30 in the morning, but Wyler and Ray had already sat through interviews by CNN, NBC, and FOX. The current program was a morning show on ABC, hosted by someone named Julie. Each interview was done remotely, and although those participating could hear the questions through earpieces, Wyler and Ray were privy to only one side of the conversation.

"Julie, what makes this event unique is really the vision of the young man sitting here beside me, Scottie Hibble," said Layton Howe. "Here's a young man, twenty-four years old, who has already been wildly successful, and yet he saw an opportunity to do something that no one else has ever done, to bring together people from all walks of life and encourage them to make a commitment. That's really what this is about. That's what makes this different from just donating to a charity or speaking out about a cause. Scottie's vision is that we will be making a commitment, taking an oath, if you will, to use whatever power or influence we have to make life better for everyone on this planet."

Wyler and Ray had met the day before to review the security footage from the New York Gemological Appraisal Institute that Ray had on his smartphone. Wyler was anxious to rewatch it to confirm his theory, but Ray insisted on hearing the details of the attack in the subway first. He was annoyed that he had heard about the incident through the cop grapevine and not directly from Wyler, so Wyler did a quick recap with enough detail to satisfy him. After that, they rewatched the footage together several times over breakfast. The more he watched the footage, the surer Wyler was of the woman's identity.

After razzing Ray for never having seen the movie *Vertigo*, Wyler went over the basic details of the plot in order to explain what had triggered his late-night epiphany. In the movie, James Stewart's fear of heights inadvertently leads to the death of the woman he loves. Months later, he sees a woman on the street who vaguely resembles his lost love and begins a romance with her. Soon, the romance turns darkly obsessive as Stewart insists on changing the woman's physical appearance in an attempt to psychologically resurrect the dead woman. In the end, Stewart discovers that his new girlfriend and the woman he thinks he killed are actually the same person, and he's been set up as an unwitting accomplice in a complicated murder plot.

When Wyler had first seen the security footage, something about the imposter seemed familiar, but it was too ambiguous to pinpoint. But as he watched Kim Novak physically transform her appearance in the movie, a connection sparked in his mind. He realized that the woman in the security footage was actually the same woman he had met a few days before at Scottie Hibble's company, RopeLine. Although her hair, glasses, clothing, and makeup were different, the body size, head shape, hands, walk, movements, and other physical mannerisms were a perfect match for Scottie Hibble's young PR assistant, Ashley Lang.

"This is not about politics, Julie." Paulo Almeida, the tennis star, was talking now in a thick Brazilian accent. "That's the problem with the world today. Politics and politicians are not able to, you know, bring about actual change. That's why we are stepping in and taking a totally different approach."

There was another interval of silence in the studio as the group listened to the interviewer's next question.

"Julie, that's a very good question, and I'm glad you asked it," said Scottie Hibble. "The reason there will be no press or cameras at Bonfire is so we can provide a safe space for our celebrities and influencers to really be themselves. We want to foster a genuine, honest dialogue, and we want everyone to openly share their views without worrying how it might impact their personal brand. That's the only way, in the end, we are going to get to the heart of some very crucial issues and come up with solutions."

Another pause, and then the whole group laughed in unison at some witty remark from the unseen host.

"I think I'm going to let Maggie handle that one!" said Hibble. Wyler couldn't help but be impressed at the sheer charisma of Scottie Hibble. He was sitting next to three of the most important people in the world, people with world-renowned achievements, and yet he seemed relaxed, poised, and in control, and acted like he was the biggest star on the stage.

"I don't think I can take much more of this," sneered Ray. Wyler didn't respond, but a few minutes later, the interview was over and a loud bell rang in the studio. Technicians and other personnel began to move about, and the celebrities on the platform stood up and stretched. Wyler and Ray decided to make their move.

They made their way toward the front of the studio, dodging busy workers and carefully stepping over thick cables that snaked in every direction. They stopped at the edge of the raised platform and waited as Scottie shared a private joke with Maggie Wells-Walling. It didn't take long for the sitcom star to notice the presence of the two strange men looking conspicuously out of place in their suits and ties, and soon Hibble followed her eyes to Wyler and Shimura.

"Could we have a brief word with you, Mr. Hibble?" Wyler called out.

Hibble made no effort to hide his annoyance at Wyler's unexpected presence, and he made them wait while he and Maggie Wells-Walling said a drawn-out goodbye.

"What's this all about, *ex*-detective Wyler?" Hibble asked, walking right by them. "I'm wondering how you were able to get past the security desk downstairs, since you're not a police officer anymore."

Wyler and Shimura followed after him.

"This helped," said Ray, flashing his badge. Hibble stopped and turned around, seeing Detective Shimura's gold shield.

"Okay, so you've brought a friend. I guess you guys stick together. Well, I'm actually super busy. Bonfire starts tomorrow, and I'm flying out myself to the island later today. So whatever it is, it'll have to be quick."

"There's just a few additional questions I'd like to ask you about Peter Lisonbee, if you don't mind."

"Okay, but I've got to get this makeup off." Hibble turned, and they followed him to a dressing room where a makeup artist was waiting for him. He sat down, and the girl began applying a cream to his face.

"Well?" said Hibble impatiently as the girl worked on him.

"You mentioned that you first met Peter on the evening of July 12th, when you happened to wander into the restaurant Nine for a late meal?"

"That's right."

Hibble was facing the mirror in the dressing room, and Wyler stood behind and spoke to his reflection.

"How did you come to stop at Nine that night? I mean, how did you choose that particular restaurant to eat?"

"I told you this before, Mr. Wyler," said Hibble. He continued in a slow, labored manner, as if indulging a stupid child. "A few of us had been at a party at a friend's apartment. We were driving back to my place. We were hungry. We decided to stop somewhere for a bite. Someone spotted this place Nine as we passed by. We decided to give it a try. We told the driver to pull over. We went in. We ate." Hibble sighed heavily, as if exhausted by having to repeat himself.

"Who was it that saw the place?" asked Wyler.

Hibble thought fast. "I'm pretty sure it was Gordon Jeffrey. He's in town starring in some awful off-Broadway play."

"Right. And where was the party you had been to?"

"Does it matter?"

Wyler waited without answering.

"The party was at Augustin Blanc's apartment in Soho. He's an installation artist. We were celebrating his newest piece—a fifteen story inverted pyramid near the seaport. You guys art lovers?"

"I read somewhere you live uptown, don't you?" Wyler asked, ignoring the question.

"Yes, my building's off East 71st, in Lenox Hill. Why?"

The makeup girl began rubbing the cream off Hibble's face with a towel.

"I'm just wondering how you ended up at Nine, going from Soho, downtown, up to Lenox Hill, which is on the East Side. Wouldn't you have taken 3rd or Madison to get uptown?"

"How do I know? This may shock you, but I don't usually sit in the back of a limo and tell the driver how to drive."

"Right, but Nine is on 2nd Avenue."

"So?"

"2nd Avenue is a one-way street running southbound."

"So?"

"So, there's no way your driver would have been on 2nd Avenue heading uptown from Soho. It runs in the opposite direction. To get on 2nd Avenue, he'd have to take a cross street over and double back. That doesn't make sense, does it?"

Frustrated, Hibble took the towel from the girl's hand and finished wiping his face with angry strokes.

"I don't know what to tell you. Maybe we asked the driver to pick a place. Maybe he had been there before. Who knows? It was almost two months ago!"

"Right, but you just said it was Gordon Jeffrey who saw the place as you drove by."

Scottie Hibble tossed the towel into the sink and swiveled around.

"I guess I was wrong about that. Why does all this matter, anyway?" he said, standing up and facing Wyler.

"You had no idea before you went into the restaurant that night that Peter Lisonbee worked there?"

"Of course not. How could I?"

"So, you didn't go there for the purpose of meeting and forming a relationship with Peter Lisonbee?"

Hibble's eyes stayed locked on Wyler's as an arrogant smirk formed at the edges of his mouth.

"What reason would I have to do that, ex-detective?"

"I don't know. Maybe there was something he had that you wanted."

"Such as?" Hibble asked, but Wyler chose to let the question hang in the air, unanswered. Hibble noticed the makeup girl was still there, nervously fussing with her kit, listening to the conversation. "You can go," Hibble said to the girl, and she scurried out of the room, leaving Hibble alone with Wyler and Shimura.

"Did Peter ever mention a family heirloom to you? A gemstone that had been passed down in this family?"

"No, I don't think so. Is there anything else? I've got people waiting for me."

"On the night that he died, Peter Lisonbee sent a text to a

friend." As Wyler spoke, Hibble crossed the room and sat down on a black leather sofa. "He said that you guys had found the perfect location for your new restaurant, a warehouse in Chelsea. He was excited because apparently you had made an offer on the place. He even gave her the address because he wanted his friend to meet him there the next day, so he could show it to her."

Hibble listened silently, with a bored expression on his face that looked forced.

"The thing is, I tracked down the building's owners yesterday. They had no idea that Scottie Hibble had any interest in the property. They were excited to hear it because they hadn't received an offer in over a year."

"That's very interesting," said Hibble, finally. "What's your point?"

"I guess I'm just wondering if you ever really intended to go into business with Peter Lisonbee, or if maybe your interest in him was based on a different motive."

"Of course I planned to open the restaurant with Peter."

"So, why did you lie to him about making an offer on the Chelsea property?"

"Look," Hibble said, leaning forward but avoiding eye contact with Wyler. "Like I told you the other day, I was starting to realize that Peter was an unstable guy. He had mad skills, don't get me wrong. He could have been a great chef. But the more I spent time with him, the more obvious it was that the guy just didn't have what it takes. He didn't have the mental toughness that all real winners have. I decided to back off and move on. That's why I didn't put the offer in on that place."

"So why lie about it?" asked Ray.

"I didn't want to hurt the kid. You could tell he was unraveling, you know, psychologically. He wasn't used to the big leagues. The stress and pressure of the whole project was getting to him. I wanted to let him down gently. He told me himself he was depressed, even suicidal. So, I told him I made an offer on that place, hoping it would cheer him up. I was going to tell him the truth the next time we met. But he killed himself before I got the chance."

"He told you he was suicidal?" Wyler asked.

"Yes, he did," Scottie Hibble nodded his head in a display of sadness and empathy. Wyler didn't buy one word of Hibble's performance. He knew a pathological liar when he saw one.

"You didn't mention that before."

"You're right. I should have mentioned that sooner. I guess I didn't believe him when he told me, and I've been feeling guilty. You of all people should understand that, Mr. Wyler. I heard your wife committed suicide."

Wyler's body immediately tensed, and Ray, who had been standing off to the side, took a precautionary step closer to Wyler and Hibble.

"What I mean is, a lot of people say they're going to kill themselves, but most people don't actually go through with it, right? When they do, we're like, shocked. I'm sure that's how you felt, right?"

Wyler glared at Hibble, feeling his blood begin to boil, but he said nothing.

"Now, you guys have got to excuse me, I really do have to head out. Big day." Hibble stood up to go, but Wyler held up the palm of a hand to stop him.

"There's one other person in your organization I'd like to speak to, if you don't mind."

"Not a problem," Hibble said, suddenly friendly and happy to oblige. "Who is it?"

"Your PR assistant, Ashley Lang. I met her when I visited your office a few days ago, and there are a couple things I'd just like to follow up with. Could you tell me how to locate her?"

Wyler studied Scottie Hibble's reaction carefully. Up until

now, he had been dancing with Hibble, provoking him with jabs to throw him off balance in hopes he would make a mistake. But Hibble had, for the most part, kept his cool during the grilling. Now, Wyler was playing the trump card he'd been saving, hoping the mention of Ashley Lang would rattle Hibble and crack his phony veneer of nonchalance.

"I'm sorry, but that won't be possible," Hibble said.

"Oh? Why is that?"

"Well, Ashley flew out to the island two days ago, to help get things ready. And, well, it's really sad, but there was a boating accident yesterday morning, and she was killed."

Scottie Hibble delivered this news with a casual cold-bloodedness that sent a chill down Wyler's spine.

"She fell off one of our yachts and drowned. I think she had too much to drink. It was a terrible tragedy. She was really looking forward to Bonfire."

CHAPTER 20

There is a moment that sometimes happens to a detective in the course of a criminal investigation. It doesn't happen in every case, and some detectives never experience it at all. It is not a moment of intellectual clarity, like in detective stories when the sleuth suddenly pieces together the puzzle in a burst of inspiration. Instead, it is a phenomenon that takes place deep within the psyche of the detective himself, like a switch suddenly being flipped. It is a moment that has countless parallels in the natural world. A shark catches the faintest whiff of blood from somewhere miles away and suddenly changes course. A circling hawk eyes the tiniest movement in the prairie below and locks on. A bloodhound picks up a scent and strains wildly to break free of its hold. It is the moment when the predator suddenly becomes aware of the presence of his prey. It is a moment, both instinctual and physical, when all internal processes instantly realign to focus exclusively on one single objective. For a detective, this moment does not necessarily mean the final resolution of the case is near. That may still be days, weeks, even months away. Proximity to the endgame does not factor in. But once this moment occurs, the detective, like the natural predator, locks on to a specific target and does not let go. Like a shark, he has smelled blood, and the scent has transformed him, dehumanized him, reduced him to a machine with but one purpose.

This moment happened to Wyler the instant that Scottie Hibble informed him of Ashley Lang's death. Wyler had met her only once. She was young, beautiful, naïve, and utterly devoted to Hibble. And it was more than just professional loyalty. She obviously had deep and sincere personal affection and admiration for Hibble. Wyler pictured the girl working days, nights, and weekends, slavishly putting her own life on hold to support the exciting vision of her charismatic boss. And yet, Scottie Hibble had delivered the news of her death—of her *murder*, Wyler had no doubt—like a shrewd chess move, with a faint, self-satisfied note in his voice.

From that moment on, Hibble had become Wyler's prey. The boy may not know it or sense it, he may not understand it or fear it, but he was now being hunted. Whatever it took, Aaron Wyler was coming for him.

Wyler was aware of all this on a subconscious level without having to think through it. Ray Shimura also sensed the change in his ex-partner—the quiet, steely determination that had settled on his friend like a dark storm cloud.

"Be careful, Aaron," he had said, in a low warning voice, as they stood together on the street outside the television studio. "You've got to forget that stuff he said about Jessica."

"This isn't about Jessica. He killed that girl."

"We don't know that."

"I know it."

"If you really think that, then let's make this official. Get Major Case involved."

"No," was Wyler's stony reply.

Ray spent a few more minutes trying to convince Wyler to stop freelancing and take things through official channels, but Wyler just listened politely and ignored him. Wyler changed the subject by asking Ray to look for any connection between Hibble and Bobby Willis or Warren Payson, his subway attackers. Before they parted, Ray made Wyler promise to keep him informed of his actions and any developments, threatening to take the case to MCS himself if Wyler didn't agree.

After separating from Ray, Wyler had knocked around Midtown by himself for about an hour, brooding and mulling things over. He knew in his gut that Ashley Lang had been acting as Scottie Hibble's agent when she gained possession of the gemstone, and he now accepted the working theory that her death had somehow been arranged to cover up her role in the plot. But how? All he knew about her death were the vague, no doubt misleading details shared by Scottie Hibble.

He decided to make a call and found a bench in Bryant Park to sit on. Two years ago in Miami, he had sat next to the chief of the Royal Bahamas Police at dinner during a conference about the nexus between Latin American drug smuggling and international terrorism. The Bahamas was a country in the Caribbean made up of hundreds of different islands, many of them privately owned. Some of these islands were used as supply chains by various drug cartels, and it was thought at the time that a similar network of private islands might host terrorist cells within striking distance of the United States.

He didn't have a direct number, but after explaining who he was to several different people and invoking the conference in Miami, he finally reached Rollie Sterling in his office at police headquarters in Nassau, the Bahamian capital located on the island of New Providence.

"Detective Wyler!" a friendly, gregarious voice said through the phone.

"Chief, how are you?"

Sterling treated him like an old friend and immediately began reminiscing about the conference in Miami. At first, Wyler thought the chief had been briefed on who he was and was only pretending to remember him out of politeness, but then Sterling asked him about his wife, the cancer doctor. Wyler informed him of Jessica's death without going into details, and he seemed genuinely sorry to hear the sad news.

After a bit more small talk, he finally said, "How can I help you today, Detective?"

Wyler told Sterling why he was calling, and asked if he had any additional details about the death of Ashley Lang. The chief said he had heard of an accidental death taking place off the island hosting the Bonfire conference but didn't know anything beyond that. Wyler told Sterling that he suspected the death may have been a homicide staged to look like an accident. Sterling said he would look into it and promised to get back to him.

After hanging up with Sterling, Wyler realized there was a problem with his theory of Ashley Lang's death. If she really had been killed the previous morning, that was just hours after Wyler himself had made the connection between her and the theft of the gemstone. How did Hibble know he was on to her? The only one he had spoken to was Ray. And yet, somehow, Wyler knew her death had not been an accident. In fact, he was now convinced that Hibble's whole relationship with Peter Lisonbee had simply been a ploy to get close to the gemstone. But why? What was Scottie Hibble's interest in the Lisonbee family gemstone? The stone was worth millions, but Hibble was already a multimillionaire.

He realized that before going forward, he needed to know everything there was to know about Scottie Hibble. And to do that, he needed internet access and a quiet place to work where he wouldn't be disturbed. Since Bryant Park was right next to the New York Public Library, he decided to make the Rose Reading Room his temporary command post.

The Rose Reading Room of the New York Public Library on Fifth Avenue is one of the largest rooms in the city, stretching the length of two entire city blocks, roughly the size of a football field. The ceiling, over 50 feet high, is decorated with gilded, ornate painted murals, like a museum or a cathedral. He wanted to be alone to concentrate on the research he had to do, and the cavernous library room seemed like an ideal place, offering solitude, anonymity, and an outlet to plug in a power cord. After checking out a laptop from the resource desk, Wyler found a spot at one of the long dark wood tables and sat down to get to work.

Wyler started his research simply by typing the name Scottie Hibble into Google. All the initial search results focused on Hibble's involvement in the upcoming Bonfire festival. Having been forced to sit through several press interviews earlier that morning, Wyler felt like he was already a reluctant expert on Bonfire, but he decided to read some of the articles anyway to see if there was anything new to learn. He found pieces in almost every major news and entertainment publication. Most of the information he read was already familiar to him, but he jotted down some additional details he was able to glean. The name of the private island in the Bahamas where the event was being held was called Caliban Cay. The event would take place over the course of three nights, beginning Saturday, August 31st, which was tomorrow, and ending on Monday, September 2nd, Labor Day. Although the invitation-only festival would be hosting some of the world's most prominent luminaries—celebrities, business leaders, social media influencers, various other VIPs—no press or cameras would be allowed on the island during the entire three days of the "Bonfire experience," a term repeated several times in the articles. Since details about what would actually happen during this "experience" were sketchy, the articles tended to focus on other things, like the private concerts by famous bands that were planned, the luxury accommodations on the island, and the gourmet menu that was being prepared by several celebrity chefs.

Even after sitting through all those press interviews, Wyler hadn't been able to quite grasp the purpose of the gathering, and the articles he read now failed to shed any new light for him. Apparently, the event would provide an opportunity for the world's elite citizens to collectively focus their attention on solving many of the planet's problems: war, poverty, race relations, climate, and so on. In several news stories, Scottie Hibble emphasized that at some point during the event, participants would be called upon to make a commitment. Words like oath, covenant, and pledge showed up in some of the articles, all without being elaborated upon.

As Wyler continued scanning the articles, he noticed something interesting. News articles and stories about the Bonfire event began showing up in mid-July. He checked the dates on the stories and found that the earliest mention of the event was in reference to a press conference held by Scottie Hibble that took place on July 15th. That was just three days after Peter Lisonbee's birthday on July 12th, the day that Peter dropped the gemstone off at the New York Gemological Appraisal Institute. Later that evening, Scottie Hibble had walked into Nine. That meant that three important events in the case—Peter Lisonbee's decision to have the gemstone appraised, his meeting with Scottie Hibble, and Hibble's press conference announcing Bonfire—had all happened right after each other, and in rapid succession. On the surface, it was an obvious interlocking chain of events, like tumbling dominoes, except for one nagging detail: Wyler couldn't find any connective tissue to link the three events, other than the coincidence of the dates.

Unable to resolve the problem, he put these thoughts aside and decided to dig deeper into Scottie Hibble's company, Rope-Line. Several news outlets and business journals had run stories about the hip new company and the exciting young tech entrepreneur who had founded it. Most of these articles were a few years old, but still available online.

He quickly read four articles that each gave different versions of the same basic facts. RopeLine had been started a few years ago by twenty-one-year-old Scottie Hibble. Hibble, a college dropout, had become a millionaire virtually overnight as a result. RopeLine was an invitation-only social media platform and mobile app. For a large monthly fee, members of RopeLine were given access to private parties, clubs, and events where they could hobnob with the beautiful and famous. A RopeLine membership had quickly become one of the most sought-after symbols of elite status. To raise awareness and create interest, RopeLine began hosting events in cities like New York, Chicago, Los Angeles, and Las Vegas. Pictures and videos from these events—showing ordinary people partying with supermodels, athletes, rappers, and the like—flooded other social media platforms and fueled the increasing demand for membership. Many of the articles attributed the success of RopeLine to Scottie Hibble's marketing genius. The more popular and fashionable RopeLine membership became, the more Hibble restricted access and raised membership fees.

The articles were not hard-hitting journalism. They were basically puff pieces, intended to show both Scottie Hibble and his company in a positive light. Hibble was presented as a visionary entrepreneur and RopeLine as the next big thing. And yet, to Wyler, the stories only reinforced the impression he already had of Hibble as arrogant, shallow, and opportunistic. In Scottie Hibble's worldview, fame and media exposure seemed to be aims unto themselves, the ultimate benchmark for measuring a person's worth. Wyler regarded the nation's mindless obsession with celebrity as a sad and destructive cultural phenomenon, but Hibble saw it as an emerging market to be exploited.

Feeling hungry, Wyler checked the time on his phone and saw

that it was close to 2:00 o'clock. Assuming he had probably learned everything about Hibble there was to learn from the internet, his thoughts turned to lunch. One of his favorite restaurants was The Peking Duck House in Chinatown, but that was all the way downtown. They had a second location in Midtown which Wyler had never been to, so he decided to try that for a late lunch. Before leaving the library, however, he decided to try one more thing.

LexisNexis was a searchable computer database that predated the internet. The database housed vast swaths of information such as news articles, court papers, corporate documents, and government records. Before search engines like Google existed, journalists, lawyers, academics, and other researchers were able to use LexisNexis to do keyword searches and bring up all publicly available information on a specific topic or person. Wyler closed his current search and navigated to the online portal for LexisNexis. He had accessed the database many times before using the NYPD's credentials, but now that he was a private citizen, he realized he would have to create his own personal account. It took him a few minutes to populate the required fields and choose a username and password, and after clicking a confirmation link, he was set up with a free trial.

He typed the words Scottie Hibble into the search box at the top of the screen, then clicked the magnifying glass icon next to it. The screen blinked and reset, showing the results of the search organized into different categories—news, company documents, court cases, forms, intellectual property, and so on. Most of the categories had a zero next to them, indicating no results for that category. The news category, however, had 3,187 results, and Wyler clicked that. A numbered list of news articles appeared on the screen, and as Wyler scanned the headlines, he saw that they were similar to the results he had gotten from Google—page after page of articles about Scottie Hibble, RopeLine, and Bonfire. Nothing new. A filter at the top of the screen allowed him to re-sort the list chronologically, and he found the earliest hit for Scottie Hibble linked to the November 2016 issue of something called *Clickbait*, which turned out to be a technology industry magazine. Wyler checked and found that RopeLine and Scottie Hibble were mentioned briefly in a story about up-and-coming apps that were already generating industry buzz before being launched.

Wyler turned back to his screen and stared at the results for Scottie Hibble. He was about to log out of LexisNexis, but he decided to try one more search before heading to The Peking Duck House. Clicking the cursor back into the search box at the top of the screen, he typed the words Scott Hibble. The search for the name Scott Hibble, instead of Scottie Hibble, generated a list of just 23 hits in the news section. Wyler began scanning the headlines. The first batch of news stories involved a Scott Hibble who served as the U.S. ambassador to the Marshall Islands during the first Bush administration. Wyler skimmed past these and came to another batch about a truck driver named Scott Hibble who had fallen asleep at the wheel in 2011, causing a multi-car accident that killed two other people. The accident had taken place on I-70 outside of Columbus, and there were articles from Ohio newspapers, transcripts of local TV news coverage, and one story from the Associated Press about the danger posed by drowsy long-haul truck drivers.

Each page only displayed 20 results, so Wyler clicked to the next page to see the final three articles. The first story on this page was also about the Ohio truck accident. The second was an obituary of an 86-year-old Korean War veteran named Scott Hibble who had died in Oregon two years ago. The last result was a separate news article, unrelated to any of the others. It was a story from *The New York Times*, dated August 16th, 2014. The headline immediately caught Wyler's interest. He clicked the link and was brought to the full article.

Drug Cartel Massacres Mormon Archeologists in Honduras

By Michael Benner

A group of amateur archeologists from the United States affiliated with the Mormon Church were slain in the remote jungles of Honduras last week in an incident the Honduran government is calling the latest example of out-of-control drug cartel violence. Fourteen individuals, most of them students, were gunned down deep in the remote jungle area known as Mosquitia on the eastern coast of Honduras. The group had been in the country for several weeks, taking part in an archeologic expedition sponsored by an organization called The Mormon Evidence Project.

The bodies were discovered several days later by authorities who were led to the site by Scott L. Hibble, a nineteen-year-old college student who was the only member of the expedition to survive the attack. After witnessing the massacre, Hibble escaped and traveled on foot through the jungle for two days before reaching the coastal town of Brus Laguna, where he reported the incident.

Authorities said the execution-style massacre was consistent with previous atrocities perpetrated by drug cartels. Still, some officials expressed surprise that the small group of archeologists had been targeted so brazenly. "This is one of the worst atrocities we've seen," said Captain Juan Alvarez of the Honduran Police Force. "It's very unusual for a cartel to travel so far from its normal zone of influence and target a group of civilians like this. It's shocking and sad."

The incident represents a dramatic escalation of violence in the ongoing, bloody feud between drug cartels and the government of Honduras. For safety reasons, the Honduran government refrains from issuing archeological permits in areas controlled by the cartels, and in the past the cartels have not openly targeted foreign citizens and groups outside their territory. Some officials have speculated that the incident may have been intended as a signal that the cartels are expanding their territorial ambitions, but no cartel has yet claimed responsibility for the attack.

According to sources familiar with its mission, the archeological group had traveled to Honduras to search for proof of historical events depicted in the Book of Mormon, a book the LDS Church considers ancient scripture similar to The Bible. Although many of the individuals participating in the expedition were members of The Church of Jesus Christ of Latter-day Saints, a spokesperson for the Utah-based religion said that The Mormon Evidence Project is a privately funded enterprise and is in no way affiliated with the Church. Earlier this year, the LDS Church took the unusual step of issuing an official statement to its members asking them not to participate in the project, citing safety concerns. However, several individuals chose to join the project despite these warnings.

Wyler read the short article all the way through twice. Could Scott L. Hibble be Scottie Hibble? Wyler quickly did the math in his head. Scottie Hibble, twenty-four years old now, would have been nineteen in 2014, the same age as the Scott L. Hibble mentioned in the story.

Keeping LexisNexis open, Wyler opened a new window in the browser and typed in the words Mormon Evidence Project. He then clicked the image search feature, which caused dozens of images to pop up and fill his screen. He didn't even have to scroll. The very first image on the page was a photograph of a dozen or so smiling people, all wearing the same t-shirt, standing with arms around shoulders under a canopy of tall trees. There were a few older adults, but most of the people in the picture seemed to be of college age. The group looked dirty and exhausted, but also eager and excited, and Wyler guessed the picture had been taken at the start of their expedition.

Wyler clicked to enlarge the photo and there, second from the left, stood Scottie Hibble, the founder of RopeLine and the visionary behind Bonfire. He was younger, thinner, and clean-shaven, but there was no mistaking who it was. As Wyler studied the picture, he noticed that Hibble's attitude and expression were slightly different from the others. He was the only one in the group whose arms weren't on the shoulders of the others. Instead, they were crossed in a smug, cocky pose. And instead of the big, hokey smile on everyone else's face, Hibble's grin was more self-conscious and reserved, like a smirk.

Wyler's brain slowly began to process the implications of what he was looking at. Five years ago, Scottie Hibble had been part of an archeological expedition that had something to do, if indirectly, with the Mormon Church. He immediately thought back to the internet search he had done at his hotel a few days ago for the words Urim and Thummim. He had been surprised that so many of the search results that popped up had referenced Latter-day Saints and Mormonism. He had found that curious at the time, but he hadn't pursued the issue because there was no reason to.

But now suddenly there was a reason.

Was there some connection between the Urim and Thummim, the Mormon religion, and Scottie Hibble?

Forgetting his hunger, Wyler sat up, moved his chair a little closer, and began reading the article a third time.

CHAPTER 21

Wyler stood on West 65th Street, waiting for the light to change. It was Friday night, and Manhattan was teeming and buzzing with noise, lights, and motion. There is a charged thrill in the air on a summer weekend night in New York City that is unlike anything else, anywhere else. Wyler couldn't help but feel the proud tug of belonging unique to New Yorkers, the sense that he was somehow part of it all, a tiny spark in the electrical grid of excitement and energy.

The light changed and Wyler joined the crowd hurrying across Columbus Avenue. Broadway ran diagonally through the intersection at this spot, creating two kissing triangles of open space called Lincoln Square. A glittering world of upscale restaurants, posh shops, and high culture, Lincoln Square was like Times Square's rich, snobby aunt. Like most rich aunts, it resided further uptown, away from the flashy squalor of its tacky, less sophisticated nephew. Where Times Square was anchored by the giant Coca-Cola jumbotron, this neighborhood's center of gravity was the stately and elegant Lincoln Center arts complex, home to the New York Philharmonic, the Metropolitan Opera, and the New York City Ballet.

As he reached the other side of Columbus Avenue, Wyler paused before a boxy, rectangular building made of light-colored granite that ran the length of the small block. The building was about seven stories high, and the upper floors jutted beyond the dimensions of the ground floor. The words The Church of Jesus Christ of Latter-day Saints were printed in plain black lettering on the overhang. A tall steeple rose from the southwest corner of the building, out of which extended a long spire and a golden statue of an angel blowing a horn.

The street-level entrance doors were open, and Wyler walked past an unmanned security desk and took an elevator to the fourth floor. When the elevator doors opened, Wyler was hit by an unexpected wave of dance music throbbing loudly through the walls. He stepped into a lobby area lined with sofas, chairs, and religious artwork, and approached a cluster of college-age kids.

"Excuse me, I'm looking for Jason Bell, do you know where I can find him?" Wyler asked a short, orange-haired young man in a bow tie standing between two taller girls.

"Um, I know he's here somewhere," the young man answered, glancing around and waving a sugar cookie like it was Geiger counter. Wyler noted with interest a large posterboard on an easel with the words "Zion's Youth in Latter-Days" handprinted in sparkling letters. "Kim!" the boy called to a girl in an aqua-colored skirt who came bouncing by. "Do you know where President Bell is?"

"Yes, I just saw him in the cultural hall! Are you looking for him?" she addressed the question eagerly to Wyler, recognizing him as the obvious outsider.

"Yes, I am."

"I'll take you to him!" she said brightly, excited to be of service. She turned and led Wyler back in the direction she had come from. "I literally just saw him a few minutes ago. He was over by the refreshment table, talking to Sister Marsh." As they went down the hall, the pulsating rhythms of dance music got louder and louder until the girl pushed open a door, and the music broke free and washed over them.

They entered a dark auditorium filled with hundreds of dancing young people, colored lights moving and flashing overhead. The girl plunged into the sea of vibrating noise, and Wyler picked up the pace to stay with her. Although the music was deafening and had the same driving, raucous beat of any nightclub, there was a chaste exuberance to the proceedings. In Wyler's experience, modern teenagers had only two settings: angry or bored. But these kids were different. They wore smiles, not snarls, as they wiggled, twisted, and bounced. Even the DJ was clean-shaven and wore a collared dress shirt.

Wyler was weaving his way through the commotion, trying to keep up with his guide, when one of the dancers accidently slammed into him, knocking him to the ground. Several people rushed to his aid, but when Wyler got to his feet, he realized the small delay had severed his connection to Kim.

He eventually found the refreshment table and saw Kim talking earnestly to a man in a tan suit, white shirt, and tie. She was glancing around with a worried expression on her face, but when she saw Wyler, she smiled with relief and waved him over like they were old friends.

"Jason Bell?" asked Wyler, extending his arm as he approached. The man switched a

half-eaten brownie to his other hand so he could shake, his huge hand swallowing Wyler's in a powerful but friendly grip.

"Yes, and I bet you're Aaron Wyler!" They both spoke in yells to be heard over the music.

Jason Bell was small but tightly packed, with broad shoulders and a barrel chest made of muscle, not fat. He seemed to be in his late thirties, with a round face, thick brown hair, and big blue eyes. He had the charismatic bearing of a star athlete, and an image flashed into Wyler's head of Bell playing high school or college football.

"Would you like a treat? We've got way too much!"

A long refreshments table was filled with an assortment of cookies, brownies, and other items. Wyler was about to say no, but he had never made it to the Peking Duck House and was starving, so he picked up a Rice Krispies treat.

"Thanks," Wyler said, raising the treat in a toast. Kim smiled once more at Wyler before melting back into the dancing throng.

"Why don't we go to an office where we can talk?" yelled Bell over the noise.

They left the auditorium, and Wyler followed Bell down a hall to an office door. "We'll be able to talk in here," Bell said.

"I appreciate you taking some time to talk to me on such short notice."

"No...problem...at...all," Bell answered, fumbling with a key ring.

"Sorry to take you away from the dance."

Bell turned back to Wyler with a conspiratorial grin. "Actually, I'm kind of grateful. It's pretty loud in there." The key Bell had inserted into the doorknob wasn't turning. "Shoot, that's not the right one." He stared down at the key ring and resumed fumbling. "Come on, Bell," he murmured to himself. "Wait a minute, I think this is it!"

The door opened into a medium-sized non-descript office with a wooden desk, matching credenza, and two blue upholstered chairs facing the desk. There was a painting on the wall behind the desk of Jesus dressed as a shepherd, a sheep slung over his shoulders. Instead of taking the seat behind the desk, Bell repositioned the two chairs in front of the desk to face each other and gestured for Wyler to take a seat.

"Is this your office?"

"No, it's one of our bishop's offices. But that's okay, we can use it."

"Sorry for the ignorance, but I heard someone call you President Bell. Are you the president of the Mormon Church here in New York?"

"Actually, I'm a counselor to our stake president." He read the confusion on Wyler's face and continued. "In our church, the individual congregations are called wards, and each ward is supervised by a bishop. A ward is like a parish, and a bishop is like a parish priest or a pastor. A group of congregations together is what we call a stake, which is kind of like a diocese in the Catholic church. So, actually, a bishop in the Catholic church is what we would call a stake president. It's kind of confusing. Are you Catholic by any chance?"

"Jewish."

"Well, you got me there," he chuckled and held up his hands in a mock surrender. "I'm not sure what the parallel would be in the Jewish faith."

"I wouldn't know either, to be honest. We've got synagogues and rabbis, but there's lots of different sects—orthodox, ultra-orthodox, reform, conservative, plus all kinds of offshoots—and they all have their own organizational approaches, I suppose."

Bell nodded attentively. He seemed fascinated by what Wyler was saying.

"I have to say, your phone call was pretty intriguing," said Bell, switching gears after a brief lull. "You said you're investigating a murder or something?"

"Well, yes, I'm investigating a couple of suspicious deaths that may be linked to the theft of a rare gemstone."

"You mentioned on the phone that you're a retired police officer?"

"I was a detective with the NYPD for over fifteen years."

"Are you some kind of private detective now?"

"Not really. The sister of one of the...deceased individuals asked me to look into it. I'm just doing her a favor."

"I see. I'm curious how you happened to get my phone number?"

"Well, I had some questions about your religion. I spent the afternoon trying to find what I needed online, but to be honest, the more I read, the more confused I got. So, I decided it would be easier to just sit down and talk to someone. I didn't realize there would be so many different phone numbers for your church in New York City, so I just started dialing. When I finally reached someone and told them I wasn't a Mormon, they gave me another number, so I called that number and spoke to someone named Elder Perry, an older gentleman. He was very nice. When I explained that I needed some historical information and background, he said the best person for me to speak to would be Jason Bell, and he gave me your number."

"I understand," Bell grinned and nodded, as if the story didn't surprise him.

"So, is that part of the job of a counselor to a stake president, to deal with questions from outsiders?"

Bell burst into laughter.

"No, not at all. You see, apart from my ecclesiastical position, which is voluntary, I also happen to work for the Church. I oversee an education program in this area for youth and college-age adults. That sometimes makes other Church members think I'm some sort of an expert on Church history and doctrine." Bell said the last part quickly, as if worried the explanation skirted the boundaries of pridefulness.

"Well, I hope you can answer some questions for me."

"I'll try, but I'm curious what our Church has to do with your investigation. Were the people killed members of our faith?"

"No, they weren't Mormons."

Wyler noticed a slight wince come to Bell's face.

"Is something wrong?" asked Wyler.

"No, it's just that…we don't actually refer to ourselves as Mormons."

"Oh, I apologize. I thought –"

"Don't worry about it at all." Bell smiled and raised a hand in a calming gesture. "It happens all the time. We prefer to be known as members of the Church of Jesus Christ of Latter-day Saints, or simply Latter-day Saints."

Wyler nodded. No skin off his nose.

"So, if they weren't members of our Church, what's the connection?" Bell asked.

Wyler didn't respond right away. He considered the question carefully, as if trying to puzzle out the answer himself. "What can you tell me about your church and the Urim and Thummim?"

"The Urim and Thummim?" Bell asked in surprise, his thick eyebrows shooting to the top of his high forehead. "Well, the Urim and Thummim are instruments prepared by God," Bell began, his voice slightly louder than it needed to be, as if he was used to addressing an entire classroom. "The purpose of the Urim and Thummim are to help a person receive revelation. They can also be used to translate languages. There are many examples of Urim and Thummim mentioned in the scriptures, in both the Old and New Testament. Abraham had Urim and Thummim. The priests in ancient Israel used Urim and Thummim. At least two of the prophets in the Book of Mormon had Urim and Thummim. Actually, the words Urim and Thummim are Hebrew words meaning Lights and Perfections." Wyler noticed that Bell gestured to him on the word Hebrew.

"You said two people in the Book of Mormon had these instruments?" Wyler asked, leaning forward slightly.

"That's right."

"What were their names?" Wyler asked the question with a clipped urgency, as if interviewing a witness at a crime scene.

"Well, there was Mosiah, and the other one is referred to only as the brother of Jared."

"And when did they live?"

"Mosiah lived about a hundred years before the birth of Christ."

"And this brother of Jared?"

"Oh, he lived thousands of years before Christ, around the same time as the events of the Tower of Babel from the Bible."

"So, this Mosiah and brother of Jared are the only connection between your religion and the Urim and Thummim?"

"No, not exactly. Joseph Smith had a Urim and Thummim."

"He was the founder of your church, right?"

"Well," Bell shifted his head from side to side, like he was trying to pick the right answer. "He was the first prophet of what we call the Restoration. You see, we believe The Church of Jesus Christ of Latter-day Saints is the same church that Jesus Christ himself established when he was on the earth, and that it was restored again to the earth in modern times to help prepare the world for the second coming of Jesus Christ. Joseph Smith was the person chosen by God to do that." Bell said all this in a low-key, matter-of-fact tone.

"And he had a Urim and Thummim set?"

"He did, yes."

"You said Urim and Thummim were instruments prepared by God. So, the ones that Joseph Smith had, what exactly were they? What I mean is, do you know what they looked like?"

"Actually..." Bell stood up and went to the bookcase where he removed a thick leatherbound volume from the shelf. Sitting back down, he began flipping through the thin pages of the book. "There's a physical description here of the Urim and Thummim that Joseph Smith used. Here it is." He put his finger down on a page and began reading. "There were two stones in silver bows, and these stones, fastened to a breastplate, constituted what is called the Urim and Thummim."

"So, the Urim and Thummim are two stones?"

"Well, yes and no," Bell responded. "The Urim and Thummim used by Joseph Smith was comprised of two stones. But he also had access to another stone, called the seer stone, which was also a Urim and Thummim."

"Now I'm totally confused," said Wyler.

"Yeah, it's a bit confusing. You see, most of the time, when the words Urim and Thummim are used in the scriptures, they're referring to two specific stones, like the stones in the breastplate described in the Old Testament. But the term Urim and Thummim can also be used to describe a single stone, or really any object, imbued by God with power."

Wyler considered this for a few moments. "So a single stone can also be a Urim and Thummim?"

"Correct."

"As long as it contains power from God?"

Bell nodded.

"What sort of power are you talking about?"

"Well, the stone Joseph had helped him to translate ancient records, including the Book of Mormon."

"So Joseph Smith didn't write the Book of Mormon?"

"No, the Book of Mormon was written by ancient prophets, like the Bible. Joseph Smith translated the Book of Mormon into our modern language."

"Using the Urim and Thummim?"

Bell nodded.

"How did he get the Book of Mormon in the first place?"

"Well, it was given to him by an angel." Bell said this with a bit of a smile, as if he understood how it might sound to a non-believer. "Or to be more accurate, an angel showed him where it was. You see, the Book of Mormon was a record engraved on metal plates by ancient prophets. The last person to write in the record was a man named Moroni who lived a few hundred years after Christ. He buried the plates in a hill, and that's where they stayed for centuries, until the same man, Moroni, appeared to Joseph Smith and showed him where it was."

"And when did all this happen?"

"Moroni first appeared to Joseph Smith in 1823."

"And these Urim and Thummim stones that Joseph Smith had, where are they now?"

"When he was done translating, Joseph returned both the plates and the Urim and Thummim to the angel Moroni."

At this point, Wyler broke eye contact and retreated into his own thoughts. Bell didn't speak, apparently sensing that Wyler needed time to process what he had heard.

"What can you tell me about the Mormon Evidence Project?" Wyler finally asked. The change in subject caught Bell off guard, and it took him a moment to search his memory.

"The group that got killed in Guatemala several years ago?"

"It was Honduras, actually."

"I don't really know much about it. The Church wasn't officially involved. It was a private group that went down there. It was a tragedy, what happened to them. Is that somehow connected to the case you're working on?"

"My understanding is they were looking for proof of the Book of Mormon. Why would they be doing that in Honduras?"

"Well, the events described in the Book of Mormon took place somewhere in the Americas between about 600 BC and 400 AD, but we don't know exactly where. Some believe the people in the Book of Mormon lived in ancient Mesoamerica, but there are other theories as well. The Church has no official position on the geography."

"Is it possible this group was looking for these Urim and Thummim stones talked about in the Book of Mormon?"

"I don't think so. Why do you ask that?"

"Have you ever heard of Scottie Hibble?" Wyler asked.

"Scottie Hibble? No, I've never heard of him. Who is he?"

"I think he's a member of your church. Or was a member, at some point. I don't know for sure. He was on this expedition. He was the only member of the group who survived."

The conversation stalled, like they had turned a corner into a dead end, and the atmosphere in the room became subdued.

"Maybe I could help you better if you told me more about this case you're investigating."

Wyler considered the request. He was growing to like Bell. He had answered Wyler's questions in a pleasant, straightforward manner, providing relevant facts without trying to evangelize or convert him. But it was late, and Wyler was tired, so he decided to just summarize the key points.

"I believe there's a connection of some kind between this archeological group that was killed in Honduras, a stolen gemstone that may or may not be one of these Urim and Thummim stones, and the recent deaths of two people. I believe this person, Scottie Hibble, is involved. He connects all of this together, but right now I don't know how. I thought that learning more about your religion might shed some light or trigger an insight, but that hasn't happened. At least not yet."

"I'm sorry I couldn't be more helpful."

"You've been very helpful," Wyler said, standing. "I appreciate your time."

They left the office, and Bell escorted Wyler back to the elevator, where they said polite goodbyes.

A few minutes later Wyler was back on 65th Street, waiting to cross Columbus in the other direction this time, when he heard his named called from behind.

"Aaron!"

Wyler turned and saw Jason Bell coming out of the church

building and hurrying toward him. Wyler moved to meet him halfway.

"I'm glad I caught you," Bell said when he reached Wyler. "I had a thought after you left. You said you were hoping to get some insight into your case by learning about our history. Well, the best way to do that would be to visit some of the sights where all of this took place."

"You mean in Central America?"

"No, I mean up in Palmyra. It's about forty minutes east of Rochester, upstate. That's where Joseph Smith lived. That's where he found the Book of Mormon plates, and the Urim and Thummim stones."

"That happened here in New York?" Wyler asked, incredulously. "I thought all that happened in Utah."

"No, it happened right here in New York. I think if you went up there, you might learn something that could help you."

Wyler took a minute to consider the suggestion as pedestrians swirled around them on the sidewalk, like a stream around two boulders.

"Would you be willing to come with me?" Wyler asked.

"You want me to go with you?"

"It would help to have you along, as kind of a guide, to answer questions. You've been very helpful. I would be happy to pay you for your time."

CHAPTER 22

At 8:00 o'clock the next morning, Wyler was in the lobby of Nora Maitland's apartment building waiting to be picked up by Bell. Bell had refused Wyler's offer of payment and volunteered to do the driving on their little road trip. In the light of day, Wyler was questioning the wisdom of his decision to leave the city for an entire day on what might be a wild goose chase. It was a move that smacked of desperation, but the truth was, he *was* desperate, and he figured he might as well grab at straws since there was nothing else to hold on to at the moment. He had no solid leads to follow and no workable theories. The whole case was like a puzzle made up of pieces from other puzzles.

As he waited for Bell, he reviewed the basic facts in his head. He believed that Scottie Hibble had engineered the theft of a gemstone believed by some to be one of the Urim and Thummim stones. Possession of the stone was important enough to him that he was willing to somehow cause the deaths of two people to obtain the stone and cover up his involvement. Although Urim and Thummim stones were mentioned in both the Bible and the Torah, Wyler had never heard the term before. However, Urim and Thummim stones seemed to play a central role in the history of the Mormon church. Hibble had been part of an archeological expedition with ties to this religion. And therefore, what? All of these facts were just bits and pieces of a larger whole that, for now, completely eluded Wyler. He had no working theory to explain Hibble's motivations. Did Hibble believe the stone had power from God? Did Hibble want to talk to God? Hibble didn't seem like the praying type. And then there was the timing. Hibble's involvement with Peter Lisonbee and the gemstone coincided directly with his announcement of the Bonfire event, a gathering of powerful and influential people taking place on a private, remote island that was scheduled to start that very day.

At that moment, Wyler saw a dark blue minivan pull up to the curb in front of the building. Bell waved from the driver's seat, and Wyler got up and went outside to meet him.

"Good morning!" Bell said, as Wyler pulled open the passenger door of the van. He was about to climb in when he noticed a woman sitting in the van directly behind Bell.

"Hi, I'm Laura. Jason's wife!" the woman said with a smile and a wave. A child's car seat was buckled to the seat next to her, and she was feeding a young toddler Cheerios from a plastic sandwich bag. Behind her, in the back row of the van, sat two young boys.

"The whole family decided to come," announced Bell with a bemused grin. The shock of encountering Bell's family froze Wyler halfway into the van. His brain searched for an acceptable excuse for backing out, but he wasn't fast enough.

"Dad, I need to go to the bathroom!" came a voice from the far back.

A few minutes later, Nora Maitland opened the door to her apartment to find Wyler, Bell, and one of Bell's sons standing in the hallway.

"Well, who's this?" Nora asked, crouching down excitedly to greet the boy.

"This is Henry," answered Bell. "And he's wondering if he could use the bathroom."

"Of course. Come on in, young man."

Henry raced in, and Nora followed, leaving Wyler and Bell to wait together in the marble foyer. Wyler saw Bell's eyes examine the bubbling water feature, then do a full sweep of the apartment.

"Beautiful place," he said to fill the silence. And then, after another moment, "We told them to go before we left. But you know kids that age."

"How old is he?" asked Wyler.

"Henry is ten. Will is twelve. And Clara, our daughter, is eighteen months. We thought we were done, but she surprised us."

It had been an uncomfortably silent elevator ride up, with Wyler unable to mask his annoyance at the situation. Bell bringing his family seemed a tone-deaf thing to do, and since Wyler couldn't think of a way to back out gracefully, he was now trapped in what would probably be a nightmare car ride, culminating in a fruitless waste of time.

"I'm sorry about bringing the family," Bell said. "I wasn't planning to, but when they heard I was going to up to Palmyra, they kind of went bananas and begged to come."

Wyler's only response was a polite smile that did little to hide the hostility he was feeling.

"Do you have any kids?"

"I have a son. He's eleven."

The night before, Wyler had gotten in late, but Gabe was still up when he stuck his head in the room to check on him. Gabe had been in the middle of a video game and hadn't even turned around. When he informed Gabe he was going upstate the next day, he had not gone bananas and had not begged to come.

Just then, Wyler had an unexpected thought and turned to Bell.

"Is there room in the van for one more?" he asked.

A short time later, the Bell family minivan was on I-87, heading north toward Albany, and Gabe Wyler was in the far back seat, sandwiched between Bell's two sons. All three were furiously pounding on handheld game devices, talking a mile a minute in their own gaming language. Gabe had surprised Wyler by agreeing to come on the trip, but he insisted on bringing his portable game console. Wyler had tried to convince him not to bring the device, fearing he would just use it as an excuse to isolate and not interact with the other boys, but for Gabe, the issue was a dealbreaker. He said he wouldn't go without it and Wyler, sensing the whole idea was about to blow up, relented. When they got to the van, it turned out that both Henry and Will had the same device, and now all three were connected to the same game and playing together like old friends. Wyler was never more grateful for losing a stand-off with Gabe.

During the first hour of the trip, as they fought their way out of Manhattan through streets and bridges clogged with New Yorkers starting weekend getaways, Jason's wife Laura asked Wyler lots of questions about his career in law enforcement. He ended up sharing a few good war stories from his early days on the job, ones that weren't too gruesome. Bell listened with one ear while negotiating traffic, but Laura seemed utterly fascinated, reacting with shock, alarm, and laughter at all the right points.

When they reached the Thruway, she had already asked about his parents, his siblings, his childhood, and what it was like to grow up in New York. She seemed genuinely interested in his family and background, but tactfully avoided any questions that might brush up against his marital history or situation. Wyler found Bell's wife both pleasant and attractive. She had long chestnut hair styled straight and simple, and dark eyebrows that arched over big brown eyes. She wore a gray top, jeans, and sneakers, and her pale face seemed to have a friendly glow that persisted in spite of being in haggard, mom mode all the time.

The baby started fussing outside of New Paltz, and they stopped at a rest area that had a gas station, convenience store, and a few fast-food choices. Laura carried the baby in to change a diaper, and everyone else came along to stretch. It was too early for lunch, but Wyler bought snacks and drinks for everyone and before they left, he paid to fill the tank. He made it clear to Bell that the entire trip was on him and he wouldn't debate the point.

When they got back on the road, Bell asked Laura to put on a movie for the boys. It took several minutes of noisy negotiation before they finally settled on one of the *Kung Fu Panda* movies. Wyler was impressed at how Laura handled the kids, with firmness that never crossed the line into anger. Once all three boys had headphones on and were staring quietly at the tiny screen hanging down from the roof of the van, Bell began speaking.

"So, I called a colleague of mine last night who lives in Utah. I don't know him that well, but we met at a conference once and I remember him mentioning at dinner one night that his daughter had gotten mixed up with the Mormon Evidence Project. She was one of the ones who went down to Honduras."

"Did she…?" Wyler asked carefully.

"Yes, she was killed, along with the others," Bell replied, gravely.

"Who was it?" asked Laura from the back.

"John Wooten. His daughter Michelle was nineteen."

"Oh no," said Laura, her hand coming to her mouth. Wyler wasn't sure if she knew the family or was just horrified in general.

"It was heartbreaking talking to him. It's been five years, but he and his wife are still torn up about it, of course. They begged her not to go."

"How did she get involved in the group in the first place?" asked Wyler.

"I asked him that. He told me she had been a student at the University of Utah studying anthropology, and this group, the

Mormon Evidence Project, had somehow gotten permission from the Honduran government for an expedition. Apparently it's not easy to do. I guess they really restrict permits for archeological digs and expeditions in certain areas, for safety reasons because of the drug cartels, but also because it's politically controversial to let outsiders come in—concerns about their cultural heritage being exploited. Anyway, somehow this group got permission, and they were looking for students to go on this expedition. They put ads in student newspapers at colleges all over Utah. It was this exciting opportunity. 'Come search for archeological evidence of the Book of Mormon. All expenses paid.' His daughter saw it as a way to get valuable field experience."

"If it was such an amazing opportunity, why did your friend beg her not go?"

"Well, the Church opposed the expedition and warned people not to participate in the project."

"Why would the Church oppose it? Wasn't the purpose of the expedition to support your church's beliefs?"

"Well, like I said yesterday, the Church has no official stance on the geography of the Book of Mormon and where it took place. And there was also the safety issue. To be honest, I don't really know why the Church came out so strongly against it. But they did, and it turns out they were right, unfortunately."

There was an explosion of laughter from the back seat at something in the movie. Wyler glanced back and saw Gabe chuckling as Henry and Will laughed hysterically on either side of him. He would take that chuckle any day of the week. He noticed the baby had fallen asleep in her car seat and that Laura's head was leaned back, her eyes blinking with sleepiness.

"Did you happen to ask your friend about Scottie Hibble?" Wyler asked quietly as he turned back around.

"Yes," Bell responded, growing animated, "and that was the most interesting part."

"What did he say?"

"Well, a lot of the parents of the kids that were killed on the expedition have stayed in touch with each other over the years, like a support group. At least that's how it started. A few of the parents in this group tried to look into what happened down there, to find out more information. They kind of launched their own investigation. Well, some of these parents are convinced that it wasn't a drug cartel at all, that there was something else going on and that the Honduran government and the company behind the expedition are lying about what really happened. John—my friend—said it's caused a real rift in the group. Most of the other parents think that the ones who believe this are just conspiracy nuts needing an outlet for their anger and grief."

"What does your friend think?"

"He's not so sure." Bell's tone insinuated darker possibilities. "He's heard what these people have to say—the group of parents that have been investigating on their own—and he said that they have uncovered some troubling things."

Wyler turned from Bell and stared ahead at the road, taking a moment to absorb this information and explore the possible implications.

"What does this have to do with Scottie Hibble?" he said, interrupting his own thoughts and turning back to Bell.

"I was getting to that. So, I told my friend John about you, that you were an ex-police detective investigating something involving this guy, Scottie Hibble. I didn't give him any details, which was easy since I don't know any. It turns out that Scottie Hibble is at the center of this conspiracy theory. According to John, when this first happened, everyone really rallied around this kid Hibble. He was considered a hero, the only survivor of the massacre, the kid who walked through the jungle for days to get help, that kind of thing. But now, the parents who have been pushing the investigation believe that he was somehow involved in what happened."

Bell glanced sideways at Wyler, as if to gauge his reaction.

"Involved in what way?"

"He wasn't really sure. He hasn't been active in the group in a while. He and his wife stopped participating when these two factions started fighting with each other."

Wyler tried to picture a group of grieving parents breaking into warring factions. Sad, but not surprising these days.

"I would really like to speak to some of these parents, the ones who think Scottie Hibble was involved in that massacre."

"I thought you would say that," said Bell with a sly grin. "I told that to John, that you would probably want to speak to some of the parents. He's going to contact the ring leaders of the conspiracy group. He thinks that for sure they will want to talk to you, because they haven't been able to get anyone interested in the case, but he just wants to check with them first before giving out their information. He's going to try to reach them today, and he said he would call me on my cell as soon as he speaks to them."

Wyler was momentarily speechless. This unexperienced civilian had behaved like a professional investigator. He had followed a lead, gotten vital, relevant information, and plotted the logical next step. Wyler suddenly felt guilty about being angry with Bell earlier.

"I'm impressed," Wyler finally said. "I mean it. I'm very impressed."

After an interlude where no one said anything for a while, Bell finally broke the silence. "It's hard to believe this boy could be involved in what happened down there," he said, his tone subdued. "What was he, eighteen or nineteen years old? How could a kid his age do something like that?"

Wyler thought the comment was naïve, but probably understandable given Bell's experiences. "You may be right. I hope you are," was Wyler's response, but inside he wasn't sure he meant it. He wanted Scottie Hibble brought to justice, and unlike Bell he had no allusions about what people were capable of at any age. He thought of the Willis brothers and what they had done to their family. He thought of Eric Harris and Dylan Klebold. Wyler himself had been in Tel-Aviv several years ago and saw firsthand the bloody aftermath of an explosion on a public bus triggered by a suicide bomber who had been fourteen years old.

They continued on in silence as Wyler stared out the passenger window. He felt his pulse quicken as his thoughts began to race. He was suddenly back in the hunt, with a new, potentially promising avenue of inquiry to pursue, and, to his surprise, he had Jason Bell to thank for it.

CHAPTER 23

They veered west on I-90 near Albany, and by the time they were approaching Utica, everyone was ready for another bathroom break and lunch. They found a McDonald's and decided to sit at two tables, one for the kids and one for the adults and the baby.

"So, Detective," Wyler addressed Bell as they unbagged their food. "How would you like to be officially read into the case?"

"What does that mean?" asked Laura, a little too excited.

"Being read into a case means you get fully briefed on all facts of the case and the status of the investigation. You're officially on the inside, up to date and in the know."

"Can you do that?" asked Bell, cautiously.

"I can do whatever I want," said Wyler. "I'm not a cop anymore, remember? Besides, I think you've earned it."

As the three of them ate, Wyler walked both Bell and his wife step by step through the events of the past week. As he spoke, his voice was calm and even. He recounted events that were, at times, shocking and bizarre, with an almost clinical detachment. He shared not only the facts, but what he thought they meant, or might mean. The summary was as thorough and meticulous as any report he had given a lieutenant or precinct captain. Hearing a true crime story told in real time by an active participant was obviously a unique experience for the Bells, and they listened in awed silence, riveted by every detail. When he got to the attack on the subway platform, Laura's mouth dropped open and she reflexively put her hand on Wyler's forearm, as if trying to protect him. When he told them about Ashley Lang's death, Jason Bell shook his head slowly as his face tightened with anger. When he finished, they were all silent for a bit.

"How did Scottie Bell know that Peter Lisonbee even had this gemstone?" Laura finally asked. "You said the family had kept it a secret."

"That's a very good question, and I don't have the answer. My mother-in-law has a theory about that." After taking a bite of his chicken sandwich, Wyler told them Nora Maitland's theory that, in seeking to sell the stone, Peter Lisonbee had violated his family's pact with God, forfeiting divine protection and somehow alerting dark, supernatural forces to the stone's existence. His tone was light and dismissive, but both Bell's seemed to take the theory seriously, nodding gravely as he spoke.

"What I don't understand is why Scottie Hibble wants the stone in the first place," said Bell. "You said yourself he's rich, so it's probably not the money. And it's not like he could use the stone to do anything. If the story is true, and this is a Urim and Thummim stone, that means it was consecrated by God, to be used for a divine purpose. It's not like anyone can just pick up one of these stones and start tapping into its power. It doesn't work that way."

These questions hung in the air unanswered as they cleared debris off both tables and got back on the road. It was almost 3:00 p.m. when the party finally reached Palmyra. They passed a sign identifying the small rural town as the historical birthplace of the Church of Jesus Christ of Latter-day Saints. Wyler had lived in New York his whole life but had never heard of the city.

Their first stop was the Hill Cumorah, the place where, according to Bell, the angel Moroni had buried the ancient metal plates that Joseph Smith eventually translated into the Book of Mormon. The hill was a large, grass-covered mound over a hundred feet tall. There was a small parking lot and a visitor's center next to the hill, and an immense, flat meadow directly in front of it. As soon as they parked, the boys exploded out the car and began running off the energy pent up from the long car ride.

Wyler walked beside Bell, asking questions, as Bell pushed the stroller and tried to give Wyler a basic overview of the things that had happened here. Laura and the boys climbed the front slope of the hill to the top, where a tall stone monument shaped like an obelisk held a golden statue of an angel identical to the one perched on top of the Mormon church in Manhattan he had seen the night before.

It was a warm, clear summer day, and a diverse cross section of visitors were scattered about walking, lying in the grass, and posing for pictures. The place seemed to be both a location of spiritual importance to the faithful and a tourist spot that attracted curious outsiders. Wyler heard some foreign languages being spoken and wondered if people had traveled from other countries to visit this small, nondescript hill, a place in his own home state he hadn't even known existed two days ago.

Wyler's phone rang and, seeing the international number, he excused himself and stepped away to take the call. It was Rollie Sterling, the police chief from the Bahamas, with an update on Ashley Lang. Wyler listened carefully, walking alone in slow circles. After hearing Sterling's news, Wyler suggested a course of action, which Sterling agreed to follow.

After the call from Sterling, Wyler caught up with the others inside the visitor's center next to the hill. They spent some time browsing displays, exhibits, and dioramas that explained significant events in Mormon history that had occurred in the region.

Wyler learned that, along with the Book of Mormon, the Urim and Thummim stones possessed by Joseph Smith had also been recovered from the hill.

At one point, Wyler asked Bell how the translation process using the stones had worked. "Did he look through them like an eyepiece?"

Bell admitted he wasn't entirely sure himself, and that there were different theories among Church historians and scholars on how it was actually done.

After the Hill Cumorah, they drove a few miles north to another Church historical site, the boyhood home of the founder of the Mormon church, Joseph Smith. Here, they filed into a crowded welcome center with about twenty other people who had arrived at roughly the same time. They were welcomed enthusiastically by a kindly white-haired couple wearing black name badges, and the man gave a brief orientation that lasted about ten minutes. Unfortunately, he spoke so softly that Wyler, all the way in the back, couldn't hear a word. Even so, Wyler saw that he spoke with deep conviction, his eyes watering with emotion toward the end of his spiel.

As they were leaving the welcome center, Bell's cellphone rang, and he peeled off to take the call while the rest of them continued to explore the Smith homestead. There were several structures on the property that had been preserved or restored, including a log cabin where the Smith family had first lived, and a larger frame house built later. Wyler noticed a steady stream of foot traffic walking along a dirt path leading to a forested area adjacent to the farm, and he asked Laura about it. The forest, she explained, was referred to by Church members as the Sacred Grove. There, Joseph Smith had been visited by God and Jesus Christ when he was fourteen years old. "It's what we call the First Vision," she added.

Laura went off to check on the boys who were huddled

around some exciting discovery in the dirt, leaving Wyler temporarily alone. He stood for a bit, observing the different people walking to and from the large grove of trees. There were individuals walking alone in contemplative reflection; there were couples of all ages, many holding hands; there were family groups of different sizes; and there was one troop of about thirty teenagers all wearing the same light blue t-shirt, obviously part of some organized excursion. Most of the people were white, but not all. Wyler saw Black, Latino, and Asian people, and other nationalities as well. He had always thought of Mormonism as a provincial religion primarily confined to western states like Utah, so the broad mix of races and cultures was an interesting surprise.

Wyler thought of other holy sites that existed in the world, such as the Western Wall of the Temple Mount in Jerusalem and the Great Mosque in Mecca, both of which he had been to personally. There was also the tree in India—Wyler couldn't remember the name—where the Buddha was said to have sat for many weeks in meditation until he obtained enlightenment. Believers and seekers from all over the world made pilgrimages to these places to demonstrate devotion, fortify their faith, and commune with a higher power. From what he could see, this remote forest on the outskirts of a small town in upstate New York held a similar sacred significance for many people.

Although Wyler found the phenomenon interesting, so far he hadn't learned anything he thought might help his investigation of Scottie Hibble, the stolen gemstone, and the deaths of Peter Lisonbee and Ashley Lang.

Bell finally caught up to him, looking like he had good news. "That was John Wooten," he said, waving his cell phone like a trophy. "He spoke to the couple I told you about, and they are really anxious to talk to you."

"That's great," said Wyler.

"John gave the couple my email address, and they are going to set up a Zoom meeting and send me a link."

"When?"

"I told John you'd want to talk to them right away. Tonight if possible."

"That's fantastic."

"And don't worry, my laptop is in the van."

From there, they drove to the downtown area of Palmyra, a small town with an old Americana charm that reminded Wyler of Mayberry from *The Andy Griffith Show*. There were other historical sites to see there, such as the printing press where the Book of Mormon was originally printed, but Wyler demurred, and the Bells didn't push the issue. Everyone was a bit worn out by that point, so they decided to just get ice cream.

As they sat at a concrete picnic table outside a local creamery eating some of the best ice cream Wyler had ever tasted, Bell checked the email on his phone and announced that he had gotten the Zoom link.

"What time do they want to meet?"

It took Bell a few minutes to decipher this part of the message, but finally he declared, "It's for 9:00 o'clock our time, tonight. The invitation is from Ron Ridgeway. That's the name John gave me."

On the drive up, Wyler had booked two rooms at the Double-Tree in Rochester, and after finishing their ice cream, they got back on I-90 heading west. They stopped briefly at a Target to buy a bathing suit for Gabe, then checked into the hotel. Bell tried to insist on paying for his family's room, but Wyler cut him off before he even got started. Dinner plans were discussed in the lobby before they went up to their rooms, but no one was hungry yet and the boys were more interested in swimming than eating.

An hour later, Wyler and Bell were seated around a glass table by the hotel's indoor pool, watching the boys as they swam and played. Laura had on a suit as well and was moving Baby Clara slowly around the shallow end in a round inflatable seat as she clapped her hands on the water and screamed with ecstasy. The baby's loud squeals echoed off the cavernous walls, and soon the boys came over to join the fun. Will and Henry begged their mom to let them take care of the baby on their own, and after stern warnings about staying in the shallow end, she left the pool and joined her husband and Wyler by the side of the pool.

"It's wonderful how they're getting along," Laura said as she wiped her face with a hotel towel, never taking her eyes off Clara.

Wyler watched as the three boys took turns pushing the baby back and forth to each other in a slow-motion game of catch. Gabe seemed to be enjoying the baby's excitement as much as her own brothers. "It's nice to see him having fun," Wyler said.

"He seems like a wonderful kid."

"He hasn't made many friends recently," Wyler added, letting a note of sadness creep into his voice. "He's been through a lot this past year."

"Aaron, where's Gabe's mother?" Laura asked carefully.

"Laura," Bell interjected.

"It's okay," said Wyler. And then, after a pause, "My wife, Gabe's mother, died a year ago. She committed suicide." After he said it, he looked squarely at each of them. It was a defiant gesture, subconsciously intended to show he accepted the reality of what happened and that he was dealing with it.

"I'm so sorry, Aaron," said Bell, quietly.

"Jessica was a pediatric oncologist. She treated children with cancer. Her father had died of pancreatic cancer when she was fifteen , so she decided to become a doctor. She really was an amazing woman."

"Not too hard, Will!" Laura yelled suddenly to the boys, who were pushing the baby faster while spinning her inflatable chair. "I'm so sorry, please go on," she said apologetically, leaning in to give Wyler her full attention.

"Pediatric oncology can be a very challenging profession, emotionally," Wyler continued. "Jessica used to complain all the time that all the training doctors receive relating to death focuses on adults, not children. We're experts at helping adults die, at providing hospice and end-of-life care, but no one teaches you how to handle the emotional and psychological issues involved when a child is dying. I mean, how and when do you tell a child that he or she is going to die? How much do you involve them? Jessica felt that children should participate as much as possible in discussions and decisions about their care, even about their own death. Children have goodbyes to say, just like adults, she used to say."

"She sounds like an incredible doctor," said Bell.

"She was one of the top pediatric oncologists in New York," Wyler said with obvious pride. "She had that reputation, but that meant she also got a lot of the toughest cases. People came from all over the country looking for hope, a lifeline for their child. Unfortunately, there usually wasn't a lifeline to give. It ate away at her, having to deal all the time with dying kids and their families. It's hard enough to deal with death when it's an adult, but having to watch children suffer and waste away, getting weaker and weaker, day after day, ravaged by a disease you're powerless to stop, it takes a toll. And she was a perfectionist, like many doctors are. It's tough being a perfectionist when you specialize in treating a disease with no real cure. She took every death personally."

"She sounds like someone with great compassion," said Laura, her eyes glistening.

"I knew she was struggling," Wyler continued, staring off into space as he spoke. "I could see it. But I didn't think it was depression or anything like that. I thought it was just normal professional burnout caused by stress and overwork. Maybe that's all it was at first. But it grew into something worse over time. Kind of like a cancer." Wyler shot them both an awkward, gallows humor grin, but they ignored it and waited for him to continue.

"Depression is actually pretty common with doctors, but they almost never seek help. Doctors are trained not to show weakness. And there's a stigma in the medical profession about mental health issues. You can get labeled quickly and derail your career by admitting you're struggling and need help, so they hide it. It's ironic."

Wyler paused here, and a few moments passed where no one spoke. "Unfortunately, I didn't help much. We had a good marriage. We didn't fight. We loved each other very much. But we both had highly demanding careers, and I was gone a lot. I couldn't talk about my work. I couldn't share it with her, and so this distance grew between us. I didn't see how bad things were getting."

Wyler turned toward the pool and was silent for a moment. He needed to summon the strength to continue, to excavate a memory that, though not old, had been buried deep.

"I wasn't even in the country when it happened," he continued, in a dull monotone. "I was in the Philippines. Two bombs had gone off in a cathedral there. Twenty-two people were killed and over a hundred were injured. We suspected an Islamic terrorist group called Abu Sayyaf was behind the attack. They had an active cell in New York, so I went there to participate in the investigation. I got a call from Jessica's mother. She had taken a helium tank from the hospital. Gabe had come home from school and found her. She had a plastic bag on her head and the helium running into the bag through a tube."

Wyler didn't realize he was crying until he felt the warm tears dripping from his face onto his hands.

"So, I retired from the force and decided to become a full-time dad, at least for now. I'm not sure I'm doing much good, to be honest. There seems to be a wall there that I just can't get around.

It's kind of always been there, to be honest, so I don't know how much of it is related to what happened. I don't know if he blames me or not. He's been seeing a therapist, but who knows if that's helping."

Laura reached over and squeezed Wyler's hand, caressing it gently.

"He probably just needs time," Bell said softly. "You both do."

CHAPTER 24

Wyler and Bell sat next to each other in Wyler's hotel room staring at Bell's laptop. It was a few minutes before 9:00 p.m., and since the Ridgeways hadn't logged into the meeting yet, all they saw was a video selfie of themselves sitting on the sofa. Bell had set up the computer for Wyler and was about to leave when Wyler invited him to stay and participate. Everyone else was in the Bells' room, eating pizzas that had been ordered and watching a movie.

"What did you say their names were?" asked Wyler.

"Ron and Cheryl Ridgeway."

"Do you know where they live?"

"John said they're from Blackfoot, Idaho."

"When they come on, why don't you get things started, since the connection was with your friend?"

Just then, the screen split into two windows as the image of Wyler and Bell shrunk and was placed next to a new window, a black box with "Ron Ridgeway" written in white letters. The room static of a live audio feed kicked in right away.

"You have to turn on the camera," a female voice said.

"Hello, Brother and Sister Ridgeway?" said Bell, leaning forward.

"Hello!" answered a deep male voice from behind the black box.

After some back and forth and fussing about the camera, the black box was replaced by an image of an older couple sitting next to each other in what looked like a master bedroom.

"We can see you now," Bell said.

The man was in his late fifties or early sixties. He had a thin face, a bald head, and wore older eyeglasses with a double bridge over the nose. The woman next to him seemed the same age and wore heavy makeup, including bright red lipstick. She had a hairdo bigger than her head, styled upward like a silver tornado.

"Brother and Sister Ridgeway, my name is Jason Bell. I'm a friend and colleague of John Wooten."

"Yes, he told us," the man answered.

"First of all, we want to thank you for being willing to talk to us."

"We're the ones who are thankful to you," said the woman, placing both hands over her heart. "We've been praying someone would take an interest in this."

"We were very excited when John called us," the man added.

"Mr. and Mrs. Ridgeway," Wyler began.

"It's Ron and Cheryl," the man interrupted.

"Ron and Cheryl, my name is Aaron Wyler."

"You're the detective." Ron Ridgeway said it as a statement, not a question.

"Yes, I was a detective with the New York City Police Department for over fifteen years, but I'm retired now."

"We're just so grateful that someone is looking into this," said Cheryl Ridgeway, her voice choked with a sudden burst of emotion as tears filled her eyes. Her husband placed his hand behind her as if to steady her, then continued speaking.

"We've spoken to the American consulate in Tegucigalpa; the national police of Honduras which is like their FBI; we've spoken to the state department in Washington—we've *been* to Washington; we've spoken to our congressman, the FBI. No one wants to do anything about what happened."

"Steven was such a wonderful boy," the wife added, wiping the tears away with a tissue. "They all were. All those kids."

"You have to understand, this has been our whole life these past few years."

"Mr. and Mrs. Ridgeway—Ron and Cheryl—first of all, I want to tell you how sorry I am about what happened to your son. I think the easiest way to do this would be for me to ask you questions, and then you try to answer them. Would that be okay?"

"Whatever you think is best. We are here to help," said Ron Ridgeway, striking a businesslike tone.

"Could you tell me how Steven got involved in the Mormon Evidence Project?"

"He was a graduate student in archeology at Texas A&M. They have one of the best programs in the country. That's what he always wanted to be, ever since he was a kid and saw those Indiana Jones movies. Also, he had served his mission in Honduras, so when he heard about this –"

"The Honduras San Pedro Sula West Mission," Cheryl Ridgeway interjected.

"Yes, so when he heard about this, about this project, he really wanted to be a part of it. Both for the archeology and for a chance to get back to Honduras."

"So he had been to Honduras before this expedition?" asked Wyler.

"Oh yes, he had lived there for two years as a missionary. He really came to love Honduras and the Honduran people during the two years he served there."

"He was one of the most experienced people on that expedition," Cheryl Ridgeway added. "A lot of the ones they recruited were just kids, but Steven was a graduate student. He had been on other digs here in the U.S. and one in Mexico. He was a real leader. And he knew almost from the beginning that something was wrong down there."

"What do you mean he knew something was wrong? What, exactly, was wrong?"

"It was kind of a bait and switch, to be honest with you," Ron Ridgeway continued. "This group, they actively recruited a lot of kids from our Church, from all over the country. They sold the whole project as a way to search out the historical sites talked about in the Book of Mormon. They had these maps on their website claiming to show places where things in the Book of Mormon might have happened, you know, like here is where the waters of Mormon are, and here is the city of Zarahemla, and here is the Temple of Nephi. These kids were excited. They thought it was going to be a spiritual experience, something to strengthen their testimonies."

Wyler nodded. He didn't know the jargon, but he got the gist.

"Actually, it started out okay. When they first got to Honduras, they were at this nice hotel in a city called Catacamas. That was their launching off point. Everyone was very excited. The man who was the head of the whole project was there to greet them. His name was Dordevic."

"Dordevic? Do you know his first name?"

"No, Steven said everyone just called him Mr. Dordevic. Anyway, this Dordevic guy could not have been nicer to the kids when they arrived. He was so excited to have them there, and the hotel was really fancy. The night before the start of the expedition, he rented a private room in this expensive restaurant and they had this big banquet. At the banquet, he explained that he had studied all the world's religions and although he wasn't a member of our Church, he had always been fascinated by Mormonism. He said he had read the Book of Mormon many times and he was excited to prove to the world that it was true. He even invited the kids who were there to share their testimonies. He said he loved listening to Latter-day Saints share their testimonies. Steven said he was an odd, eccentric sort of character. He had long white hair, a black mustache, a white goatee, and big, wild eyes. And he was giant, at least seven feet tall and over 300 pounds, Steven said."

Wyler thought about this. Something about the statement seem to tickle a memory or thought in the trunk of his mind, but he pushed it aside for the moment.

"So, there were no signs of trouble at the hotel. When did that change?"

"It changed when they left for the archeological site. Dordevic stayed at the hotel, and the group was led in the field by these two other men."

"Where was the actual site?" asked Wyler.

"That's one of the first things that Steven thought was strange. You see, from Catacamas, they went by helicopter to a place called Mosquitia, this big, jungle area on the eastern slope of Honduras that runs down into Nicaragua—totally cut off from civilization."

"Is that what concerned Steven, that is was so remote?"

"No, not at all. That's what they all expected. They knew they'd be going deep into unexplored territory. But Steven had studied the maps and the locations provided by the organization before going on the trip, and the site that they went to was not on any of those maps. It didn't match up with any of the sites they were told they would be exploring. Steven tried to ask about that, and they just kind of brushed him off, told him that they had some new information or something. And once they were in the jungle, these two guys started acting really badly. They were smoking, drinking, using really bad language, that kind of thing. It made the kids really uncomfortable. And Steven realized pretty quickly that these guys were not even archeologists. They were supposed to be in charge, but they didn't know even the basic things about archeological research. They didn't follow any of the normal rules and procedures for an expedition like this. That really upset Steven. The way these guys talked and acted, Steven suspected they were raiders, you know, people who loot archeological sites and sell artifacts on the black market."

"And they treated the kids like slaves," added Cheryl Ridgeway.

"That's right. Look, all these kids knew it would be hard, grueling work, that's what they signed up for, but they also thought it would be a learning experience. But no one was learning anything. They made the kids work all day long, hacking through the jungle, all without telling them anything about what they were looking for. They had their own maps, which they wouldn't show anyone. And then at night, these guys would sit around the campsite getting drunk and acting obnoxious. The kids were scared of them."

"And there was nothing that any of the kids could do about it at that point," said Mrs. Ridgeway. "They were so deep in the jungle that they became trapped there. None of their cellphones worked, and there were no roads in or out of the place. A couple of kids wanted to leave, but the only way to leave would have been by helicopter, and these guys said they didn't have the fuel for the extra trip."

"Excuse me for asking this, Mr. and Mrs. Ridgeway, but how do you know all of this? If none of the kids could talk by phone, and then...after what happened...I'm just wondering how you have all this information."

The Ridgeways exchanged a look, then Cheryl Ridgeway stood up and left the room.

"You're right," the husband began. "We never would have known any of this, except for a boy named Doug McBride. He was one of the kids on the expedition. He got bitten by a snake, a fer-de-lance, one of the most poisonous snakes down there. This boy had to be evacuated by helicopter before the tragedy happened."

"So you spoke to this boy?"

"No, he died at a hospital in Tegucigalpa a few days later. But before he left the jungle, Steven secretly gave the McBride boy his journal. Steven always kept a detailed journal when he was on any kind of research project, and he gave the journal to the McBride boy and made him promise to mail it to us."

"Steven knew that something bad was going to happen," Mrs. Ridgeway added as she came back into the room, waving a book in her hand. "He didn't think he would be coming back." She sat down and held the book up to the camera until it filled the whole screen. It was a leather-bound journal closed by a brown strap. The cover was faded and sun blotched.

"So, this boy mailed the journal to you from a hospital in Honduras?"

"Either that or he got someone else to do it, maybe a nurse or something," the husband continued. "To this day we don't know for sure. We didn't get it till six months after Steven and the others were killed. It just showed up in our mailbox one day. You can imagine how we reacted."

"That's how the mail is down there," Mrs. Ridgeway added. "When Steven was on his mission, sometimes we'd get a letter from him months after he mailed it. Some we never got."

Wyler tried to imagine the shock of opening the mailbox and finding an unexpected package from your dead son.

"We had accepted the story of what happened just like everyone else. But then, when we read Steven's journal, we realized that there was more to the story than we had been told."

"So, what did he say that makes you think the killing was not the work of one of the cartels, like the authorities say?"

"Lots of things. For one thing, they found something down there."

"What do you mean? What did they find?"

"We don't know for sure, and neither did Steven. But in his journal, he said these guys leading the expedition seemed to be looking for something specific. They were not interested in mapping or exploring the area as an archeological site. They ignored lots of things that a normal expedition would have been interested in."

"Like what?"

"Well, at one point they came upon several giant mounds of dirt that seemed to be man-made, surrounding a large, flat area bordered by stones. Steven said it looked like the remains of a small city or plaza, one that had been completely swallowed up by the jungle and hadn't been seen in hundreds of years. Steven said it was potentially a major discovery, but they weren't allowed to examine or explore the site. These guys weren't interested. It's like they had a treasure map, and they were just looking for the X."

"And they found the X?"

"When they got to this certain area in the jungle, the men made the kids spend several days clearing it. Then, they organized the kids into small groups and made them start digging all around the cleared area in random places. Steven said it made absolutely no sense from an archeological standpoint. It was like they were digging for buried treasure or something. Then, one of the groups found something."

"What was it?"

"Steven couldn't say for sure. He wasn't in the group that found it. The boy who sent the journal, Doug McBride, had been in the group that found it, but he only got a glimpse of it because as soon as this thing was discovered, they made all the kids back off and stop digging. They wouldn't let anyone near it. But this boy Doug told Steven it looked like a stone box, about four feet by four feet. The next day, Doug tried to sneak out in the middle of the night to get a better look at it. That's when he was bitten by the fer-de-lance. The boy's whole leg started to swell and rot right away. Steven and the others insisted that the boy needed to be evacuated immediately, but these two slime bags running the expedition refused. Then, the next morning, this Mr. Dordevic, the head of the project, showed up at the site in a helicopter, but he wasn't alone. According to Steven, he had two men with him with machine guns. Dordevic told them he had hired the men to protect the expedition, because of rumors of drug cartels in the area, but Steven didn't believe that."

"Why not?"

"He said this guy Dordevic acted totally different than he had been in the hotel. He ignored the kids, didn't speak to them. They tried to tell him what had been going on this whole time, what a nightmare it had been, but he didn't care. He didn't even care about the boy with the snakebite. He made the boy wait a whole day before allowing him to be flown out. By then, the boy's leg was so badly infected that he didn't have much of a chance. That's when Steven decided to send his journal with this boy and get it to us."

Wyler took a few moments to absorb and process all this. The couple waited and watched Wyler with eager expressions.

"This still doesn't explain why you are so sure that the killing wasn't a drug cartel, and why you think Scottie Hibble was involved."

"Scottie Hibble was just a bad kid," Cheryl Ridgeway said with undisguised contempt. "He got kicked out of SVU for violating the honor code."

"SVU?" asked Wyler.

"Southern Virginia University," explained Bell to Wyler. "It's a private college in Virginia that is unofficially affiliated with our Church. It's not owned and operated by the Church, like BYU, but most of the board members are Latter-day Saints, and the school aligns itself openly with the Church's values."

"We spoke to someone whose daughter was there the same time he was, and she said he got caught cheating. He also drank and did drugs. She thinks he even tried to sell drugs on campus." She said the last part in a quasi-whisper, like she was sharing classified intel.

"That doesn't make him a mass murderer," Wyler said.

"His whole story doesn't add up," Mr. Ridgeway took over. "He says this massacre occurred on August 14th. He says he was away from camp, that he ran and hid when he heard the gunshots. Then he says he walked through the jungle on foot, arriving at Brus Laguna two days later. That's totally impossible. Brus Laguna is a coastal town, hundreds of miles through thick jungle. It would have taken him at least a week on foot, and that's if he knew exactly where he was going, which he says he didn't."

"What are you suggesting?"

"We think he was taken to that city and dropped off just outside the village so he could stumble into town and play the part of the only survivor," Mrs. Ridgeway said.

"Taken by who?"

"The same people who killed our son and all those other kids."

"And then there's the discovery they made, this stone box," Ron Ridgeway continued. "When the authorities got to the site, the box was gone. There was nothing there but a bunch of empty holes."

"It could have been taken by the cartel," said Wyler. "You said yourself there's a lot of looting, and people sell artifacts on the black market."

"There was no cartel. Yes, Mosquitia is used as a route for illegal drug smuggling, but not the area where they were. The Honduran National Police admitted that there's too much swamp land in that part, that's why cartels usually bypass it."

"*Usually* bypass it. They could have gone that route. They could have stumbled unexpectedly upon the group."

"If that's true, then where is this Dordevic guy? And the two gunmen who were with him? What happened to them? Their bodies weren't found at the site. They were gone, along with the stone box and whatever was inside of it. And not only that—the whole Mormon Evidence Project seemed to just disappear overnight. We used to go on the website every day to check for updates on the expedition because Steven was out of contact. Well, their website was taken down on August 14th—the same day of the massacre, and a day before Scottie Hibble came out of the jungle. Why would they do that if they didn't know something had happened, and how would they know about it if they weren't involved?"

Wyler didn't have an answer, but the date a website was taken down seemed like a flimsy fact to hang a theory on.

"We've tried to pursue legal action against the Mormon Evidence Project, but all we could find out was that it's not a U.S. company or organization. It was set up in Nigeria, of all places. And now it's gone, and no one knows anything about it."

"It does sound like a shady organization," conceded Wyler. "And there are a lot of unanswered questions, but I'm not sure there's any real proof that this was some kind of conspiracy or that Scottie Hibble was directly involved."

"Read him the note," said Cheryl Ridgeway. Her husband opened the journal and removed a folded page of torn-out notebook paper.

"This was a note that Steven wrote to us that was in the journal when we got it." He unfolded the paper and began reading.

> Mom and Dad, I don't have much time to write this. One of the kids is being taken out of here by helicopter, and I'm going to give him this journal and your address and ask him to mail this to you. I'm doing this because I'm not sure if any

of us on this expedition will ever be coming back. You'll understand when you've read the journal. There are men here with machine guns now who say they are here to protect us, but I think they are here to make sure that no one ever finds out what was discovered here. Mom and Dad, remember what happened to Joseph Smith in the Sacred Grove right before the First Vision? When he first started to pray, he said an evil power suddenly came upon him unlike anything he had ever felt before. He said that he felt the presence of some actual evil being with incredible power. He thought he was going to be destroyed. I never really understood what he meant until a few days ago, when we found the box you will read about in this book. As soon as we unearthed it, an evil presence flowed into this part of the jungle. It's been here ever since. It feels tangible and real, like thick smoke or fog, even though you can't see it. Some of the other kids have felt it too. I hope, like Joseph Smith, we are saved by a pillar of light. But if something happens and I don't come back, I wanted you to have this book and know the full story. I love you. Please tell Hannah and Rachel and Tommy that I love them too. I've got to go now.

CHAPTER 25

After the Zoom meeting with the Ridgeways, Bell went back to his room, and a few minutes later, Gabe knocked on the door, back for the night.

"Did you have fun?" Wyler asked.

"Yeah," Gabe replied as he entered the room carrying a pizza box. "Mrs. Bell said I should bring this back for you in case you were hungry."

"Thanks."

The room was divided into a small family room area and another sleeping area with two queen beds. Gabe put the pizza box down by the TV and headed for the bathroom. Wyler opened the box and saw a half moon made up of slices from different pizzas, but he decided he wasn't hungry.

"The toothbrushes are in the bag by the sink," Wyler said through the bathroom door.

"Okay," came the reply after a pause.

Wyler plopped down in a chair to wait his turn. It had been a long day, he was feeling frustrated and mentally exhausted, and he wanted to go to bed. The interview with the Ridgeways had uncovered new information, some of it interesting, but overall it had been a disappointment. There was lots of suspicion and conjecture colored by the emotions of grieving parents, but no hard evidence, and no smoking gun implicating Scottie Hibble in anything other than some college hijinks. There was circumstantial evidence that something sordid, maybe even illegal, was going on during that expedition before they were killed, but Wyler wasn't convinced it had any bearing on the case at hand. Still, as he waited for the bathroom, he took out his phone, opened Google, and did a search for the name Dordevic. All the results focused on a college hockey player from the University of Minnesota. No help. Next he paired the name Dordevic with Mormon Evidence Project, but the results were an oil-and-water mishmash of the hockey player and the expedition, with no overlaps. An image search of Dordevic and Mormon Evidence Project generated pictures he had already seen the day before, with no one resembling Steven Ridgeway's description of the strange man. Whoever this guy was, he knew how to cover his cyber tracks. Before putting his phone away, he sent a quick text to Ray Shimura:

Background check—Dordevic (sp?). No first name.

Gabe came out of the bathroom, and Wyler got up and went in. They passed each other like two strangers on the street. When Wyler came out twenty minutes later, Gabe was already under the covers of the bed nearest the window, lying on his side with his back to Wyler. The room was dark except for two lamps extending from the wall between the beds. The one closest to Wyler's bed had been left on, and Wyler took it as an act of courtesy on his son's part. He stripped down to boxers and climbed into the other bed, but as soon as he did, Gabe flipped over onto his back, surprising Wyler by being wide awake. As Wyler arranged his pillows, Gabe laid on his back, staring up at the ceiling.

"So, what do you think of the Bell boys?" asked Wyler, hoping to spark something resembling a conversation between two human beings.

"They're cool," replied his son in a surprisingly light tone. "They invited me over."

"To their house?" asked Wyler, realizing the lameness of the question too late.

"Yeah."

"Where do they live?"

"Inwood. They live in an apartment, like we used to."

"Do you want to go?"

"Maybe," Gabe said, as if carefully weighing the pros and cons. "Where's Inwood?"

"It's a neighborhood at the northern tip of Manhattan, just below the Bronx."

"Oh."

"You've been there before. Remember when we went to the Cloisters?"

Gabe had to search his memory for a moment, then said, "That castle museum thing?"

"Yep, the castle museum thing. That's up near Inwood."

There was silence between the beds for a bit.

"When did they invite you to come over?"

"We didn't set a specific day or anything, they just said I should come hang out." And then, a moment later, "I think I'll go."

Wyler nodded casually. He didn't want Gabe to sense that his dad was more excited than he was.

"Did you invite them to our place?"

"No."

"Why not?"

"I don't know. I just didn't think of it."

Wyler turned on his side to face Gabe's bed. "Gabe, the house in Rhinebeck, that's your house as much as our apartment in the city used to be. You know that, right?"

Gabe didn't say anything for a few seconds. Then, just a quiet "Yeah."

"Don't you like the house?"

Gabe answered with a slight shoulder shrug. Wyler tried hard to interpret what his son was thinking and feeling, but as usual, he came up empty.

"Would you rather move back to Manhattan?"

"Rhinebeck's fine."

Suddenly and for the first time, Wyler began second guessing the decision to buy the house in Dutchess County and move out of Manhattan. At the time, he thought he was giving them both a fresh start. It never occurred to him that Gabe might not want a fresh start. Maybe what he had needed most was a sense of continuity, of sameness. But Wyler had ripped him from all that he knew and stranded him in an unfamiliar place. Thanks to Wyler, the boy was now a stranger in strange land, lost as well as motherless. At the moment, Wyler didn't have the physical or mental energy to bear the weight of these new self-recriminations, so he just reached up and turned out the light.

"Goodnight, son," he said.

With the lights out, Wyler took his phone off the nightstand and plugged in his wired earphones. He usually didn't use the earphones when he slept, but he didn't want to disturb Gabe. He tapped open an app on his phone that looked like an old-fashioned radio and began scrolling through options.

"What are you listening to?" asked Gabe, a voice in the dark.

Wyler popped the earphones out of his ears.

"You'll probably think it's silly," he said. "Sometimes I listen to old radio programs at night while I'm falling asleep." Wyler couldn't see Gabe's reaction, so he just continued. "In the old days, they didn't have television. They had radio. And people would gather around the radio and listen to shows, like they do with TV shows today. Only there weren't any pictures."

"Was this when you were a kid?"

"No, this was when your grandfather was a kid. When I was a kid, they had TV, but only a few channels. Not hundreds of channels like today. And no Netflix or YouTube."

"So, how did you get into listening to these old shows?"

Wyler turned on his side, and Gabe reciprocated so they were facing each other across the beds. Their faces were lit just barely by the faint glow of downtown Rochester sneaking through a slit in the closed curtains.

"Well, the truth is, I sometimes have a really hard time getting to sleep, and this helps me."

"Why can't you sleep?"

"Sometimes, when I lie down at night, my mind starts racing. My body's really tired, but my brain isn't, and it keeps thinking. Especially when I'm working on a case. I lie down, turn off the lights, but I can't turn off my brain. Instead of going to sleep, I just lay there, thinking a mile a minute, turning things over in my head."

"You mean like clues and stuff?"

"Yeah, sometimes. I went to a doctor years ago, before I met your mom, and he prescribed these pills to help me. But I never took them."

"Why not?"

"I don't know. I think I was worried that if I started to take them to help me sleep, eventually I would *have* to take them to sleep, and I didn't want to be dependent on them."

"You mean addicted?"

"Something like that. So anyway, I started looking for something to distract my mind when I was going to bed. I tried listening to music, but that just kept me awake. TV was no good, because of the light. And so one night, I was browsing online, and

I stumbled on a website with all these old-time radio programs posted, like from the 1930s and '40s. I remembered my dad and my grandpa talking about listening to these shows when they were growing up, so I put one on. Now I'm hooked."

"I think that's cool," said Gabe. "What kind of shows do you listen to?"

"All kinds. There's comedy shows, like Jack Benny and the Life of Riley. Scary shows, westerns, science fiction shows like Dimension X, even detective shows, like Philip Marlowe and The Shadow."

"What's The Shadow?"

"The Shadow is this detective who has the power to make himself invisible."

Gabe took a moment to think about that. "And listening to these shows helps you sleep?"

"It does. What happens is, I find that if I'm listening to one of these shows, my mind lets go of all the other thoughts that are swirling around in my brain, and I'm able to fall asleep."

Gabe thought about that for a bit.

"But don't you need to think about the case you're working on, to figure things out?"

"Not always. Sometimes it's better to stop thinking about a case, to take a break."

"What do you mean?"

"Well, like now, for example. I'm working on this case. And tonight, I just learned a lot of new information. But sometimes the best thing to do when you get new information is to force yourself not to think about it for a while. It's a trick I learned years ago. You just set the information aside and clear your head completely. Focus on something else. Then, you wait and see what aspects of the new information start creeping back into your subconscious mind. Doing that has helped me on some difficult cases."

For a few minutes neither of them spoke, but they both stayed on their sides, facing each other.

"Wait a minute," said Gabe, finally.

"What?"

"If you listen to these radio shows to fall asleep, don't you miss the end of the show?"

Wyler laughed. "Yes, a lot of the time I do, but it doesn't matter, because I'm asleep and that was the main point. A lot of the shows are kind of corny by today's standards anyway, so missing the end isn't a big deal. If it's something really good, I just finish it the next night."

There was another lull, and then Gabe said, "You like old things a lot, don't you?"

"What do you mean?"

"You're always watching old movies. The music you like is old. You listen to old radio shows."

Gabe's statement caught Wyler off guard. As obvious as it was now that Gabe mentioned it, the pattern had never occurred to him before. That fascinated him.

"I guess you're right."

"So, why do you like old stuff so much?"

Wyler considered the question carefully. He knew he could give a throw-away answer, like "old things are better," but he didn't want to do that. It was a surprisingly penetrating question, and he wanted to try to answer it, not just for Gabe, but for himself.

"I don't know, really," Wyler began, thinking out loud. "I got exposed to a lot of that stuff by my parents when I was growing up, so I always assumed that was why I liked it. But now that you ask, I think maybe it's more than that. Maybe it's because of the work I do. In my job, I have to deal with some really horrible things. I see a lot of violence and destruction, a lot of hate and anger and cruelty, and the pain and suffering it leaves behind. It can seem like, day in and day out, you're facing the very worst of humanity. Maybe I like older things because it allows me to escape into a more innocent time. Or at least pretend to escape. The truth is there's always been violence and cruelty in the world, but it seems like the art from old times was more focused on providing people an escape from that stuff. Today, it's more about imitating the worst things about the world instead of escaping from it."

As Wyler spoke, Gabe nodded slowly in an adult way, like a psychiatrist listening to a patient. Then, suddenly, he flipped over onto his back in sleeping position, and Wyler did the same.

"Dad?" he asked after a minute.

"Yes?"

"Did Mom listen to the shows with you at night?"

"Well, she was always there next to me in bed, but I don't think she listened very much. Your mom was always so tired by the time she laid down that she used to drop off to sleep right away. She told me once that doctors get really good at grabbing sleep when they can because they get so little of it. When she was a resident, she used to work eighty hours a week. A single shift could last thirty hours. Sometimes she'd be asleep before I even had the chance to say goodnight."

Wyler felt a surge of unexpected emotion, for the second time that day, and was grateful he had the cover of darkness this time to hide in.

"Dad?"

"Hmm?"

"Can I listen, too?"

"Of course," Wyler whispered. "What are you in the mood for?"

"Can you put on that one you said—The Shadow?"

Moments later, the staticky crackle of vintage lo-fi broadcasting pierced the quiet of the dark hotel room, and a tinny voice spoke with melodramatic spookiness, *"Who knows...what evil... lurks... in the hearts of men? The Shadow knows..."*

* * *

Wyler's eyes opened instantly and easily, as if he had just closed them moments ago. His body had no memory of sleep, and he felt no drowsiness or fatigue. Only vague outlines of shapes were visible in the unfamiliar darkness, and he was temporarily disorientated. The soft purr of rhythmic breathing coming from the other bed gave him back his bearings, like an auditory north star.

The red analog numbers on the clock radio next to the bed informed him it was 1:08 a.m. What had woken him? Had it been a noise or sound? He waited in the stillness, bracing for the sound to repeat and identify itself. But no sound came, and Wyler realized that it hadn't been a sound that had stirred him. It had been a thought. He sensed the presence of a thought, an idea, just out of reach, waiting for him behind his conscious perception, like a child playing hide and seek.

He sat up. He had been here before, and he knew not to force things. He had to let it happen. He waited. His head rotated slowly, an unaroused searchlight surveying the room. He was giving his conscious mind something mundane to do, leaving space for the unconscious to assert itself. As his eyes adjusted to the dark, outlines and shapes turned into objects: the chair in the corner, his clothes draped over the back; the pizza box by the TV; his son's body, sprawled crookedly on the bed, partially wrapped in a tangle of sheets and blankets.

And then, it happened. The mental fog dissipated, as if scattered by a sudden, gentle gust, and he saw it clearly. The thought that had awoken him.

He got up and started to get dressed.

CHAPTER 26

Wyler was surprised to see Bell already waiting for him on a leather sofa in the hotel lobby when he stepped off the elevator. Wyler had sent a text asking Bell to meet him in the lobby with his laptop. When Bell responded right away, Wyler assumed it was because he was a light sleeper. He didn't expect Bell to beat him down to the lobby.

"Were you still up?" asked Wyler as he sat in the chair nearest the sofa. It was the middle of the night, and the spacious lobby was completely deserted. The girl in charge of the front desk came out of a little side office when she heard the elevator, but she was gone again before Wyler sat down.

"Yes, I was." Bell seemed anxious about something.

"Is everything okay?" asked Wyler.

"Yes," replied Bell after hesitating briefly. Wyler sensed Bell had something on his mind, but he chose not to pursue it.

"Thanks for bringing the laptop. There's something I want to show you."

Bell logged in and handed him the laptop. Wyler navigated to his own email account and signed in. He scanned the inbox, searching for the email from Detective Rob Moretti.

"There's a video I want you to watch."

He found the email and double-clicked the attached video clip. A window opened up with playback controls at the bottom of the screen.

"This isn't the video of that suicide, is it?"

"It is, but it's not the actual death I want you to see."

Wyler used the computer's trackpad to search for a specific spot in the video.

"There was something about this video that stuck in my mind, something that bothered me. Bothered might even be too strong a word. Let's just say there was something unusual about it that I couldn't put my finger on. I've watched it a few times, but I could never figure out what kept drawing me back."

"And now you have?"

"Actually, it was something the Ridgeways said that put it together for me, but it was a delayed reaction."

Wyler positioned the laptop between them so they could both see the screen.

"This is almost four minutes after Peter Lisonbee jumped from his balcony. The kids were still filming. Now watch."

Wyler tapped a button and jerky, handheld footage began playing. The video showed the chaotic aftermath on the street just minutes after Peter Lisonbee's body had slammed into the pavement. A shocked crowd of pedestrians and onlookers formed a makeshift perimeter around the body on the sidewalk. Some people were screaming. Some were crying. Others were just gawking with morbid fascination. A couple of random guys were shouting orders, trying to take charge of the pandemonium before the authorities arrived. The camera was constantly moving, panning from left to right, trying to capture the scene. Either the person holding the phone or someone standing right next to him kept saying *"I can't believe it"* over and over. At one point, the glass double door entrance to Peter Lisonbee's apartment building was briefly visible on the right of the screen.

"There he is," said Wyler, pointing to a man exiting the apartment building.

"Who?"

"Mr. Dordevic," Wyler said, putting the words in verbal quotes.

Bell leaned forward to get a closer look, but the camera had already jerked away. He turned and looked at Wyler. "How do you know?"

"For one, he matches the physical description we heard last night. The long white hair, the two-tone beard. He's the right general age. But most importantly, remember what the Ridgeway boy said? He said Dordevic was a giant, almost seven feet tall."

"How can you tell how tall that guy is? He's only in the video for a few seconds."

"That's true. And it's usually very hard to judge someone's height on film. Bogart was pretty short, but you'd never guess it from watching his movies. Same with Stallone and Cruise."

"So what makes you think this guy is seven feet tall?"

"Watch the clip again." Wyler backed up the video a few seconds. "This time, keep your eye on the sculpture hanging in the lobby."

The video started again. They watched closely as the screen panned to the building entrance just as a middle-aged man with long white hair, a black mustache, and a white goatee left the building, his hands stuffed in the pockets of a dark overcoat. After clearing the doors, the man walked directly forward, then to the left, disappearing from the frame. In the lobby behind the man, a large modern art sculpture hung from the high ceiling. It was a giant mobile, made up of hundreds of multicolored shapes dangling from wires. The shapes hanging at the bottom of the sculpture were swirling about restlessly, colliding with each other as if reacting to some disturbance.

"Pieces of that sculpture are moving," said Bell.

"That's right," Wyler declared. "That moving sculpture is what lodged in my brain. There was no explanation for it, so my mind just held on to it, like a loose end."

"I'm not following you."

"I was in that same lobby a week ago. I walked right under that sculpture. I'm almost six feet tall and my head didn't get anywhere near it. A few seconds later, I saw a girl carrying a potted tree walk under the same sculpture. The tree brushed against the bottom of the thing, causing the exact same reaction we're seeing here, pieces moving and twisting. The tree, the way she was carrying it, was at least a foot taller than I was. I know because she walked right by me."

Bell was silent and thoughtful, his expression blank.

"So, why was that sculpture moving?" Wyler continued, walking Bell through his thought process. "The idea of a seven-foot-tall man never occurred to me, until we spoke to the Ridgeways tonight. It didn't actually click until twenty minutes ago, then it woke me up out of a dead sleep."

"Are you sure it wasn't a gust of wind or something?"

"There was no wind that night. That's obvious from other parts of the video. There's a pub with an Irish flag on a pole that is just hanging there, totally inert. But even if there was a sudden gust of wind when the door opened, it would have impacted the whole sculpture, not just those pieces at the very bottom. Something or someone at least seven feet tall bumped into that sculpture."

"How do you know it was him and not someone else, like the lady with the plant?"

"You can see when the camera first pans over that the lobby is completely empty. No one else is there. I'm guessing that anyone who was in that lobby ran out to see what happened as soon as Lisonbee's body hit the street. You've probably never heard the sound of a body hitting the pavement after a suicide jump, but believe me, it's not a thud, it's a loud explosion, like a bomb."

"Maybe someone bumped the sculpture when they ran out of the lobby," Bell offered, but Wyler was already shaking his head before he finished.

"The way those pieces are moving, it looks like they were just knocked a moment ago. Not four minutes ago. They're not settling down yet. Besides, once you notice the swinging sculpture, you can go back and check the guy's height in relation to the doorway. Which I did."

Bell was nodding slowly, as if the theory was taking hold in his mind.

"And another thing," Wyler continued, becoming more animated. "Notice how this guy, when he leaves the building, doesn't pause to look at what is happening on the sidewalk right in front of him, just a few feet away? He doesn't even turn his head to glance in that direction. That's just not how human nature works. Maybe you don't stop and join the looky-loos, but you at least turn and look at a dead body. Unless, of course, you're the one who put it there."

As Bell listened to Wyler, he seemed to retreat into his own thoughts and feelings. Instead of sharing Wyler's excitement, the revelation about Dordevic appeared to disturb Bell on some deep level that Wyler didn't understand.

"What's wrong?" asked Wyler.

For a few moments, Bell was a million miles away, then he came back and deflected Wyler's question with one of his own. "Are you saying that this Mr. Dordevic killed Peter Lisonbee?"

"Yes," said Wyler. "There are too many coincidences to explain it any other way. I now believe this guy Dordevic was in the apartment with Peter Lisonbee when he jumped off that balcony. I believe he showed up at his apartment unexpectedly that night. I say that because, based on what I saw, Lisonbee had settled in for the night and was working on a project. He had ordered food for one and wasn't expecting visitors. So Dordevic shows up, and Peter lets him in. Maybe they already knew each other, through Scottie Hibble. See, Hibble is the connection. We know that Dordevic knew Hibble from the expedition in Honduras, and Hibble obviously knew Lisonbee. So let's say Dordevic comes into Peter's apartment, then pulls a gun. I'm just speculating here, but it fits. He could have held the gun on Lisonbee and made him give up the code he needed to get the gemstone from the appraisers, and then he could have forced him to jump off the balcony at gunpoint, thereby clearing the way for Ashley Lang to pose as Sarah Miller and pick up the stone. I think Dordevic and Hibble have been working together this whole time."

"Why?" asked Bell.

"We know from Honduras that Dordevic is interested in religious artifacts. If the Lisonbee family stone was one of these Urim and Thummim stones, that would certainly qualify."

"But what are they planning to do with the stone?"

Here, Wyler closed the laptop and handed it back to Bell, leaning back in his chair with an air of defeat. "That I still don't know."

"Wait a minute," said Bell, after a moment. "I thought you said the door to Peter Lisonbee's apartment was chained from the inside. How could anyone have been in the apartment with him when he killed himself?"

"I have a theory about that," said Wyler, sitting up again and leaning forward. "I think, after Peter Lisonbee jumped, this guy Dordevic put the chain on the door himself, from the inside. Then, I think he pulled the door open, breaking the chain off when he was still in the apartment. This idea only came to me when I realized the size of the man we are dealing with. This guy Dordevic is huge. He's got hands like two catcher's mitts. I'm guessing he's strong enough to pull the door open and break the chain. Then, he leaves the apartment, jamming the key in the lock before he goes, making it necessary for the police to bust down the door to get in. When they did that, they saw the broken chain and just assumed they were the ones who broke it when they kicked in the door. It never occurred to them that it had already been broken, deliberately, from the inside, to make it seem like Peter was alone when he jumped."

Bell furrowed his eyebrows thoughtfully, then said, "I don't know. It seems like pretty circumstantial evidence to me."

Wyler erupted in sudden laughter that echoed around the empty lobby.

"What?" asked Bell, wounded.

"You've seen too many episodes of *Law and Order*," said Wyler, smiling and shaking his head. "Let me tell you something about circumstantial evidence. It's the best kind there is. People who watch cop shows and read mystery books think it all hinges on one big clue suddenly discovered, or on eyewitness testimony that comes out in some dramatic courtroom revelation. The truth is eyewitness testimony is the least reliable. Witnesses can be pulled apart like string cheese by any decent defense lawyer. A witness is a person, and a person can have a bias, an ulterior motive. They can lie, they can be stupid, or they can just get it wrong because everyone's memory plays tricks. But when you take a series of objective facts, facts you can prove, little facts that don't seem important or significant on their own, and string them together into a chain of logic, the truth becomes obvious to everyone nine times out of ten. Ask any real-life prosecutor if they'd rather build a case on witnesses or circumstantial evidence, and they'll go with circumstantial evidence every time."

As Wyler spoke, Bell nodded along, yielding to Wyler's expertise and experience. But when he finished, Wyler noticed that Bell still looked troubled.

"You've had something on your mind since I sat down. What is it?"

"I was doing some research of my own," replied Bell. "That's why I was up when you texted."

"Research about what?"

"About Urim and Thummim stones."

"What did you find out?"

Bell leaned forward, putting his head right next to Wyler's. He glanced quickly around the hotel lobby to make sure they were alone, then spoke in a hushed tone, almost a whisper.

"Remember what I said at lunch yesterday, that there was really no point in Hibble or anyone else trying to steal a Urim and Thummim stone, because the power of such a stone came only from God and they wouldn't be able to use it anyway?"

"Yes," said Wyler, cautiously.

"Well, it turns out, I may have been wrong about that."

Wyler shot him a quizzical look.

"I came across a story in a book that was published just recently. I had never heard this story before, so I've spent the past few hours trying to determine the original source. It turns out the story was first told in the unpublished autobiography of a man named Wandle Mace, an early Latter-day Saint convert who lived at the same time as Joseph Smith. He was an engineer who helped build the Nauvoo temple, then he and his family moved west with Brigham Young."

Wyler began to fidget impatiently, and Bell sped up.

"Anyway, according to this story, and keep in mind this was a story told to Wandle Mace by someone who had heard it from someone else, so it's really—"

"What's the story?" Wyler cut in.

"Well, the story is that one of the early apostles of our Church, a man named George A. Smith, encountered some stones while on a mission to England, stones he thought might be Urim and

Thummim stones. He brought the stones back to the United States to show the prophet Joseph Smith, and apparently, Joseph Smith said that the stones were in fact Urim and Thummim stones. But, according to this story, Joseph Smith went on to say that these Urim and Thummim stones had been corrupted by the devil, consecrated for use by Satan's followers. That really surprised me because it had never occurred to me that Urim and Thummim stones could be used for an evil purpose."

Bell paused here and looked at Wyler, but Wyler had no readable expression.

"You don't believe any of this, do you?"

Wyler thought for a moment before answering.

"What I do or don't believe doesn't matter. What matters is what other people may or may not believe, and how those beliefs could motivate their actions. Certain members of the Lisonbee family believed—for centuries—that this gemstone was a sacred stone that had been possessed by ancient biblical prophets, and that it had been entrusted to their family. They acted accordingly. There's a jeweler in Brooklyn named Howard Gelb who believes that same stone is one of the Urim and Thummim stones spoken of in the Torah. If they believe that, then it seems possible that other people, like Dordevic or Hibble, might believe the same stone could be used for an evil purpose of some kind. Learning about these various belief systems and how they interact helps me to understand the motivations and actions of people involved in this case. I don't have to share those beliefs."

Wyler knew that his answer, though technically correct, carefully avoided providing a direct response to Bell's question about Wyler's personal beliefs, but he had been unexpectedly open and vulnerable with Bell and his wife earlier that day. Now he felt the need to retreat a bit and reassert an emotional boundary.

"I have no idea if this story about Joseph Smith and these evil

Urim and Thummim stones is true," Bell continued. "But even if it isn't, the story itself made me think of things differently."

"How so?"

"Well, maybe it's not too farfetched to think that something that was originally consecrated for a holy or divine purpose could, if it fell into the wrong hands, be corrupted and used for an evil purpose."

"What evil purpose?"

It was Bell's turn to look defeated.

"I don't know," he sighed heavily. "I've been trying to think of some reason, some dark use or purpose an evil Urim and Thummim stone could be put to. But I can't think of anything."

For several minutes they just sat next to each other in silence, as if hoping their combined frustration would somehow conjure a new insight. And then, the fatigue of the long day seemed to overcome them both simultaneously, and they stood up to head back to their rooms.

CHAPTER 27

Wyler was woken up by the sound of knocking at the hotel room door. He rubbed the sleep out of his eyes and saw Gabe, already dressed, sitting in a chair in the corner, playing his handheld game. As Gabe popped up to answer the door, Wyler glanced at the clock beside the bed and saw that it was 8:34 a.m. The darkness in the room mixed unsettlingly with a bright sliver of sunlight that divided the curtains, creating an overall effect of dreariness. A moment later, Gabe came back into the bedroom area, accompanied by Jason Bell, Will, and Henry. All three of the Bell men were wearing white dress shirts and ties.

"Good morning," said Bell in a stage whisper after seeing Wyler in bed. "Sorry to get you up."

"Morning," said Wyler, guiltily propping himself up on his elbows.

"Would you mind if we slipped away for an hour? Our church has a congregation near here that meets at nine. We figured we could go while you and Gabe have breakfast, then we could swing back and pick you guys up around ten."

"I was hoping to get on the road right way," said Wyler, tossing the sheets aside and sitting up. "I can be ready in five minutes."

For a few moments there was an awkward standoff between Wyler and Bell. It ended when Gabe asked, "Can I go with them, Dad?"

Will and Henry, flanking him on either side, made excited noises at the idea. Wyler was stunned by Gabe's request. For months, Gabe had willingly gone along with everything Wyler had invited him to do, but he had never asked himself to do anything. This was an earthquake. Still, Wyler wasn't sure it was a good idea. He liked the Bells and was glad Gabe had made two new friends, but going to their church didn't feel right.

"You don't have any good clothes," said Wyler, searching for a diplomatic out.

"That's not an issue at all," said Bell brightly, to Wyler's irritation.

An hour later, Wyler was sitting alone in the front passenger seat of the Bell's minivan, finishing his second cup of coffee from Dunkin Donuts. The van was parked in front of a Mormon church somewhere in Rochester. Wyler had reluctantly given in to Gabe's request, then decided to come along himself and wait in the van so that they could start back as soon as the service was over. On the way there, Wyler had asked Bell to go through a drive thru for the coffee. He hadn't slept much the night before, and he needed to clear the cobwebs out of his brain.

He took a sip and listened for the second time to an intriguing phone message. . The call had come in the day before, but Wyler hadn't recognized the number and had let it go to voicemail. With time to kill in the van, he had finally listened to the message, expecting the usual robocall nonsense, and was surprised to hear the voice of Cheryl Branford, the detective from the 88th precinct in Brooklyn. She said she was following up with him to see how he was doing, and reported that they hadn't been able to establish any link between Bobby Willis and Warren Payson, his two subway attackers. Then, before disconnecting, her voice modulated to a friendlier tone, and she renewed her invitation to meet Wyler for a drink sometime. She was free any night that week but Thursday and hoped to hear from him.

After hearing the message a second time, Wyler still wasn't sure how he was going to respond. He had known Cheryl for years, and he had heard she was divorced from another cop in the department, but he didn't know who. On the surface, they had a lot in common and they seemed to have an easy rapport. She was also very attractive, which never hurts. But the issue wasn't her, of course, it was him. Her invitation forced him to confront the question of whether or not he was ready to start dating again.

His entire focus, since Jessica's death, had been Gabe. At first, even taking on the Lisonbee case had felt like a small betrayal of the commitment he had made to himself to give Gabe his undivided focus. But the decision seemed to have worked out well for Gabe; he had picked up two new friends in the bargain. Dating another woman, however, was entirely different from working on a new case, and he wasn't sure how his son would react. On the other hand, maybe he was just using Gabe as an excuse to hide from the world.

As he continued debating the pros and cons, he finished the second cup of coffee and realized he needed to use the bathroom. This presented a problem as he wasn't crazy about going into a church just for this purpose. It didn't seem right, somehow. Bell had left the key in the ignition, and Wyler briefly considered switching to the driver's seat and trying to find a gas station somewhere, but the pressure on his bladder was quickly increasing.

The church building was different from the cathedral-like churches that seemed to be on almost every street when he was growing up—there was a reason Brooklyn was nicknamed the "City of Churches". This was a low-rise building, with a triangular, steepled roof in the center and two long, one-story wings on each side. He entered the church through two layers of glass doors and passed through a lobby area with couches and soft chairs. He walked down a long, deserted hallway that bordered the outer perimeter of the building until he found a restroom. After a few minutes in the bathroom, he retraced his steps down the hall back toward the entrance. The sounds of congregational singing began rumbling from the center of the building as he reached the lobby. He was about to exit when his phone started chirping, and he saw that Ray Shimura was calling him.

"Hey," said Wyler in a hushed tone, sitting down on the empty sofa in the lobby to take the call. "You got something for me on Dordevic?"

"I might," said Ray. And then, "Where are you? I hear music in the background."

"I'm at a church up in Rochester."

"I thought Jews went to church on Saturday."

"It's a long story. What have you got?"

"Well, without a first name, it wasn't easy. I couldn't find anyone in any of our databases under Dordevic."

"Did you check Interpol?"

"Nah, cause I've only been doing this for fifteen years."

"Settle down."

"Nothing from Interpol either," offered Shimura.

"So, nothing?" said Wyler, disappointed.

"I didn't say that. I think I found the guy you're looking for. His name is Edgar Dordevic."

"Edgar Dordevic," Wyler repeated the name slowly, as if trying it out. "How'd you find him?"

"Well, in my free time I've been looking into our friend Scottie Hibble's finances."

"Really?"

"That little punk really rubbed me the wrong way, so I got curious."

"Excellent. What did you find?"

"Well, you know that website of his where he made all his money?"

"RopeLine."

"Right, RopeLine. Well, I wanted to know where he got the company's seed money. I found out it was originally funded by a private hedge fund based in Turkey, which I thought was pretty bizarre."

"That does sound strange. Who goes to Turkey for start-up capital for a tech company?"

"Scottie Hibble for some reason. But that's not all that's strange about it. Hedge funds almost never invest in business start-ups. They're usually into quick turnarounds with high returns."

"So why would they invest in Scottie Hibble's website idea?"

"That's what I wanted to know. I looked into the company, and it seems legitimate. It has investments all over the world. The only unusual thing about it was the investment in the Scottie Hibble startup. And even that wasn't criminal. It was just odd."

"What's the name of this hedge fund?"

"I can't even pronounce it. It's about eight Slavic words strung together, with maybe three vowels between them."

"Slavic? I thought you said it was based in Turkey?"

"It is."

"So why the Slavic name?"

"I wondered about that too, but I didn't pursue it at first."

"Why not?"

"Because I have a full-time job with the New York City Police Department that takes up some of my time. Anyway, when you sent me that name last night, Dordevic, I checked the usual databases and came up empty, but the name sounded Slavic to me, so I went back to this Turkish hedge fund to cross check their major investors. At first it was a dead end because, over there, hedge funds don't have to disclose their investors. But I found out that any fund with over a hundred million in assets has to file with the SEC if they want to invest in an American company."

"Like RopeLine."

"Like RopeLine. So I went back a few years and pulled the SEC paperwork. Turns out, the principal investor in the fund is a Serbian named Edgar Dordevic."

Wyler took a moment to let the information sink in. It was too much of a coincidence to believe this wasn't the same Mr. Dordevic who had sponsored the Mormon Evidence Project expedition. An expedition that had included one Scottie Hibble.

"So, who is this guy?" he asked.

"No one really knows for sure. He showed up in Melbourne, Australia in 2004, claiming to be a Serbian civilian who fled Kosovo during the war with nothing but the shirt on his back. Since then, he's taken over most of the iron ore and coal mining in Australia."

"How did he do that?"

"If I knew that, I would have done it."

"Are we sure Dordevic is his real name?"

Shimura laughed. "Of course not. No one knows anything for sure about this guy. He has no traceable background or history. He claims all his records were destroyed in the NATO bombing campaign. Which is possible, of course. There were over a million refugees from that war."

"But if you wanted to reinvent yourself and create a new identity in the 2000s, claiming to be a Serbian refugee wouldn't be a bad strategy."

"Also true. Oh, and I almost forgot. He owns an island in the Bahamas."

"Let me guess."

"That's right. Caliban Cay. The soon-to-be location of the Bonfire festival."

Wyler's phone emitted a sad-sounding chime to warn him of a low battery.

"I've got to go. My battery's dying. Look, thanks for doing this, Ray."

"No problem. Keep in touch, okay?"

"You got it."

Wyler disconnected the call. It was 9:47 a.m., and Bell had said the service would be over by ten. He thought about going back to the van, but now that he was in the church, the comfortable, air-conditioned lobby seemed like a better place to wait. As he sat alone on the sofa, he felt his heart racing in his chest from the second cup of coffee, twice his usual intake.

He looked up and noticed a painting on the opposite wall that looked familiar for some reason. Then he remembered he had seen the same painting at the Mormon church in Lincoln Square two nights ago. It was a picture of Jesus talking to a young man dressed in expensive robes. The young man had his hands on his hips and was turning away from Jesus like a defiant teenager.

The more Wyler waited, the more the caffeine made him fidget. Unfinished thoughts passed through his head like horses on a runaway carousel. He thought of Edgar Dordevic, Scottie Hibble, Steven Ridgeway, Peter Lisonbee, and Ashley Lang. And he thought of Cheryl Branford.

Looking for a distraction, he took out his phone again, but it was dead.

There was a small table next to the lobby sofa with a lamp on it that he noticed was unplugged. Next to the lamp was a shallow carboard box, and the words "Take One" were written on the side with a black marker. He pulled the box closer and saw that it was filled with old, worn magazines. Curious, he picked one off the top of the pile. The magazine, dated July 2007, was called "The Friend." A Norman Rockwell-like painting on the cover depicted an excited father teaching his son to ride a bike, while the young boy's eyes bugged out in terror. Wyler flipped through the magazine and saw that it was a mix of short stories, games, and colorful illustrations, obviously intended for children. He put it down and picked up the next one in the stack and looked through it. This one was the opposite of the first one, with almost no pictures or art. Just white pages filled with text. He was about to put it down when he noticed the date on the ripped cover: November 2001. He was curious to see if this religious magazine, published so soon after 9/11, would mention the event in some way.

He flipped through the pages, casually skimming the titles of the articles. He saw articles titled "Prayer," "Gratitude," "Our Duty to God," "Our Father's Plan," and then he landed on one right in the middle fold, titled "The Times in Which We Live."

He glanced down at the beginning of the second paragraph and read,

> I have just been handed a note that says that a U.S. missile attack is under way. I need not remind you that we live in perilous times. I desire to speak concerning these times...

That got Wyler's attention. The article was obviously a transcript of a live address of some kind that must have been given on October 7th, 2001, the date U.S. missile strikes in Afghanistan began. The name at the top of the article was Gordon B. Hinckley. Wyler continued reading:

> You are acutely aware of the events of September 11, less than a month ago. Out of that vicious and ugly attack we are plunged into a state of war. It is the first war of the 21st century. The last century has been described as the most war-torn in human history. Now we are off on another dangerous undertaking, the unfolding of which and the end thereof we do not know. For the first time since we became a

nation, the United States has been seriously attacked on its mainland soil. But this was not an attack on the United States alone. It was an attack on men and nations of goodwill everywhere.

Wyler was impressed. He remembered a few other Christian preachers at the time who tried to place the blame for the attacks on the United States. But there was no America bashing or equivocating here. He kept reading:

Recently, in company with a few national religious leaders, I was invited to the White House to meet with the president. In talking to us he was frank and straightforward. That same evening he spoke to the Congress and the nation in unmistakable language concerning the resolve of America and its friends to hunt down the terrorists who were responsible for the planning of this terrible thing and any who harbored such.

Wyler's mind flashed back to the days directly following September 11th. Without thinking, he had immediately rushed to the scene and spent the next several days working alongside firefighters, cops, EMTs, and other random New Yorkers from all walks of life who, like him, had felt compelled to do something, anything, to help. That week had been the turning point in his entire life. He abandoned his law career and, a few months later, he was a cop with the NYPD. A few years after that, his work in counterterrorism had led directly to his meeting Jessica Maitland, his future wife.

Wyler skipped forward a bit and landed on the following paragraph:

We of this Church know something of such groups. The Book of Mormon speaks of the Gadianton robbers, a vicious, oath-bound, and secret organization bent on evil and destruction. In their day they did all in their power, by whatever means available, to bring down the Church, to woo the people with sophistry, and to take control of the society. We see the same thing in the present situation.

Wyler paused, then slowly read the paragraph a second time. Before he could finish, however, the doors leading to the chapel swung open and a stream of people flooded into the hallway and foyer. Wyler, who had been sitting alone in the quiet lobby, suddenly found himself surrounded by a sea of suits and dresses. In just a few moments he found himself boxed in by people talking, laughing, and socializing in small groups, and he stood up, almost in self-defense. The volume of white noise kept increasing, punctuated occasionally by loud bursts of laughter. He heard his name called, and turned to see Bell making his way toward him.

"Laura's talking to a friend she ran into from one of our old wards," Bell said with a smile as approached Wyler.

"I need to talk to you," said Wyler, in an urgent tone that contrasted with the boisterous levity around them. "Can we go outside?"

Wyler and Bell went outside and walked to a tree in a narrow strip of grass next to the parking lot. Wyler noticed new cars were pulling in to replace the ones leaving, and a fresh wave of churchgoers were flocking to the church's entrance.

"What's up?" asked Bell as they faced each other.

Wyler still had the magazine in his hand, and he flipped it open where his finger was saving a place.

"Who are the...Gadianton Robbers?" Wyler read the word from the page.

Bell saw the magazine in Wyler's hands.

"You've been reading The Ensign? I'm impressed." Bell nodded goofily, as if gently ribbing an old friend. But when he saw Wyler's serious expression, he changed his tone. "The Gadianton Robbers were a secret society of wicked people who existed during the time of the Book of Mormon. They tried to infiltrate and overthrow the government, they plotted assassinations, they robbed and murdered and basically terrorized society from within."

"What about secret oaths?"

Bell paused, as if wanting to ask a question, but Wyler's cold earnestness warded him off.

"That's true. The organization was bound together by secret oaths."

"What kind of oaths?" asked Wyler.

"Satanic." The word came out a bit too loud, just as a young family in their Sunday best passed by the tree. The mother of the family briefly glanced in their direction and kept walking. In synch, Wyler and Bell both moved a few steps away from the foot traffic. When Bell continued, it was in a hushed tone. "The oaths and plans the group used came directly from the devil. These secret oaths bound the members of this organization together."

"What can you tell me about the nature of these oaths?"

"Why are you so interested in the Gadianton Society?"

"Scottie Hibble is hosting an event this weekend on an island in the Bahamas. An island, I just found out, that is owned by Edgar Dordevic."

"*Edgar* Dordevic? You found out his first name?"

Wyler nodded. "Shimura called me a few minutes ago. It turns out that Dordevic was the one who originally funded Scottie Hibble's website three years ago."

"Wow. What else did you find out about him?"

"Not much. He showed up for the first time on the radar in 2004, claiming to be a Serbian refugee from the Kosovo war. There are no records of him and no way to trace his background before that."

Bell looked away for a moment, as if searching for the answer to an unspoken question. "What does this have to do with the Gadianton Society?" Bell asked, turning back to Wyler. "Maybe nothing, but this event is a gathering of some very important and influential people. It's also very secretive, with no outsiders or cameras allowed, which is pretty unusual in itself for people who love to see themselves in the news. There's also been talk of an oath of some kind taking place. So, when I read in this magazine about an evil society that took a secret oath, I got curious. Especially because of the connection both Dordevic and Hibble have to Mormon archeology."

"What are you saying, exactly?" Bell asked, looking confused.

"I'm wondering if maybe they are trying to recreate this ancient society in some way, using the same oaths this group used. I know it sounds farfetched, but my tolerance for entertaining outlandish theories has increased exponentially over the past week."

"That would be impossible," Bell said, shaking his head. "At least in the way you're talking about."

"Why?"

"Because, according to the Book of Mormon, this group was ultimately defeated and destroyed."

"So what? That was a long time ago."

"I know, but after the group was destroyed, the people took all the secret oaths and hid them away so that no one would be able to use them ever again."

"They hid them? Where?"

"No one knows that, of course. That was the point. All we know is they were…" Bell's voice suddenly trailed off.

"They were what?" asked Wyler.

Bell's expression had suddenly darkened, and his eyes seemed to be filled with dread.

"What?" demanded Wyler.

"They were buried," Bell said flatly.

Wyler paused for a moment, then physically turned away from Bell. He began pacing in a small circle, taking slow, deliberate steps, like he was working something out in his mind, but needed his whole body to do it.

"So, these oaths," Wyler said, speaking to the air, "that supposedly came from the devil...were somehow written down hundreds —or maybe even thousands—of years ago...and they would have been recorded in an ancient language...a dead language that no longer exists. To use them, you would have to have some way to translate them into a modern language."

Wyler glanced at Bell, who suddenly looked pale and sick. Bell nodded helplessly, as if silently apologizing for the answer as he was giving it.

"There you guys are!" Laura said, as she and the boys approached the tree where Wyler and Bell were standing.

CHAPTER 28

During the first part of the drive home, Laura Bell told the story of how she and Jason met at college in Idaho. It turned out that Bell was a NCAA division wrestler, not a football player as Wyler had supposed. But Wyler was only half listening. His mind was elsewhere.

It was about 12:30 p.m. when they decided to pull over for lunch, and they ended up at the same McDonald's in Utica where they had eaten the day before. As the kids were climbing out of the van, Wyler pulled both Bell and Laura aside for a private conference.

"I have a favor to ask," said Wyler.

"What is it?" asked Laura.

"I'm wondering if you could drop me off at my home in Rhinebeck. It's on the way, just north of Poughkeepsie."

"Sure," they both nodded.

"But *just* me—not Gabe. That's the favor. Would you be willing to keep Gabe with you and drop him back at his grandma's apartment in the city? I'm sorry to ask, but I have something I need to do in Rhinebeck."

"I don't see any problem," said Laura. She looked at Wyler

with concern and touched his arm. "Are you okay, Aaron?" But before Wyler could reply, the boys were out of the van and bouncing toward the McDonald's entrance. Laura peeled off to follow them, the baby's car seat slung over her arm like a giant purse.

Bell hung back for a private moment with Wyler.

"What are you planning?" Bell asked, but Wyler just looked at him without answering. "Look, I know I don't have any right to ask. It's none of my business, but I'm asking anyway."

"I've got to get to that island somehow," said Wyler, his voice dull like a murmured threat. "That's where Hibble is, that's where Dordevic is, and that's where the stone is."

"And then what are you going to do?"

"Among other things, I'm going to get Peter Lisonbee's stone back and return it to its rightful owner, Sarah Miller."

"How are you going to do that?"

"TBD," said Wyler. "I probably won't know that until I get to the island."

After a pause, Bell asked, "What's in Rhinebeck?"

"Something I'll need."

Wyler looked at Bell with a blank, cold stare, almost daring him to ask the follow-up question, but Bell stepped back, and they both turned and walked toward the restaurant in silence.

Two hours later, Wyler was turning the key to the front door of his house in Rhinebeck, having said his goodbyes to Gabe and the Bells. As the door opened, he turned and saw that the van was still parked in the driveway with the engine running. Were they waiting to make sure he got inside, like a child dropped off by a friend's parents? He waved politely, then went in and closed the door behind him.

Once inside, he headed up the stairs. When he got to his bedroom, he glanced through the window and saw the van pulling out of the driveway and onto the road. Good. He knew his son was in good hands, both with the Bells and with Nora, so he was able to focus his mind on other things, like planning his next move.

On the wall next to his bed hung a series of three framed prints by the French impressionist George Seurat, each about the size of a wall calendar. The one in the middle showed a lone horse in a field pulling a cart. Wyler moved his hand along the top of the frame until he found the small, almost imperceptible trigger. He pressed it, and a mechanism gently moved the painting aside along a hidden track, revealing a safe in the wall. Wyler placed his index finger on the small biometric scanner at the base of the safe, and, a second later, the door popped open.

There were two handguns in the safe, a Glock 22 and a Beretta 92. He liked the feel of the Beretta more, but the Glock was more powerful. He pulled out the Glock and ejected the clip. The magazine was about half full, so he removed a box of bullets from the safe. Next, he took out a small wallet and flipped it open. As he stood and stared at his NYPD badge, he suddenly heard someone knocking loudly on the front door to the house. He paused and waited, then the knocking repeated. He stowed the bullets and badge wallet back in the safe, closed the safe's door, and slid the clip back into the gun.

As he moved down the stairs, the Glock ready in his hand, there was a third, louder round of knocking at the front door. Wyler wasn't expecting trouble, but too much had happened the past few days for him not to be careful. Approaching the door cautiously, he peered out the spy hole, then relaxed and opened the door.

Bell was standing on the porch. He glanced down and saw the gun in Wyler's hand.

"You didn't waste any time," Bell said.

"What are you doing?" asked Wyler, stuffing the gun into the waist of his pants.

"I'm going with you."

Wyler immediately pushed past Bell onto the porch and began searching the driveway and street.

"The van is long gone," Bell said. "I knew you wouldn't say yes at first, that's why I waited for Laura to drive away."

"I hope you don't think that gives me no choice. I'll pay for the Uber," said Wyler, with irritation bordering on hostility, as he passed Bell and went back in the house. Bell followed him in uninvited.

"You need my help," said Bell, closing the door and following Wyler into the living room. Wyler forced a mocking laugh, then dropped his body onto the sofa in an exasperated heap.

"Look, I admit you've been helpful. But this whole thing is about to get messy." Wyler didn't look at Bell as he spoke, but stared straight forward, as if imagining all the worst-case scenarios.

"You can't do this alone."

"I appreciate your tactical assessment, but if I wanted backup there are at least twenty guys—and a few girls—I would call before you."

"Okay, so maybe I'm not backup. That's fine. You can think of me as a consultant."

"A consultant?"

"Admit it. There are things going on in this case that I understand better than you. So, I can come along as a consultant."

"You're not coming along."

"Why not?"

"Because *I* shouldn't even be going. I'm about to cross a line here, a line I've never crossed in my professional career, and the last thing I need is a curious civilian along for the ride who just wants a story to tell his friends."

There was a tense moment of silence, and then Bell asked, "Is that really what you think of me?"

Wyler looked up at him. "Yes, it is." But Wyler said it quietly, without conviction.

Bell stood for a while, then crossed and sat in a chair on the other side of the room, facing Wyler.

"You said last night that it doesn't matter what you personally believe, as long as you understand what other people believe and how those beliefs motivate them. Well, I want to share something with you. Something about my beliefs. I don't expect you to accept what I'm going to say, or even believe it, but I need to share it with you, so you understand my motives in this."

Bell paused a few moments, as if waiting for Wyler's full attention. Eventually Wyler turned to him, then showed both his palms to Bell in an "it's your move" gesture.

"First of all, I believe that God can and does speak to us, to all of us, in different ways. I believe that sometimes he places thoughts or ideas in our minds. I also believe that he speaks to us through our feelings. Sometimes those feelings are feelings of happiness or peace, or they can be strong emotions of love for other people, or a desire to help someone, or feelings of humility, or compassion, or forgiveness. But these feelings that come from God, let's call it the spirit of God, can also take the form of a sudden pull to do something, an urge to take some sort of action that we might never have considered taking the moment before. Well, when you told me you were going to that island, I felt something. I suddenly felt that I had to go with you. And I believe, I know, that this feeling didn't come from inside myself, from Jason Bell. It wasn't a personal whim based on my ego or curiosity or anything else you might think. I'm telling you it was a feeling, a communication, a prompting, that came from God."

"So, you're telling me that God told you to come with me?"

"Look," Bell said, scooting forward to the edge of his seat. "I accept that you are an expert in your field. I'd be a fool not to, right? You've spent your entire life in law enforcement and criminal justice, with years of training and experience. I have complete trust that you know what you're talking about and what you're doing when it comes to detective work. All I ask is that you extend to me the same professional courtesy."

Wyler furrowed his eyebrows. As if in response, Bell stood up, sighed with his whole body, then continued, raising his voice and gesturing with his hands for emphasis.

"I know what spiritual communication from God feels like. In my own way, I guess you could say I'm an expert in that. I've spent my entire life praying to God and listening for his answers, Aaron. I've learned how to distinguish his voice from my own feelings and thoughts. So when I tell you I felt a strong spiritual prompting that I needed to go with you, well, you may not believe it, but I expect you to take it seriously."

Wyler didn't respond, and Bell sat down next to him on the couch.

"I know I'm not the kind of backup that a cop or a detective like you would normally need on a case. But like you've been telling me, this is not a normal case."

Wyler's head was moving slowly from side to side, either in agreement about the strangeness of the case, or in opposition to Bell's proposal, or a mix of both. Wyler himself wasn't sure.

"I'm sorry, Jason. I appreciate all you've done, and your passion, and I do respect your beliefs. But this is not about that. This is about your own personal safety. I cannot allow a civilian bystander to come into a situation this high risk with so many unknown variables. I'm sorry, but that's just the way it is."

Bell took a moment to absorb the disappointment, but then his body straightened and stiffened with resolve, like he was bracing himself against a gale-force wind.

"Okay, then there's this," Bell began, speaking slowly, in a grave tone. "The truth is, I haven't told you everything I know about this situation."

"What are you talking about?"

"There's something else. Something important."

Wyler got up and stood in front of Bell. "I'm waiting," Wyler said.

"I'll tell you on the plane," said Bell.

"I'm not kidding around."

"Neither am I."

Wyler glared fiercely at Bell, his eyes burning with grim seriousness, but Bell met Wyler's deadly stare with one of his own, holding his ground. The two men stood less than a foot apart in a tense, silent standoff.

CHAPTER 29

Wyler and Bell were the only passengers in the spacious cabin of the Cessna Citation Excel as it cruised at 40,000 feet over the Atlantic. The cost of renting the mid-size luxury private jet was such an obscene figure that Wyler chose to block it out of his mind. Unfortunately, both tactically and strategically, he had no choice. Tactically, there was no practical way to get to the island in time without chartering a flight. Strategically, their arrival needed to attract as little attention as possible, and, in this unusual situation, blending in required flamboyant extravagance.

The luxurious cabin was thick with tension between Wyler and Bell. They hadn't spoken much beyond what was absolutely necessary during the past day as Wyler had prepared for the trip, and now they sat alone at opposite ends of the plane like squabbling children sent to neutral corners. Bell had essentially blackmailed his way onto the plane, and Wyler resented him for it. He was giving Bell the silent treatment even though he knew it was petty and childish. Still, as Wyler sat alone, staring out at the Atlantic, he had to admit to grudgingly admiring the inner strength Bell had displayed in holding firm and not buckling under Wyler's pressure. It also took guts for Bell to risk his life over something that wasn't even his problem. Wyler decided it was time to let it go, and he stood up and walked down the aisle toward the front of the plane.

"Okay, consultant, start consulting," said Wyler as he sat down in a tan leather seat facing Bell.

"So, am I out of the penalty box now?" asked Bell, sulkily.

"You're lucky you weren't ejected from the game," countered Wyler, but his tone was more playful than biting. "You still might be if you don't tell me what you know."

Bell hesitated briefly, then seemed to quickly drop any hard feelings.

"First of all," said Bell, suddenly leaning forward and becoming animated, "While you were ignoring me yesterday, I took the time to study every reference to the secret oaths and the society that used them in the Book of Mormon." As Bell spoke, he referred to a yellow legal pad filled with scribbled notes as well as a thick leather book with thin pages that looked like a Bible, flipping back and forth through the pages of each. "The first mention of the secret Gadianton society takes place about fifty years before the birth of Christ."

"How did it start?"

"That's not entirely clear. What we know is that members of this secret society were hidden but scattered through all levels of society, many in positions of power and influence. No one knew exactly how many there were. They were bound together by these satanic oaths, and they used secret signs to identify one another. They even had their own clandestine justice system for enforcing loyalty, holding trials, and executing anyone who stepped out of line. A man named Gadianton was the leader."

"Where did they get these oaths and signs, did they just make them up?"

"No, they didn't. The oaths and covenants used by this group came directly from Satan." Bell flipped to a page in the leather book and began reading. "'He who is the author of all sin and doth carry on his works of darkness, doth hand down their plots, and their oaths, and their covenants, and their plans of awful wickedness, from generation to generation.' The purpose of the society was 'to spread the works of darkness and abominations over all the face of the land' in order to 'drag people down to destruction and everlasting hell.'"

"So, what happened to this group? You said they were defeated."

"They were. In about 20 BC, the people were able to root out and destroy the secret society. And they buried all the secret oaths and signs so that no one could ever use them again. But, a few years later, the society sprang up again, and members of the group found and dug up all the secret oaths and signs. This iteration of the group was destroyed in 20 AD, and again the satanic oaths and signs were hidden away. But then, in about 245 AD, the group sprang up yet again."

"So, this secret group, which you say was founded by the devil, kept being destroyed and then, after time, it would spring up again?"

Bell nodded.

"So how does this story end?" asked Wyler.

"According to the Book of Mormon prophets, it was this secret society that eventually led to the destruction of this entire civilization around 400 AD."

"So what happened to these oaths after that?"

"Well, that's where we get into speculation. The last prophet to record anything in the Book of Mormon was a man named Moroni."

"He was the one you said buried the Book of Mormon and then came back as an angel to deliver it to Joseph Smith?"

"That's right."

"What does he have to do with these satanic oaths?"

"Maybe nothing. Like I said, this is all speculation, educated guesswork on my part."

"But you have a theory?"

"I've started to form one."

"Let's hear it."

"Well, this man, Moroni, knew firsthand how dangerous and destructive these secret oaths were. He had witnessed the destruction of his entire civilization because of them. I think it makes sense to assume that he didn't want those writings and plans to fall into the hands of anyone ever again. I think it's possible that, like others before him, he buried the secret signs and oaths of the Gadianton society, to hide them from the world for all time."

Wyler considered that for a few moments, then asked a question.

"You told me the other day that scholars and historians from your church don't agree on where the events described in the Book of Mormon took place?"

"That's right."

"Well, if that expedition in Honduras really did unearth this stuff buried by Moroni, doesn't that prove that that's where all the other things happened?"

"I've thought about that, but actually, no, I don't think so."

"Why not?"

"Well, we know that Moroni buried the metal plates containing the Book of Mormon in upstate New York. If the events in the Book of Mormon happened in Central America, and my theory about his burying the Gadianton oaths is correct, that means, after burying the oaths in the jungle in what is now modern-day Honduras, he walked from Central America to New York. That's entirely possible, since the scriptures say he wandered alone for many years."

"So, doesn't that prove then that it all happened in Central America?"

"I thought that at first, but then I realized he just as easily could have done the opposite. If the events in the Book of Mormon took place somewhere else, for example, like in the Great Lakes region of the United States, which is another theory, Moroni could have buried the Book of Mormon first in New York and then walked down to Central America to bury the oaths. It would make sense that he'd want to get them as far away as possible, to a remote, hidden land. Believe me, I've been thinking about this from every angle, and I've concluded that even knowing the location where these oaths were buried doesn't tell us anything definite about the location of the other events in the Book of Mormon."

Wyler thought about this, then asked, "Is this the important information you've been holding back?"

Bell leaned back in his chair and shook his head slowly. "There's something else." His voice was grave, like a doctor bracing a patient for bad news.

"Well?"

"Remember how you told me that you sensed a dark presence of some kind, a force permeating this case? You said it was similar to feelings you used to have tracking down terrorist networks."

Wyler gave no response but stared at Bell and waited for him to continue.

"I said a few minutes ago that the evil oaths originated in the Book of Mormon stories about the society of Gadianton, but that's not really accurate."

"What do you mean?"

"Well, the truth is, the birth of these secret oaths date all the way back to the story of Cain and Abel."

"You mean Cain and Abel, from The Bible?"

"That's right. The Book of Genesis says that after murdering Abel, Cain ran away to the land of Nod, east of Eden. There's not much said about him after that in the Bible, but scriptures translated by Joseph Smith contain details about Cain that aren't in the Bible."

"Like what?"

"The story of Cain didn't end after he killed Abel. Satan continued plotting with Cain and his followers."

"He had followers?"

Bell nodded, then leaned forward, gripping the sides of the table with both of his hands, as if to steady himself.

"Please understand, what I am about to suggest may not be true. In fact, it probably *isn't* true. It's just a theory. Actually, it's really not even a theory. It just crossed my mind when we were on the Zoom call with the Ridgeways, and they mentioned this man, Mr. Dordevic."

"What about him?"

"Well, for one, who is he? Why is he involved in this? What explains his interest in Book of Mormon archeology? The Ridgeways mentioned that he was almost seven feet tall, with large, wild eyes. And then, you made the connection with the man leaving the building where Peter Lisonbee died. The guy was so tall his head brushed against that hanging sculpture in the lobby. And then the next day, you discovered that this man didn't have any traceable history before the early 2000s. No record of his birth. No way of knowing anything about where he came from. And then, when you stumbled on that article about the secret oaths and the Gadianton society, that was another connection."

"Connection to what? I'm not following you."

"After Cain killed Abel, he was cursed by God."

"Right," said Wyler. "A mark of some kind was placed on him."

"That's right, but that wasn't the only part of the curse. He was cursed in another way."

"What other way?"

"He was denied a natural death. He was cursed to go on living, to wander the earth as a miserable outcast. And that's not all. He entered into a secret agreement with Satan, a pact with the devil that included secret oaths—oaths that he kept and passed down to others, like a caretaker. He's actually referred to as the 'master' of the evil oaths and covenants. There was another civilization called the Jaredites that was also destroyed by these secret oaths—long before Gadianton—and the oaths were introduced into their society by a man named Akish, who received them from Cain."

"I'm not seeing how any of this is relevant. You said you had important information about this case."

"There are stories. I knew of one story, but in the past couple of days I've discovered several more."

"What stories?" asked Wyler, impatiently.

"There is a story told by David W. Patton, one of the early apostles of our Church, of something that happened to him in 1835. He was out riding a horse on his way to visit someone when he encountered a man who was so tall that he stood almost even with him as he sat in the saddle. The man introduced himself by name, and said his mission was to wander the earth to destroy the souls of men. There was another story, from 1921, that happened in Hawaii, to the son of the prophet Joseph F. Smith. This time, the strange man came to the door to his home right before the dedication of the Hawaii temple. He was so tall he had to stoop to enter. He had wild eyes, and long hair and fingernails. There are other stories as well, and all these stories describe similar encounters with the same man. A man cursed to roam the earth as a living emissary of evil, secretly conspiring with Satan down through the ages."

There was a long pause before Wyler spoke again.

"Are you suggesting that this man, Edgar Dordevic, is Cain, as in Cain and Abel?"

"I know it sounds crazy, but there's a clue even in his name. The Bible says that Abel was a shepherd, and the offering he gave to the Lord was the firstlings of his flock, which was accepted by God. But Cain wasn't a shepherd. He was a farmer, a gardener, and his offering, which God rejected, came from the soil. Do you know what the name Dordevic means? I looked it up last night. It's a Slavic name, and it means farmer. Literally, it means tiller of the soil."

Wyler stared blankly at Bell.

"I said before I told you that it was just a theory, an idea. It's probably not true."

Wyler shook his head in disbelief.

"Look, I'm not a fool," Bell continued. "I knew you would have this reaction. I knew as soon as I told you this I'd go from consultant to kook. That's why I didn't want to tell you until we were already on the plane. I knew if I told you, you'd think I was nuts and you wouldn't have let me come. I knew it would destroy any shred of trust you might have in me or my judgment. But it was a risk I felt was worth taking, because even if there's a small, tiny, miniscule chance that this theory is true, I felt like you needed to know about it."

"Why?"

"Because, Aaron, the person you are dealing with here may be much more dangerous, much more powerful, than any mere man, and you need to understand that."

"Well, I know that, in your own way, you felt that you were doing the right—"

But Wyler was interrupted by the sound of his phone chirping. When he saw who was calling, he said, "I'm sorry, I have to take this."

Wyler stood up and answered the phone. "This is Wyler," he said in an eager voice as he walked back down the aisle toward his seat on the other side of the cabin.

"You were right," said the voice on the other end.

"Really?" replied Wyler, excitedly.

"Exactly as you said. If you hadn't called, we would have missed it for sure."

"I knew it!" Wyler said, punching the air with his fist like a gambler who had won a bet. For the next few minutes, as Wyler listened to Rollie Sterling, he grew more and more animated, pacing up and down the narrow aisle like a caged tiger before feeding time. When he finally disconnected the call, he stood for a while in silence, mentally debriefing himself on what had just happened.

Eventually, he noticed Bell staring at him, and walked over.

"What was that?" asked Bell.

Wyler didn't answer at first, he just stood and grinned. His mood had completely changed.

"We've got him!" Wyler said.

"What do you mean?" Bell asked, but Wyler was already on his way to the cockpit to talk to the pilot.

CHAPTER 30

It was just after 9:00 o'clock when they landed on the private Bahamian island of Caliban Cay. The Cessna taxied beyond the island's exclusive airstrip to an area crowded with dozens of other private jets, parked in rows like new cars on a dealership lot. After coming to a stop, the clamshell-style door on the side of the plane popped opened and became a staircase that Wyler descended carefully, followed by Bell. Wyler immediately noticed a full moon hanging low over the sea, ominously large and threateningly close. A pair of golf carts were just pulling up as Wyler and Bell reached the bottom of the plane's steps.

"Hello, I'm Carol Reinert, one of the event coordinators." A woman in a pantsuit wearing a headset stood up from the front passenger seat of the first golf cart. "Could I just get your names, please?" She held an iPad and began tapping on the screen. The second golf cart was a security vehicle with an orange dome light mounted on a pole. Two armed men in gray security uniforms sat in the second cart but didn't get out.

"I need to see Mr. Hibble, right away," Wyler said, removing the expired badge from his jacket and making sure the rent-a-cops got a glimpse of the Glock 22 strapped to his shoulder.

"What is this about? This is a private event."

"Not for very long," said Wyler. "Where's Hibble?"

As the woman stepped closer to examine Wyler's badge, Wyler caught a questioning look from Bell, who was obviously surprised by Wyler's direct approach. The truth was, Wyler had planned to infiltrate the proceedings secretly, but things changed after the phone call he took on the plane.

"NYPD?" she said, straightening up. "You don't have any jurisdiction here. This is an island in the Bahamas."

"Do you want to take responsibility for involving the RBP? Fine. Give them a call. Ask for Rollie Sterling. He's the chief. Look," Wyler continued, leaning in and lowering his voice. "I'm trying to handle this discreetly. I know this island is full of VIPs and A-listers. If you want to call the police, go ahead, but where they go, the press follows. Is that what you want?"

Her face darkened as she imagined a full-blown fiasco with her name on it.

"Where's Hibble?"

"Mr. Hibble is at the oath ceremony with most of the other conference attendees. It's the final event of festival."

Wyler and Bell exchanged a look.

"Take us there," Wyler said, climbing into the back of the first golf cart. Following his lead, Bell climbed in next to him.

The woman, obviously perturbed, glanced nervously back to the security guards, as if trying to draw strength from their presence or will them to do something, but they just sat in the golf cart, inert. Wyler's badge, gun, and take-command presence had had the intended effect of neutering them.

"Now!" Wyler barked.

Reluctantly, the woman climbed into the front passenger seat. "This is a private event," she repeated weakly, almost to herself, as if making sure her official protest was on the record.

"Let's go," said Wyler to the driver, a man with a blond handlebar mustache wearing a polo shirt and a baseball cap.

"Take us to the west pavilion," the woman instructed the driver, and the cart zoomed forward and made a U-turn. Wyler looked back and saw the security vehicle was following, but not too closely.

After leaving the smooth concrete of the island's airstrip, the golf cart began crunching and bumping along a pebbled path. For the first few minutes, the scenery all around was featureless and flat, marked only by a few shallow sandbars and patches of dense shrubs. Wyler was starting to wonder if owning a private island in the Bahamas sounded better than it actually was. Then, the cart passed over a paved bridge under a series of sprawling white arches. On the other side, the path was lined by tall palm trees swaying in the nighttime breeze. Wyler couldn't see the ocean from where they were, but the sound of waves crashing into the shore came from all directions, like a surround sound system in a movie theater. Through the trees, Wyler noticed a series of identical bungalows along the beach, linked together by raised wooden walkways, like sidewalks on the sand. He counted over thirty of these small, luxury cottages before the cart swerved off in another direction.

The woman with the headset turned around to face Wyler.

"Can you tell me what this is about?" She had dropped the official tone and seemed to be asking for herself, afraid that somehow she had gotten entangled in something.

"How long to the pavilion?" asked Wyler.

"It's just over that ridge," she answered, giving up and turning back to face the front.

The cart path curved again, and they were suddenly moving along the outer perimeter of a large inlet cove surrounded on all sides by a narrow sandy beach. The beach was studded with lounge furniture and glass tables where people were eating, drinking, smoking, laughing, and dancing around bonfires to blasting music. Staff in polo shirts ferried trays of drinks and food among the partyers, which included several famous faces that Wyler recognized. There was a carnival-like atmosphere on the beach, with some people fully dressed, others wearing bathing suits or parts of bathing suits, and some who weren't bothering with clothing at all. A gentle breeze blew in from the water, and Wyler suddenly felt like he was in the back of a hippie's van. He caught the cleaning chemical aroma of methamphetamine, the vinegary, acidic scent of heroin, and the heavy, distinctive odor of cannabis, all mixed together like a bouquet of illegal smells. He exchanged a look with Bell, whose face was scrunched up in reaction.

On the other side of the cart path, a series of large villas the size of small hotels had been built into the rocky landscape, and each overhanging patio and courtyard was hosting its own crowded party. In one house, Wyler saw several famous people, including a well-respected news anchor, sitting around a table covered in a small mountain of white powder.

"I thought you said everyone was at this oath ceremony," Wyler said to the woman in the front seat.

"Not everyone chose to go to the ceremony. It was optional," she answered huffily without turning around.

The cart moved past the beach and traveled up and over a gentle slope, then gradually down a long hill that cut through a dense forest. Wyler could hear a man's voice, amplified by loudspeakers, echoing through the trees, getting louder as they approached. As the cart turned a corner, they came upon an incredible sight: a large outdoor stadium made up of rows of stone ledges carved into a cliff face overlooking the beach below like an ancient Greek amphitheater. Wyler estimated the crowd size at just over a thousand people.

"Stop here," said Wyler, and both he and Bell jumped out of the cart before it had time to stop. They moved quickly and quietly and found a spot between two palm trees just behind the last row of seating. On the beach below, Layton Howe, the tech billionaire who had participated in the television interviews Wyler had sat through the week before, was holding a microphone and addressing the crowd. Tall arc lights mounted on metal scaffolds lit the arena around the narrow slip of beach that functioned as the stage. He was flanked by two giant screens that projected his image, while ocean waves behind him provided a dramatic backdrop.

"Gandhi said that poverty is the greatest form of violence, and we agree," Howe was saying to the crowd. "But solutions cannot be focused simply on providing immediate relief, as important and necessary as that may be. In the poverty working group, we decided to go beyond relief and focus on long-term, sustainable economic development targeted at the root causes of human poverty. We came up with a seven-point plan."

About half a dozen individuals were sharing the stage with Howe, all seated on tall stools. Wyler recognized most of them: Maggie Wells-Walling, the TV sitcom actress; movie director Arthur Mapleton; Gustav Muck, celebrity scientist and host of the popular series *Spacetime* on public television. Standing off to the side was Scottie Hibble, listening and nodding along as Howe spoke.

"What is this?" whispered Bell. "What's going on?"

But Wyler didn't answer. He kept watching as Howe read from a sheet of paper, reciting a bland series of wonky policy proposals and initiatives designed to combat poverty in developing countries around the world. When he finished, Hibble stepped forward and began clapping. The crowd answered with enthusiastic applause mixed with a few hoots and hollers.

Hibble handed the microphone next to an elderly, dark-skinned woman with white hair peeking out from under a colorful headscarf. She stood hunched over in front of her stool and began speaking in a thick Indian accent about climate change. She held the microphone too close and yelled into it, distorting her voice and making her words difficult to understand.

As Wyler continued to watch and listen, he became fascinated by the sheer dullness, the utter tedium, of the spectacle.

When the old woman finished, Hibble took control of the microphone again. He thanked those on the stage for their service over the past few days as facilitators. He also thanked the entire audience and all those who had participated in the various working groups dealing with topics such as women's health, education, structural racism, technology, poverty, and climate change.

"But it's not enough to simply develop plans and to make promises," Hibble continued, walking to the front of the sand and looking out over the crowd. "What sets Bonfire apart, what makes this event special—no, special is not the right word—what will make this event *impactful* is the willingness of all of us to make a commitment. To take an oath, together."

"What are we going to do?" Bell said in a whispered panic.

"The oath that we take together this night will bind all of us together in a sacred pact. There are no cameras here to record what is about to happen. No one will be asked to sign anything. The oath that this group, on this island, will take here tonight, is more powerful than any legal document. It will reach into your very heart and soul and forge a united fellowship of solemn, sanctified purpose."

"We should get down there and stop this," Bell insisted.

"Just wait," Wyler said, without taking his eyes off Hibble.

"I ask all of you now to please stand," said Hibble, spreading his arms out like wings as the sound of hundreds of people simultaneously rising from their seats rumbled like a shock wave through the night air. Wyler and Bell, still hidden in the trees, unseen and unnoticed, stared in mesmerized silence, afraid to move or breathe.

"Please repeat after me," began Hibble. As he spoke, he paused between phrases, allowing the crowd to echo his words in a thunderous mantra. "I solemnly vow...to live my life in accordance with the values and principals of Bonfire...I will consecrate my power, passion, and influence...to implement the plans and programs discussed here...I vow to channel... my physical and spiritual and psychic energy...in a positive direction...toward the betterment of all people...of all races and genders...and to work toward common solutions to the world's problems."

When the crowd finished repeating the last phrase, there was a brief interlude of reverent silence, and then, suddenly, a wild cheer rose up from the crowd, and a party atmosphere broke out. A loud explosion was heard, and Wyler and Bell instinctively ducked for cover, but then fireworks began bursting overhead, filling the sky over the outdoor amphitheater with bright streaks of color and light. A live rock band began playing on the beach below as people stood up and started to leave and mingle.

Wyler turned to Bell.

"What just happened?" asked Bell, confused.

"That didn't sound to me like a satanic oath," said Wyler.

CHAPTER 31

The golf cart that had dropped them off was still waiting where they had left it at the top of the amphitheater. The security vehicle was gone, however, as was Carol Reinert.

"Can you get us down to the stage area?" Wyler asked the waiting driver as he climbed into the front seat.

"No problem," said the driver.

But driving down to the beach turned out to be a problem after all, as the cart path was congested with people leaving the oath ceremony. Wyler was tempted at several points to hop out of the golf cart and continue down the hill on foot.

When they finally reached the bottom of the path, Wyler turned to the driver.

"Could you wait here please?"

"Yes, sir," responded the man.

Wyler, followed by Bell, approached the narrow strip of sheltered beach that had served as a stage for the ceremony. It was empty now, except for Scottie Hibble, who was standing in the middle of the beach listening to an anxious report from Carol Reinert, who looked positively stricken. She was obviously briefing Hibble on Wyler's presence on the island, a fact confirmed by the reaction she gave when she glanced over and saw Wyler approaching.

"Hi, Scottie," said Wyler calmly, as he stepped onto the beach.

"Carol, get on the radio and have security send some people here right away." Hibble spoke with authority, but then he turned and yelled at Wyler like a surly teenager, "You're trespassing on private property!"

Wyler casually removed his gun from the shoulder holster and pointed it at Hibble. Carol's mouth dropped open in a violent intake of breath, and she let out a half scream. Hibble's eyes grew wide and he stepped back, putting Carol, who had frozen in place, between himself and the gun.

"What are you doing?" Hibble stammered, his voice quivering.

"Scottie Hibble, you're under arrest," Wyler said calmly as he took a step forward to counter Hibble's step back.

"Yeah, right! You're not even a cop anymore!" Hibble sneered.

"I can legally detain you until law enforcement arrives, and they're on the way."

"Who's on the way? What are you talking about?"

"In a few minutes, this island will be swarming with the Royal Bahamas Police."

"Idiot! This is private island!"

"Yes, it is. And it also falls under the jurisdiction of the RBP. They're coming to arrest you, Scottie, for the murder of Ashley Lang."

Hibble forced a fake laugh.

"That's stupid. Ashley died in a boating accident. I wasn't even here!"

"Yes, I heard your story. She fell off one of your yachts and drowned."

"That's right! It was an accident! It wasn't murder!" As Hibble spoke, he maintained a tight grip on Carol Reinert's arm, using her like a human shield.

"You're wrong, Scottie. According to the chemicals found in her body, Ashley was drugged and dumped off the side of the boat. That's murder."

For a moment, Hibble's eyes became wild and fearful, like a cornered animal, then he recovered.

"That's a lie! There weren't any drugs in her system!"

"I know why you think that, Scottie. And you're right, the original blood test done after her death showed no signs of chemicals. That's why the drug you used, Flunitrazepam, is such a popular date rape drug, because it washes out of the system so quickly. Normal tests, like blood and saliva, don't detect it after twenty-four hours. But what you don't know is a new test has recently been developed. It turns out that Flunitrazepam actually stays in the hair for up to a month. I understand why you didn't know that. My friend Rollie Sterling, chief of the Royal Bahamas Police, also wasn't aware of the new test. Until I told him about it."

Hibble listened in silence. The rhythm of waves crashing violently against the jagged rocks behind him seemed to increase in tempo and intensity, as if nature were providing a soundtrack to the tense standoff.

"Even if that's true, which is probably isn't," Hibble said, in a subdued voice, "I didn't have anything to do with that. I wasn't even here."

"This morning the RBP arrested the two men who had been on the boat with Ashley, and though I can't say I approve of all the methods they used to extract information, both men gave detailed statements about your involvement. According to them, they were hired by you and working under your orders."

"I'm an American citizen! They don't have any authority over me!"

"That would have been true if you hadn't come to Caliban Cay. But you're here, Scottie."

Wyler took a step toward Hibble.

"It's over, Scottie. We know about everything. About Honduras. About Mosquitia. We know about Doug McBride and Steve Ridgeway."

Wyler saw the shock register in Hibble's eyes at the sound of those two names.

"We know you killed all those kids in the jungle. You killed your friends."

Hibble's eyes suddenly lost focus, as if his mind was in another place, another time.

"We know about the gemstone, about the Urim and Thummim."

Wyler saw the brazen defiance in Hibble's face begin to slip.

"We know about Edgar Dordevic!"

At this, Scottie Hibble suddenly shoved his human shield toward Wyler and took off running. As Carol Reinert screamed, Hibble climbed over the rocks, tumbled to the other side, then took off down the shoreline and into the night.

Wyler holstered his gun and started to chase after him, but Jason Bell streaked passed him like a runaway train. Bell soared over the giant boulders like it was an Olympic event he had medaled in. Wyler awkwardly scaled the rocks, scraping his leg in the process, and dropped onto the other side just in time to see Bell overtake and slam into Hibble like a guided missile.

When Wyler finally caught up to them on the beach, Bell was on top of Hibble, pinning him down. Hibble, flat on his back on the sand, was blubbering like a baby.

"It wasn't me! It wasn't me! It was him!"

"Who? Dordevic?"

Hibble looked at Wyler, and Wyler saw terror in his eyes.

"I can't tell you. He'll kill me. Or worse."

"It's over Scottie. You might as well think of yourself now."

But Hibble was shaking his head from side to side like a baby facing a forkful of veggies.

"Start from the beginning Scottie. What happened in Honduras? Why did you kill all those kids? Your friends!"

Scottie Hibble began sobbing.

"It was Dordevic. He murdered them. He had them gunned down right in front of me."

"That's not true! You're the one who did it! You were part of it!"

"No! I swear! It was him!"

"So why did he spare you?"

"He said he liked me. He said I was smarter, savvier than the others. He said they were just a bunch of naïve, brainwashed fools, but I had real talent and could think for myself. He said he needed someone like me. He said if I listened to him, he could make me famous and rich. He gave me the idea for RopeLine. He gave me the money to do it. It was all him!"

"What did you find on that expedition? What was in that stone box?"

Hibble looked shocked at Wyler's knowledge, but then said, "I don't know. I swear. He never let me see it."

"What about Peter Lisonbee?"

"That was Dordevic, too. He's the one who made me become friends with him. I hadn't seen Dordevic in years, then he showed up out of the blue a couple months ago and told me to get close to Peter Lisonbee. He said I had to arrange to meet him that same night. I couldn't say no to him."

"Is that all he said about Peter?"

"He said Peter had messed up or something. Made a big mistake. He'd gotten greedy and now Dordevic finally knew who he was. I don't know! I never understood half of what that guy said!"

"Did he kill Peter Lisonbee?"

"I don't know."

"Come on, Scottie! He held a gun on Peter and made him jump!"

"I don't know what happened to Peter! I swear! Dordevic said he wanted me to tell Peter I'd go into business with him so he wouldn't sell this gemstone that he had. So I did. Then Peter died, and Dordevic told me he needed help getting the gemstone from this place in Brooklyn. He had it all arranged, he just needed a woman to pose as the sister."

"So that's where Ashley Lang came in."

"Ashley agreed to do it for me, and she got the gemstone. But then, after you showed up that day, Dordevic said Ashley had to die." Hibble started a new round of sobbing.

"So you sent her on a business trip down here and arranged for her to be murdered."

"I didn't want to do it. I really liked Ashley. It was Dordevic. You don't understand!"

"What about the people you sent to kill me?"

"I don't know anything about that! That was him! He has this power over people! You don't understand!"

"Where's the gemstone?"

"He has it."

"And where is Dordevic now?"

"He's here, on the island."

"Where?" demanded Wyler.

"There's a cave on the eastern slope, near the cliffs."

"What's he doing there?"

Hibble didn't answer. He seemed to slip into a state of shock, and just shook his head slowly from side to side. "You don't understand...you don't understand..." mumbled Hibble, repeating the words over and over. Seeing that Hibble was lost now, Wyler spoke to Bell.

"Can you stay with him?"

"He's not going anywhere," said Bell.

"Hold him here until the police arrive."

Bell nodded, then said, "Go!"

Wyler turned and started running east.

CHAPTER 32

As Wyler ran east, the golf cart driven by the guy with the blond handlebar mustache pulled up alongside him.

"Hop in," the man said, slowing the golf cart enough for Wyler to jump in.

"There's a cave, on the eastern slope of the island, by the cliffs," Wyler said, catching his breath.

"We'll find it," the man said, speeding on. They followed the cart path behind the outdoor amphitheater and continued east through a dense forest of pine trees. Wyler looked at the man in the driver's seat. He had a lined, leathery face that seemed to have weathered a lot of life.

"What's your name?" Wyler asked.

"Dennis. Dennis Wilkinson." His spoke in short, laconic phrases that reminded Wyler of an old western cowboy.

"Do you work here full-time, Dennis?"

"No sir, I do not. I was hired on just last week through an agency in Nassau. Based on what I've seen on this island over the past few days, I can't say I'm very surprised by the things you were saying down on the beach."

As they emerged from the trees, the cart path arced in a wide horseshoe back toward the center of the island. Dennis brought the cart to a stop at the turn in front of a wild, undeveloped dirt field that stretched out as far as they could see.

"The path ends here, but the eastern cliffs are that way."

"Let's go," Wyler said.

"It's going to get bumpy," Dennis said, as they left the path and continued east.

The terrain was rugged, and the cart bounced and shook violently, swerving between rocks, patches of shrubs, and large cactus plants. As the cart's batteries drained, the headlights dimmed and cut the visibility to just a few feet.

Eventually, they came to a cliff lined by low, jagged rocks, and Dennis slammed on the brakes just in time.

"Looks like these are the east cliffs," said Dennis.

"Let's try to find a way down."

They turned right and headed south, carefully following the border of the cliffs at a safe distance. Eventually, they found a break in the rocks and turned into it, dropping down a steep incline that twisted back on itself and dead ended at a grove of palm trees too thick to navigate in the cart.

"Cut the lights," Wyler whispered.

Off in the distance, Wyler could see several tiny points of light flickering through the trees. He brought his finger to his lips, and they both listened, straining to pick up any unnatural sound. At first, there was nothing, but when the warm breeze stroking the palm trees momentarily died, the low, sporadic rumble of human speech reached them.

Wyler climbed out of the cart, and then stopped and looked up. Another unnatural sound was buzzing in the distance. It started as a dull growl, then grew louder and louder, approaching the island from the north sky. A few moments later, a noisy pack of helicopters shattered the soundscape completely, roaring past them directly overhead and continuing on to the center of the island.

"Can you make it back from here?" Wyler asked Dennis.

"I think I'd better wait for you."

"Dennis, listen to me. I need you to head back and find Chief Sterling. He's the chief of the RBP. He's on one of those choppers. Find him and tell him where I am. Tell him to send some backup my way."

Dennis nodded, then backed up the cart, executed a three-point turn, and drove off.

Wyler unholstered his gun.

CHAPTER 33

Wyler moved carefully and stealthily through the trees, taking great care with each footstep. He held his gun in one hand and his cellphone in the other, angling it down and using the glow from the screen to light a path.

As he approached the edge of the forest, he stopped, then cautiously inched forward.

The flickering points of light Wyler had glimpsed through the trees turned out to be about two dozen tiki torches staked in a wide, circular pattern around a small clearing in the woods. The area was bordered on three sides by the forest and on the far side by the towering cliff face.

Wyler paused and remained perfectly still. From his vantage point tucked several feet within the tree line, he had a clear view of what was taking place.

The clearing was filled with dozens of people, perhaps fifty or sixty, seated on folding chairs arranged in semicircular rows pointed toward a large cave in the cliff wall. Most people were facing away from Wyler, and he could only see the backs of their heads. But those positioned on each side of the semicircle sat at a slight angle, and the profiles of some of them were visible to

Wyler by the light of the torches. Wesley Tanner, the host of one of the most popular cable news programs in the country, was seated at the far end of one of the rows. Wyler recognized self-help author Ariana Primrose a few seats down from Tanner. As he scanned the crowd, he saw other faces that were familiar. Movie star Jack Wade, whom he had seen the week before at Scottie Hibble's office, was there, along with Dr. Rita Hopkins, a former surgeon general. In one row, British comedian Derick Stiles was sitting next to Senator Mark Sheffield. Based on the diverse variety of clothing styles, Wyler guessed that many different countries were represented in the gathering. One man with his back to Wyler was wearing the white robe and head covering common to members of the Saudi royal family.

Positioned at the center, just in front of the blackness of the cave opening, was a podium. Behind the podium stood a large man, almost seven feet tall. He had broad shoulders and a large square head that looked as if it had been chiseled from granite that had faded for centuries in the sun. He had long white hair and thick, bushy eyebrows that arched over a pair of bulging, wild eyes. An unruly black mustache tapered down the sides of his face and merged into a sharp, white goatee. A long, heavy black cloth was draped over one of his shoulders like a toga.

The man wore an unusual apparatus strapped around his forehead. It looked somewhat like a jeweler's loupe, with a half-visor that extended outward from his face on one side. But instead of the usual magnifying eyepiece, the visor held a small, black gemstone which hung down in front of the man's eyes, illuminated by a tiny light fastened to the apparatus. The tall man was leaning over, speaking in a low voice as he peered through the gemstone at something on the podium.

As he spoke, the man paused after each phrase, allowing the people in the crowd to repeat or answer his words.

Wyler strained but couldn't make out what was being said.

The man at the podium was too far away, and the murmured response from the crowd mixed with the island breeze reached him as a hushed, indecipherable chant.

Then, Wyler remembered the camera feature on his phone. He held the phone up and began recording, but as he looked at the screen, he could see that the bright flames of the tiki torches were washing out the rest of the image, making everything else a dark blur.

Frustrated, Wyler's mind raced, searching for tactical options. In the end, he was swayed by the merits of a direct approach.

He suddenly stepped out of the trees and into the clearing, held up his Glock 22, and fired three shots into the air.

The loud explosions pierced the air like bolts of lightning, provoking a collective gasp and scattered screams from the conclave's participants. All heads turned, and the focus of the secret assembly shifted immediately from the podium in front to Wyler in back.

"Those helicopters you heard a few minutes ago belong to the Royal Bahamas Police," Wyler announced, stepping forward through the torches. "They've landed by now and have arrested Scottie Hibble for murder. Oh, and I should mention that they've brought the media with them and are on their way to this very spot right now."

As soon as Wyler mentioned the word media, pandemonium broke out. People immediately stood and began leaving. Some knocked over folding chairs as they rushed to get away as quickly as possible. Before long, the exodus turned into a mad scramble. Wyler noticed a line of golf carts parked on the opposite side of the clearing. In the chaos and panic that ensued some people jumped into empty carts and drove off alone, leaving several celebrities and dignitaries to pile into overcrowded vehicles and others to scurry off into the night on foot. Wyler wryly noted the sudden desperation of the group to distance themselves from what, moments ago, had probably been considered the most elite and exclusive event on the island.

There was only one person who didn't move at all.

Edgar Dordevic stood motionless behind the podium like a stationary lighthouse in the raging storm. In the midst of all the commotion, his eyes remain fixed calmly and deliberately on Wyler, even as he removed papers from the podium and placed them in an inner garment pocket.

Wyler, gun in hand and pointed forward, began moving slowly toward Dordevic.

"That stone you have there doesn't belong to you," Wyler said as he approached the podium carefully.

Dordevic continued to stare in silence at Wyler. Then, as Wyler reached the podium, Dordevic slowly removed the apparatus from his head. Wyler tensed the arm holding the gun, but Dordevic surprised him by gently removing the stone from the apparatus, then tossing it to the ground. It landed in front of Wyler with a soft thud.

Without taking his eyes off Dordevic, Wyler bent down slowly. Then, quickly but carefully, he picked up the stone and stuffed it in his pocket.

"I'm arresting you for the murder of Ashley Lang and Peter Lisonbee."

As Wyler said this, the corners of Dordevic's mouth curled upward slightly, but only for a moment, before collapsing back into expressionlessness.

They stood for a long minute, facing each other in a frozen tableau. Only the sound of the night breeze rustling the trees and ocean waves breaking against the shore filled the silence.

Then, Dordevic turned and began slowly walking away.

"Stop!" cried Wyler, firing another shot into the air just as Dordevic disappeared from the clearing.

Wyler followed him into the jungle of tall palm trees a

moment later. It was like walking into a dark room, with the light of the moon providing only a few feet of visibility. He relied on his ears, and soon heard the sound of Dordevic's footsteps moving through the foliage. He followed.

He cursed himself for not restraining Dordevic back in the clearing. The darkness and unfamiliar landscape had robbed him of his tactical advantage, evening the odds and making him vulnerable. In the blackness of the jungle, Wyler was forced to move slowly and pause every few steps to listen for Dordevic. If he risked pursuing any faster, the noise of his own movements could block out the sound of Dordevic, causing Wyler to lose the trail or worse, opening himself up to a surprise ambush in the dark.

Up ahead, the audio trail he was pursuing veered to the left, and soon Wyler was on a sloping incline, feeling in the dark for branches to steady himself. He stumbled in the dirt and rocks more than once but kept moving, at times using tree trunks as leverage to propel himself forward. The pain from his bandaged hand began to bite, and he wondered if the knife wound had reopened.

As he fought his way to the top of the hill, Wyler suddenly realized that the sound of Dordevic's movements had ceased. He froze in place and listened for several moments, but there was nothing. In a panic, Wyler scrambled to the top of the hill, emerging from the forest of trees onto a flat, rocky ridge.

About fifteen yards away, standing in the moonlight facing Wyler, was Edgar Dordevic. Wyler panted heavily, wiping his forehead and trying to catch his breath as perspiration dripped down his face. Dordevic, on the other hand, stood still and quiet, patiently waiting for Wyler.

Wyler suddenly remembered the gun in his hand and pointed it at Dordevic.

As he moved toward Dordevic, gradually closing the distance

between them, he saw that Dordevic was standing on the edge of steep cliff. Wyler glanced over the precipice down to the ocean smashing into a rocky beach hundreds of feet below, then quickly met Dordevic's gaze head on.

"I will shoot you if I have to," said Wyler, coming to a stop about ten feet away, and for the second time that night he saw the corner of Dordevic's mouth twitch upward, hinting at a grin that vanished before it began.

In truth, Wyler knew the threat to shoot Dordevic was an empty one. He had no real authority. If he shot Dordevic, it would be murder, plain and simple, like the ones he himself had investigated, back when he was a real cop. But he wasn't a cop anymore. He was just pretending to be one. Even the badge in his pocket was a useless trinket, like an expired driver's license or a teenager's fake ID. It was phony. Fake. Just like his threat to Dordevic. If the threat rang hollow in his own mind, then what must Dordevic be thinking? Suddenly, Wyler saw himself in a new, unpleasant light. He had once had a job, and a real purpose in life. He fit into things, was part of the machinery of the world that, for better or worse, cranked forward, day by day. Now, he was just an extra piece that didn't fit anywhere. What was he doing, standing out here alone in the middle of the night on this island, playing cops and robbers, pretending to be something that he wasn't? Wyler suddenly felt like a complete and utter fool. Clown was a better word for it. He saw clearly now that since Jessica's death, his life had spiraled downward and completely out of control. The image of Detective Bonavitch of the 6th precinct sneering and laughing at him flashed in his mind. He imagined colleagues and former supervisors having a field day, sharing the news about the pitiful joke that Aaron Wyler had become. The news about him would probably even spread to people he had put behind bars. He imagined the faces of criminals, laughing at him, laughing at his wife's suicide.

But it really wasn't suicide, was it? It was more like murder. He had murdered Jessica. Murdered her as surely as if he had forced the bag onto her head and held it there as he turned on the gas. He should be in prison, right next to those laughing at him. Or perhaps instead of them, because his crimes were worse. So what if he hadn't directly caused her death? If she had been married to a stable, loving man, someone who was emotionally available and caring, she would be alive today. He had seen the signs and chosen to ignore them. He had known Jessica was suffering and did nothing. And now she was dead. Murdered by him. And not only her. What about all the people she could have cared for and saved as a doctor? He was responsible for their deaths, too. Their blood was on his hands.

Standing there, at that moment, Wyler saw his life completely and clearly for the first time. He was finally looking at himself honestly, without the hundreds of lies he had to tell himself day in and day out just to function. His life had been like a runaway train that had hopped the tracks in a peaceful suburban neighborhood, plowing through and destroying innumerable homes and families, wrecking and smashing everything it touched.

He snickered at the irony of it all. He had spent his so-called career trying to prevent the slaughter of innocents from a bomb or some other weapon, all the while he himself was a walking weapon of mass destruction, tearing through the lives of people he loved. People like Gabe.

Poor Gabe. His poor, tragic, innocent son! What had he done to him? It wasn't enough for him to wreck his own life and destroy Jessica, but now he was maiming his son's future. He wasn't capable of providing the love and support that his son needed! Even Gabe was smart enough to sense that, to see him for who and what he was—an emotionally abusive and destructive monster. That's why Gabe was so distant! His son had put a wall between them. Good for Gabe! Wyler realized now that Gabe had erected the emotional barrier as a form of self-defense, to protect himself from his father, hoping to avoid his mother's fate. His own efforts to break through that wall had probably terrified Gabe all along.

Jason and Laura Bell and their children were a real family, while his was a depressing freak show that served no purpose other than as a cautionary tale. He could see that now. Gabe needed to get out, to get away from him. It was his only hope. It was the only chance he had of having a normal, healthy life. He needed to free his son of his own destructive influence. That was the only thing he could do for Gabe that would matter; the one gesture he could offer that would actually help him. The way to rescue Gabe was to eliminate himself completely from the picture. Then, Gabe would finally be free to live, to breathe, to grow, to flourish, to prosper! He wanted that for his son. He wanted that for him more than anything in the world!

Tears began to flow down Wyler's cheeks, moistening the dirt crusted to his face. Slowly, he raised the hand that was holding the gun. He brought it up to his shoulder, then to his chin. The gun was heavy, heavier than it ever felt before. It was like lifting a barbell, but he kept going, bringing the gun up to his face. Then, finally, he raised it to just below his hairline. It had been a long journey up to his temple, and his arm was tired. Bracing the gun against his head made the gun lighter, easier to handle. It felt like the gun was finally home, and it was relaxing.

Gabe was going to be free! Finally, the boy would have peace. The doors of his dungeon would fly open. He would be released from the dark, harrowing torture chamber of his life with Aaron Wyler, the beast, the destroyer of people's lives.

All he had to do now was make a slight movement with his finger. It was a movement he had practiced hundreds, no, thousands, of times before. Only this would be the last time. In all the rehearsals that had come before, he had conjured an imaginary villain on the receiving end of his bullet. Now, at the end, he had finally found the one and only real villain in his life, and there was no chance of missing.

Time seemed to stop. He had to act now. He knew that. He had reached the final moment of his life on earth. He felt all the emotion and energy drain from his body, leaving behind an empty husk.

The final mystery, of death itself, would soon be revealed to him. What would it be like?

Death was calling to him now. He could hear it, summoning him by name. His name.

"Aaron!"

The voice was far off.

"Aaron! Aaron!" The voice kept calling to him, urgent and pleading, and then, suddenly, Aaron recognized the voice. He glanced over the face of the cliff and saw the small figure of a man standing hundreds of feet below on the sand. Jason Bell had a frenzied look of panic on his face as he called up to Aaron.

"Aaron!"

And then Wyler became aware of physical pain. He felt a pinching or biting sensation, like a bee sting or the bite of a scorpion. Where was it coming from?

It was his head. The pain was coming from the side of his head.

What was it? He was confused, like waking up from a strange dream in an unfamiliar place.

And then, Wyler realized the source of the pain was the cold, sharp metallic muzzle of a gun being pressed forcefully against the side of his head.

He realized it was his own gun, and he himself was holding it.

He tried to focus, to emerge from the black cavern of his own thoughts, but it was a struggle.

A dark shape several feet away suddenly formed into the

outline of a man. There was another man here with him. The man was looking at him, staring at him. He knew the man and didn't know him at the same time. It was a strange, foreign sensation. He felt lost, disoriented.

Where was he? What was he doing? How long had he been standing here?

His mind desperately searched for guideposts, but there were none. There was only the man.

The man.

He knew that man!

But from where? Where had he seen him before?

And then, he remembered. It was the same man who had come out of Peter Lisonbee's apartment, the night he jumped to his death.

It was Edgar Dordevic, and he was...staring at Wyler.

And as he realized this, his mind seemed to wake up from the dream, and, like a computer rebooting, it processed several different levels of information simultaneously. Wyler knew, at that moment, that no pointed gun had threatened Peter Lisonbee the night that he took his own life. Dordevic needed no such weapon. Somehow, in some way, he had turned the boy's own thoughts against him. Wielding some power Wyler didn't understand and couldn't even conceive of, Dordevic had plowed the hidden trenches of the boy's mind, searching for weakness, for vulnerability. What buried insecurities he had found in the young man to exploit, Wyler didn't know. Perhaps it had been unresolved feelings of guilt and shame about his relationship with his father, or perhaps his own identity. In the end, it didn't matter. There are chips and cracks hidden in the deepest recesses of every human ego, and Dordevic had somehow insinuated himself into those razor thin crevices and violently ripped them open, letting the bile overflow and spill out to drench and soak his mind in a deluge of self-loathing. That was the extreme stress event that had injured the young man's heart in the last minutes of his life. Of course the young man had jumped.

And in the same instant that all of this became clear to Wyler, the two other incidents from Peter's apartment building suddenly made sense to Wyler. The dark energy emanating from Dordevic that night had rippled outward like a shockwave, randomly effecting other people, causing one heart attack and one senseless act of murderous violence. Collateral damage.

Quickly and without thinking, Wyler drew back his arm and with all the strength he could muster he threw the gun over the side of the cliff. It spun down and out of sight and fell noiselessly into the dark void beyond the cliff's edge.

As soon as he completed the action, some unseen force took hold of Wyler and forced him to the ground. It was a real, tangible force that he could feel pressing against him, overwhelming and restraining him. It was not human, and yet Wyler was aware of a malevolent intelligence. It was not a physical entity and yet it had a force and substance a thousand times stronger than anything Wyler had ever experienced before, beyond anything he had ever conceived of. Wyler was pinned to the ground by this force and lay there, completely helpless under its power and influence. Like a living nightmare, he was aware of what was happening but was paralyzed and mute, unable to move or to speak.

As he lay prostrate and inert on his side, he glimpsed Dordevic's feet and legs moving toward him. But then, a moment later, the darkness of the night seemed to gather and close in around him, blocking out the light of the moon and stars and abandoning him in a black void.

In that moment, the moment before his death, Wyler's heart filled with love for Gabe, and for Jessica, and for his parents, and his brother, and for all those lives that had touched his for good or ill throughout his life.

And then suddenly, in the blackness, he heard a sound

coming from Dordevic, or from where Dordevic had been standing. It was unlike anything he had ever heard before. It was a tortured wail, sickening and sad, the anguished shriek of an animal howling in pain. It was so loud, so piercing, that Wyler's hands reflexively pressed against his ears to block it out.

And then, the horrible inhuman scream receded, echoing in every direction for a moment and then disappearing. He knew somehow that Dordevic was gone, and as the horrible sound faded away, the invisible force restraining him instantly dissipated.

Wyler lay still on the ground for a period of time. Minutes? Hours? He didn't know. He did know that the evil presence that had seized hold of him and bound him in its power had ceased to exist. It had left him, along with Dordevic.

But as he sensed this, he sensed also that he was not alone.

Realizing his eyes were closed, he slowly opened them.

When he did, he was surprised to find that he was no longer in darkness. The night had ended. There was light around him. He could clearly see things lying next to him. The brown dirt, a few gray rocks, the green grass. Had he been lying here all night? Had morning come?

No, he realized, it hadn't. He now noticed that the light around him extended only a few feet and then ended in a wall of blackness. It was still nighttime, but he was in a small pool of light. The light was coming from some source directly above him.

He looked up and saw a figure standing over him. It was the figure of a man. It wasn't Dordevic. He knew that. Dordevic was gone. This was a different man, a man whose body seemed to be emitting a soft, warm glow that was the source of the light in which he now lay. As Wyler stared up at the man, he was reminded of creatures in nature, like fireflies or jellyfish, whose bodies glow with bioluminescence.

And at that same moment, every bit of fear or pain or anger or sadness he had ever felt in his life instantly left him, like a candle snuffed out in the breeze, and an overwhelming sensation of peace and calm flooded into Wyler's soul. It sanctified him, cleansed him, flushing away in an instant a lifetime of accumulated burdens and sorrows.

He continued staring up at the glowing figure above him, and then, before he could form any additional thoughts, the light around this man began to dim. Slowly and gradually it died out, leaving behind a human face and form, with natural texture and definition.

It was a face that Wyler recognized.

It was Eugene, Wyler and Gabe's friend from the hobby shop in Poughkeepsie.

Only, it couldn't be. It was impossible for Eugene to be here.

Wyler realized he must be hallucinating.

He must have passed out at that point, for the next thing he knew, his body was levitating. Up and down in a gentle rhythm, he moved forward in the darkness, cutting through the warm breeze of the island. But how could he be moving? He was still lying down. And then he realized he was being carried. He felt disembodied, with no sense of space, but he forced his head to flop to one side and, just before he passed out for the second time, he saw Eugene's face again, closer now, hovering just above him, staring forward.

When he woke up again, he was on the chartered plane that had brought him to the island. The plane was in flight, and Jason Bell was standing over him this time.

"Are you okay?" he asked.

"What happened?" asked Wyler. "How did I...?"

"I don't know. When I finally got to the top of that cliff, you were gone. Then, when I got back to the plane, you were already here, out like a light."

"Where's Eugene?"

"Who?" asked Bell. Wyler saw the confused look on Bell's face.

"Where's Hibble?" Wyler asked, straightening up and collecting himself.

"Your friend, Rollie Sterling, has him."

The two men stared at each other for a long time, until Wyler finally spoke.

"Thank you," Wyler said. The understanding that Bell had saved his life back at the cliff passed between them, unspoken. Bell looked into Wyler's eyes, read what was there, and nodded.

Wyler slept.

CHAPTER 34

The news about Scottie Hibble ricocheted through media outlets around the world for days, with video clips of his arrest on the island playing over and over. The controversy cast a bright spotlight on the Bonfire event, but not for the reasons originally hoped for by those in attendance. Local news outlets that accompanied the Royal Bahamas Police to the island had captured unflattering footage of many rich and famous people partying in a hedonistic atmosphere of drugs, alcohol, and excess. The picture painted was a caricature, unfair to the majority of participants who had probably attended the event with the sincere hope of doing some good in the world. But any good that was originally intended was drowned out by gossipy headlines and salacious video clips. Only public relations firms specializing in celebrity damage control had reason to be pleased.

There was no mention of the name Edgar Dordevic in any of the news stories about the event, nor of the small, private ceremony disrupted by Aaron Wyler that had taken place near the eastern cliffs that night.

Two months later, Hibble, who was being held at Her Majesty's Prison in Nassau awaiting trial, was found dead in his cell. He was discovered in the morning, the victim of multiple stab wounds to the chest. So far, no charges had been filed, and there were no known suspects.

A few days after returning from Caliban Cay, Wyler met with Sarah Miller. They sat together at the same table in the hospital cafeteria at Westchester Medical Center where they had first met. He removed the small, black onyx stone from his pocket and slid it across the table toward her. At first she just stared down at it, making no move to take it. He told her everything that had happened, leaving nothing out, including details and events that he himself could not explain completely. As he spoke, she listened quietly, asking very few questions, at times letting her eyes drift away in an effort to concentrate and take it all in. It took almost two full hours to tell the whole story, and at one point he took out and handed to her the certification and appraisal of the Lisonbee family gemstone produced by the New York Gemological Appraisal Institute. The documents estimated the worth of the stone sitting on the table between them as being between eleven and twelve million dollars. She read the documents without expression, and when she was done, they sat together in silence. Finally, she told him that his story confirmed what she had believed in her heart all along. Her brother hadn't committed suicide. He had, in fact, been murdered. Wyler said that he agreed with her but added that it was a crime that couldn't be prosecuted in any courtroom, to which she responded, "Not one on this earth, anyway."

Before they parted, he asked what she was going to do with the stone, and she said she wasn't sure. Two weeks later, he received a handwritten letter from Sarah Miller explaining that she had taken the stone to Bishop Joel Cariani, the pastor of the Catholic Church she attended in Newburgh, seeking his advice. She told Bishop Cariani the history of the stone, and the recent events surrounding it. After consulting with his ecclesiastical superiors, Bishop Cariani felt the best course of action would be to destroy the stone. At the close of her letter, she reported to Wyler that this had been done, in a ceremony of some kind presided over by Bishop Cariani that she herself had attended. She gave no further details. As he read the letter, Wyler couldn't help but feel tremendous admiration for this woman. Two working parents, trying to raise a family on modest incomes, could have used the financial windfall that would have come from selling the stone. Had she chosen to, she could have justified the action in any number of ways. It could have paid for a new home, cars, college tuition, weddings, vacations, retirement. It could have provided financial peace of mind for the rest of their lives. But she had chosen a different kind of peace. Wyler had to admire that.

Aaron Wyler's experience that night on the cliffs of Caliban Cay changed him. For a few moments, his own mind had become so distorted that taking his own life seemed to be the only logical avenue available to him. He realized that, in the light of day, this perspective might seem absurd, but we don't always live in the light of day. Sometimes night falls, and it blinds us to things that we should see, but can't.

One evening, soon after returning from the island, Wyler sat on the corner of Gabe's bed and tried to convey all this to his son. They talked about Jessica and her death openly and honestly for the first time. Wyler reminded Gabe of the day, many years ago, when they had gone to the Bronx Zoo early in the morning, only to have their day ruined by a rainstorm. The storm had come on suddenly and unexpectedly, darkening the sky and blocking out the sun. Eventually, Wyler, Jessica, and Gabe had made a break for it and ran back to the parking lot, but they were all completely drenched by the time they reached the car. He and Gabe smiled together at the shared memory.

"What do you think happened to the sun during that storm? Did it go away?" Wyler had asked him.

"Of course not. It was just blocked by the storm and the clouds."

Wyler explained that sometimes storms like that happen inside a person's mind and, like dark clouds blocking out the sun, it keeps them from seeing everything good and positive. Wyler told Gabe that he believed his mother's perspective had somehow become distorted. Wyler didn't need to evoke supernatural powers to explain this. There were plenty of forces all around and inside a person that could get the job done. Feelings, thoughts, situations, chemicals in the brain. All this could combine to twist and warp a person's view of reality, blinding them from seeing the good around them, and in them.

He told his son how much he still loved Jessica, and how important it was to understand that what happened wasn't her fault.

He opened up further by confessing to Gabe that he had been blaming himself for what had happened, and he apologized for letting his own feelings of guilt and shame put distance between them.

Gabe shared that he, too, had felt that he might in some way be responsible, and that he had worried that his father blamed him for his mother's death. These words broke Wyler's heart and, as he choked back tears, he confessed that he thought that Gabe had blamed him.

This frank and heartfelt exchange served to dress the wounds that each had been carrying, allowing the healing process to finally begin for both of them.

Over the next few months, Gabe's close friendship with the Bell boys continued. Will and Henry came up to Rhinebeck a few times, but usually Wyler would bring Gabe into town, and when he did, they stayed with Nora. They were spending so much time in Manhattan that they began talking openly about moving back, a prospect that thrilled Nora, and also pleased Jason and Laura Bell.

It was a drizzly Saturday afternoon in early October, the anniversary of Jessica's death, when Wyler, Gabe, and Nora, accompanied by the entire Bell family, visited Jessica's grave in Greenwood Cemetery in Brooklyn. They stood by the headstone in silence together for a while, each taking turns laying flowers. Even the Bells brought a basket of carnations and white lilies.

Afterward, on the street by the cemetery, as they were climbing into the Bells' van, Wyler noticed something and stopped. He stood and stared for a moment into the window of the coffee shop across the street.

After everyone was inside the van but Wyler, he came around to the driver's side of the car. Bell rolled down the window.

"What's up?" he asked.

"Look, I want you to go on ahead without me. I'll meet you there."

The group had decided to have lunch at the Peking Duck House in Chinatown in Jessica's honor.

"Are you sure?" Bell asked.

"Yes," Wyler replied. "I just need to spend a little more time here, by myself." When Bell looked concerned, Wyler added, lightheartedly, "I'll take the F train in ten minutes and probably beat you to the restaurant." And then, after a pause, he said, "Please."

A minute later, the van drove off. Wyler followed it with his eyes and waited for it to disappear around the corner. Then, he crossed the street to the coffee shop.

The coffee shop was a throwback, with a bell on the door, maroon vinyl booths, a dessert display under glass by the register, and waitresses in blue skirts and white aprons. Wyler walked slowly to a booth tucked away in the back corner by the window, where a man was sitting with his back to him.

"Sit down, Aaron," the man said without turning his head, pointing at the booth opposite with a forkful of eggs.

Wyler took the seat across from the man and looked at him.

"Hello, Eugene," Wyler said.

Wyler had not seen Eugene since the island. Gabe's friendship with the Bell boys had caused his son to lose interest, at least for now, in RC planes. Even so, Wyler had visited the hobby shop a few times by himself over the past months, not to buy anything, but to look for Eugene. Once or twice he had come close to asking one of the other employees about him, but he never did. Deep down, he was afraid of what the answer might be. It might be something simple and expected like, "Oh, Eugene doesn't work here anymore," but Wyler thought there was a 50/50 chance the answer might be something out of *The Twilight Zone* like "Eugene? Why, we don't know any Eugene. No one by that name has ever worked here before," and Wyler didn't know how he would deal with that.

"It's good to see you, Aaron," said Eugene, still working on his plate of eggs. "How's Gabe?"

"He's doing good," replied Wyler, staring at the man. He felt a strange mix of curiosity, fear, and, for some reason, nervous excitement.

"He seems to have made some new friends," Eugene said, taking a bite of toast.

"Yes, he did."

"You, too," Eugene added, and Wyler conceded the point with a nod.

"They're good people," Wyler said.

"Yes, they are," said Eugene.

"You know them?" Wyler asked. Eugene paused, looked up from his eggs and grinned at Wyler, then continued eating.

Since the island, Wyler had wondered endlessly about Eugene. It had been Eugene who had put him on the Lisonbee case in the first place, and it had also been Eugene who, that night on the train, had cleverly redirected him when he was ready to give up.

And it had been Eugene who had saved his life on the island, after Bell had saved it just minutes before.

"Who are you?" Wyler asked. "What I mean is, *what are you?*" Wyler leaned forward, whispering the last three words. When Eugene didn't answer, Wyler added, "Are you…an angel or something like that?"

Eugene calmly laid down his knife and fork, then lifted a folded cloth napkin to his face and dabbed his lips with it.

"I'm not an angel, Aaron. I'm a man."

"You're more than just a man."

"That's true. I am," he said, putting down the napkin.

"What does that mean?"

"It means that I am a man, but I am also more than that."

Wyler scrutinized Eugene like an abstract painting with an obscure, hidden meaning.

"You see, Aaron, there was a gift given to me, many years ago, almost two thousand years ago, actually. I realize this may be hard to accept, but I've lived on this earth all that time."

Wyler didn't know what to make of that statement. Was it the truth? Recently, Wyler had seen and experienced things he couldn't explain, things that didn't fit neatly into reality as he understood it. He hadn't succeeded in figuring out what all of it meant. The truth was, he hadn't really tried. He had chosen instead to simply file away certain events in his mind, to coexist with them, without forcing the need to understand them.

"If that's true, what have you been doing all that time?" Wyler asked in the dull, flat tone that had been perfected in hundreds of interviews with suspects and witnesses.

"*Good*, Aaron. I've been trying to do good. Isn't that what you try to do, each day?"

"So, you've been alive for two thousand years, and you've spent that time trying to do good?"

Eugene conceded the point with a nod.

"How is that possible?"

"I told you, I was given a gift."

"Who gave you this gift?" Wyler asked, continuing the interrogation.

Eugene looked at him. "I could answer that question, but that's not the question you really want to ask me, is it?"

It was true. There was one question that had been burning inside Wyler for months. It was the question he planned to ask Eugene if he had found him in the hobby shop.

"Go ahead and ask," Eugene said, as if reading his thoughts.

"Why me? Why did you come to me? Why did you get me involved in this?"

After a long pause, Eugene said, "Because I needed your help." And then, after a shorter pause, he continued. "And, because I felt that you needed mine. You *and* Gabe."

"What do you mean?"

"Aaron, I saw how you and Gabe were suffering. I knew there were things you needed to learn. Things that would help both you and Gabe to heal."

Eugene was right. Wyler couldn't deny the positive impact his involvement in the case had had upon both him and Gabe.

"But couldn't you have just...spoken to me?"

"Maybe," Eugene said with a chuckle. "But I doubt a few wise words from me would have helped you much. Besides, as I told you, I needed your help."

"How could someone like you need help from someone like me?"

Eugene pushed the plate of eggs away and leaned back in the booth. He stared at Wyler for a few moments, as if taking his full measure. When he spoke again, it was in a tone more serious and purposeful than Wyler had ever heard him use before.

"You're a man of very special abilities, Aaron. You see the world in a certain way. Your professional training has taught you to look for connections that others don't see. You have years of experience waging a certain kind of war, a war involving global conspiracies, secretly plotting and planning, with hidden cells linked together by invisible chains and networks. You've spent your career tracking down and exposing these invisible networks, anticipating their moves, sensing their very presence, sometimes with nothing but your own instinct and intuition. You did the same thing on this case."

"What do you mean?"

"You didn't believe Peter Lisonbee committed suicide, even though all the evidence pointed to that conclusion. You had the ability to look beyond what the physical, material facts were telling you! You sensed that other forces were somehow in play, things beyond your own senses. Forgive me, but where I come from, we call that faith. Is it really that hard to see how someone like you, with those skills, could be valuable to us?"

"*Us*? There are others like you?"

"A few."

"How many?"

"A few."

"And what, exactly, do you want from me?"

"Aaron, I want you to listen to me. You may not realize this, but you are living in a very special time." Eugene pointed to Aaron, and his whole face seemed to radiate excitement. "The Heavens are open, Aaron! Light is breaking forth in the world in a glorious way!" As he said this, he raised both his hands in a sweeping gesture that seemed to take in the whole of everything. Then, suddenly, Eugene's expression changed, and he lowered his arms and gripped the sides of the table. "But Aaron, you must understand." He leaned forward now, staring directly at Wyler. "*Light always casts a shadow!*" He said it slowly, punctuating and emphasizing each word individually. "And in those shadows, parallel to the wonderful work of light that is rolling forth, another work is taking place. It's a work that is organized, but hidden. It's powerful and deadly and thrives off secrecy and darkness. You've been brushing up against it for years, in your previous career, but all that was just peripheral, the outer edges. Deeper in the shadows, Aaron, you'll find a much purer strain of evil, in a more concentrated form. You glimpsed it on that island. You felt it. You know now that it exists. In times like these, Aaron, men such as you *are* needed. Men who can, from time to time, infiltrate the shadows and disrupt the work of evil going on there."

They sat in silence for a while as Wyler thought about this.

"But what about Dordevic? What happened to him?"

"Oh, he's still around," Eugene said casually. And then, more thoughtfully, as if to himself, "He's been around, and he'll be around."

"And what about those other people, the ones who were with him that night? There were a lot of important people there."

"That's true, but most of them were just misguided, or foolish, or stupid. And thanks to you, their little ceremony was interrupted before any real harm could be done."

"Why did Dordevic go to the trouble of staging that whole, elaborate festival in the first place, when the real event was being held in secret?"

"Why do you think?"

Wyler thought about this for a bit, then answered, "My guess is that the larger festival may have served two purposes, as a decoy for the smaller, main event, but also, perhaps, an opportunity to meet and, maybe, recruit others?"

"As I said before, you have an instinct for these things."

"What about the oaths? The secret oaths? He still has them!"

"Aaron, I realize you just got into this game, but it's been going on for a long time, and believe me, it will continue."

"But—" Wyler began to protest, but Eugene raised his hand in a gesture to silence him.

"That's enough for now," said Eugene, with finality.

Eugene stood up and laid some money on the table.

"Goodbye, Aaron," he said. "Enjoy your lunch at the Peking Duck House. Best steamed dumplings in the city."

Wyler remained in the booth, overwhelmed by the words that had been spoken, trying to reconcile their meaning and significance with all in his life that had come before.

Eugene turned as if to leave, but then he paused and came back.

"Don't worry, Aaron," Eugene said, placing his hand on Wyler's shoulder. "Remember," he began, and then Eugene spoke to Aaron in perfect Hebrew, quoting a passage from the Torah. It was the same passage that Aaron Wyler, at age thirteen, had struggled to memorize and recite at his own bar mitzvah.

> *For I know the plans I have for you, saith the Lord,*
> *plans to prosper you and not to harm you, plans*
> *to give you hope, and a future.*

Eugene left Wyler sitting by himself at the table and walked down the aisle toward the exit. Wyler continued watching him through the coffee shop window as he crossed the street and headed south along the sidewalk past the cemetery, eventually disappearing from view.

THE END

ACKNOWLEDGMENTS

There are many people to thank, but I'll start at the top: without the constant love and support of my wife, Valdete, this book would never have been possible.

I owe a huge debt to author Richie Franklin, who was the first to read a few chapters of the unfinished manuscript. Without his early support and enthusiasm, I would not have continued working on it.

Another author and friend, Rick Sherman, was a mentor, therapist, and cheerleader throughout the entire process, and this book would not have been published without his continual encouragement and assistance.

Additionally, I'll be forever grateful to the following individuals for being foolish enough to agree to read an unpublished manuscript by a first time author: Danny Brock, Marty Oestreicher, Megan Burt, Lynn Whipple, Don Markham, Michael Baker, Steve Harvey, Kimberly Ishoy, Justin Hansen, Dan Hogan, Vera Silva, Lynn Deppe, Jim Baird, Rick Sherman, Richie Franklin, and Jeanna Jones. Without the feedback and encouragement of each of these individuals, this book would never have made it across the finish line.

I am grateful for the contribution of a wonderful editor, Kevin Breen, who helped to shape and improve the material, to Jerry Todd for his excellent cover design, and to Dave Pasquantonio for the interior layout and for his patient and generous guidance throughout.

And finally, I am grateful to a loving and loyal mother who believed that children actually benefit from early and continuous exposure to the culture, events, ideas, and challenging complexity of the adult world.

ABOUT THE AUTHOR

Joe Doria is an award-winning filmmaker and the author of several short stories and feature-length screenplays. He studied theater at Oberlin College and Film Production at New York University, earning a Bachelor of Fine Arts. He and his wife Valdete live in South Jordan, Utah. They have been married for 25 years and are the parents of four wonderful children. *Lights & Shadows* is his first novel, and will be followed shortly by *Last Responder*, the second book in the Aaron Wyler detective series. Visit his website at www.JoeDoria.com.

Scan here to get a free sneak peek at the first 3 chapters of *Last Responder*, the 2nd book in the Aaron Wyler series!

ALSO BY JOE DORIA

Coming in 2023: *Last Responder*, Aaron Wyler book 2

Made in the USA
Coppell, TX
08 July 2023